Accidental Attachment

max monroe

New York Times & USA Today Bestselling Author

Accidental Attachment
Published by Max Monroe LLC © 2023, Max Monroe

ISBN: 979-8-9881190-0-5

Editing by Silently Correcting Your Grammar
Formatting by Champagne Book Design
Cover Design by Peter Alderweireld

Author's Note

Accidental Attachment is a full-length romantic comedy stand-alone novel that tells a tale as old as time. Not the one where a Beast keeps you captive inside his castle that showcases a library only dreams are made of, but the tale where you accidentally send the wrong file (or message) to someone (and that someone just so happens to be your crush and the file you send them just so happens to be an entire romance book you wrote about them).

VERY IMPORTANT WARNING: You're not just going to be a fan of Chase and Brooke's story, but we guarantee, after you read this hilarious, lovable, all-the-things book, you're going to be a whole damn air conditioner.

VERY IMPORTANT FUN FACT: This is one of our longest books to date! And some of the most fun we've ever had while writing. Seriously, to us, this book is magic. We needed it. And we think you might need it too.

Also, due to the hilarious and addictive nature of this book's content, the following things are *not* recommended: *reading in public places, reading in bed next to a light-sleeping spouse and/or pet and/or child, reading on a date, reading on your wedding day, reading during the birth of your child, reading while eating and/or drinking, reading at work, reading this book to your boss, and/or reading while operating heavy machinery. Also, if suffering from bladder incontinence due to age/pregnancy/childbirth/etc., we recommend wearing sanitary products and/or reading while sitting directly on a toilet.* It might seem like a long list of places not to read, but we assure you, if you do it in the right setting, it'll be worth it.

Happy Reading!

All our love,
Max & Monroe

Dedication

To anyone who has ever crushed on someone so hard it made them do stupid things.

And to Henry Cavill's right testicle. Some might say it's his best testicle, and well, we agree.

Intro

Brooke

Spending a week with a serial killer, a car-crushing interstate pileup, and deadline day.

This may not seem like a list of events you'd group together, but the truth is, they all have a bevy of horrible things in common.

Bloodshed. Tears. Begging to be put out of your misery.

I realize that may sound *a tad* dramatic to say about a writing deadline, but I'm in the pits of deadline hell, and I won't apologize for it. I'm a writer. A novelist. It's my duty to paint a portrait with my words. To reel a reader into my web of description in such a way that they'll never escape its clutches.

This is what I do, and normally, I revel in the task. In the past, I've even been praised and awarded for it. I've been on the *New York Times*, *USA Today*, and *Wall Street Journal* best-seller lists, have topped the charts on online retailers like Amazon and iBooks, and was awarded Author of the Year by the Author's Guild two years ago.

I have three of the most successful books of the last decade with one of the biggest publishers in the United States—Longstrand Publishing—and have even become somewhat of a household name, thanks to an upcoming show on Netflix about my first series.

At least, that's what you'd learn about me if you took to Google. My Wikipedia page is just one big *"Everyone come see how great Brooke Baker is!"* commentary, but none of it even scratches the surface.

On the inside, I'm a no-good, talentless hack, and the book I'm about to turn in to my new editor at Longstrand might as well find a home at the bottom of the Staten Island dump.

In defense of my inward pointing offensiveness, writers *are* known for being self-deprecating, no matter how successful they might be on paper. Pretty sure it's part of the job description.

Still, this book is a piece of crap.

Frustrated, I huff out a breath, shove away from my keyboard, and stand. But in the process, I bump into my sweet German shepherd Benji who's curled up at my feet. The abrupt motion propels me forward into a running fall.

"Shit, Benji," I mutter as I bang my foot on the coffee table, do a three-sixty spin, and finally come to a stop when my lower back slams into the edge of the sofa just as my Dolly Parton CD gets to the crescendo about a woman named "Jolene."

Dramatically, I let myself slide to the hardwood floor of my apartment and release a long exhale when my ass gently hits the floor. The motion makes my glasses slide to the bridge of my nose, and I reach up to adjust them on my face.

Benji stands up, crooking his head in concern. His ears perk up and his snout alarms into a frown, but the Batman costume he's currently sporting makes it hard to see him as anything but adorable.

Note to self: Benji in a Batman costume is impossible to get annoyed with, even when he sends me careening across my apartment like I'm a stuntwoman in the movie Jackass.

I might be biased, but my furry buddy is a superhero, and I always make sure he's dressed the part. His closet is nearly as big as mine, containing every superhero outfit from DC to Marvel because we don't choose one over the other in this household. We are superhero connoisseurs who don't discriminate. From Batman to Thor, we are fully inclusive.

"Okay, Batman Benji," I say, looking into his big and assessing brown eyes. "I'm going to overlook this little problem we just had because, first of all, you're so dang cute I can't even stand it. And secondly, the number of times you've saved my life far outweighs this endangerment."

He tilts his head to the side, and I get to my feet and walk toward him because I can't resist giving my canine superhero a rubdown.

Plus, he always lies at my feet when I'm writing. *Always.* So, it shouldn't have been a surprise and, therefore, shouldn't have caused me to nearly split my head open.

"Sorry, buddy," I apologize and scratch between his ears. "I'm not myself tonight, you know that. I'm in severe emotional distress about the fact that I'm a piece-of-garbage writer. Thank goodness for the Netflix deal on the Shadow Brothers, huh? Otherwise, I'd be worried about keeping us in kibble."

I head toward the kitchen, intent on pouring myself a glass of wine as my CD ticks over to the next song, "Living on Memories of You." As Dolly sings about a lack of sunshine during both day and night, I'm reminded why Dolly Parton, to me, is life.

Thanks to my fun (not fun at all) medical condition otherwise known as vasovagal syncope, I'm always one anxiety-ridden meltdown from passing out, and let me tell you, living in that kind of vacuum can turn someone cynical.

Dolly's music, though, I've decided, always has an answer.

I'm not obsessive or anything, but one of the rules of my house is that Dolly's CDs always take priority over other music. A new song comes out that Benji really likes to jam to? Great. But as the sun sets and the wine kicks in, Dolly's coming back. You really can't beat paying the price of a CD for therapy.

And yes, I'm a thirty-one-year-old woman who still buys CDs and plays them from a nineties-style boom box I found at a secondhand shop years ago. I'm nostalgic like that. A Time Life dream customer, if you will.

I swing open the cabinet and pull out the bottle of Pinot Noir I just bought yesterday. It's not long before I have a glass filled and I'm taking my first—*and very much needed*—sip of wine.

Benji's paws tip-tap across the floor as he meanders into the kitchen and finds a spot beside the island to lie down. However, I can tell he's making sure his eyes are on me at all times.

But that's his job. He's my service dog.

Basically, vasovagal syncope is a neurological condition that involves a drop in my blood pressure, heart rate, or both at the same time, and sends me into a brief—but severely inconvenient—loss of consciousness. It can happen when I'm sitting or standing or walking or talking or pretty much doing anything at all, and for many years, I had to manage recognizing the signs and symptoms myself in order to do something about it before catastrophe struck. My success rate was marginal at best.

Enter Benji.

Five years ago, just about a year after my divorce from my ex-husband Jamie, my four-legged friend came into my world and changed my life forever.

My superhero canine knows when my blood pressure and heart rate drop way before I do and makes sure I do something about it *before* I whack my head on the floor. He's a literal lifesaver, and now, after almost half a decade together, he's also my best friend.

A little pathetic, sure, that the main man in my life has paws and a propensity for drooling whenever the smell of meat is in the air, but I swear I've never met a human who outshines him. He's a great listener, he's calm, cool, and collected, and as made obvious tonight by his new Batman costume, he looks aces in pleather.

I don't know when or why I started putting Benji in superhero costumes, but it just kind of happened, and it's gotten to the point where it doesn't feel right unless he's Iron Man or Superman or any of the other mans that dominate the superhero stratosphere.

"You know, Benj, you almost look risqué in that getup. It's probably good that we're testing it out at home before we take it to the streets. I wouldn't want you attracting the wrong kind of attention." He groans, and I hold up a hand defensively. "I swear I won't be a nightmare mother-in-law when you meet your soul mate, but I need her to be at least a little respectable. Kind, understanding, doesn't bark after midnight—that kind of thing."

He woofs lightly—at a volume that doesn't anger the neighbors—and I smile. "I know. Dating is hard for me too. But we're going to find our happily ever afters eventually…I'm sure of it."

I'm not sure of it, but I heard you're supposed to put the things you want out into the universe. Positive reinforcement or manifestation or whatever they call it on TikTok.

Truthfully, I'm making exactly zero progress on the love-life front. Pretty sure I can count on one hand the number of dates I've had since my divorce from my childhood sweetheart six years ago.

Jamie and I got married at twenty-three, right after graduating from Middle Ohio University, and spent two mediocre years trying to criticize each other into different people. I wish I could say there was some big cataclysmic event that broke us up, but sometimes the biggest changes come out of living a life with no change at all.

We lived in small-town Ohio, going to the same jobs, seeing the same people day after day, and for my ex-husband, that meant contentment. It was peace; it was comfort. Unfortunately for me, the longer I sat behind my desk at the high school with my plaque that said School Counselor, the more I felt like I was coming out of my skin.

He was a good guy with good intentions, but good intent doesn't always equate to good results. In the end, it led to resentment from him and me, and he left the marriage emotionally. I don't have specific evidence that he was cheating, and to be honest, I wouldn't blame him too much if he had been. We were about as much of lovers as a couple of old, worn gym socks are haute couture.

We were the essence of "it wasn't meant to be."

I take another sip of my wine and look down at Benji. "We just need to keep trying. That's all. One day, we'll find our soul mates."

Benji lets out another little woof and tilts his head. I sigh. "Don't be like that. Just because I spend ninety-nine percent of my time here in this apartment in some form of pajamas with you and the characters inside my head does *not* mean I'm not trying."

He rests his head on his paws, and I swear, he rolls his eyes at me.

"Hey! Don't be so judgy. You know I have issues putting myself out there. I have a lot going on, you know? I'm pseudo-famous, which is a joke, but I am, and I have *very* nearsighted eyes and a limited ability to poke my eyeballs with contacts." I put a hand to my hip. "On top of that, I have a voyeur dog who has to be with me all the time to make sure I don't pass out and, you know, die. I'm a lot to handle compared to the superfit Insta-models with no structured job and the flexibility of an Olympic gymnast."

Climbing back into my computer chair like a complicated mix of spider monkey and shriveled old lady, I pull the chunky knit blanket from my ottoman and drape it across my legs. It only takes a few clicks to open my manuscript back up and start reading again while Dolly serenades softly in the background.

I mouth the words as I read through my final draft of *Garden of Forever*, hearing the words in my head and picturing them as though my glasses are a portal to a film-dimension.

But the garden is that of a flower's life cycle—forever and futile all at once. We're here for a good time, not for a long time and all that jazz.

Fabian lets out a deep, unsteady exhale, the realization of his demise all-consuming.

Life is, after all, life.

"If only I'd unsheathed my sword when Swanson asked, I might not be here, bleeding into the grass."

Dread settles into the base of my neck and shoots pain behind my eyes. *I cannot believe my new, hot-as-facckkk editor Chase Dawson is going to read this pile of garbage as his first taste of me.*

It doesn't seem fair, and it doesn't seem real. This is awful—hardly even coherent, if I'm honest—and nothing like my successful first trilogy, *The Shadow Brothers*. They were pithy and witty and smart.

This…this is like something Benji left on the sidewalk for me to pick up.

Chase Dawson is going to think I used a ghostwriter for my first series. Either that, or I suffered a very traumatic brain injury in between the publication of those and this.

Gah.

Garden of Forever and I never found our stride.

And I'm saying that *after* I've written "The End" and revised this WIP for the past month until I've reached the point that every time I look at it, I feel nauseated.

Not a good sign for a book that's supposed to be my next big release after a series that landed me a Netflix deal.

I imagine my readers using their copies of *Garden of Forever* for toilet paper and kindling on cold nights, and it's enough to make me wonder if Longstrand is going to drop me like a bad habit after they read this steaming pile of trash.

The thing is, though, it's not like I can't write *anything*. I know for a fact that my brain still works, because anytime the block has really gotten me in a bind on *Garden of Forever*, I've moved over to a different project—a manuscript of a different color, if you will. One that, under no circumstances, is ever to be shown the light of day.

On a whim, I minimize the window for *Garden of Forever* and search my other recent documents. *Accidental Attachment*, my contemporary romance about TV anchor River Rollins and her producer Clive Watts, isn't far from the top, and consequently, it's only a brief moment before it's open on my screen.

Involuntarily, my breasts swell in my tank top, and the pace of my breathing escalates. Clive and River together are…*hot.* The five-alarm kind that is a roller coaster of intense passion and emotional devastation. But they're not what my readers are used to, and the inspiration…well, it comes from a little bit of a personal place.

I scroll down into the Intro and start to read.

Strong, unhurried fingertips lift at the edge of my pencil skirt, scraping it up the skin of my thighs, and my head lolls back. This anchor desk is big and cumbersome—both normally great features that I use to hide my slippers when I have to rush to make live time—and it conceals Clive as he breathes a warm puff of air against the burning flesh beneath my lace panties.

Today, I'm being naughty. Daring, bold…wanton, even—I can't wait another second, even as we're about to broadcast live on the air, to feel Clive's mouth against my sensitive skin.

He takes his time, tracing his tongue along the hem of my panties. His mouth is warm and intense and a shock of pleasure rolls up my spine. My hips fidget, and two strong hands grip my thighs, forcing my legs to spread open as far as they can go.

Everyone around me is hustling to get in position. Cameras click on. Spotlights shine down on me from the ceiling. And the guy behind the teleprompter gets into place.

But Clive doesn't stop, and no one else but me is aware of his presence beneath my news desk.

The mere thought makes me feel bad, dirty, insane. And it's so arousing that I can feel how wet I am without even touching myself.

My fingers clutch at the edge of the desk, and a moan sits at the base of my throat when I feel my panties slide to the side.

I can't see Clive, but God, I can feel him.

His mouth is right there, hovering over where I ache and throb. My heartbeat has relocated to between my thighs, and a steady bum-bum-bum makes my toes curl inside my heels.

"Quiet on the set," fills my ears just as Clive's mouth latches on to me, and the rush of pleasure that floods my veins is so intense, my eyes threaten to roll into the back of my head.

"And we're live in three, two, one..."

Even though I know that River is just having the kind of explicitly vivid dreams I've had a time or two about my new editor Chase Dawson, and not actually getting her vahooch licked live on the evening news, my hands feel clammy and sweat rests uncomfortably above my top lip. The second-hand embarrassment is almost overbearing. To be honest, I'm one grease-and-debris-smeared T-shirt away from looking like a main character in a Michael Bay movie.

I need to walk. Take a shot. Smoke a cigarette. Something. Although, I probably shouldn't do either of the latter two because the last time I took a shot of liquor, I threw up instantly, and since I've never smoked anything in my life, I'm pretty sure I'd just hack myself over the rail of my balcony. But I should definitely do *something* that gets me away from my computer and dulls the edges of both my unbridled manuscript disgust and my in-appropriate lust for my very nice—*and far too attractive for my own good*—book editor.

I stand up in a huff again, but this time, Benji manages to scoot out of my way. I grab my glass of wine and chug it down for the sole purpose of cre-ating an empty vessel for my next heavy pour.

I may not be the kind of woman who can do shots of hard liquor on a Sunday evening without re-creating *The Exorcist*, but by God, I can handle a bottle of wine.

After one cold, hard swig from the bottle, I fill my stemware again and take a deep breath and try to reassure myself before I fall off the cliff of crazy.

Okay, so it's not that big of a deal, right?

I mean, sure, I have a little crush on my editor, but it's completely healthy...*I think*. Instead of bumbling my way into a sexual harassment suit, I put my feelings to the cursor and, as a bonus, got to put good practice hours into my writing craft.

Even if the content of *Accidental Attachment* is a little off genre for my career, it's still exercising the sensitive muscles of my creativity. It's honing. It's refining. It's breathing new dimensions into my prose.

Right? *Right.*

I look at the time and see it's nearing midnight, which means I have about forty minutes left of my final deadline day for *Garden of Forever.*

Wow, Brooke. You're really cutting this one close…

I puff out a breath that blows a few loose pieces of my brown hair out of my face, and I quickly readjust the messy bun on top of my head, my eyes never leaving my computer screen.

This is it. I have to send it. I have no more time left.

I look down at Benji, who is in a half-asleep, half-awake phase of his napping by my feet.

"I should just bite the bullet and do it, huh?" I question, and he barely moves his eyes up to meet mine. "I could do another thousand read-throughs of *Garden of Forever,* but it's not going to change anything, Benji. Not to mention, I don't have any more time."

He searches my face but, eventually, settles his snout back between his paws and lets his eyes start to get heavy again. I imagine this is his way of saying, *Look, lady, you handle the writing, and I handle the vasovagal syncope. I can't help you here.*

I take off my glasses, scrub a hand down my face, and sneak another drink of wine before I slip my glasses back on and refocus my attention on the screen.

Just do it.

Newly determined to put myself out of my misery by turning in my *Garden of Forever* file, I return to my computer and click frantically on Clive and River's story to minimize it. I don't close it just yet—because, well…I have a feeling after I get a little deeper into this wine, I'm going to want to "read" a little more to settle my mind before I go to sleep.

With a few hasty clicks into my email, a trip into my recent documents folder, and a simple search, a list of my files starting with "WIP" and ending with the title acronyms and dates populates. I don't give myself any wiggle room to rethink my next move and attach *Garden of Forever* to the email and address the message to my editor Chase Dawson.

Click, click. *Sent.*

There. It's done.

No more time to dwell. *Garden of Forever* is officially in Chase Dawson's inbox, and I don't have to think about it anymore. Well, technically, I don't have to think about it *until* my already scheduled meeting on April 26th with my editor.

But minor details.

Until then, I think I might sleep for the next fourteen days. Maybe wake up occasionally to eat takeout and down more wine and be temporarily oblivious to the fact that I might have to face the career-shattering music that would be my hot editor telling me I'm a rubbish writer and Longstrand can no longer publish me.

April 26th can take its sweet time.

Chapter
One

Brooke

April 26th came too soon.

I sit in a fancy, plush cream chair in the waiting area of my editor's office, and my knees bounce with the kind of nervous energy that threatens to catapult me into outer space without needing Jeff Bezos's penis rocket.

My purse digs into my back from its awkward spot behind me, and it paints the perfect picture of how anxious I'm feeling about being face-to-face with Chase Dawson again. It's not every day that you diddle your doodle to the distinct image of someone's uber-attractive face to put yourself to sleep every night, and then have a professional meeting with them.

It's just not that common.

I wrestle the offending bag like it's a gator in a swamp, and Benji lifts his head off the carpet quizzically. It's not hard to tell what he's thinking—*you, lady, are a psychopath.*

After three deep breaths in and out to calm my racing heart, I finally manage the transition of my bag from the chair to the floor, and Benji lays his head back down with a soft groan.

I know, Benj. I'm annoyed with myself too.

Chase comes around the corner suddenly—not really, I'm just at DEFCON level one—and I startle in the chair hard enough to make it rock onto its back legs. I swear I see Benji roll his eyes from the floor, but he doesn't bother to pick up his head. Saving his energy, I presume, for when I'm *interacting* with my crush, and he has to be on alert to make sure I don't pass out.

Or, if I do pass out, make sure I do it with the kind of grace that prevents head contusions and stitches.

Chase doesn't notice me at first, which is probably for the best, and I try to remind myself that a lady shouldn't gawk or have drool dripping out of her mouth.

"Good morning," he chirps cheerfully to his assistant, who's stationed at the desk ten feet in front of me. He picks up his messages from her waiting hand and smiles so brilliantly my chest hurts.

"Good morning, Mr. Dawson," she returns easily.

God, he's a beautiful human being. High cheekbones, a strong jaw, and a perfect complexion are just the tip of the iceberg when it comes to his Clark Kent-esque charm. He's tall, but not too tall, and just fit enough to see the hint of muscular bulges beneath his crisp, collared shirt. He also has the algorithm for grooming balance nailed. Kempt, but not super feminine, Chase Dawson might as well be red-hot candy in human form.

He turns on his heel, and that brilliant smile is now focused on yours truly.

God help me.

"Brooke," he croons deeply, closing the distance between us and kneeling down to give Benji a scratch behind the ears. My sweet canine moans that it feels so good. I only wish I knew the feeling.

"It's great to see both of you, and I'm so sorry to have kept you waiting," he continues, that smile never wavering despite the risks it's causing to my sanity. "Morning meeting ran a little long. They apparently didn't get the memo about who my visitors were for today."

I return his smile, still unable to form actual words. *Pathetic, Brooke. Pathetic.*

"I also have one quick phone call to make, if that's okay with you," he adds, and his full, perfect lips turn down at the corners. "I feel terrible to keep you and Benji waiting any more than you already have, but I'm afraid if I don't make this call, they won't keep me around to edit for you, and I'd absolutely hate that."

"Uh-huh." I nod, and it feels like my neck doesn't understand there's a point where you need to stop nodding before you look like one of those bobble-head toys they give away at baseball games. "That's...of cour...mm...fine," I mumble. My tongue trips over itself because apparently I am a toddler learning how to speak for the first time.

For the love of everything, get it together.

I swallow. Clear my throat. And attempt my best impression of a casual woman who hasn't been having sexual fantasies about the wickedly handsome man standing in front of her. Though, my impression is more of a silent film version, where I don't say a word but offer a far-too-big smile in his direction.

If Benji were wearing his Batman costume today, I could be his Joker.

"Do you want any coffee? Some tea? Maybe a cookie or two?" He winks. *He winks.* At me. "If you snack on the good stuff, they let me have some too."

"U-um, suuu...sure." I clear my throat again, trying to remind my vocal cords they have thirty-one years of experience at their job and need to start using it. "Coffee would be great." *As would a lobotomy with a rusty knife and no anesthesia at this stage of discomfiture.*

Chase chuckles a little, and I panic that I've just said the line about the brain removal aloud. I look at Benji, who's studying me closely, thanks to many rapid changes in my heart rate. *Did I just say that out loud?*

The backstabbing, adorable bastard in the Thor getup and service dog vest doesn't answer, instead tilting his head to get another scratch from Chase. *That's it. I'm canceling the Captain America costume order when I get home.*

Chase's assistant gets up with a nod, not even having to be told to carry out my coffee and cookie order directly, and Chase gives Benji one final rub behind his ears and stands up straight.

"I'll just be one minute," he promises, his impressive white line of teeth on display, courtesy of his smile.

I nod. A minute is good. A minute gives me time to gather myself out of the pile of goo on the floor and try to remember how to put a motherflipping sentence together.

Chase glances over at me for a moment, and then, even though I didn't think it was possible, his grin grows. "You look great in purple, Brooke."

"T-thank you." *Your tongue would look great on my nipples.*

His grin turns megawatt, and again, I have a brief moment of panic, wondering if I said the thing I didn't mean to say. Of course I didn't say that out loud. Lord knows he wouldn't be grinning. He'd be, like, running for the hills or something. *But holy shit, why can't I distinguish reality anymore, especially when my thoughts are this demented?*

Chase heads into his office behind me, and the glass door to my right falls closed almost painfully slowly.

His voice is distinct, cheerful, and confident as I hear him at the beginning of his call. "Jim, I got your message about the Beranski deal. I have a couple of ideas for strategy if you're ready…"

His voice fades out as the door finally settles into place, and I let go of the tension I didn't know I'd rammed into the base of my spine like a rod. I've been white-knuckling the armrests of this chair so tightly that my fingerprints are visible in the creamy velvet. My palms are also sweaty, and I discreetly wipe them down the front of the lavender dress Chase said I look good in.

News flash: He said you look good in the color. Not good in the dress.

I want to smack myself across the face but decide that's not a good look since the office behind me that contains the man who makes me turn into a moony-eyed crazy person is made of a glass door and glass windows. Pretty sure witnessing someone slap themselves is a *huge* red flag.

Of course, Benji is on his feet now, likely sensing the impending disaster my little emotional breakdown is liable to cause.

Using the breathing techniques I've learned over the years, I work vigorously to bring myself back from the brink of unconsciousness, glancing over my shoulder briefly to get another look at Chase's comforting smile.

Because for as much as he riles me up, he also calms me down, and yes, I *am* aware I've never sounded more insane than I do right now. Thanks for asking.

Since Chase's assistant, whose name my fogged-up brain can't seem to remember, is down the hall and Benji and I are alone, I don't censor myself while trying to regain control. I take several deep breaths—enough that I'm pretty sure I'm responsible for the entirety of the oxygen-carbon dioxide exchange on the planet—until I've melted back into a semi-recognizable version of the woman I aspire to be.

Come on, Brooke. You're acting a little immature right now, don't you think? Adults can have crushes without melting down, for heaven's sake.

There she is—the voice I paid one hundred dollars an hour to find in post-divorce therapy.

And even better, she's right. Sure, I find Chase Dawson dreamy in the way that suggests I should participate in a sleep study or two, but as a rational, professional, compartmentalizing-capable adult, there's no reason I can't find a way to be "Work Brooke" for the next thirty to forty-five minutes. She's a badass. She knows her worth. She, unlike the anxious me, sometimes recognizes how meaningful it is to have landed a Netflix deal and live in an apartment in Lenox Hill that doesn't inherently smell like moldy cheese and farts.

Newly pepped, I straighten the line of my spine and sit up tall in my chair. Benji notices, giving me a canine nod of pride.

We got this. I wink at him.

I fold my hands in my lap and try to position myself in my chair until my legs are crossed and I look like a professional woman who isn't at all on the brink of a nervous breakdown. I am victorious.

Squeaky wheels chatter with Chase's assistant Dawn's—*go me, remembering her name and everything!*—return, the chocolate cookies atop the cart she's pushing harkening my mental win like a siren on a slot machine in Vegas.

She smiles politely, parking the catering rollaway right in front of me and locking the wheels. "I thought you might want to go ahead and have a cookie or two while you're waiting—though, he shouldn't be long."

"Thanks," I reply, my voice belying my now obvious affection for Dawn. *She's, like, really nice.*

With a quick nod and a wink, she returns to her desk and dives right back into work. I'm almost astonished. I mean, she didn't even pick up her phone and scroll TikTok or anything.

If only you had her willpower, maybe Garden of Forever *would've ended up good and you wouldn't be here stressing—*

I squash that thought before it can even grow legs.

I look down at Benji and note that he is studying Dawn too, and I'm sure it's because he's never seen such focus before. Her fingers roll across her keyboard like they're one memo away from solving world peace, and I'm convinced the modern me would never make it in a job outside of writing.

Thanks to my fascination with Dawn, I don't realize that Chase has opened the door until he's standing right next to me, his smile nearly all the way wound up.

"You ready?" he asks, causing a jerk in the muscles of my neck so violent that a shooting zing of pain rolls up the side of my face. No doubt, I'll be working out that new kink for the next week.

"O-oh," I stutter. "Y-yes. Let's do it!" My fist pumps in the air as though it has a very Jersey mind of its own, and Chase laughs. Like, throws back his head while his chuckles make his vocal cords pump at the line of his sexy throat.

By God. No wonder I wrote a book about this guy.

"Fantastic!" he cheers then, holding out a hand to help me out of my chair. "I love the enthusiasm."

It'd be so easy to get embarrassed again right now, but thanks to all the willpower I can fit inside my five-foot-six body and desperation born from years of dealing with my own awkwardness, I manage to place my sweaty, clammy hand into his completely dry one and stand. Benji pushes to his feet at our sides and follows us into the office obediently.

I don't realize until we're entirely through the door that I'm still gripping his hand and drop it like it has the power to burn my skin right off my bones. But Chase continues to maintain so much nonchalance that I'm honestly not even sure if he noticed.

The door falls closed behind us, its path still creepily slow, and Chase rounds his desk to the other side, all while holding out a hand to the chairs at the front.

"Take a seat," he suggests warmly, tucking his tie close to his abdomen so that it doesn't get caught on his desk as he sinks into his chair.

He's a professional suit guy, but not in the way that's boring. Of course not. He could never be boring. Everything he wears, every pair of dress pants and every collared shirt and suit jacket, fits his body like a glove. I'm certain he gets his clothes tailored. It's either that or he just has one of those perfect bodies where everything fits him.

I, on the other hand, have one of those bodies where finding a good pair of jeans that fits me is like finding the golden ticket in a Willy Wonka chocolate bar.

"You know, Brooke, I've been looking forward to this meeting for weeks," Chase admits unabashedly, rolling up the sleeves of his white button-down shirt almost recklessly until both veiny forearms are exposed.

"You have?" I hear my mouth question with an apparent mind of its own.

"Heck yeah. Longstrand wanted me because of the book I hand-picked at my old publishing house landing on the New York Times for twenty-nine weeks. And you're the reason I wanted Longstrand."

I can't be too sure, but I seem to have swallowed my tongue. *Seriously, I think I can feel it in my throat.*

He chuckles a little, his cheeks heating to the most subtle color of rose. "That sounds pretty creepy the more I think about it. But I'm a fan of your work, and my sister...well, she's a superfan. I'd have been excommunicated from the family tree if I didn't jump at a chance to work with you."

I'm flattered and flabbergasted all at once. I'm flattergasted.

"You'd read my stuff before you came here?"

"Yes. I think I read the first book in your Shadow Brothers Trilogy within the first month of its release, before the presses even heated up too much. I knew instantly it was going to be a hit. You've got an ease of prose that lulls the reader into submission. To be honest, being so familiar with your work is what made this one all the more of a surprise."

A surprise? Surprisingly bad, he means.

And just like that, the whole reason I'm here, sitting across from the most handsome man who has ever lived, hits me like a semitruck careening off the highway.

Today's conversation is about *Garden of Forever*. And I know that manuscript isn't worthy of publication. I knew it when I was writing it. I knew it when I wrote The End. And I definitely knew it when I hit send on the email addressed to Chase Dawson at Longstrand Publishing.

Shit, shit, shit. I knew they'd never let that heaping pile of fly-covered cow manure go to print.

The need for flight pounds in my temples, and I consider just up and darting out of the office like one of those little psychotic birds—barn swallows. My grandparents had a barn swallow problem when I was a kid, and it was fascinating to see the way those feathered lunatics would just recklessly fly all over the place.

"That said," Chase continues. "I'm seriously impressed by the seamlessness of the transition."

What? What transition? *Transition from being a successful novelist to a rock-bottom hack who can't write?*

"Brooke." Chase smiles like he's really proud. "This is good. Really *fucking* good, if you'll excuse the language."

Um…*what?* "Y-you…you like it?"

"Yes." He nods. "I have some modest ideas that I think can really turn up the emotional tug to an eleven, but Clive and River's chemistry is undeniable. Their story is magnetic, Brooke. Truly captivating."

Did he just say Clive and River? Brain cells wither, and a blinding light cut only by the shadow of a dark man with a scythe paralyzes me. Sweet Lord and the land of Jesus, I know this man did not just say the name of the character I've written *about him*.

Right? Tell me for the love of everything holy that's not possible. Those words were never meant to see the light of day, let alone land on *his* desktop. Inside that fangirl fiction book that no one should have ever seen, I wrote some seriously sexy fantasies, described down to the minutest of details. I put my pen to the paper—*fingers to the keyboard*—in the hope that I'd bleed out any and all feelings for my hot editor from my system. I did *not* write any of those words with the intention of having them read.

As a matter of fact, if I had, I'm more than certain I would have omitted ninety-nine percent of them. If I'd known Chase, of all people, would see that manuscript, the book would've been so fade to black that all that would've been left would have been two lines of dialogue that overutilized the word hello.

"Hello, River. I'm Clive."... "Hello, Clive. I'm River."... The End.

Chase is still smiling at me, and my heart is taking it personal. Up-up-*up* the rate of my ventricles pumping blood throughout my body increases. I grip the armrests of the chair, and white dots start to take over my peripheral vision.

"Accidental Attachment is fantastic, Brooke. Clive and River together are fire. Their passion has an intensity you can *feel."*

Okay, yeah, I'm no longer on the brink of passing out. It's coming; I can *feel* it.

It makes me think of this blooper reel I saw on YouTube where a man passed out live on air while in the middle of a conversation with a news anchor. His face went from red to white, and his final words were "I'm gone" before he fell like a stack of dominoes to the floor.

"Honestly, their sex is some of the hottest I've ever read in my life," Chase adds, and yeah...

I'm gone.

Benji jumps to his feet in front of me and starts nudging, trying to keep my attention long enough to get me into a suitable position. You wouldn't necessarily think of the fact that there are both good and bad ways to hit the floor when your body turns into a limp sack of noodles, but as a resident expert on the issue, I'm here to tell you it's true.

Benji's primary purpose is to alert me before I'm past the brink of lights-out-ville, but in the event—such as this—that the tank in my blood pressure is too fast for even a SuperDog, he has to settle for finding a way to prevent me from splitting my head open.

The room spins, and vomit percolates, right there, just at the back of my throat, waiting to spray its embarrassing chunks all over the hunkiest man I've ever seen's office.

It really wouldn't be so surprising, though. Because for as successful as I seem on paper, I'm also in the top one percenters of awkwardness. This is all just par for the course in Brooke Baker world.

"Brooke? You okay?" I hear Chase question foggily, almost like he's standing on the other side of a bridge in a distant haze.

I try to answer, I think, but my words are nothing more than garbled gravel on my lethargic tongue. Benji gets impatient, shoving his body between mine and the side of the chair and effectively sliding me off the front edge like a rubber waterfall. I land none-too-gently on my ass, but the sting is nothing compared to the one I feel seeping into every vestige of my pride.

With quick paws and a soft bark, Benji rounds the space behind me and jumps on my back, forcing my head between my legs and a slight awareness to return to my mind.

"Oh my God, Brooke," Chase croons in a way that seems both distressed and controlled from right in front of my face. I'd love to be able to focus on the perfect, passionate blue of his dreamboat eyes from this unexpectedly close position, but to be quite honest, I'm a little too occupied with using all my basic functions to avoid peeing myself.

Yep. That's right. Unfortunately for me and the universe, one of the main side effects of going unconscious unexpectedly is losing control of your bladder.

As if the humiliation of the whole thing isn't enough for people like me, the Almighty decided, "Hey, why don't we also let them piss themselves?"

No offense to God or anything. He obviously did a good job with everything else. I'm just a little bitter about this one tiny thing.

Benji woofs softly beside me, licking at the apple of my cheek and bringing a tingle to my face. I'm coming back from the precipice—hallelujah—but all my thoughts are still sluggish.

Still, I fight hard, and I manage a horrifying fake smile for Chase. His eyebrows draw together in concern, and I pointedly ignore them.

"I'm okay, I think. Just ensuring my memories last longer by making them dramatic." The joke falls flat, but that's okay. I'm sure he'd find me funnier if all the blood hadn't drained from my face.

"Can I get you anything at all? Some water? A soda? What would help?"

What would help most is to go back in time and not fall off my chair and nearly pass out during a work-related meeting, but since that's not really an option, the soda is probably ranked at number two.

"I'll take a Coke if you've got one. It usually helps."

"Dawn, get me a Coke, please. Quick!" Chase yells through the glass wall of his office from his knees beside me, not even bothering to explain. Given my little-girl crush on the Super Secretary, I'm really hoping she doesn't take offense at her boss's barking orders on my behalf.

I focus on breathing—and you know, not looking Chase directly in the eye—for the next minute at least. Normally, I'd be dedicated to focusing on how he was feeling about the situation, about me, about the book—*dear God, the book*—but if I'm ever going to make it off this tan Berber carpet floor of his, I'm going to have to spend a little time on me.

The sound of Chase's glass door's hinges sliding open comes quickly, and Dawn's presence looms over the two of us. "Oh my gosh, is she okay?"

"Just testing out the floor as my zen space," I tease. "As the British would say, it's rubbish."

Chase chuckles, thankfully, and the momentary excitement of having my humor land is enough to get me up onto my knees and into the chair. Chase keeps a hand on my back to steady me, Dawn braces the seat, and Benji crowds the front of my legs to ensure I keep moving in the right direction.

Dear Lord. A hunk, a costume-wearing canine, and a powerhouse woman who obviously has a heart of gold. Somewhere, there's a writer just wishing they could write a scene like this. I know it.

Dawn twists off the top of the bottle of Coke and places it in my hand, even going so far as to curl my fingers around the bottle for me. "Got it?" she asks, and I nod.

"If you need anything else at all, you just let me know. There's a deli a couple of buildings over. I could get you a sandwich or some soup or—"

"Thank you so much," I interrupt as politely as possible. "But just the Coke should help. Plus, you already brought those cookies, and I think they'll be really disappointed if I don't eat them."

Dawn moves so she's easily in my line of sight and gives me a warm smile before going back out the door. Chase nods at her over my shoulder, and as much as my nosy ass would like to, I don't know why.

Benji, evidently satisfied with my progress, finally abandons his alert and curls himself up on the floor at the side of my chair. Chase notices. "Hey, that seems like a good sign."

I nod softly. "I'm no longer posing a threat to your carpet's security."

He laughs before joking, "Was it something I said?"

Sheesh. If he only knew the power of his words. Or his smile. Or his blue-as-the-sky eyes.

"No, no," I cover. "Just…probably didn't eat enough this morning or didn't have as much caffeine as I normally do." *Liar, liar, five-cups-of-coffee-drinker's pants on fire.* "I'm feeling better, I promise."

"Okay, good." Instead of heading back for his chair, he leans his hips into the edge of the desk behind him and crosses his feet at the ankles, pressing his palms into the surface. "Still, just in case, I'll try to keep the rest of this as short as possible. I really just wanted you to come in so I could give you an idea of the process we have ahead of us."

"The process?" I ask dumbly. I mean, I'm three traditionally published books in with this publisher. Shouldn't I know what to expect by now?

"Yes," he says excitedly, rubbing his hands together. "It could be a little confusing since you have a contract with terms for *Garden of Forever* and we're switching it up with this different manuscript."

I feel clammy again, and by the look on Chase's face, I'm guessing my skin is a matching shade of putrid.

"No, no, don't worry, Brooke. I don't think we're in the weeds here. In fact, I think we're ahead of the game. This new direction from you is just fresh enough to throw the market into overdrive. It showcases your talent in a way I don't think Longstrand ever even considered. Going with this book is the right move. I'm confident in that. But now it's my job to convince the other editors."

"Convince them how?"

He smiles. "With my unrivaled pitching skills, of course. You did the hard work by writing a great book, and next Friday, I'm going to make sure everyone else understands just how confident I feel about it."

"Do you think there's going to be pushback about not complying with the terms of the title and content?" I ask through a thick throat. I mean, I have the correct book just sitting on my computer, waiting for someone who's not an idiot to send the right file. It's crap, but at least it's what they asked for—and a little less life-ruining for me too.

"No," Chase assures. "It's a simple change for the reward of a bang-up best seller."

I swallow hard. Some withered part of me is still screaming, *I can't believe this is happening!*

"Once I get the go-ahead in the pitch, it'll be up to us to work through all the content editing changes and potential improvements. I hate to be the bearer of bad news, but you're probably going to be sick of me by the time this thing goes to print."

"Why?"

"I've never believed in the potential of characters like I do River and Clive, and I know this isn't your problem, but I have a hell of a lot to prove since this is my first fully solo project here. I won't sleep until it's perfect."

"So…we're going to be working really closely."

"Most definitely," he agrees, like that isn't the biggest bombshell to the heart I could get.

Clive and River are a collection of everything I've ever dreamed about this man and me together.

And now, I'm going to have to dissect every single part of it while staring at his handsome face?

Better dry-clean your black outfits, ladies and gentlemen. Brooke Baker's funeral is sure to be soon.

Chapter
Two

Brooke

I pace the kitchen like a madwoman, blood pressure cuff on my arm and inflating. My problems with the vampire juice don't normally run on the high end, but with the way I've been feeling since my meeting with Chase this afternoon, I'm convinced hypertension is my new normal.

Don't stand too close to this flesh balloon, folks—she's about to pop.

Benji cranes his head at me and groans, flopping his body down onto the floor and looking up at me with judgy eyes. I scoff. Nobody likes a smartass dog—even in a Thor costume.

"No, actually, I *don't* think I'm making a bigger deal of this than it is. He has *the* book, Benj. You know…the one where I wrote an entire scene dedicated to the way I imagine he would eat me out?" I huff three sharp breaths in an attempt to keep myself from hyperventilating and reach a shaking hand out to pour more wine into my glass, ripping off the blood pressure cuff before it can finish. "I'd have to stage a terrorist attack to be blowing this out of proportion, and believe you me, I've considered that a whole *three* times in order to come to the conclusion that blowing up the city I love and a bunch of innocent people is over the top."

Benji cocks his head to the side, and he paws me on the shin in sympathy. *There, there, you crazy woman. There, there.*

I chug a thick swig of Cabernet and bow my head with a lingering sigh afterward. Only I would get myself into this kind of situation. *What kind of professional keeps their manuscript for the thing they hope never sees the light of day right next to the one that's supposed to, for Pete's sake?*

Probably the same kind who allows themselves to fall into an obsessive infatuation with their editor and turns it into a book, that's who.

I know it's crazy, *I know*, lusting after him, but I don't even completely know how it happened other than to say…the day I met Chase Dawson was the day the earth stood still.

There were bright lights and powerful auras, and I'm pretty sure the whole "circle around the sun" thing paused for ten to fifteen solid seconds.

He was something out of a fantasy I'd never dared to dream. Dark hair, strong cheekbones, and the friendliest smile. I swear you could melt a Catholic toward the devil if Chase just introduced the two.

He had a perfect touch of a Southern accent—not thick, just…there—and the things he said to me with ease will forever live in the very core of my memory.

"I knew meeting you would be one of the highlights of my career, Brooke, but I didn't know your banter would be the highlight of my day. If I could carry you home with me, I doubt I'd need any other entertainment at all."

Ha-ha-ha. Complimenting my work and my humor and managing somehow not to sound like it was scripted? I was sold. Down the river, swallowed up, fully on my way into a crush tailspin.

Obviously—*obviously*—my mind took liberties in its imaginings of Chase Dawson from the start. Realistically, he's no more than a handsome human man with good people skills and charisma. Somewhere deep down, I *knew* that.

But then there were funny, but still professional, text messages checking in on the status of *Garden of Forever*, and phone calls where I had to hear his sexy voice and laugh. The calls were brief, but they sure as shit didn't help dissipate my crush.

And the next two times I saw him at Longstrand, you could have knocked me over with a feather's memory at the sight of his muscled shoulders and sent me straight to detention for the things my mind started to imagine.

From there, every sexual impulse inside me ran wild.

I barely know him—don't even know his favorite color—but as far as my imagination is concerned, he's the man the universe created just for me.

And in this reimagining of the astral plane I've created in my manuscript of *Accidental Attachment*, Clive Watts—aka Chase Dawson reincarnated as a dreamy TV producer—feels the exact same way about River Rollins—aka fictional news anchor me.

Burning, obsessive passion. Smooth, effortless banter. Hot, dirty-as-fuck sex. All produced from the little visualizations in my head.

And now…everyone is going to read it.

Oh God. I'm going to vomit—big, ugly chunks too, not the delicate warning that stays in your throat.

I take off at a run for the bathroom and slide into the toilet like a baller stealing a base. I hit my knee so hard the porcelain rings like a bell, and a groan involuntarily jumps from my lips.

"Jiminy Cricket!" I yell, the nausea still swelling up the walls of my throat. Battered kneecap forgotten, I heave myself up into a squat and tuck my head into the lip of the toilet bowl just nanoseconds before I spew red wine all over the white walls.

It's disgusting to say the least, and beyond that, very, very telling.

I'm not just upset about having my innermost thoughts exposed—I'm sick over it. And it's not even a full reality yet. If by some twisted fate, the publisher agrees to switch my contract, this thing is going to be pushed and shoved and publicized into almost every corner of the planet.

If I'm this much of a mess now, I don't see how I'll ever survive when it publishes.

I won't.

My skin tingles, and a hair-raising chill at the back of my neck makes me lean into the toilet fully again. I don't get sick, though. Instead, my mind takes off at a run. Searching, looking, begging for some way to get out of this.

A plan. A con. A turn of the tables. If I want to keep food down in this lifetime, I've got to eighty-six the hell out of my dream man's drive to publish this book.

Maybe I can worm my way on to the catering staff for next Friday's meeting…give them a mild case of food poisoning or something?

Not, like, sick with a need for the hospital kind of thing, but a small mindfuck about the taste of my book in their mouths. I've heard Jonah Perish, Longstrand's president, is the superstitious type. Maybe putting him off a little would work.

Of course, I'd have to know who they normally use for their catering, somehow convince them that Friday's meeting needed something special, and then also come off as a convincing chef—all without being recognized by Chase or anyone else associated with the publisher. It's risky. Deranged, really. So, I have a strong feeling I'm going to have to move in a different direction.

Perhaps, I could send anonymous messages to the rest of the editors undercutting Chase's pitch? Warn them off the book kind of thing.

I shake my head. Not only is forming a coup against the man of my dreams a touch distasteful, it's also far too exposing. Since no one other than my publisher and I are supposed to have access to the manuscript, it might be a little messy to create a fictitious third party that's both believable and practical for the continuation of my career.

I mean, I'm doing well, but not well enough to toss my shit in the fire and quit it all.

Surely there's something else. Something simple in nature without being generally harmful…

An excuse. That's it. I need an excuse to convince him that what he read is not, in fact, worthy of publishing, let alone taking it to the other editors and risking his own career. I need to give him a reason to throw that thing in a dumpster and never look at it again *before* he makes a fool of himself in front of his peers.

Picking up my phone off the kitchen island while Benji sits at my side, an undeniably worried look on his handsome canine face, I type frantically in a draft with no number attached yet, you know, because apparently I tend to send the wrong things to the wrong people. Once I get the message I want, I'll add his contact, but I'll be goddamned if I'm going to send another clusterfuck right into the middle of my first one—*Hank Baker didn't raise no fool.* At least, not a full-fledged one.

So, that book you're thinking of pitching next Friday…the thing is, I plagiarized it.

HA-HA. Oh look, it's the sight of me flushing my career down the toilet. *No.* Delete.

I know you saw potential in that manuscript, but the thing is, I'm not really done with it. I've got another part to write, and it changes the whole story and basically nullifies all the good parts of this one.

Ugh. No. Delete.

Hahaha I've got a funny story for you. As it turns out, I sent you the wrong book. I have a whole other manuscript to send you that's much more in line with what you were expecting. Other than the fact that it's a heaping pile of garbage, of course.

Doing great here, Brooke. Really making progress on sending him a message that will *help* the situation.

Are you sure the book is good enough?

Finally, a message that might work. It's vulnerable and damn near soul-crushing, but it doesn't make me sound like a fracking idiot or a con. Adding his contact in at the top, I send the message and drop my phone on the counter like a hot potato before I can reconsider.

It dings so fast with a response that a wrecking ball of lead with a caricature of Miley Cyrus riding on top swings itself into the lining of my stomach.

Chase: Better than. Brooke, it's one of the best books I've ever read.

Oh God, what have I done?

His words should make me feel better. Bring me peace of mind and a settled stomach. Instead, they inflict more fear than I'm equipped to handle, and Benji goes into service-dog mode, gently knocking me right to the floor to push my head between my knees.

The explicit book I wrote about myself and my editor while he has no freaking idea he's the protagonist is the best book he's ever read?

That's what I was afraid of.

Chapter
Three

Chase

After work, I run home to change out of my suit and into something a little less business. The apartment is quiet as a mouse, and once I toss on my favorite pair of Levi's and switch out the suit jacket and tie for a T-shirt and light bomber jacket, I grab my phone and keys off the kitchen counter and head for the door.

It's nearing seven in the evening, and I leave the light on in the entryway to make it easier to see when I get back from my sister and brother-in-law's place later tonight.

I step out into the hallway and pull the door closed behind me, but when I turn to insert my key into the lock, the dead bolt slides home all on its own. Just for shits and giggles, I stick my key in anyway and *unlock* it. But I've no more than pulled my key back out for a second when it locks again with a clack.

Is my apartment haunted? I wish, but sadly, no.

The culprit is my freaky temporary roommate Glenn.

I didn't even know he was home, but I never know when he's home. Glenn moves like a ninja at all hours of the day, a dark hoodie pulled up over his side profile to keep me from ever actually getting a look at it. He doesn't talk and he doesn't socialize, and to be honest, those have been perks. But when I find random carafes of liquid outside my door every morning and barely get the front door closed before it locks behind me, I understand why the guy living in my room before me left a complicated series of bolts on the bedroom door.

I don't know Glenn's last name. I don't know if he has a job. I don't even know how old he is. Glenn is an enigma. And I'm kind of hoping to move out before I find out exactly what that is.

How did I find myself in this living situation? Great question. One I ask myself about twenty times a day.

Seven months ago, I was hired by Longstrand Publishing and moved to New York after spending nearly a decade in the booming Southern city of Nashville. And I was used to hustle and bustle, and even a lot of weirdness, but what I wasn't prepared for in the Big Apple was a roommate by the name of Glenn.

Renting isn't cheap in New York, and finding an apartment I wanted to invest money in wasn't easy. And since I didn't want to waste cash on living in a hotel, I ended up finding a roommate arrangement with low rent and a convenient commute. It was one of those "a friend of a friend knows someone who needs a roommate" kinds of situations.

In my defense, I didn't realize I was signing on to live with Glenn, but here I am, living with Glenn.

Thankfully, the apartment I purchased and have been renovating a couple blocks away in Nolita should be ready in a month or two, and my roommate and his bizarre tendencies will be in the past.

My expenses will be higher living alone, but I won't have to keep a butcher knife under my pillow either.

When I consider where my life was two years ago, I still can't believe how much it's changed. I was social—sometimes overly so—newly engaged, and only half-baked into my focus on my career.

If there's one constant with life, it's that it changes and evolves—sometimes to the point where it feels like a real hit to the nuts—but in the end, it usually gets you where you need to be. In my case, it got me here—working at, arguably, the biggest publisher in the country, with one of the top authors in the world right now, and hyping myself up to turn my whole career inside out to make sure the books on my roster are a success.

I rarely engage with any social activity, other than the occasional dinner night with my sister and her husband like I'm doing now. It's a big change from the barhopping life I lived with my ex-fiancée Caroline, and yet, somehow, I'm happy. *Happier*, really.

I feel engaged with my life, not just in a *fake it till you make it* kind of way, but in a main character energy, "I'm driving this car" kind of way.

It's invigorating. And scary. Because when you're in charge of your destiny, *everything* is yours to gain or lose. The choices you make can't scapegoat themselves on to other people, and the reality you face is one of your own making.

You can fail. Or you can succeed bigger than you ever dreamed.

As I walk out of the elevator, I step out of the way for an elderly lady with a white poodle and hold the door until she and her little dog can get on safely. She thanks me with a smile, and I offer her the same in return before heading on my way.

The front door of my building resists my push, a gust of wind visibly sending debris of papers and leaves swirling down the street through the glass. As I lean my weight into it, the pressure breaks free and reverses, damn near jerking my shoulder out of its socket when the wind catches the door and rips it out toward the sidewalk.

The literary freak in me wants to use the simple action as symbolism for the next week and a half and how any shift in the wind could violently blow my existence in a new direction—but I'll spare you the pain and drama.

Put simply, next Friday afternoon, I take Brooke Baker's manuscript and every vestige of my hopes and dreams to the weekly editors' meeting at Longstrand with a single goal: convince the president of the company (and everyone else) to publish in an untested genre with little notice, instead of the long-awaited spin-off to an already successful series, and to do it with gusto.

Longstrand is expecting *Garden of Forever*. It was pitched as a stand-alone book that is a spin-off from Brooke Baker's worldwide blockbuster series called *The Shadow Brothers*.

And I'm about to give them something that isn't even in the same fantasy genre.

Clearly, it's going to take big balls, a lot of luck, and a hell of a pitch because the odds aren't in my favor. Jonah Perish, Longstrand's president and my boss, is amped to see what *Garden of Forever* will do on the tails of *The Shadow Brothers'* Netflix success.

But after reading *Accidental Attachment*, I'm convinced Brooke Baker has created something unlike anything I've read before. And it deserves to be published. It deserves to be experienced and talked about and devoured by every reader imaginable, and I'm the guy who needs to make that happen.

No pressure or anything.

Ha. Yeah, right. It's so much pressure that it's practically choking me alive, and it's why I convinced my sister Maureen into talking her husband Vinny, a world-renowned chef, into making my absolute favorite comfort food to-night—chicken parmigiana, extra mozzarella—on a night they would normally be working at the restaurant. It was a lot of work for them to find coverage, but I begged.

I need the comfort, and thankfully, Vinny's parents are Italian, coming here just in time to make their bouncing baby boy first-generation American. He can cook sauce in his sleep, and when he's awake, it's even better.

The cool spring wind is brutal, making couples walk close and businessmen pop the collars on their suit jackets in an attempt to keep the whoosh of it off their necks. Friends chatter as they pop in and out of basement-level bars, and the neon open signs for restaurants flash in the windows.

I take the steps down to the subway at a jog and tuck myself down the tracks to escape the entrance of the wind. Several people on the platform have the same idea, but I keep a big enough distance not to have to make conversation.

The funny thing is that no one in New York who isn't crazy tries to talk to you, but I'm so used to living in Nashville that I automatically assume small talk will be a part of my every journey.

The steel rails whine and shriek as the B train approaches, and I shove off my spot at the tiled wall and wait for the door to find its home. When it comes to a stop and a crowd of people exits, I wander into the car closest to me and take a seat in the most remote location possible—right at the front.

Once the train starts to move, I pull out my phone and open the manuscript for *Accidental Attachment*. I could call it research, I suppose, but that wouldn't be fair to the genuine interest I have in reading some of these scenes over and over again. The emotional tug is powerful, and there's nothing more exciting for a book lover than the feeling you get from a book you can *believe*.

The way she looks at me tells the story of a woman who knows. A woman who can see the dulling of the sparkle in my eyes and the flattening of the bounce in my step. A woman who's been trod on just enough times to know the weight of my stomp is coming.

A woman who deserves so much better than the cowardly behavior of a man who's worried about something as trivial as our jobs. A man who can see past the embarrassment we'd both face and will defend our love aggressively.

I want to be that man so badly. But I can't let River lose her job over me or any other man. The work she put in to get here…it'd all be down the drain and washed away for good. Because no other station would hire her. The cloud of disgrace is both broad and dense, and the news world is far too petty to rise above it.

The subway jostles and shrieks as we approach the station on 34th Avenue, so I skip down the page to read closer to the end of the chapter.

"I'm sorry, River. But we knew this wouldn't last—that it couldn't. Getting involved with a coworker never ends well. I knew that."

"But you did it anyway, Clive. We both did. You can't tell me you didn't know my heart was involved or that yours isn't either. Because if you do, you're a liar."

River's face is streaked with tears—the wetness of hurt I fueled and caused. It's so different from the unmarred façade of her work appearance, but so is the messiness of all the perfect imperfections of her larger-than-life personality.

She's so much more than an anchor voice and a pretty smile, so much more than a vessel to deliver the news. She's mustard stains and late-night I Love Lucy reruns. She's erotic midnight swims in someone else's pool and on-time arrivals that border on being too early. She's the cream and the cookie, and I'll be goddamned if I didn't take a hammer to her just to watch her crumble.

Coworkers like us aren't supposed to be together. It's a complication that doesn't mix. But when I hear her laugh, I hear my own. When I think of happiness, I think of her. And I don't know a man on the planet who'd throw that away for something less than.

I don't know a man on the planet who'd feel her heartbeat during her climax and do anything but chase a re-creation of that feeling for the rest of his existence.

My heart thumps a little louder than normal in my chest as I read over the emotion-provoking words of Clive's innermost thoughts, and the corners of my mouth curve all the way to the tops of my cheeks.

This. *This* is great literature. It's not highbrow or intellectual, but it's an *experience*. It makes the reader live and breathe and cry and mourn the losses of its characters before they celebrate the victories. It touches on passion and personal poignancy. There's a reason romance is one of the most popular genres in the world, whether snooty-falooty people want to believe it or not.

My phone buzzes with a text message. The sender? The brilliant author of this very book.

Brooke: *Are you sure the book is good enough?*

I can't blame her for asking.

Hell, I've been asking myself since the moment I decided to see it through to the end, consequences be damned.

But I can say with absolutely certainty, sitting here now, feeling the way I feel after reading this scene again, this book is worth everything I'm putting into it and then some. It's wreck and ruin and healing all in one.

It's smart, it's fresh, and it's fucking captivating. But it's also unlike anything I've ever read, which tells me it's a new literary meta that will capture an audience. This is the kind of book Hollywood drools over. It's power. It's relatable. It's the human condition and the kind of love story people will remember.

And it's why I feel zero hesitation when I text her back.

Me: Better than. Brooke, it's one of the best books I've ever read.

I put my knuckles to the posh cream door of my sister and brother-in-law's penthouse-level apartment in the Chelsea Landmark, and it isn't but one knock before it swings open with a whoosh.

My sister's smile of greeting is of the creepy variety, but I don't dare ask why. The evening is just getting started, and I'd like to cruise along without incident as long as possible.

"Chase! Hi! Hi! Come in!" She waves frantically, offering a hand for my light jacket, and, when I don't comply quick enough, reaching out and just ripping it off herself.

I turn and duck and nearly lose my balance as she snatches it from my back and smooths it onto a hanger in the hall closet.

"Jeez, Mo."

"Come on in! I've got some apps in the living room, and Vinny's finishing up dinner in the kitchen."

I pass her slowly, keeping my eyes on the strange, chaotic line of her face with suspicion. The thing is, my older sister isn't normally manic and pushy and edging toward psychotic. I know it's hard to believe in the face of her behavior now, but being the eldest Dawson sibling by four years, she's usually the more even-tempered of the two of us.

When she blows past me at the mouth of the hallway and starts patting the seat of the sofa and calling me like a dog, I've had just about enough.

"What's the deal, Mo?"

"The deal? What deal? There's no deal!"

"No deal, huh? You're honestly scaring me. Did you take a hit of speed or something?"

"Nooo," she practically growls, waving a hand in front of her face and grabbing the plate of apps from the coffee table to shove them into my chest. "Take a popper."

My eyes narrow as I study her closely, cautiously reaching for one of Vinny's famous poppers. I'm half convinced she's going to bite off a finger or two with the opportunity, but I'll be honest, Vinny's poppers are usually worth the risk. If I really had to, I could learn to type with a couple of nubs.

When she bounces up and down while watching every chew I make, I know I can't survive an entire dinner like this. I came here to relax and wind down before my meeting on Friday, not to be lured into a manic episode that will require treatment.

"Okay, Mo, what's going on? You're seriously freaking me out."

Positively bubbling, she hops up from her seat and vibrates with excitement. I brace myself for impact as she jumps toward me and plants her ass on the coffee table in front of me, leaving only six inches of space between us. "You have to tell me. I've been *dying* all week, knowing you had a meeting with *the* Brooke Baker! What did she say? What did she do? Did she have any top-secret news? Was she chic or relatable or—"

"Mo-Mo—" I edge in carefully.

"No, no, stop right there." She holds up her hand in front of my face, close enough that I can make out the lines of her fingerprints. "Don't try to soften me up with nicknames and affection and shit, and then try to beg off by claiming editor-client privilege or whatever. I want the details about what she's like, and I want them now. You can formally address me as Maureen for the rest of the evening, just to ensure things stay professional."

My sister has officially lost her mind. "Exactly. Things have to stay professional. And you know that means I can't tell you anything, *Maureen*."

"Ugh!" Her arms fling into the air before landing with a slap on her knees. "Don't give me that shit, Chase! Mom and Dad already gave you the better name, you can't keep this from me too."

"What the hell does one have to do with the other?"

"You'd better just tell her, bro," my brother-in-law Vinny interjects, popping his head outside of the kitchen briefly. "I haven't stopped hearing about this since you told her it was happening last week."

With the way my sister is panting like a dog over any insight into Brooke Baker, you'd think I've been working with her for years. Which I haven't. This will be the first book I've worked with Brooke on. Prior to this, we've only had a few meetings together. Chatted on the phone several times. Texted occasionally. Other than that, it's still pretty early in our author-editor relationship.

Though, I can't deny I do see the appeal. Brooke Baker is fantastic. She's easygoing and sweet, and her smile never comes across as anything but genuine. She's a class act, but she's also relatable and endearing.

"Chase! Details! *Now*," my sister nearly growls again, and her eyes start doing this weird thing where I feel concerned they're going to pop straight out of their sockets.

I sigh heavily, not wanting to go into the details of everything that happened to Brooke during our meeting—obviously, my sister couldn't know that she had a health episode while she was in my office, and the level of confidentiality I feel is important because of it—but I have to give her something if I don't want her to peck off one of my limbs.

"It was a really exciting meeting." *In every way possible.* "She's just as hilarious in person as she is in print, which is really refreshing since that's not always the case. And her newest book is…well, I think it's seriously special. It's different, though. So, I'm going to have to sell it to the other editors pretty hard."

"Different?" Maureen asks, leaning in eagerly. "Different how?"

"Just the whole vibe of it. It's still really witty writing, but the genre is a bit of a sidestep."

"Ooh, I am so intrigued right now," my sister coos. "I need the manuscript."

I snort, roll my eyes, and grab a popper and toss it into my mouth before sinking into the cushy pillow on the back of Mo's expensive couch. "You know I can't give it to you."

"No, I don't. Andrea Sachs got *Harry Potter* for Miranda Priestly. Why can't you do this for me?"

"Maybe because I value my new job and don't want to lose it? Or, I don't know, this isn't a Hollywood movie? It's my actual life."

"Oh!" she grumbles, waving a hand in the air. "You always were such a do-gooder."

"Look, all I can say is that it's not a mistake for you to keep fangirling over her. She's a great writer and, from what contact I've had, though limited, a truly awesome human too." I shrug, trying to keep myself collected under Maureen's scrutiny. It's weird. And unnerving. And I don't know why she's doing it, but I'm not going to ask. When it comes to my sister, you must never, ever ask. "Her dog is pretty cool too."

"She has a dog?" Mo breathes, like canine ownership is something reserved for the Messiah.

"Yes. His name is Benji."

"Oh my God, Benji! I love that so much!" She turns to the kitchen. "We need a dog named Benji, Vinny!"

"You live in a top-floor skyscraper with limited roof access," I mutter, knowing that nothing I say at this point will even make it inside her ears.

"What kind of dog, hun?" Vinny calls back, never one to disappoint my sister. It's normally an endearing quality—one that makes me sure he's the right guy for her and then some—but right now, it makes me roll my eyes into the back of my head.

My sister turns to me without even blinking. "What kind of dog?"

I guffaw. "You sound deranged right now, I hope you know that. Like a freaking stalker."

"What kind of dog, Chase!" she demands, her question not very question-y at all.

"Brooke has a German shepherd."

"A German shepherd, Vin!" she calls back excitedly, and all I can do is shake my head in dismay. It was so nice, having a sane sister for thirty-three years of life. I'll miss it.

"I'll look into it, hun," Vinnie responds from the kitchen, and I look down at their ivory rug to hide my smile. At least someone hasn't lost their mind yet. Vinny's accommodating her, sure, but the brother-in-law I know would be on the phone right now with dog rescue organizations if he had even an ounce of interest in owning a dog.

Frankly, it's impressive how well he knows how to handle my sister in moments like this.

Mo, mollified for now, turns back to me again, excitement still alight in her eyes. "What else? Tell me everything about her!"

"I don't even know her that well, Mo."

She scowls, and I sigh.

"*Maureen*," I correct, and she nods. "I've only been in her company a few times, and most of the meetings were brief, at that."

Maureen jumps up from the coffee table and starts to pace, pointing several angry fingers at me every chance she gets. "That doesn't mean you don't know things. I know you well enough to know that you make it a point to know anyone you're going to be working with. You know her. You just don't want to tell me what you know."

I groan, stretch out an arm along the top of the couch, and let my head fall back. "She's nice, okay? Funny." I pick up my head from the back and meet her eyes again, shrugging. "Very funny, actually. Both in her writing and in person. And she's...well, she's beautiful. Big, honest, green eyes and perfect skin and teeth. Everything I know about her is pretty much...perfect."

A visual of Brooke in my office this afternoon fills my head. *Light purple dress that complemented her skin—and her body—in the best kind of way. It just barely brushed above her knees, revealing a modest amount of her long legs. Her long, thick brown hair hung past her shoulders and—*

"Ohh, you think she's beautiful *and* perfect," she hems, rubbing her hands together and jumping onto the couch beside me on her knees so she's uncomfortably close. Immediately, I regret my choice of words *and* my rogue, irrational thoughts.

"Stop, Mo. I don't mean it like that. I just mean that if you're going to fangirl over someone, it seems like you've picked a good choice. You might want to dial it back a bit, but that's just my personal preference for keeping myself from having to attend a lengthy trial on your behalf. You do you, sis."

She sighs happily. "And the book… You said it's different?"

"Good different." I find myself clarifying with a nod.

"Oh man, I love the sound of that." She claps and bounces on her knees, and I find the corners of my mouth curling up without permission. "Can you at least give me something? A little tiny nugget of hopes and dreams and exclusivity that I can rub in my reader friends' faces. Pleeeeeeease," she begs, clenching her hands together and wiggling back and forth.

"When you get done with it, yours and Vinny's love story won't be the only one you're invested in," I say, finding I can't help but play into her excitement just this little bit. I mean, it is a damn good book, and technically, it's part of my job to make people want to read it. Leaning into Mo's hype alone will probably do half of the legwork for me. With her current state, it'll be less than twenty-four hours before she shares my sentiments with half the city.

She shrieks so loud the windows shake, and I sit back on the couch, satisfied.

I've compelled my audience into an actual fit of glee, and I can only hope I walk away from my meeting next Friday with the same results.

My career and Brooke's next big success are counting on it.

Chapter
Four

Friday, May 5ᵗʰ

Chase

Today, I can honestly say, I'm scared.

Scared of the possibilities ahead of me in today's editors' meeting and all that entails for the future and, more urgently, scared that Glenn, evidently, does not appear to have a job.

I've been home for three extra hours this morning, trying to lessen the tense time in the office before one of the most important meetings of my life, and Glenn has shown absolutely no signs of leaving.

I haven't actually seen him, of course, but I've heard him moving around, and the pitcher of unknown liquid—*it's blue today*—I found outside my door first thing this morning was gone by the time I made it back to my room with my first cup of coffee.

The first time he left liquid outside my door, I feared it was a gift for me or some kind of bad omen of what's to come. But after a few more odd-colored carafes of mystery fluid, I've learned that they never stay there for long. Eventually, he takes it away and does… Well, I don't know what he does with it. I don't even know what it is. I'm also pretty sure I probably don't want to know. Some things are truly better left unsaid.

I grab my tan canvas bag—one that's reminiscent of Peter McCallister's bag in *Home Alone: Lost in New York* and a complete manifestation of my generational influences—swig the last drops of my third cup of coffee from my mug, and put in the sink. I fill the mug with water to make sure the coffee doesn't stain, but I'll have to wash it later. The editors' meeting at Longstrand waits for no one—especially not me—and between how long I've waited to head into the office and the commute itself, I'm going to be cutting it close.

A little too close for my punctual taste, to be honest.

Music starts to play from Glenn's room, loud and aggressive and slightly on the edge of what might be satanic in nature, and I move even quicker to get the hell out of here. I grab my phone and keys and head for the door.

I pull it closed behind myself and ready my keys at the lock to secure the dead bolt, but before I can even stick it inside, I hear the mechanism turn, just like always.

Glenn, the bizarre bastard. *How the hell did he even know I was leaving with his music playing that loud?*

I need my place in Nolita to get done like I need my next breath.

And I should probably consider checking the apartment—and my room—again for hidden cameras. Yes, *again*, because I've already been down this road three times before, and every time, I've come up empty-handed.

But I'll save that dilemma for another time.

Right now, I need to focus like I'm Jason Bourne on the run from the CIA and trying to figure out my father's true identity.

I glance down at my phone as I step onto the elevator and hit the button for the ground floor. The screen showcases two missed calls—one occurred while I was sleeping last night, and the other came in this morning while I was getting ready. The first one makes me roll my eyes—there's not a chance in hell I'm calling Mo back right now—and the other one can wait until I get into the office.

My assistant Dawn knows I don't want her working outside of business hours anyway, and I don't want to encourage the behavior. This industry is stressful enough. I might work at all hours of the night, but Dawn doesn't get paid enough to do the same. She works hard during the day, and quite frankly, that's enough.

I'm out of my building and down the block to the D train before I know it, headed toward my stop at 7th Avenue and West 53rd.

The subway is relatively quiet this morning, and that's mostly because I'm a good four hours behind the normal morning rush commute. Most people in New York need to bleed as many hours into their work as humanly possible to afford their rent, so they head for the office by seven a.m. at the latest.

I can't say my life is entirely different on any normal day, but today, I knew my stomach was going to be playing host to several very energetic butterflies who require as much breathing room as possible. I need to get in there and go straight for the meat and potatoes of the day to keep my visitors from trashing the place and from turning over its contents in the upheaval.

I use the quiet to pull my paper version of *Accidental Attachment* from my bag so I can scan through it and feed off the scenes to drive my campaign.

One of the most memorable to me is the first time Clive meets River. She's shy and unassuming and even awkward at times, but there's something about her from the start that tugs at Clive's sensibilities. He's never dreamed of mixing his personal life with work, but River makes the task of maintaining that boundary much, much harder.

"River Rollins, I presume?" I greet with a smile, reaching out a hand for the woman of the hour. As the new female anchor on our staff, she's held court with just about every other employee in the building at this point.

"Yes!" she says excitedly, her smile touching the greenest part of her eyes in earnest. "That's me. And you must be Clive Watts. I've heard so much about you from everyone today, I think I could draw a picture of you in my sleep." Her words make her startle, and her eyebrows climb to her hairline. "Not that I…would…you know, do something like that. I don't draw anything at night other than a bath. Truthfully, I'm pretty much shit artistically."

I start to smile, start to respond, but she cuts me off with a little gasp as her hand covers her mouth. "And now I've gone and said 'shit' on my first day to my…well, my boss. So, so sorry. I promise not to curse on air."

I smile warmly—at this point, my face is unable to consider any other expression. "That's all right. That's what we have Nate and the beeper for. I'll tell him to keep one hand at the ready."

"I don't normally need a censor handy, I swear."

"Really?" I ask, to which she replies with a fervent nod. My smile changes slightly, I can feel it, and yet, not even the warning can stop me from uttering my next words. "That's a shame."

River's cheeks flood with a blush so pretty, I feel it in my thighs. I like it way too much. And if I give myself more time, I'd try to search for a way to make that gorgeous blush of hers grow deeper.

I've just met this woman, and I already feel like I can't be trusted around her. Shouldn't be in her orbit for more than a few seconds.

What in the hell is wrong with me?

The train squeals as the brakes engage, and I pick my head up out of the book for the first time since I opened it. It's so easy to get lost in—so easy to fall in love with. God, I hope I can convey that to Jonah Perish properly.

I close my binder and shove it into my bag as the train slows to a stop, and I exit the car upon the opening of the doors. I have a few blocks to walk, and with a light sprinkle having just started while I was leaving my building, the last thing I need is to soak the pages of my copy of the manuscript until they're illegible.

I could print another copy, sure, but this one is already well-read and well-loved and filled with hours' worth of notes.

Experiencing this book for the first time—getting those notes back again—is something I'd never re-create correctly.

And that's a much greater risk than I'm willing to take.

Despite the light sprinkle that turned into a near downpour when I still had a block left to walk to my office, I was able to make it on time.

I even managed to run into the bathroom and dry my hair and suit jacket underneath the automatic hand dryer.

But now, whether I feel ready or not, it's time to face the music.

I step out of my office, and the glass door falls closed behind me just as my assistant's eyes lift from her computer screen to meet mine.

Instantly, I look down the hallway, toward the conference room I can't even see, and my heart rate kicks up about fifty notches. Realization is a son of a bitch, reminding me of what I'm about to attempt, and my stomach relocates to my throat.

Right now, I may as well be a fifteen-year-old boy with a face full of acne who is about to give a presentation to his class that just so happens to contain his crush.

Get it together, man.

And my assistant is still looking at me, most likely trying to understand why I'm just standing outside my office door.

"All right, Dawn," I say with a deep breath as I straighten my tie in front of her desk. "Tell me I've got this."

"You've got this," she says immediately and dutifully...and with no enthusiasm at all.

"Dawn!" I whisper-yell.

"What?" she asks, a smile lurking at the corners of her mouth. "I said it."

"Say it again and mean it," I order a little too brusquely, and then reel myself back in by softening my voice exponentially. "Please. Sorry, sorry, I'm sorry. I'm just nervous."

"Don't be nervous, sir," she replies. Thankfully, this time with vigor. "I've never seen anyone believe in anything as much as you believe in this book, and they're going to notice that too. You've got this, Chase Dawson. You've so got this."

"Okay, that was really good. So good that I've completely forgotten the first lame attempt." I sigh heavily and smile. "Thank you."

"I'd do almost anything for someone in as pathetic a state as you."

"Well, thank you. How kind," I say with an almost scoff sticking at the top of my throat.

Dawn laughs. "I have a husband and two sons at home. I only have so much energy left for taking care of a man. Don't take it personally."

I consider her for a moment. She's put together perfectly with an ironed blouse and made-up face and well-placed hair. But if you look closely, the skin beneath her eyes is darkened with fatigue, and she has a small stain on her blouse that has been worked over with a Tide pen.

She carries the façade well, but the truth, I fear, is that my assistant Dawn is a nightwalker of sorts, doing her best to survive.

"I'm really lucky you put up with me, aren't I?"

She shrugs. "You're the easiest male I deal with—usually—and you pay me. So, you're in a pretty good position. Still, there's a reason that show *Snapped* is a thing."

I laugh, my eyebrows rising to my hairline. "So, I'll make a mental note of that horrifying fact and keep it in mind moving forward."

Dawn stands up to give me a firm pat on the shoulder and then pushes me in the direction of the conference room so hard I have to jog to keep my footing. "Go get 'em, tiger."

I thought I'd stall a little bit more, but as I walk down the hallway and approach the glass-walled conference room in the center of our office floor, I see that Dawn was right to push me.

Three of the other editors have already arrived and are shooting the shit while they wait for the big man, Jonah Perish himself.

Jonah is the grandson of Carl Longstrand, the founder of Longstrand Publishing and the main reason we're as big as we are today. It'd be easy to dismiss his position as president and CEO of Longstrand as a showing of nepotism, but anyone who knows Jonah knows he's a shark in his own right. Not only has he modernized his grandfather's vision, but he's also taken an ever-changing publishing landscape and flourished in it. When other publishers saw downturns because of KDP and self-publishing, Jonah saw to it that business at Longstrand picked up.

He saw an opening to give authors the kind of support they were longing for—one of the only things missing from the setup of a one-person self-publishing show.

We market and distribute at a higher level than anyone else and carry a lot of the workload when it comes to all the things a self-publisher would have to contract out to freelancers. But overall, what really sets us apart in my eyes is the willingness to fuss over our authors. They're the value of the company, and keeping them happy and comfortable is our number one goal. In the end, it benefits everyone.

I enter through the door with a stack of synopses clutched to my chest, and the heads of my colleagues turn in my direction.

"Oh, man. You brought props?" Frank Bowman asks with a teasing smile. "This oughta be good."

I shake my head with a smile and toss one in his direction quickly enough that he has to scramble to catch it. Regina Swanson and Meryl Hargrove, two of the best editors in the business, laugh.

"He's still in his honeymoon, suck-up phase, Frank. It'll pass," Regina adds with a wink that's friendly enough to make me move right past her remark without addressing it.

"It's going to be great, Frank," I announce with the kind of confident smile that is the opposite of how the inside of my body feels. "Prepare to be amazed."

He smirks with a shake of his head. "Man, I remember when I used to be a cocky little shit like you. The good old days. Now if I let my dick swell too much, my back hurts."

Regina and Meryl laugh again, coughing to correct it as Jonah enters the room, his assistant shutting the door behind him.

"Good morning, ladies." Meryl and Regina smile and return the sentiment before Jonah turns to us, his face transforming from jovial to serious. "Don't disappoint me, gentlemen."

Frank and I both smile at Jonah's less-than-enthusiastic greeting and, quite frankly, thrive on it. At some point in his career, Jonah figured out that women thrive with affection and men thrive with pressure, and he started employing it. We're all at our best working under him. I'm still in the fledgling part of my career here at Longstrand, but I have no doubt that taking the job here and mentoring under a man like him will get me much further than any other moves would have.

"All right, people, I have a busy day and a busier night. I promised my wife to quit early and take her on a date, and I think you all know I'm a man of follow-through." Jonah looks at us with an amused smile, and we all nod back in response. "So, who's first?"

I raise my hand like a kid in school, knowing if I don't get this whole thing out of the way, I'm liable to spontaneously combust with anticipation. I'm in Upchuck Alley, and too many minutes hanging out here is bound to end with chunks of my lunchtime chicken salad sandwich all over my socks.

"Dawson. Great." Jonah pulls out his chair at the head of the table and unbuttons the front of his suit coat before taking a seat. He grabs his reading glasses out of his chest pocket and slides them over the bridge of his nose to glance through the packet I've placed in his spot.

As he reads, he talks. "You've received *Garden of Forever* from Brooke Baker, correct? How are we looking with the manuscript? Can we make a three- or four-month timeline, or do we need longer? No reason to shit the bed by waiting too long and letting the Netflix buzz cool off. We've got to strike while the iron is still in the fire."

And here we go…

"Actually, sir…" I clear my throat. "It's not *Garden of Forever*…" Jonah's eyes come to me over the edge of his black-framed glasses, and the steeliness makes me swallow twice. "Brooke turned in a different book…called *Accidental Attachment*."

"A different book?" he scoffs, and to be honest, I can't blame him. An author going that far off legal script is highly unusual.

"Yes, sir," I make myself reply confidently. "I assure you, though, I feel very strongly that this book option is much better. I know it's unorthodox, but I believe we're getting the better end of the deal here."

He blinks. Just one, long, hard blink. "Did Brooke Baker supply a reason for the change?"

I shake my head. "No, sir. And truth be told, I was too excited about the book she did submit to even think to ask her."

Jonah removes his glasses and tosses them on the table, leaning back and crossing his arms over his chest.

"You didn't think to ask her?"

"No...sir." Boy, my throat feels thicker than usual.

Jonah studies me closely for several seconds, and I spend every one of them wondering if I should be filling them with babble. Unable to come up with any, I settle for meeting his gaze with a steadiness I have no idea how I'm producing.

Swath of smooth peppered hair bouncing slightly, he shifts in his chair and purses his lips before speaking. "Junior editor at Brentwood Books in Nashville for five years. Senior editor for three years after that, with three debut authors unexpectedly hitting the *New York Times* and staying there for several weeks under your leadership. Have I got that right?"

I swallow a nervous burp and nod. "Yes, sir."

"Your track record is impressive, Dawson, and one of the reasons I personally voted to hire you."

"Thank you, sir. I—"

"But this isn't the kind of thing we do—switching out an approved manuscript for one we've never seen or heard of before."

"I understand that, sir. Really, I do. I know that the algorithm for sales is made up of one part writing, two parts marketing, and three parts similarity to things people have a proven history of liking before. I know it's highly unusual to switch to an untested genre, even with a vetted, proven author like Brooke, but I wouldn't be presenting this idea to you without merit. This book is worth it. I promise you that."

"You sound pretty damn sure."

"Yes, sir. I am."

"Sure enough to bet your job on it?"

The question isn't theoretical—I can tell from the sharp inhalation of all the air in the room by everyone in it. If I don't make this book a hit, I might as well pack my shit.

Fuck, I'm rhyming. Now I know I'm nervous.

Of all the major moments I've had in my life, this one somehow feels like the biggest. Like the decision to go for this or not—the choice to take this challenge by the balls instead of sitting around and twiddling my thumbs—will be a huge factor in the outcome of the rest of my life.

I don't know if that's true or if it's some sort of coping mechanism I've acquired to keep myself from literally shitting my pants while one of the most powerful men in publishing stares me down, but I have to roll with it. I can't back down now.

"Yes, sir. I am." All the air in the room shrinks as if sucked up by a vacuum, and wide eyes stare back at me from every department.

Holy shit. I actually said it.

Frank's face, in particular, looks like someone just threatened him with a knife. *Don't worry, Frankie. I can't believe I said it either.*

Mr. Perish surveys me closely, his knowledgeable brown eyes looking for something I'm not sure I know how to convey. And the conference room is so quiet that all I can hear is the pounding of my heart roaring inside my ears.

The clock on the wall, above Jonah Perish's head, ticks through the seconds, and it feels like the seconds turn to minutes. Many, *many* minutes. But Jonah remains stoic, and I can't get a read on him while he's trying to get a read on me, and it is an otherwise psychological mindfuck.

It reminds me of the time I egged Bobby Tubertille's house when I was fourteen, and my dad spent the night interrogating me and every other kid on my street. His glare was so hard I could feel it in my spine. But I didn't break then, and I'm not going to break now. My insides may be vibrating themselves into Jell-O, but I'm not backing down.

I want Longstrand to publish this book. Brooke Baker deserves for Longstrand to stand behind her, even if she went off script and gave us something that wasn't in the contract.

"All right, Dawson," Jonah finally announces. "We'll stand behind your decision. But I hope you know what you're getting yourself into and just how much it'll cost *all* of us if you're wrong."

His meaning is clear as crystal. The price for Longstrand will be money. The price for me? A very bloody end to my entire career.

I nod. It's all I can manage with a lump the size of Texas in my throat.

"Good. Now that that's settled, what's next?" Mr. Perish directs, thankfully moving the attention away from me before anyone notices the sweat that is most likely dripping from every pore of my body.

Clearly, though, I'm happy. I'm *thrilled*. This is what I wanted. Brooke's book deserves to be read, and I deserve the shot to prove it.

But, dear God, please help my body withstand the pressure.

Chapter
Five

Brooke

Belinda Carlisle plays from the boom box in the corner of my living room, and I scrub at the crusty food on the seat of my barstool. My pink vinyl gloves squeak against the wood with every wipe of my rag.

I'm not a neat freak in the traditional sense. In fact, I'm not nearly disciplined enough to be that steady in any aspect of my life. I mostly live in fits and starts, bingeing in my mess and then attacking the consequences like a woman possessed when the clutter overwhelms my sense of peace.

There's a lot of other stuff infringing on my kumbaya vibes these days—*one thing, in particular, that involves my publisher and a book I'm choosing not to think about,* but for the sanctity of my survival, I've compartmentalized all that out of my thoughts and am choosing to fixate obsessively on cleaning and scrubbing my kitchen.

It's called *Advanced Avoidance,* and I could teach a honors-level course at Harvard.

I toss the rag onto the countertop and round the tiny island only a New York apartment could call spacious, stepping to the sink in the corner. Bending to the cabinet underneath, I grab an industrial-strength cleaner that has the power to resurface almost anything. Or at least, that's what the late-night informercial that convinced me to buy it said. Vinyl gloves still on, you know, because I'd like to keep my skin, I uncap the bottle and shoot the foam from the nozzle over every inch of exposed stainless steel of my sink. It coats it evenly and intensely, and I hack a cough from the potency of its chemical smell.

Then, I hack again.

And *again.*

"Shit!" I sputter through several choking coughs from my lungs. Tears coat my eyeballs when an abnormal sting wreaks havoc on my vision.

Fearful that I'm about to poison myself from toxic fumes, I stumble over to the window at the end of the counter and shove it open. I can hear Benji's paws tap across the kitchen floor behind me, but I'm too busy hanging my head out the window and gasping for untainted oxygen. The air is stale in a way I'm used to after this many years in New York, but it's still better than the vicious stuff I just sprayed in my kitchen.

A slight breeze blows past me and into the apartment, swirling the untouched air and setting some of the potency free. I fill my lungs with a few more breaths of NYC oxygen and wipe the tears from my eyes before carefully backing out of my window guillotine and pulling my gloves from my hands with a snap.

Suddenly, cleaning has lost some of its mystique. I can't be sure if it's from the health risks that I didn't realize were involved, but it certainly didn't help my motivation.

I trudge back to the sink, and without scrubbing, I rinse the industrial cleaner down the drain. Once I'm confident the toxic product is headed for the sewer system, I relocate myself to my semi-clean island and proceed to slouch over the surface. Benji snuggles closer to me now that I'm returning to a more normal state, and I welcome the warmth of his soft fur on my bare feet. I grab the remote to my boom box and switch off my cleaning music—Belinda— and put it back to the woman who tells it best—Dolly.

"You know, Benj, I'm not sure I'm cut out for this cleaning stuff. Maybe I should just hire someone to do it," I remark, tossing the remote back down to the counter and leaning into my elbows again.

Benji responds by nuzzling his snout closer to my toes. I take that as his agreement. *Yes, you should definitely hire someone instead of risking our lungs.*

Dolly's barely three lines into "9 to 5" when three sharp, pounding knocks on the other side of my door pull my spine straight from its usual hunch-backed position—*desk workers unite!*—and the skin between my eyebrows knits. Benji's curious too, jumping up from his place on the floor beside my feet and tilting his head to the side.

I'm going to be really impressed if he already called someone at a cleaning service. Paw dialing is tricky.

The thing is…we don't get visitors very often. Other than a yearly visit from my Midwestern parents, Benji and I pretty much rule this roost. It's not that I don't have a couple of acquaintances in the city, but they're not the kind of people I invite over for wine and cheese on a weekly basis. Truth be told, I save the vast majority of my social energy for my characters.

They need to be interesting a whole hell of a lot more than I do.

I bend over to give Benji a swift scratch on the head to reassure him he shouldn't be worried. It's a lie—we both know it, given my heart rate—but my dog is sophisticated enough to understand it's the thought that counts.

On hurried legs, I dash across the open space to shut off Dolly—the power button on my 1990s remote gave out a long time ago—and then head back in the direction of the door. Another knock sounds, and it feels like whoever is on the other side is growing impatient.

I cross the living room, and when I reach the entry, I take a deep breath before leaning in to look through the peephole. I don't want whoever it is to hear me hyperventilating through the wood.

Chase's handsome face is distorted and ballooned thanks to the fish-eye effect of the view, but I'd recognize his features anywhere.

Though, I'll be honest, I never expected any of the *anywheres* to be right outside my apartment door.

What is he doing here?

Panic rushes over me, and Benji bumps into my legs in warning. I take three deep breaths and try to steady my voice as I call out, "Yes? Who is it?" like I don't know who the motherflipping fox just outside my henhouse is.

"It's Chase! Dawson. Your editor!" he stammers, quickly sucked into my game of stupidity. I shake my head, glance down at my shirt before giving it a sniff test, take another cleansing breath, and finally open the door.

Benji stands at attention next to me, and to be honest, I can't blame him. Last time I was around this guy, I totally flubbed the whole consciousness thing.

"Chase?" I greet, still sounding unsure as to who and what he is. An alien, an amoeba? He could be anything at this point.

His cheeks are full and bright with blush, and his hair is standing on end as though he's run his hands through it a million and one times.

"We did it, Brooke! We did it."

The words ring in my ears as I try avidly not to make sense of them. To ignore them completely. To transport my brain to a little, tiny island with cute umbrella drinks and no work whatsoever.

But my pulse pounds in my throat, and Benji crowds my legs like a little doggie couch.

Chase reaches out and grabs my face, both cheeks at once like you'd do if you were about to kiss someone, and the action momentarily gets my erratic heart's attention. "They agreed to make the change and take the chance!"

He searches my gaze, his hands still cupping my cheeks, and he is so close that I can see the swirls of blue and light gray within his eyes. There's even a hint of gold around the edges, and if I leaned my face a few more inches, our lips would touch.

Our lips. Mine and Chase's.

"*Accidental Attachment* is getting published!" he exclaims, and his voice bounces with the kind of enthusiasm that grabs my focus with an ironclad fist. "We have the green light to let the world fall in love with Clive and River!"

Oh noooooooo.

My eyes widen so much the skin around them pulls, and Benji knocks me right off my feet, bringing Chase down on top of me as a result. His weight is heavy, but the rest of my senses spin like a toy top that's been released from a child's hands.

Holy shit, how could I have forgotten what day it is? It's Friday. *The* Friday! *Probably because you decided to try your hand at a career as the next Merry Maid instead of thinking about it.*

But now, I *have* to think about it, and the worst possible verdict is in—the book I wrote about the guy lying on top of me without his knowledge is getting published.

My ears buzz with that familiar ringing sound, and my peripheral vision rivals that of a drunk person.

I'm about to go night-night, I can feel it...

"Brooke, are you okay? Brooke!" I can hear the words being yelled, but the voice in my throat and edge of my consciousness are too muddled to respond.

I haven't passed out completely in quite some time. I've skirted the brink, danced with the syncope devil, but never went fully lights-out. But this time, I can tell by the tingle in my palms and the wonky sound of Chase's voice that all good streaks eventually come to an end.

Especially under the duress of finding out that the book you wrote about yourself and a man who has no fucking clue is going to be in bookstores worldwide, just waiting for people to read every dirty, salacious word.

Dear God and the Holy Ghost—I'm pretty sure Clive and River even devolve into anal play at the end of that one chapter I wrote after drowning in two bottles of wine.

And just like that—there's a gap in the space-time continuum of Brooke Baker.

For all I know, the world stops turning.

Chase snaps his fingers in front of my face, and Benji barks directly in my ear as I start to come to, trying to make sense of where I am and who I'm with and what the hell is going on.

The thing about passing out I've never been able to come to terms with is that it doesn't exactly read well with details in first-person POV. I don't know what happens when my lights are out—I can only piece it together from the clues I find when they come back on.

"God, Brooke, are you okay?" Chase asks, half muttering to himself as he cradles my head in one hand and looks manically around my apartment for something. Benji licks at my face—a fun treat since his breath still smells like his dog food dinner—and I surreptitiously reach down to feel if my pants are peed.

When the pajama fabric brushes dry against my fingertips, relief escapes my lungs in a lengthy exhale.

"Brooke? Hello? Can you hear me?" Chase tries again, this time sounding even more desperate. He shakes his head then, scrambling to dig in his back pocket while still crouching and holding my head in his other hand. It's pretty impressive, and I'm not sure I was generous enough with Clive's flexibility when I was writing the book.

"I'm calling for an ambulance," he declares, and *that* wakes me out of my slumber.

"No, no," I say, my throat just dry enough that my words sound raspy. "I'm okay. I don't need a ten-thousand-dollar joyride today."

"Then let me drive you, or—" He curses under his breath. "I walked here. Wait…I could get a cab!"

Sadly, I think Chase Dawson is even cuter when he's problem-solving.

"I'm okay, really. I mean, my head isn't spurting a scary liquid, right?"

"No. No liquid coming from your head," he replies, testing the feel of his fingers in my hair just to be sure. It feels stimulating, like a good scalp massage at the hairdresser.

In a seriously problematic way, given the circumstances, my mind takes out its notepad to scribble down yet another thing that Chase Dawson is capable of on a master's level: Shampoo Girl. Immediately entranced, I picture Chase in some trendy NYC salon, all the women flocking to his tip jar to stuff their bras inside.

Good grief, maybe I do need a ride in the meat wagon. Destination: psych ward.

"Brooke? Please, let me take you to get checked out. You're still scaring me."

Well, that's convenient, Chase. Because I'm also scaring myself in ways you can't even imagine.

Using the muscles of my core, I force myself to sit up, and Chase backs away just enough to give me room. He doesn't stand or retreat, and our breaths are left to commingle in a pretty tight space.

Ignore it, ignore it, ignore it, I chant in my head three times fast. I really don't want to do a blood panel at the hospital, and I definitely don't feel like losing access to wine if this thing is really going to market.

I need to get it together, and I need to do it quick.

"I'm sorry...you know, for scaring you," I start and briefly shut my eyes to focus on breathing in a few heart-calming breaths. "I'm okay, I promise...just overwhelmed and medically inept."

Chase's eyebrows draw together as I gather myself enough to stand, his capable hands steadying me at the forearms.

"Overwhelmed in a good way, right?" he clarifies, searching my eyes with an intensity I'm in no way ready to give myself over to. I look to the floor, trying to find a sliver of my dignity on the tile surface. Unfortunately, in the face of finding out the book I wrote in secret about this man and me and all of my kinkiest fantasies is going to be spread around the world like butter, fainting into his arms, and just barely pulling myself together enough not to piss myself, all the shreds of my pride are gone.

When I glance back up and into his pretty blue eyes, they're desperate—silently begging me for the confirmation that I'm ready and willing to tackle the effort it's going to take to get this entirely different book published successfully.

Which, of course, I am *not*. Not even close. I'd get to the moon in a go-kart faster than I'm going to get comfortable with this book.

But his puppy-dog eyes and excited spirit are too much to deny. I have no option but to lie my ass off.

"Y-yes. In the best way. Just…I… Well, I didn't expect a warm reception, and I think it doesn't feel real."

My B-size boobs suddenly becoming double Ds with no surgical intervention seems more in line with reality, if I'm honest.

"Oh, it's real. *Accidental Attachment* is going to market, and it's doing it soon. As a matter of fact, we only have four weeks to get it in final draft shape."

"Four weeks?" I wheeze. He's got to be kidding me. I haven't done edits that fast…well, ever.

"I know. It's tight. But we're going to work together on this thing every step of the way. I'm not going to leave you alone in this, I promise."

Ha. Ha. Yeah. That's kind of what I was afraid of. More scary words from the frighteningly handsome man.

The buzz of light-headedness returns with a vengeance, and Benji crowds my legs. Chase notices the change in my position and jumps into action, shoving me back with a gentle and guiding hold at my arms until I'm seated at one of the freshly cleaned kitchen counter barstools.

"Brooke. Jesus. Look at me, Brooke."

I shake my head and swivel my hips to lift my legs up onto the counter in front of me, forcing the blood away from my extremities and back toward my brain. The relief that comes with the change of the tide is swift and true, and I gulp a deep lungful of fresh air.

"That's it. Come on, I'm taking you to the hospital on my damn back if I have to."

"No!" I snap at first, before steadying my voice and softening my approach when he looks disappointed in me. "Sorry. I just… This happens a lot. I don't need to go, I promise."

"A lot? How much is a lot?"

"Are you looking for the subjective conjecture held by society or, like, my own opinion on a number?"

"Brooke."

I dig my teeth into my bottom lip. "I have a condition called vasovagal syncope. Basically, something triggers a drop in my blood pressure, and boop, I'm dropping into a fainted state like a cast member on *Days of Our Lives*. It's not horribly uncommon—maybe you know someone who can't stand the sight of blood or whatever and passes out—but I'm kind of a standout student in the class. This, well…this makes about nine hundred and seventy-six times I've passed out in my lifetime."

His eyes couldn't be any bigger right now. "*About* nine hundred and seventy-six?"

"Okay, *exactly* nine hundred and seventy-six, but most of those are from my childhood, honestly, before my parents really had a handle on just how much of a nuisance I was." I offer a nonchalant shrug of my shoulder. "And I almost never get to the point of unconsciousness since I've had Benji at my back. He's specifically trained to catch all the warning signs and get me into a position that optimizes bringing my blood pressure back up to normal."

Almost subconsciously, Chase reaches down and scratches at my good boy's ears, and the sweet gesture causes an unfortunate skip in my heart.

"So, what? You just live like this? There's no treatment?"

I shake my head and shrug at the same time. "Avoid triggers. Stay really hydrated. Move slowly if I'm going to be changing positions, like from sitting to standing or lying down to sitting, et cetera. Other than that, I'm just special, I guess."

He frowns, entirely unhappy with my answer. "What about medication? There's got to be something."

"They tried putting me on anxiety meds, but it made my management of the whole thing worse. It kind of numbed me, I guess, and I was missing all my normal warning signs. Benji takes that period of our lives very personally."

"Well, shit."

I almost laugh but, instead, allow myself a bemused smile. "On the positive side, it's not contagious. So other than catching my bloated carcass every once in a while, you don't have anything to worry about."

He frowns so hard this time, the normally perfect skin between his eyebrows mars itself with a jagged wrinkle. "I'm not worried about *me*. I'm worried about *you*."

Hearing those words from his very specific set of lips is almost enough to trigger me into a backslide. But I fight the feeling, shoving the excitement of having my crush's interest in anything about me down into the depths of my stomach.

"And that's seriously so nice of you. But I swear, I don't get into too much excitement on the regular. This is a rarity, really. Nothing to worry about."

He scoffs. "The last two times I've seen you this has happened."

That, of course, is true. But Chase Dawson and his strong jaw are definitely considered extenuating circumstances. How to explain that to him, however, is quite the dilemma.

Unsure of any other option, I settle on avoidance. "It's okay, I swear."

He stares at me for a long, long moment. So long that I find myself sinking into the depths of his eyes for a nice cool-down swim. They're so blue and perfect and welcoming, like the gentle lull of the waters on the shores of Aruba. Or, at least, I think. I've never been to Aruba, but I've included it in a novel, and everything I researched said that's how it is.

"I'm going to drop this because I can sense by the tense line of your mouth that you want me to drop this."

My mouth is that visibly tense?

"But I want the record to show that I don't believe you when you say it's not a big deal."

"I'll be sure to notify the court reporter," I tease, using a joke to wiggle my way out from under the overwhelming discomfort sitting atop my chest. I don't like the look of Chase Dawson frowning at me. I don't like it at all.

"Good." He nods, and one corner of his mouth lifts. "Now, I'd like to take you to dinner."

I sputter so hard at the non sequitur, I can see a droplet of my own spit land on the front of Chase's dress shirt and spread. I expect him to break character at any moment, possibly find the horror in my saliva bomb, but instead, he stands there, staring at me, his invitation lying in wait.

He wants to take me to dinner?

I shake my head and try to get my bearings, but when I come up empty-handed, I flutter into the kitchen to start cleaning up all my random cleaning supplies.

Chase watches, tucking his fingertips into the tops of his pockets with an ease that puts me on edge enough to provide some kind of answer to his insane question.

"I…I'm not exactly in the physical state of a dinner guest. I've been cleaning, and I haven't showered, and my hair is—"

"Perfect. You don't need to look any differently than you look right now."

Perfect? My hair is perfect? I call bullshit, Mr. Dawson. Not to mention, I'm in my favorite velour pants from the early 2000s. No adult woman in her right mind would walk the city streets with the word "Juicy" plastered across her ass.

"I also usually have to warn places that I'm going to be bringing Benji." I continue to plead my case. "He's a registered service animal, so I don't technically have to, but I know from experience that people get touchy when food is involved."

"That's okay. I know a place where that won't be an issue at all. They love dogs. Specifically, German shepherds. Last time I spoke to them, they were even considering getting one."

Good grief. It's like none of my excuses are getting me anywhere.

"Chase—"

"Come on. If we hurry, we can make it in time for happy hour. Two drinks for the price of one."

I have to admit, for the first time tonight, I'm hearing something that sounds like a good idea. If I drown myself in enough wine, maybe I won't know what's happening or who I'm with anymore. The prospect has potential.

He startles then, unsure of himself. "But wait…is it okay for you to drink now?"

It's probably the best thing for me.

"Yep. It's fine." *So fine, it's perfect.* "The good news about my whole ordeal is that it takes virtually no time to bounce back. Once my blood pressure comes back up to normal, I'm good to go."

"That is good news." He smiles at me. "It would be a shame if we couldn't do a champagne toast to celebrate the book."

Oh yes, I muse. *Ha. A crying shame.*

I'm so, so fucked here.

With no more outs in sight, I do the only thing I can—dive headfirst into the fire.

"So, I guess I'll just go throw on a different set of clothes, and then we can go?" Why I'm asking him for permission is beyond me. Deep down, I think I'm hoping he'll still change his mind and decide to go to dinner by himself and leave my crazy ass here.

"Sounds like a plan."

But of course, he doesn't say no. If anything, his responding smile looks far too happy to accommodate.

Duh-duh. Someone call *Law & Order.* There's about to be a new special victim for their unit, and she's coming in hot.

Chapter

Six

Brooke

I bang around in my room like a maniac, looking for the kinds of makeup products that can turn a train wreck of a woman into one from the magazines. Incidentally, I don't own any of those products, nor do I possess the sort of expertise required to use them, but a woman as desperate as I am doesn't need to be bothered with those details.

From my vanity mirror, I see Benji stare at me from his spot on my bed. His eyes say everything that needs to be said, *Agreeing to dinner with a man who makes you pass out is the second-worst idea you've ever had.*

He doesn't even have to tell me my first-worst idea. I'm currently in the middle of living the consequences of it. This dinner is in the name of celebrating it, in fact.

"Don't look at me like that, Benj," I whisper toward him. "And trust me, I know. I freaking know."

A doggie scoff escapes his snout, and I smack my eye shadow palette from three years ago onto the surface of my vanity and speed-click through a YouTube tutorial video. My phone rests against the mirror so I can multitask.

She's a lovely woman, KatVonMakeup or whatever, but she's spent five minutes on contouring so far, and I really need her to get to the meat and potatoes of this showdown. Shaping my face into another—or shape-shifting, as some idiot men like to call it—is a little too far above my skill level on this kind of time scale.

Chase is in my living room waiting—and that means he has access to snoop through anything and everything in my apartment. I don't have any CIA files or drugs or even any nude photos of myself, but for some reason, I'm convinced he's going to stumble upon all three and turn me in to *America's Most Wanted.*

Click, click, click, I tap my finger on the screen, fast-forwarding through the next two minutes of video, fifteen seconds at a time, until I finally reach the beginning of her tutorial on the eyes. I watch carefully as she smooths on a primer I don't have, and then I huff one more click forward.

Finally, she sweeps at her eyelid with a special brush after pointing at the color in her palette that's the most neutral. She covers the entire eyelid, so I do the same. It's instantly clear that my skill is lacking, but I push forward anyway, gripping the tiny foam applicator that was included with my drug-store shadow.

She points to another color in the palette—evidently meant for the crease of the eyelid—and I lean in to try to get a closer look at how she's doing it. The color choice is far more obvious now, so I have a feeling if I really flub it, everyone in the city is going to notice.

"You okay in there?" Chase calls down the hallway when I drop the applicator on the floor and bang the top of my head on my vanity on the way back from picking it up.

I rub at the sensitive bump I've caused and yell back with as much normalcy as possible, "Oh yeah! All good! Nothing to worry about in here!"

I roll my eyes at myself, bite my lip, and then push on. "I should be ready soon!" *Dear God, I hope I'm ready soon.*

"Take your time!" he booms back, making my spine tingle. He's hot and he's considerate and he's patient. *And he's waiting to take me to dinner.*

It's a business dinner, of course, but I don't know that my loins have been trained to distinguish the difference. They're fired up and roasting—practically begging to warm the surface of Chase Dawson's face.

Jesus, Mary, and Joseph, Brooke, calm down, would you?!

I chuckle a little as I consider myself in the mirror, mumbling, "Definitely won't be needing blush tonight…"

Quickly as I can manage, I follow along with the rest of the tutorial, skipping the liner and fake lashes and settling for a couple of coats of year-old mascara. I study myself in the mirror for a long moment—pink cheeks, mostly smooth skin, and mildly stylish eyes—and it'll have to do.

Shockingly, I don't have bad self-esteem on a regular basis. I'm okay with the way I look. But something about the dreamboat that is Chase Dawson makes me want to be *more*. Sexier, more confident, *vibrant*. Those are the things a man like him deserves.

Which is probably why I wrote River that way—at least, as her personality progressed and grew. She became vivacious and alluring and all the things I wish I could be when it comes to men like Chase. Sadly, it's much easier to give those qualities to a character than to find them in myself.

I shove away from my vanity, rush into my closet, and pull the first chunky sweater I locate off a hanger. It's not exactly *Cosmopolitan* feature style, but it's flattering and comfortable, and with its golden color, any mustard I drop on myself will blend right in.

Three quick flicks of the light switches in my closet, bathroom, and bedroom, and I'm on my way back down the hall to my dinner date, with Benji following dutifully in tow.

My professional dinner companion, I correct. Professional. Dinner. Companion.

I plaster on a smile as I step into my living room, and Chase tosses my *People* magazine back down onto my coffee table and stands. Seeing him sitting there, reading about the Kardashians so casually, is weird. Almost too weird for even the alternate universe I'm apparently living in these days.

"All set?" he asks, his voice friendly and not at all tired. It's almost as if sitting out here and waiting for me all this time really didn't bother him, but I know that can't be true. My dad and my ex-husband Jamie were both doers. Once a decision was made to go, it was time to go, no dillydallying. If you weren't five minutes early, you were five minutes late, and any other annoying man-phrase you can think of.

"Yes. I'm really sorry it took me as long as it did, but I had to at least rinse off the cleaning chemicals in the shower."

"Cleaning chemicals?" he asks.

"I was doing a little cleaning before you got here."

"Gotcha. Place looks great." He nods and then waves me off with a smile. "And no worries. I popped in on you without warning and demanded your company at dinner. I'm pretty sure you could have made me wait all night if you wanted to without any foul play."

"But then we'd miss dinner."

Chase shrugs. "There's always breakfast."

Okay, jeez. That's a good-ass line if I've ever heard one.

I smile—I couldn't stop that shit if I tried—and Chase holds out a hand toward the door. "Shall we?"

"Sure. Let me just grab my purse." I jerk my chin at the small bag on the kitchen stool, and Chase picks it up to hand it to me.

Ever so slightly, our fingers brush in the exchange, and everything inside me stops. My eyes flick up to meet his, to search for a sign that he feels whatever this is too, but I can't see anything other than the endless pools of sparkling blue I always do.

"Thanks," I whisper, the raspy purr all my stolen voice can manage.

Chase's smile climbs, the corners of his mouth carving just the slightest of dimples in his cheeks. I've never noticed them before—maybe because I was too busy looking at other features or because I haven't been this close to his soft smile—but every remaining air particle in my lungs vacates. *Poof, pow, my breath has left the building.*

Clearly, I better get the hell out of this apartment and on with this dinner if I have any chance of surviving the rapid pace of my pride's deterioration.

Benji's snout bumps against the back of my thighs, his silent agreement that we really do need to get a move on it, urging me to grab his leash and snap it in place on his collar. I secure his service dog vest over his Superman cape.

The heels of my booties clack on my wood floor as we head for the door with Chase behind me, and I swear I feel the whisper of his hand at the small of my back. It's not firm enough to know for sure, and I'm sure as hell not going to turn back to look, but in the deepest recesses of my mind, neurons fire at the potential contact.

Benji and I exit first, and then I wait for Chase so that I can lock the door behind us. We all make our way down in the elevator to the main floor below. My doorman nods as we walk out onto the street, and for the first time tonight, it occurs to me that Chase never even rang up before he was knocking at my door.

"How did you, uh…how'd you get to my door without calling up first?"

He shrugs. "I might've told the doorman it was a surprise?"

My eyebrows climb the distance of my forehead—which is saying something because I've got a decent-sized forehead—concern making my limbs feel a little numb. "And he just…believed you?"

Chase shakes his head then, reaching out to squeeze my forearm. "Oh, Brooke. I'm sorry. I can see now how inappropriate that was and how much it would worry you, but I promise he made me show my Longstrand ID and driver's license to confirm my identity before he let me go anywhere near the elevator."

"Oh. Okay."

"Still, you should have a talk with him just to be sure the security is tight enough for your liking. I know the safety of your apartment building is one of the most basic needs of a woman, and you deserve to be able to be at home without the constant worry that someone might find their way to you who shouldn't. Especially with all the publicity you're going to be getting soon."

"I'm sure it's fine."

"No," Chase argues. "You really opened my eyes here, Brooke. And at the risk of being inappropriate again, I'll just offer that I'd be happy to talk with your doorman myself if the conversation makes you uncomfortable in any way."

Chase talking to my building staff like he's responsible for my well-being? Like a boyfriend or something? *Ha. Ha-ha.*

"No, no. That's sweet, but I can handle it myself, really."

"Okay," Chase agrees easily, raising his hand in the air to hail a cab. It's such a casual action to perform while holding my eye contact perfectly that it's a little disarming. "Whatever you want. This is your decision, but I'm here for support if you need it."

Man, I didn't think guys like this existed. At least, I've never had any experience with them before. No bravado, no false posturing. Just an honest apology and an open-minded discussion about solutions.

A cab pulls up just in the nick of time, saving me from myself and all of the ridiculous things I might say in the face of his honesty.

Chase holds open the door, and Benji and I climb inside. "Hey, you can't bring dogs in here—" the cabbie starts to yell but then shuts his trap when he notices the service vest over Benji's Superman cape. "Sorry. The dog's no problem."

Chase smiles at me and then winks as he climbs in behind us and gives Benji a pointed scratch of his ears, leaning down to whisper, "Biggest compliment there is, buddy, blending in despite your superhero status."

I turn to face the opposite window to conceal my smile at the sweet attempt to comfort my dog, who's not offended in the slightest. Not only is Benji used to getting the stiff arm from most establishments, he's got the confidence not to care.

Unlike me, he's not affected by awkward uncertainty on a daily basis. In fact, he's the exact opposite.

He's got swagger and style, and quite frankly, I don't know what I'd do without him. Even aside from the whole passing out and cracking my head open thing—Benji is often the balm to my raging soul.

"Where to?" the cab driver asks, and Chase is quick to answer.

"La Croissette. 59th and Amsterdam."

La Croissette? Dayum, I'm really glad I hosed off now.

It's a fancy-dancy kind of place, and I've only heard about it in random articles highlighting the best restaurants in the city.

"Okay." I look over at Chase. "I have to know your secret now. You said you know a restaurant we can get into last minute, without a reservation, with a dog, without a problem, and it turns out it's *La Croissette?*" I shake my head on a laugh. "What's the secret? And when is Ashton Kutcher showing up with his crew from *Punk'd?*"

"That's a pretty old reference, you know, Ashton and *Punk'd,*" he teases. "You better be careful using that around the Gen-Zers."

I scoff and giggle at the same time. "I'm old, and I'm never around Gen-Zers. Now, stop stalling. What's the secret? How on earth do you think you're going to get us into this restaurant? I mean, the whole thing is a tough deal for any restaurant in the city, but La Croissette? No way. They're booked up months out."

"I know the owner. I have an open-ended reservation. I can show up anytime, with anyone, and they'll find a way to seat me."

I scrunch up my nose. "Are you their bookie or something? They owe you money?"

Chase chuckles. "Something like that."

"*Pfft,*" I blow out an audible breath through my lips. "It'd have to be."

I've got a stout feeling, influenced by the look on Chase Dawson's face, that there's a lot more to this story than he's letting on, and not only that, but he's not going to tell me anytime soon.

I take the small moment as a reminder that we are not, in fact, lovers on a romantic date sharing a meal—the kind of occasion where we might reveal our innermost secrets to each other—but instead work associates, celebrating a professional victory (for him) in a food-centric setting.

This can be snappy and entertaining and full of banter, but this isn't the opportunity to expose my thoughts and unearth my crush. This is a trade meal, and I should treat it as such. Doing so will probably make it that much easier to behave with a little bit of dignity and confidence, to be honest.

I don't have to try to be sexy or flirty or attractive. I can be bookish and literature-focused. The characters can be the stars, just like I'm used to.

For the purposes of tonight, Clive Watts and River Rollins are just that—Clive and River, a fiction-based meandering of my creative mind, in no way rooted in reality.

They're my Romeo and Juliet, and I'm their Shakespeare. And if I'm really lucky, they even understand that vague-as-shit analogy better than I do.

Before I know it, the cab pulls up in front of the restaurant without another word spoken between us. The inner trappings of my head have been far too distracting. Immediately, I wonder what on earth Chase has been thinking all this time with me sitting lost in my thoughts.

I don't have time to wonder long, though, as Chase exits the cab and runs around the car to open my door for me rather than make me slide across the bench seat. He blocks the direct path to the street and hands me Benji's leash when it gets stuck between the edge of the seat and the seat belt.

He's every ounce of a gentleman, and I do my very best to ignore it.

"Thanks," I say instead, in the interest of being distantly polite.

Professional. Dinner. Companion, I repeat to myself five times fast.

He's my editor. I am a writer. And his interest in me is the kind that's rooted entirely in my characters, their story, and the power of those both together to sell books off bookshelves in spectacular fashion.

I know his push for this book is there—in his belief for success in the market. Not in his connection to the character of Clive or the obvious likeness of River to me. This isn't the live action of his crush. It's mine. And he's an innocent bystander to it all.

We move quickly off the street and into the crowded vestibule of the restaurant, only to be shuffled through the throng by Chase. He approaches the hostess while Benji and I hang back just a bit. She smiles in recognition and nods vigorously as he points back at us and asks for a table.

I still don't know what his secret connection to this place is, but it's good. That's for sure.

I look around the rose-colored room, taking in the chandeliers and flower-covered center wall. It's a beautiful place—every bit of the social media frenzy spot I've heard it is—and if the food is half as good, I have a feeling I'm in for one hell of a meal.

"Come on," Chase says in my ear, surprising me with his proximity, thanks to my distracted survey of the dining room. "Our table's ready. Right in the corner with a good spot for Benji to lie out of the way and everything."

I shake my head. "I swear if I find out you're a part of the Illuminati…"

"What?" His grin is addictive, and his eyes are light with humor. "What will you do?"

"Well…I guess, first, I'll be impressed."

Chase laughs, and the sound is every bit as pretty as our surroundings. "And after you've come to terms with the impressiveness of my Illuminati status?"

"Start fielding offers from you to see if it's enough money to sell my soul," I tell him. "I mean, I love writing, but I also love the idea of spending the rest of my days on a beach in the Bahamas where my only concern is if my piña colada needs a refill."

"Of course." His smile is a mix of secretive and jovial. It also gets punctuated by the kind of sexy wink I feel in my kneecaps. "But we should probably get to the table before I start throwing out numbers."

Oh boy. Benji might be Superman tonight, but this man is my kryptonite.

I nod and precede him as he indicates I should, following the hostess with Benji close to my side through what feels like every inch of the dining room. People do a double take at Benji's Superman costume, smiling when they realize what his vest says and how cute he looks in the red cape.

It's a godsend, actually, all the attention that flocks to my best friend—because that means it's not on me at all.

When our arrival at our table finally comes, I see why we did all the traipsing through God's creation to get here. It's an intimate booth in the back corner, with a small empty space for Benji to lie out of the way but close enough to do his job. I don't know where they got it or how, but there's a padded blanket on the floor waiting for him, almost as if they knew he was coming and wanted to make it as comfortable for him as possible.

It's so damn thoughtful, I have to swallow against the unwanted emotion in my throat.

At this point in my monthly hormonal cycle, I could easily cry. My period is just one big sneeze away, but I hold in the tears with every vestige of my being because I'll be damned if I'm going to embarrass myself any more than I already have as of late.

There are only so many times you can faint in someone's presence before they start to take the hint and move out of it. And even if it's a true risk for sanity and well-being, I want Chase Dawson in my orbit pretty badly. I don't think you write books about people you don't want.

He gestures to the booth, standing behind it as I lead Benji to the floor pad on his leash and give him a rub as he gets settled.

I try to hurry, but when it comes to dog lovin's, I'm not exactly great at time management.

I half expect Chase to give up and take a seat or, at the very least, be sporting an irritated frown or something when I turn back around, but instead, he's smiling, the corners of his mouth so curled up they almost take on a bemused personality of their own.

"Sorry," I apologize through a slight blush as I rush to take my seat.

"No worries. I'm planning to buy Benji a steak for his heroic acts earlier. He deserves all the scratches and good pets tonight."

"He's a good dog." I almost scoff at myself, and Chase notices.

"What?" he asks, curiosity making one eyebrow rise just a touch higher than the other.

"Truth be told, he's my best friend in the universe, and I'm not sure what I'd do without him."

Chase considers me for a long moment and then looks to Benji, murmuring, "Maybe I'll get him two steaks."

"Great." I laugh. "He'll start to like you more, and before you know it, I'll be the third wheel in the friendship. That never ends well."

"I'm sure it would take more than a couple of steaks to buy Benji's love."

"I don't know," I singsong. "I tend to be pretty cheap with his red meat intake."

"Ah, I'm sure you're just worried about his cholesterol."

"You're painting me in a pretty good light, and I appreciate that, but I've also got some flaws, you know."

Chase smiles a little too big for my liking—though my vagina seems quite thrilled with it—and I'm immediately on edge.

"What?" I ask. "What's that look for?"

"Oh, nothing. You've just stumbled perfectly into my trap for talking about the book."

"What book?" I ask.

"The *book*. The next big best seller by Brooke Baker. *Accidental Attachment*."

Oh. The *book*.

Ha-ha-ha-ha. Wow. I almost forgot about the life-ruining publishing news that brought Chase Dawson to my door tonight in the first place. I can't believe myself, just sitting here, pretending Chase is in love with me and we're on a romantic date or something. *What a fool.*

"Brooke? Are you all right? Do you need a Coke or something?"

"Oh no, I'm fine." *Stupid, but fine.* "So, you were saying something about the book?" I question to distract his attention away from my current state of mania, but instantly, I feel annoyed with myself. That book is the last thing I want to talk about.

Ironically, it's probably the only thing he wants to talk about. It's the whole damn reason we're here.

Chase smiles, and I nearly die inside all over again. How in the world did I put myself in this position?

"Yes. The book," he says like it's a brilliant plan to talk about the book I thought was going to be my dirty little secret and stay locked away on my computer. "Now, don't get annoyed, but the editor in me can't wait to start into the nitty-gritty. The special stuff. The attention to detail that's going to sky-rocket this thing to the number one spot on every best-seller list in existence."

"Wow," I mutter and have to clear the discomfort out of my throat. "Those are some…big goals."

Chase shakes his head vehemently. "No, they're not. Not with this book. Not if we work together to make it the very best it can be."

Inside, I choke. He's got one thing right. The combination of Brooke Baker and Chase Dawson is incredibly vital to this storyline.

The storyline I want to act like doesn't exist, but I have zero fallback plan. The man is fresh off fighting for *Accidental Attachment* to go to print, and the book I was supposed to turn in to Longstrand is in the kind of shape that would require a good trash compactor to handle it properly.

There's no getting around this, Brooke. You're going to have to talk about the book.

I swallow my pride and try to pretend that Clive and River are just some fictional people I made up. From here on out, they have nothing to do with me or Chase or the many fantasies I've had about the combination of the two.

They are just fictional characters in a fictional novel that in no way reflects real life.

"Okay. So, what did you have in mind?" I eventually question. "What did I say that triggered this detour to the book?"

"Flaws," Chase responds without hesitation. "People have them."

"Yes…they always do."

"Which means your characters should too. And right now, Clive Watts doesn't have many."

I roll my eyes. "Clive has flaws."

I mean, he's got to. I always give characters their special brand of quirks, and there's no way I wrote this guy any different…right?

"Name one."

I search my mind, scrolling through the chapters from the book. "Well, in the scene with…" I pause. "Oh, that time that the other producer…" I stop again. "When they go for a swim in the pool in…" Yet another pause.

"He makes right of every situation immediately." Chase verbalizes my thoughts.

I frown.

"Even in the breakup scene with River, he sees the error of his ways, *and* at the base of it all, he's trying to protect her." He reaches out to pat my hand that rests on the table. His touch makes the nerve endings in my fingertips zing to life. "All I'm saying is to take another look at this guy. Give him some human mistakes—some tiny annoyances. It'll make the book that much better."

Oh, you have no idea what you're asking me to do.

"Don't look so sad," he adds. "Everybody's got flaws, remember?"

I almost sigh, but when a little "Cheer up, Brooke" chuckle leaves his perfect mouth, I find myself smiling instead.

I'll tell you one thing—Chase's laugh doesn't have any flaws at all.

Chapter
Seven

Chase

La Croissette is packed to the brim, but I hardly notice the chatter of the other guests around us, but that's probably because my dinner partner has kept me wildly entertained with her infectious laugh and sense of humor.

The dim but cozy lighting only makes Brooke look more enchanting beneath its glow, and it makes me wonder if she knows how beautiful she really is. She's good at laughing at herself in the best way, a truly endearing quality, but I don't know if she truly understands how she looks from other people's eyes.

Does she know she's an incredibly attractive woman?

The thought pulls me up short, and I mentally berate myself. She's one of my authors, for fuck's sake. The last thing I need to be doing is taking inventory of her allure.

Brooke's green eyes are filled with light and humor, and her hair hangs past her shoulders in soft waves. She reaches out to take a sip from her glass of wine, and I find myself watching the way her full lips perch around the edge.

It's a good night. A great night, actually, and everything feels pretty damn perfect.

Everything *except* for the fact that my sister Maureen keeps peeking her head out of the kitchen door every other minute. Currently, she is trying to get my attention or stare actual holes through my skull, I'm not sure, but I refuse to engage.

Instead, I focus on Brooke.

She sets her wineglass back on the table and glances toward Benji for a brief moment before meeting my eyes again.

"Okay, I've got one for you."

A smile is already on my lips. "Hit me with it."

"What did the writer say to the other writer?" Brooke asks, setting up another joke I'm sure will have me snorting my Old Fashioned through my nose. But my sister's eyes have turned wild now, the top half of her body hanging entirely out of the kitchen door, and I'm not sure how much longer I can let this go on without the entire restaurant erupting into a scene.

Mo's arm waves like she's ushering in a 747 for a low-visibility landing, and when she puts two fingers to her lips in what I'm sure is preparation for a whistle, I interrupt Brooke.

"You know what? Can you hold that thought?" I question, but it's entirely rhetorical. She's going to have to hold that thought or else my sister is going to make a scene in her own fucking restaurant. "I'm really sorry, but I need to run to the restroom for a minute."

Brooke's eyes widen in surprise, but other than that, she takes my weird bathroom emergency behavior in stride. "Uh…yeah. Sure."

I smile as genuinely as possible and jump up from the table, my legs churning toward Mo like a New York Marathon runner.

"Get back in the kitchen, for God's sake," I say through gritted teeth, grabbing her by the elbow to force my suggestion into action as I get to her.

We tumble through the swinging door like a couple of newborn horses, and at least three kitchen staffers jerk to a surprised halt. Mo ignores them, the rabid nature of her obsession superseding even her own business.

"What are you doing here with Brooke Baker?" she asks with big eyes and an even bigger, over-the-top, and super-unnerving clownlike smile. She might as well be all teeth and eyeballs. "Does she know you have a sister? Does she know this is my restaurant? Did you bring her here to meet me?"

"No, Mo." I shake my head. "No, to all of the above. We're on a business dinner, and she needed a place that could accommodate her service dog Benji on short notice." She shakes me by the shoulders, so I add, "Trust me, I would have gone anywhere else if I'd have been able to be choosy."

"Don't be rude."

"Then don't be crazy. The whole restaurant was five seconds away from calling the police on your little show for a wellness check."

She scoffs. "I didn't look that crazy."

I eye her knowingly. "Yes, my dear sister, you did."

Vinny shoves through the two of us with a bowl full of who knows what, a focused but frantic look on his face. "You two mind having this little quarrel somewhere other than my kitchen?"

"No problem," Mo agrees straightaway. "Chase was just about to take me out to meet Brooke Baker."

"Mo, no!" I exclaim, but she lunges and bobs, and I have to body-block her like an offensive lineman for the New York Mavericks. "Mo! No! You can't go out there and make a scene."

She grabs a knife off Vinny's prep table and lunges toward me at an alarming rate. My eyes grow so wide they nearly span the space of my forehead, and I move back with a shuffle that knocks me into a rack of pots.

"What the hell?! Have you lost your mind?"

"What?" she asks as she picks up a zucchini the size of a football and starts hacking at it over a chopping board like her intention for the knife was vegetable-focused and not trying to commit homicide on her own flesh and blood.

"You just tried to stab me because I won't let you harass Brooke Baker!"

She rolls her eyes. "Don't be so dramatic. If I wanted to stab you, you'd be bleeding."

My brother-in-law Vinny laughs from across the table, and far from the first time, I question the health of their pairing.

"But what I don't understand," Mo says while she continues to chop at the zucchini like it personally harmed her, "is why you thought it'd be a good idea to bring my *favorite freaking author* here, to my restaurant, if you didn't plan to let me meet her. It's like you wanted to torture me."

"I needed a last-minute reservation, and seeing as I kind of have an in here, it was the natural choice."

"Not anymore," she states firmly.

"What?"

"You don't have an *in* here anymore." She pushes her nose toward the ceiling and continues roughly chopping the zucchini.

"Seriously? I'm your brother."

She shakes her head. "Wrong. From now on, you're the Judas formerly known as my brother."

"Vinny?" I try, but he holds both of his hands up in self-defense, putting a pause on the meat he's slicing and everything.

"Oh no. Don't you try to drag me into this."

Suddenly, Mo makes one last attempt, dropping the knife and lunging at the swinging door that leads out of the kitchen. I juke to stop her, and she grabs me by the tie, nearly choking me as she pulls and tugs at it, trying to free herself.

"Mo, stop it," I chastise, setting her away as gently as I can while being firm. "Another time, I promise. But this has already been a big, stressful night for Brooke, and I don't want to add to it."

Mo frowns, picking up the knife from the table again and stabbing it into a loaf of bread with sadistically dramatic fashion. That bread, I imagine, is now the highest form of voodoo doll for my organs.

"I'm sorry," I apologize one last time to her and Vinny and make my exit from the kitchen. I feel like I've worked out and am, perhaps, even drenched in sweat, but I've already taken a far too long leave of absence to stop by the actual bathroom on my way back to the table.

When I take my seat again, Brooke is slathering a pat of butter onto another piece of bread. She's obviously hungry, so I don't dare tell her that I've just delayed our meal by another fifteen minutes by distracting the chef with a brawl in the kitchen.

"Everything okay?" she asks, probably because I've been gone "to the bathroom" longer than *Ace Ventura, Pet Detective*.

"Yeah, of course. It's great."

She nods then, a little smile curving up the corners of her pink mouth. It's suspiciously knowing, and I'm not sure why.

"What? What is it? Why are you looking at me like that?"

Her eyes flit to my neck. "Your tie is in a knot around your throat."

My hand scrambles, going to the silk material at my chest, only to find it missing, just like she noted. I look down, and even with as awkward as it is to try to look at your own neck, I can see it's around my throat like a scarf, tied in a loose knot with the top of itself in the front.

How in the hell did Mo manage that without my noticing? And just how serious does that mean she was about choking me?

I scramble to untie it and put it back in place, but Brooke is eyeing me with unending curiosity. The kind that sticks like molasses. She's not going to let me get away without explaining this one, I can feel it in my bones.

I run a hand through my hair before allowing myself a little chuckle. "You see, what had happened was…"

Brooke laughs and chews on another piece of bread. We've been sitting without food for quite a while now, and my kitchen catastrophe is at least partly to blame. With her having a fainting spell right before this, I can't imagine waiting this long is the best thing to bring her equilibrium back to normal. The guilt of her starvation is enough to push me right over the proverbial cliff into the land of truth.

"This is my sister and brother-in-law's restaurant."

"Really?" she asks, her perfect green eyes getting broad as she talks around her bread and almost choking on it. "Your *sister* owns *La Croissette*?"

I nod.

"Your sister owns one of the most popular restaurants in New York City?"

I nod again, but this time, it's followed by a sigh. "It's not as glamorous as you might think," I remark, gesturing to the place where my knotted tie used to be.

"Oh man. The tea feels hot tonight. Please, I beg of you, pour me some," Brooke replies, leaning in eagerly.

"Um…" I pause slightly to allow room for an awkward chuckle. "Well. My sister is one of your fans. She's actually the one who originally pushed me to read The Shadow Brothers Trilogy. And…she kind of harangued me in the kitchen in an effort to convince me to let her come out and talk to you."

Brooke's eyes widen even more, and she drops the piece of crusty bread on her plate, dusting off her hands.

"I tried to tell her it wasn't a good idea or good timing, with us discussing all the changes coming up, but she didn't take that very well."

"Tell her to come out now," she says without hesitation, looking around the room as though Maureen is just waiting for the go-ahead.

Truthfully, she may very well be doing just that, but I refuse to look over Brooke's shoulder and toward the kitchen door.

"I didn't tell you so you'd feel bad and say yes, Brooke. In fact, I'd have rather done just about anything else, but—"

"What, does she have horns and lasers for eyes or something? If she's not an evil sociopath with superpowers, I think it's fine." She is so relaxed and laid-back about it, but at the same time, she didn't just see my sister try to stab me.

"Well, she did make a knot around my throat without my knowing, so I can't guarantee she doesn't have the powers of a witch."

Brooke's face dances with humor. "I've never met a witch before. It'd probably be cool."

I close my eyes briefly before opening them with a groan. When I speak again, my voice is a whisper. "You don't have to do this, Brooke."

Benji stands up, pawing at Brooke's leg underneath the table. She jerks her head toward him. "Oh, come on. Even Benji wants to meet a real-life witch. See?" Benji yips just loud enough for me to hear his confirmation without disturbing the other diners. "Tell her to come out here."

When I don't say anything, she adds, "It'll be fine."

I sigh. Run a hand through my hair again. "I'd like to sincerely apologize in advance if this turns into something you regret."

"Chase, relax. Any sibling of yours has to be at least half cool. And since I'm about half cool at maximum myself, that really works out. The universe won't explode at our overwhelming power."

At the thought of the look I left in Mo's eyes, I reconsider trying so hard to talk Brooke out of the whole ordeal and consider maintaining an intact, untwisted set of balls instead. For as weird of an organ as they are, I really like them as is, and Lord knows, the next face-to-face conversation I'd have with my sister if she doesn't get to meet Brooke tonight could very well end in castration. "My future children thank you."

Brooke laughs, and it causes her to choke on her drink slightly. I reach around to pat her on the back. I'm not sure that patting someone on the back while they're choking on liquid helps, but it feels better than doing nothing.

"Are you okay? Is it something I said? You really don't have to meet her if you—"

"*Chase.* Go get your scythe-carrying sister and bring her out here, would you? If I'm going to meet my maker, I'd like to do it before I bloat up on veal Parmigiana."

I stand up without saying another word and head straight toward the kitchen to get Mo.

When I peek my head in the swinging door, I crane it inward slightly like a turtle tucking into its protective shell. I'm not sure how crazy I think my sister might get, but I know for a fact there are a lot of sharp objects back here.

"Mo?" I call out when she doesn't instantly pop out of a corner and take a machete to my neck.

Vinny is the first to see me, and the expression on his face—well, let's just call it disbelieving. "You didn't get enough the first time, bro? Are you crazy?"

"Yes. I definitely am. Because I just talked with Brooke, and she wants to meet her."

Mo's head pops out from the walk-in freezer like a cartoon jack-in-the-box. I swear her head doesn't even look attached to the rest of her body. "What?" she asks, her voice horribly high-pitched and frightening.

"Brooke said she wants to meet you. Come on."

Mo's legs move like a sprinter out of the gate, and I have to grab her by the elbow before she goes running out the door and crawls right in my star author's lap. "Listen, this is really nice of her to do. I need you to be cool."

"Oh yeah. No problem," Mo says, bobbing and weaving to get around me at the same time.

I grab her other elbow and pull her to a stop in front of me, engaging my most serious of brotherly voices. "No, Mo. Really. I need you to be cool, please."

"I'm ice, baby brother, swear."

I look deep into her midnight-blue eyes, studying them for a long moment for any signs of lasers or, I don't know, psychosis.

But they look normal enough, and I can't really justify any more time spent in this kitchen while Brooke Baker sits at a table waiting for me.

"All right, then. Come on. Let's get this over with."

"*Get this over with*," she mocks in the voice of a petulant child. "Why so humdrum about it, Chase?"

"Because this woman is extremely important to me."

She raises her eyebrows, and I roll my eyes. "Extremely important to my *career*. Remember? I put my ass on the line with my boss over this new book."

"Well, you can relax. I'm just as in love with Brooke Baker's writing career as you are. I'm not going to do anything to jeopardize your precious book deal."

On that final note, Mo shoves me all the way out of her path and marches toward Brooke Baker's table with false confidence. I recognize the *fake it till you make it* gesture a mile away, likely because I just had a similar performance at my editors' meeting today.

Like it or not, I can tell we're siblings without sampling for DNA.

I rush to catch up as she comes to a stop next to a smiling Brooke and sticks out an aggressively friendly hand for a shake. Brooke's hair swooshes against her shoulders as she postures her head back and forth, climbs from her seat, and pulls my sister in for a hug.

Mo's body tenses at the same time mine does, but within the span of one deep breath, I can practically see the joy radiating directly off her.

"Oh my God," I hear her croon sweetly and shyly as I approach the two of them. "I can't believe Brooke Baker just hugged me."

"You know, I've heard that before, this one time in high school, but the inflection had a little more disgust," Brooke replies easily, her ability to make any moment humorous uncanny.

"I just…just…" Mo stutters. "I can't believe I'm really meeting you." Brooke smiles, and a hint of rosiness warms her cheeks. "I've read *The Shadow Brothers* at least twenty times. Anytime I'm in a rut, I go right back to them."

"Well, thank you. That means a lot. It really helps to keep you from getting admitted to a padded room when other people enjoy hearing about the voices in your head too."

My sister laughs, but she also keeps blathering on and on. "I told my brother he had to read your stuff, and I swear, now he's even more obsessed with you than I am."

I roll my eyes heavenward.

"Well, sisters are often the wiser ones," Brooke says teasingly. "Which makes sense. Women in general tend to catch on faster."

Mo laughs again, and I smile. Brooke's personality really is magnetic. It's no wonder her charm translates directly into her writing.

"Well, I'd say he's convinced now. He pretty much threatened death and dismemberment to his own sister if I came out here and made a fool of him."

My God, I could strangle her. "I never said that." I turn directly to Brooke, who's smirking in a way that makes me squirm. "I never said that, Brooke." I glare at my sister. "I just didn't want someone's excitement to get the better of her and end up launching Brooke's chair to the moon or something."

"A moon landing takes precision and planning, Chasey-wasey. I don't think it's the kind of thing you achieve by accident," my sister teases, making the back of my neck flare hot.

"Chasey-wasey?" Brooke asks, confirming that she caught the nickname.

I clear my throat to try to find the words, but Mo has a much easier time, the witch. "Oh yeah. It's my nickname for him. According to our mother, I had a flair for the dramatic when he was first born and treated him like a doll or something. Even dressed him up in a couple frilly dresses a time or two."

"Mo," I say low, under my breath, and without much thought.

My sister grins, whispering, "I guess I'd better stop sharing all his secrets since the two of you work together."

"No, no," Brooke begs. "Please keep sharing."

I narrow my eyes at her, and she giggles. "Sorry. I can't help but enjoy when someone else is the butt of the joke. So often, it's me, passed out on the floor with pee running down my leg, you know?"

I chuckle, and Mo's eyebrows shoot to the ceiling.

Brooke laughs too, realizing she's now left an open-ended point of interest with my sister to explain.

"I, uh, have a condition called vasovagal syncope," Brooke elucidates. "Hence, my best buddy superhero Benji. I tend to pass out a lot without a whole lot of notice."

"Holy cow! That's wild," Mo comforts and even steps toward Brooke's dog to give him a few pets and scratches. "You and Benji and pee running down your leg are welcome here anytime."

I smack a hand to one side of my face as Brooke's laugh overcomes the space around us. "Wow, this place really is accommodating of special circumstances, Chase. You were right."

"Okay, sis," I declare, moving to grab Mo's arm and direct her back toward the swinging door. "Maybe you should head back to the kitchen and see what you can do to expedite our food. We've been waiting quite a while."

Mo's starstruck, smiley face moves from Brooke to me ever so slowly and then fades into realization as she gets a good look at me. I'm on the brink of not keeping my shit together anymore, and for as much of a pain in the ass as she can be, some small part of her feels sorry for me.

"Right, right," she mutters with a paced, repetitive nod. "I'll…uh…just go back and check on everything." My head bounces with excitement. "I'll see to bringing it out myself." The bounce stops immediately.

"Mo," I start, only to be stopped by a tiny punch to my stomach. It's not even really a blow, but the flinch I make when tightening my abs is enough to make me stop talking.

"Relax, brother," Mo says with a wink. "I'll be right back with your food."

Brooke's smile is unrepentant. "I like her."

"I was afraid you'd say that."

Brooke's laugh is soft, not the cackle I know she's capable of, but it's enough to make her green eyes dance and her long brown hair sway. Involuntarily, I'm broken of all my grumpiness.

"Really? I was more afraid she'd be carrying a scythe."

Goddamn, her power to disarm a situation—*disarm me*—is otherworldly.

I swear, when it comes to Brooke Baker, she's my perfect match…when it comes to work, obviously. The editor-author relationship is an important one. If neither party understands the other, it can turn a good book into a disaster.

But that's not what's going to happen with us. Together, we're going to take the book world by storm. *You better hope that's the case or else you'll have to get used to living with Glenn permanently because you'll be out of a job and have to sell off the apartment you haven't even gotten to move in to yet.*

It's going to be good. Brooke and I have got this. *Accidental Attachment* is going to be life-changing in the best way. I can feel it…I think. I hope. *I fucking pray.*

Chapter
Eight

Monday, May 8th

Brooke

As a writer, I know that any good character has flaws. They chew too loudly or they pick at their nails or they have memory issues that prohibit them from remembering new acquaintances' names, no matter how hard they try.

And I know this is important because human nature is imperfect. If a character doesn't have flaws, they don't have realism, and the whole story becomes a one-dimensional caricature of life.

I get it. I do. I just wish it felt that easy to write some wrongs—*ha! Punny*—for the awesomeness that is Clive Watts—and by proxy of my inspiration, Chase Dawson.

His smiles. His wit. His charming deference to other people's feelings. They're all outstanding.

Honestly, he's so far above the bare minimum I've come to expect from men that red flags have ceased to flap in the wind.

After eating dinner with him Friday night, I can't even say that his table manners are underdeveloped. No, whoever raised Chase Dawson—*or my future mother-in-law, as the psychotic part of me likes to refer to her*—did a mighty fine job.

I lean forward and bang my head against my desk a couple of times to stun my brain back into the realm of existence.

Okay, Brooke, get it together. This is the book that's going to be published three or four months from now—*holy shit!*—which means this is the book you have to find some way to be at peace with working on. I gave myself the weekend off to meld into the surface of my couch and avoid any and all career responsibilities, but now it's time to get to work.

Sure, maybe I can't see Chase's flaws right now, but I should be able to come up with some for his character, right?

I purse my lips and think really hard about Clive. Sexy. Self-confident without being cocky. Friendly, caring, a great sense of humor, not afraid to be self-deprecating like so many macho men are.

Jeez Louise. *Think, think, think.*

When I'm still mooning over how dreamy he is five minutes later, I decide to try something else—starting with River. She is, after all, mirrored after me, and if I'm not my own worst critic, I'm nothing.

It's a little bit of a kick to the shin how easy it is for me to pick apart a woman after struggling so vastly to do the same to two men, but I'm just desperate enough not to worry about it. I have several scenes to make changes to in the next couple of weeks, and I don't have time to focus on the patriarchy's role in my psyche *and* meet the deadline.

"Okey dokey." I crack my knuckles and stretch my arms out in front of me before putting my hands to the keyboard and typing with swift fingers. "River is…too preoccupied with what other people think. Awkwardly chatty in uncomfortable situations." I snort as more and more flaws come pouring out of me. "Sexually unconfident. She picks at the skin around her nails and chews at the inside of her lip when she's nervous."

I laugh, muttering, "Wow. List is getting a little long there, Riv. I might have to dial you back from me a little bit."

I start typing again, the click-clack of my keys echoing in my otherwise quiet apartment until the trill of my phone ringing from the kitchen counter makes my eyes narrow and my hands come to a stop.

What in the world? Who could be calling me now?

I get so few calls altogether that I can hardly imagine getting one at ten p.m. Still, I jump up and run over to it, only narrowly missing stubbing my toe on the coffee table as I sidestep around a sleeping Benji.

"Shew," I breathe, looking back at the offending item. "That was clos—oh, *fucker-nucker!*" I yelp, cringing in pain as the blinding throb of the feeling of my toe meeting the metal leg of my barstool runs all the way into my calf muscle.

There's just something about excruciating pain that turns my otherwise modest mouth X-rated.

"Holy *shit!*" I cry out and blink a sheen of tears from my eyes. "It's fucking gone. It has to be. I'm down to four toes now on this foot." I dance around on one leg, muttering more obscenities to myself, and somehow, manage to pick up my phone off the counter in the process.

Thanks to my murdered toe, I don't even bother to look at who the caller is before putting my cell to my ear. Instead, I'm squinting and glancing down to see if it's still attached or hanging out by the barstool. "Hello?" I greet as I'm glad to find out that, despite the pain, I still have all five toes.

"What?" the caller replies on a chuckle, and I instantly know who it is. "No mocking greeting?"

It's my agent, Wilson Phillips, and for the first time in the history of our pairing, I've failed to address him with the title of a song from the musical group Wilson Phillips. It's my thing when it comes to him. He hates it. I love it. Which means, I'll never quit doing it, and I really dropped the punny ball this time.

Momentarily agitated enough to forget about my dang toe, I stomp my foot and instantly howl in pain.

"Jeez, you don't have to cry out like a wounded rabbit, Baker. I'll call back so you can amuse yourself at my expense."

Before I can explain or stop him, Wilson hangs up and then instantly calls back, my phone ringing violently in my hand.

It wasn't the point, but I don't take the opportunity lightly when I answer this time.

"Hey, Will. Thanks for calling back. It really gives me 'Good Vibrations,'" I snicker, my mangled toe long forgotten. Will sighs. I continue on, of course, like he's enjoying it. "What brings you to call at such an hour? Do you have news that gives me a 'Reason to Believe'?"

Will grumbles something, but it is nearly unintelligible through the shake of my laugh. The funniest part of this whole bit is that I had to *study* Wilson Phillips to be able to do it. I knew a couple of songs, but I wasn't anywhere close to their all-time most frequent listener, so it took actual research and memorization to get to where we are now.

I figure that just goes to show, I can achieve anything I put my mind to, no matter how stupid.

"What was that, Will?"

"I *said*, 'No wonder TikTok's mindless bullshit is as popular as it is.' This is the kind of crap people find entertaining."

I play dumb to his insults, which I know will annoy him even further. "If you're trying to say I should put this on TikTok, that's a great idea. No wonder I pay you fifteen percent."

"Far be it for me to condone this shitty bit of yours, but it would probably be better than the content that's on TikTok about you right now."

I tilt my head to the side in surprise. "They talk about me on TikTok?"

"Uh, yeah. Mostly about you being a recluse and the great possibility that you might just be as much of a ghost as the Shadow Brothers. But yeah, they talk about you."

I ignore the negatives of his statement and focus on the most important part. "Wouldn't you have to have a TikTok account to actually know what's happening on TikTok?" I question. "Is there something you're not telling me, Will? If I locate your account, will I find my agent dancing to Nicki Minaj or something?"

Will scoffs. "I have a TikTok account because I'm your agent and need to be proactive when it comes to your publicity. Though, I think we both know what I'm going to say next…"

He wants me to start posting on my TikTok account. He's been on my ass about it for the past year. In my defense, I already post on Facebook and Instagram and Twitter, and I honestly feel like those are enough, even if my content is scarce.

"You know I'm not good socially, Will. I don't think parading my awkwardness on a global scale is going to help sales."

He's silent after I say that. Silent in a way that means something. Silent for a duration of time that's way too long. Silent in a way that *scares* me.

"What aren't you telling me right now?"

"Nothing."

"Wilson, I swear to Carnie you'd better 'Hold On' if you're lying to me."

His deep exhale is so loud it echoes inside my ears "It's Netflix. They want you to do a tour, prior to the premiere of the show."

"No way," I whisper.

"Yes, but it's just eight cities in two weeks. You'll do quick flights and five-star hotels the whole time. It'll be easy peasy," he updates like it's no big thing.

But it is a big thing. A *huge* thing.

Flights? Mamma Mia.

I shut my eyes and try to fight off an impending headache with three fingers to the bridge of my nose. "Listen, the last thing I want to do is come across as a drama llama with the good people at Netflix, but if you'll remember, the last time I was on a plane, 250 people who didn't want to be in Buffalo made a screaming-fun landing there just in time for the Bills game, and I had to pay twenty thousand freaking dollars to cover my out-of-pocket maximum on my medical insurance."

The last time I was on a plane, it took a grievous toll on my mental health.

As it turns out, being the reason for a plane's emergency landing is the kind of thing that really sticks with a girl.

"I can't do the planes, Will. I can't," I add, my voice edging on desperation. "Trains, automobiles, buses, sure, but I can't do the planes."

"Brooke, come on. You know the tour would take significantly longer with those methods of transportation."

I huff out a breath. "Not as long as it'll be if I down a plane before I make it to the first stop. I'm telling you, Will, no planes."

"Okay, fine," he acquiesces, though his voice indicates an annoyance. "I'll talk to Netflix. See what we can work out."

"Good." I don't mention that I'm hoping the thing they work out is that I'm too much trouble for a tour because I know that'll set Wilson off in the kind of way my song bit never could. But I'm not built for public consumption, you know? I'm an inside, in pajamas, at my desk kind of gal.

"I'll get back to you when I nail down the details, okay? 'The Dream is Still Alive.'"

"Did you…" I pause, and my mouth forms a little "O" of its own accord. "Did you just do my own bit to me?"

Wilson lets out a husky laugh. "Bye, Brooke."

The click of the line going dead kills my opportunity for a rebuttal, but nothing can put a damper on my smile. Because by joining in just now, poor Wilson Phillips has solidified that my game of music with him will never, ever die.

When my phone rings again before I can even put it back in its place on the counter, I look at Benji as though he's Alexander Graham Bell reincarnated. I mean, I feel like the inventor of the phone would have some kind of insight into the coincidental circumstances that have led to my newfound popularity.

My sister's name is the last one I expect to see. Not because I don't talk to her regularly—we've spoken so much since her divorce you'd think I was her new lover—but *I'm* usually the one to call *her*.

She has two young, wild boys that keep her on defense ninety-nine percent of the time, and that's the kind of lifestyle you just barely survive. She doesn't have time to think about calling me—at least, normally—so I don't mind doing the legwork.

"Sammy!" I greet enthusiastically. My big sister is really going through it right now, but don't let that fool you. She's one of the best, most supportive, good-hearted humans I've ever met. I only wish I could take away some of her hurt—rewind some of the years she wasted on that puckered entrance, Todd. "How's it going?" I ask just a shriek of terror and hell demand attention in the background.

"Oh, great," she replies sarcastically, the grind of her teeth giving her words a real edge. "I'm forty years old with two demon hooligans who don't know their cup from a hand grenade, facking divorced, and currently living with our mom and dad—a man, by the way, who's told my kids that they'll find themselves at the bottom of the back creek bed if they interrupt his after-dinner personal time twice since my arrival."

Yikes. Only Hank Baker could say something like that to his own grandchildren. Don't get me wrong, he's a good father and grandpa, but finesse definitely skipped his generation of Bakers.

"Okay, well, that's…it's… I'm sure it'll be…" I sigh. "Shit. I'm sorry, Sam, but I'm pretty sure your life has just developed a kink for sucking balls right now."

I cross the room to my desk and plop my ass into my swivel desk chair. I don't know how long this conversation is going to last, but in the name of being fully supportive, I don't want to get tired from standing.

And yes, I realize that makes me sound ninety years old, but my hips just don't like that position, okay? I can sit, I can walk—I can even run short distances—but standing for more than two minutes at a time sends my hips into a spiral of shame and dismay.

Another screeching scream fills the silence, and she groans. "Tell me something I don't know, Brooke."

"The earth's rotation has been getting faster lately by, like, a millisecond or something. So, I know the days are long, but technically, they are getting shorter."

She snorts. "The fact that you know this makes it so, so obvious that you're not living the life I am right now."

I pick at the very corner of my lacquered IKEA desk that's just starting to come apart, and I swallow all of my thoughts—about my ex Jamie and how I thought life would be, about the book that is ruining my life, about my unrelenting crush on my editor and the potential Netflix tour I'm in no way equipped to handle, and how I'm still lost as all hell, though definitely more in charge of my time. Because Sam is looking to vent, and I know the feeling well enough to let her.

No one likes a one-upper during story time. Especially when their one-up isn't a one-up at all. Instead, I venture to lighten her mood with some humor—just a little.

"I also peed by myself and managed a shower today," I tease, making her laugh.

"Whore."

"I know, I know. But trust me," I say, snapping the stretchy waistband of my sweatpants against my stomach, "not everyone is prepared to live a life of luxury like me."

I can hear the slow creak of Sam's childhood room door, and my nephews' tiny voices go from boisterous to muffled.

"Wow. It's like entering a sound booth."

Sam laughs. "Yeah. They should be in bed by now, but Mom got them all hopped up on sugar."

"What?" My jaw hits my knees. "Mom? Sugar before bedtime?"

"Oh yeah. Mom and Gammy are two *very* different people, Brookie. Gammy thinks cookies and milk solve everything. And Gammy tries to help *all* the time." Sam lets out a groan that feels like it comes from her freaking toes. "If it weren't for Dad yelling at her, I think she'd sneak sugar into their rooms in the middle of the night, too."

"Just repeat to yourself that this is temporary, Sam. Because it is. I know it doesn't feel like it right now, but you're going to be out of there and on your feet before you know it."

"I know. I do. It just doesn't feel like it right now."

God, I feel for her. Her life has been upended by her asshole ex-husband. Not only did he go through some kind of pathetic midlife crisis, but he decided he wanted a "cool life" that didn't include his wife and two kids. In what felt like a blink of an eye, Todd, the douche, wanted a divorce, and my sister went from being the stay-at-home mom who put her family above every-thing—including herself—to a woman trying to find her way again, with two kids in tow.

Now, Todd is living in Cincinnati, doing God knows what, and barely sees his boys, and my sister is trying to clean up the disaster he created for her.

I open my mouth to reassure her again, when a shriek and the sound of shattering glass travel undeniably through her door. I wince, and she curses. *Loudly.*

"Sorry, B. I gotta go. We'll catch up on what's going on with you next time."

"No worries," I rush to say. I know she's likely already pulling the phone away from her ear, but I at least want to try in case she can hear me. "Love you."

She's hurried and discombobulated, but she still finds the headspace to say it back. "Love you too, sis. To the moon and back."

I listen for the click on her end and then slowly pull the phone away from my ear. Benji is staring at me with his head cocked in question, and I can't help but chuckle.

"I don't know, Benj. I think the people who say dogs are like kids are lying to themselves."

My conscience is quick to mock me ruthlessly. *They're not the only ones lying to themselves right now…*

Instantly, my eyes flit to the screen of my computer, and I scan River's flaw list before glancing down at the minimized file that reads *Accidental Attachment.*

I think about Clive and River, and I think about Chase and the fact that whenever I'm in his close proximity, it tends not to end well.

If there's any hope of getting through edits on this book, I'm going to need to keep my distance from that man. Emails, text messages, and a limited number of phone calls. Anytime he wants to meet in person, I'll tell him I have the flu or some shit.

But what about when the book actually publishes? You going to come down with a chronic illness that requires years-long isolation?

Considering I have no guarantees that I'll even live through edits, I'll cross that bridge if I get to it.

Chapter
Nine

Sunday, May 14th

Chase

A half a pound of pastrami and rye fills the balloon of my stomach, and a balmy sixty-eight degrees fills the pee-smelling air.

What a day to be alive and in New York City.

My Sundays are normally spent wandering aimlessly from the gym to lunch and onward to any number of people-watching locations, and today is no different. By nature, I'm more of a homebody, but when you have a room-mate like Glenn, home is not where the heart is, if you know what I'm saying.

I stroll through the southern end of Central Park where I've been for the last hour or so and out onto the street at Columbus Circle to walk in the direction of home.

Granted, home is approximately one million blocks away, so I'll have to hop on the subway at some point, but for now, I'm content to stroll.

An elderly woman with a flowered cap brushes past me on her way into the park and gives me a lift of her chin in acknowledgment. It's miles above what I normally get from strangers on the street in this city, and for some reason, it makes me smile.

I crane my neck around to watch her retreat, and the pace she's keeping is entirely impressive for someone her age. I hope I'm still as spry and adventurous as she is when I'm closing out my life's circle.

With a shake of my head and a jumbo-size grin, I turn back in the direction I'm heading and pick up my pace. People are out and about in droves, both locals and visitors alike, wanting to take advantage of the weather before rain sets in tomorrow.

The thing about spring flowers is that they're created by showers. Some of those age-old sayings are commonplace because they sound nice, but this one...this one is true.

Thanks to my proximity to Longstrand, I detour from 8th Avenue to make a pass on the building for shits and giggles. As stupid as it sounds, sometimes I take a moment out of my days off just to look at the building and remind myself how hard I worked to get here.

To be valuable enough that the number one publisher in the country would want me, and to be confident enough in my ability to read the market that I can push for unorthodox decisions like Brooke's new book.

I've always loved to read, but right now—reading books unknown to anyone but me and crafting them into a position to take the literary world by storm—I've found a whole other level of invigoration for it.

New path set, I keep walking in the direction of the subway stop I use when I come to the office and catch the D train headed back toward my temporary apartment.

It's relatively empty for as crowded as the streets are, but I figure people are sticking to walking in the enjoyable weather.

When the train pulls into Chelsea, I get off at my sister and brother-in-law's stop so I can go to their Trader Joe's for my basic weekly groceries.

Eggs, bagels, coffee, and half-and-half are the gist of it, but I'm feeling a little wild today, so I might even pick out a snooty cheese too.

Look out world, it's getting crazy!

Off the train and up the metal-trimmed steps, I jog onto the streets of New York like I never left them in the first place. My pace automatically matches the crowd, and my nose drifts between the scents of bread flour and pizza grease. I avoid a woman with two little girls in frilly dresses and bows holding hands on her right and two boys in baseball caps and gym shoes on her left by carefully stepping off the curb and into the street, and then back up when she's passed.

I can't imagine navigating this city with four kids on my own, but in some twisted way, I want to. I've always wanted a family and to settle down—people to spend my aimless Sundays with.

I'm still looking back when my phone starts to ring, and the quick grab I make for my pocket accidentally sends me bumping into a beautiful woman with dark hair and bright-blue eyes with a camera bag slung over her shoulder.

"Shit," I mutter when the bag slips down her arm and careens toward the ground. "I'm so sorry."

"No worries," she replies through a smile, catching the bag just before it hits the sidewalk and lifting it back onto her shoulder. "I reserve my dick punches for my husband."

My eyebrows jump to my hairline, and the woman with all the kids stops in her tracks to turn around and yell at her. "God, Cassie. Could you not with the strangers, please?"

"Relax, Georgie." Cassie—apparently—just shrugs and winks at me before continuing on her way.

My phone starts to ring again, me having missed the first call entirely during the scuffle. But when I see Dawn's name, my good mood shrivels. She wouldn't be calling me on a Sunday if it weren't important—I know that for a fact.

"Hello?" I say, putting my phone to my ear and my feet to the sidewalk. I don't know where I'm going, but it's somewhere other than here. According to my sister, I've always been a phone pacer—completely incapable of standing in one position while I'm talking. Even if I'm on the corded one behind my desk, I wiggle like a Labrador following a swinging piece of meat.

"Hi, boss. Sorry to bother you on Sunday, but…" She pauses, and I don't like the hesitant tone of her voice.

"But what? What don't I want to hear?"

"I hate to be the bearer of bad news, but I just took a call from Wilson Phillips."

"Carnie, Chynna, or Wendy?"

Dawn chuckles at my pathetic joke, and an immediate suspicion comes to mind. "You're laughing because I pay you, aren't you?"

"Yes. Though, technically, my payroll is completed by Longstrand Publishing, so I basically laughed for free."

"Right. Okay, then, hit me with the bad news before I crack another one that costs the company money."

"Wilson says they're still verifying final logistics like a driver and confirming all the stops, but it looks like the Netflix tour for Brooke is going to happen, and it's going to happen soon—as in, sometime this upcoming week. They're on a short leash with the premiere in LA, so they're moving quickly. There's absolutely no way they're going to hold this thing, deadline or not."

"*Shi—oot!*"

"I know," she replies, understanding the situation well enough to know this isn't a good thing for *Accidental Attachment*. "Should I talk to marketing? See what would happen if we pushed publishing back by a month or two to give you more time for first edits?"

I rub at my temples with a spread hand while I keep my phone to my ear with the other.

"No. The last thing I need is Jonah knowing about anything even mildly related to shaky ground with this book. I'm going to have to figure out some way to make it work."

"Okay, boss. Whatever you think."

Whatever I think? I'm not thinking anything right now besides impending doom.

I stare up at the blue sky and shut my eyes for a second. "How sure did Wilson sound that this thing was going to happen? Any chance at all of it falling through?" I open my eyes slowly, like the answer to her question is going to appear in human form and scare the shit out of me. "I know they nixed the planes because of Brooke's condition, but what exactly is their backup plan?"

"That's why they're looking for a driver," she explains. "Evidently, they're going to do three weeks by motor home rather than two by plane. He seemed pretty confident it was going to go through. Maybe even chipper? Though, he did mention he had to make a call to Brooke with the details still."

I jerk my head back in surprise. "He called us before her?"

"Yes. Something about being afraid of getting blackballed by Mr. Perish."

"Shit! I mean, shoot." The last person who needs to get involved in this is my boss.

Dawn laughs. "It's okay, sir. You can curse. I live in New York. I've heard it before."

"Of course…I just…"

"You were trying to be professional, but you're having an existential crisis. I understand."

I groan and run an erratic hand through my hair. "How much do you charge per hour as a therapist exactly?"

"What do you want me to do?" Dawn questions, humor that I'm in no way feeling right now tap-dancing in her voice.

What do I *want* her to do? Fuck if I know. I don't even know what I *should* do.

"I can try to get Wilson Phillips back on the phone and inquire a little harder?"

"No." I shake my head. "Just hang tight while I think for a little bit and see if I can come up with something that's helpful."

"10-4," Dawn replies, hanging up without expecting anything else.

I look up from my phone, tuck it into my pocket, and take stock of where I am. I've been power walking for the entire length of the call without environmental awareness. But as luck would have it, my feet have taken me right to the front door of my sister and brother-in-law's building. I don't know that they're home, but I *do* know that the restaurant is closed on Sundays and Mondays, so I've got a halfway decent shot.

Without pause, I shove inside the door, wave to the doorman Dave, who is familiar with me, and make my way to the elevator at the back of the lobby. Normally, I'd call and warn my sister of my arrival, but under these circumstances, I'm hopeful that the element of surprise will help her think of solutions to my problem.

The elevator dings its arrival on the top floor pretty quickly, and I step off before the doors have even opened all the way. My long legs eat up the distance to their door quickly, and I lay my finger into the ceramic white of their fancy doorbell button with gusto.

When Mo doesn't answer right away, I change tactics to an obnoxious knock.

She's got curlers in her hair and a scowl on her face, but the sight of my sister on the other side of an open door is all I need to barge my way into their apartment.

"Well, hello," she remarks, just barely swinging her shoulder out of the way before I bowl her over. "What is it I can do for you today, dear brother?"

"Sorry. My feet just came here," I say nonsensically as I collapse on her couch and look to the ceiling in an effort to think all the thoughts.

The thing about publishing is that you never run out of problems or surprises. I've been in this career for a decade, editing for nearly that, and I can count on one hand the number of times things have gone exactly as planned or, for that matter, similarly to how they'd ever gone before.

"Oh-kay," Mo responds, shutting the door with a shove and coming to take a seat on the coffee table beside my couch-lounger. "Are you sick? In the body or the head? Because you're not making any sense."

"I just found out that in all likelihood, Brooke Baker is going on a *three-week* Netflix motor home tour soon, right in the middle of our extremely tight deadline."

My sister still doesn't get it. "And…you feel deeply disturbed that…she's doing this in a prime number of days?"

"I'm afraid we're not going to finish the edits on her new book in time, Mo!"

"Oh, *oh*. Got it." She widens her eyes comically. "Sorry, just thought it was weird we were being so mad about Brooke Baker getting something as accomplished as a Netflix tour."

I roll my eyes, practically yelling, "I'm not mad about the tour! I'm mad about the timing. Three weeks! Three freaking weeks, right in the middle of our deadline for first edits. Her agent said they're looking for a driver still, but in the age of Uber and Door Dash, I doubt it'll take a modern miracle to find one."

"Bro." She scrunches up her nose at me. "You're kind of being a drama queen. It's unbecoming, to say the least."

"I'm not being dramatic, Mo. One of literature's great stories is on the line here—and oh yeah, so is my job, in case you've forgotten."

"You're such a book dork, putting the *fate of the story* ahead of yourself. I love it."

I ignore her mocking. "We're going to fall too far behind on edits. There is no way we can make the deadline if she's on a three-week fucking tour."

"So…go on the stupid motor home tour thing with her, then?" She shrugs like her words make actual sense. "Drive the bus like you used to on Dawson family vacations. Stay on top of it. Work on edits in between tour stops and shit like that."

I scoff. "That's highly irregular. Editing is kind of a remote job. Not traditionally done while living together on a damn motor home."

"And Brooke Baker turning in a book the publisher wasn't expecting is highly irregular too, wouldn't you say?" she retorts back. "Pretty sure you can take your job at Longstrand on the road for a few weeks in the name of *the fate of the story*." She's still mocking me, but I'm also considering her crazy solution.

However, I only consider it for one foolish moment. "No way." I shake my head. "I can't do that. That'd be crazy."

"Sorry, I thought you were worried about your job, having just upended your life in Nashville to move to New York with a roommate who I'm pretty sure is just an illegal squatter or a paranormal entity with a penchant for liquid, but hey, if you're not, that's cool."

I stare at her. "I'm struggling to remember why I thought living close to you would be such a good thing."

She has the audacity to laugh. "This is what they call a shit-or-get-off-the-pot moment, Chasey-wasey. What's it gonna be? Undeniable relief or chronic, painful constipation?"

I snort and scoff at the same time. "I really hate how much sense that just made."

"No, babe. You don't." She pats my knee. "Do the damn thing, okay? And send me a postcard while you're at it."

Mo gets up from the coffee table and heads down the hallway toward the bedrooms, leaving me to sit here and ponder my choices all on my own.

My stomach churns and my throat burns… *Am I really going to do this?*

I've got the phone in my hand before my brain even answers the question.

The man of the hour picks up by the second ring. "Hello?"

"Hi, Wilson. Chase Dawson here. I've got a proposition for you."

Chapter *Ten*

Brooke

Benji pulls at his leash in an uncharacteristic fashion as we stroll the Mall in Central Park, and for the second time this week, I give myself a mental lashing for being so deep within my own head that I've been neglectful. Benji needs his exercise just as much as I need my wine, and yet, I've only managed to give him two walks to my three bottles.

Don't judge me, okay? I'm going through a whole new level of a personal crisis.

Maybe that's why I've taken us this far from home, deep into the center of the park to the historic promenade through statues of literary figures, to turn one walk into four by proxy of length.

Or maybe it's because of the comfort I get from being surrounded by the memories of like-minded people. Surely, I convince myself, American poet Fitz-Greene Halleck also spent most of his days alone, shut in with nothing but his pajamas, his words, and a big bottle of wine. And William Shakespeare had to have had a crush on someone he shouldn't have, right? I mean, isn't that the whole freaking basis of star-crossed lovers?

"I'm sorry, Benj," I tell him again when there's an opening in the hordes of people around us. It's not that I'm embarrassed to talk to him in public, or that a crazy lady talking to herself in New York is all that uncommon, but whatever twinge of personal responsibility I have for my outward appearance usually shows up in the most public of locations with people I don't even know. As if strangers' opinions are somehow the most important.

Caring what people I'm undoubtedly never going to see again think is twisted. But it's real. I'm sure if I pursued it hard enough, I could find a mental illness diagnosis that supports it.

Benji, thankfully, seems unaffected by my slight.

His step is high, and his mood is a strut as we pass by several other sexy dog babes and their owners. His pleather Batman costume is really working for him in this lighting, and the dramatic cast of the sidewalk-lined trees makes him seem like the true superhero among canine commoners.

"I'll admit it, Benj. You look good. I wasn't convinced this getup was the right move, but as always, you were right. I'll try to make myself listen to you sooner next time, but I think we both know that's not exactly likely." I laugh at myself. "Hardheaded runs in the family."

Benji barks to get my attention—and I can't blame him since I've devolved into a full-on one-person conversation—but when I look up and follow the direction of his gaze, what I find isn't at all what I expect.

A very large, attractive man wearing what I'd guess is an incredibly expensive custom suit is walking a pig on a long lead line. A tiny purple service vest is wrapped around his pink body as he struts through the park with his nose held high in the air.

Benji turns to look back at me as if to say, "Hey, don't get any ideas on the purple vest," and I nearly chortle.

"It's cute, for sure," I chide softly. "But it's not exactly your color, my man."

But Chase thinks it's your color...

I roll my eyes at myself and focus on the larger-than-life man and pig duo walking through the park. What a set of characters this pair would make. I imagine a man that size walking a pig that small has some outrageous stories to tell and a lot of vibrant life to live. He's probably got a crazy girlfriend or wife who can talk him into just about anything and a group of friends who both love and hate him. In fact, with the way his mouth appears to be in a perpetual smirk, he looks mischievous and fun, like the kind of man who could pull off one hell of a prank.

I pull Benji over to the bench on the side of the walk path and pull my phone out of my pocket to jot down some notes. Benji groans at my inability to get my brain off books, and I nod. "I know. I'm sorry. I'll make it up to you."

An old lady with a flowered knit cap stares at me from the bench ten feet away, and for some insane reason, I feel the need to explain myself. "I'm just talking to my dog."

She bites her bottom lip to stop a laugh—I can tell—and hums before turning the other direction.

I take a deep breath and focus back on my notes app.

Big guy with pig, I write, making myself laugh. *God, I'm crazy.* **Potential character in a city series about a friend group with him at the center. Bold personality with soft, gooey center. Wealthy, funny, and always the life of the party.**

I read my notes back and blow out a breath of incredulity. I can only imagine how on earth I'm going to interpret this jumble when I finally get around to doing something with it. It's not like I have free writing time right now—ha-ha-ha. All of my current time and concentration belongs to the book that shouldn't be. The life-ruiner, as it were.

But just for the hell of it, I try to jot down some names—whatever comes to mind—just to set myself up when I come back to this in the future. One might call this a pathetic attempt to avoid the book I should be working on, but I'm certainly not the person who is going to call that out.

What kind of guy does he look like?

Paul? *Ha, hard no.*

Nathan? *Definitely not.*

Calvin? *No. Still wrong.*

Parker? *Not bold enough.*

Brooks? *Seems better as a last name.*

Kline? *Hmm. That one's got some merit.*

I'm about to continue when Benji pulls at his leash so hard I'm catapulted up from the bench in one smooth motion. It's jarring and surprising, but when I see the border collie coming our way with a bow in her hair, it starts to make a little more sense.

I shake my head to clear the giant pain radiating up my neck and rub at the soreness in my leash-holding forearm. "Dang, Benj. Keep it in your pants, would you?"

The old lady with the flower cap looks my way again, her lip curled up in slight wariness this time. I choose to ignore her once and for all. She'll be dead in a couple of years anyway.

Okay, okay, Brooke, that was a little too far. I glance over at her again and search my conscience for inner forgiveness. All I can muster is an extension on her timeline by three or four years.

That's it. I'm really going to hell now. This poor old woman hasn't even done anything to me. Something about her just puts me on edge. Like I should know her or something.

Standing, I wrap Benji's leash around my hand to get better control and drag him—nicely, I swear—in the opposite direction of his lover. His eyes are a little sad, but I've already painted this park red with crazy today, and I think going over to talk to the collie's owner about how my German shepherd is experiencing love at first sight would really put me over the quota.

Benji falls in line, dutiful as always, but when he looks over his shoulder one last time before we turn the corner, I start to feel more than a little bad.

Did I just mess up here? Have I let my best friend down in immeasurable ways? I don't know if I can stand the thought of being a disappointment to Benji—denying him something he both wants and deserves. He's always had my back, even when I'm being nuts, and at the first sign of insanity from him, I'm just going to turn on him?

No. No, I can't do that. I have to let him have a chance at love!

Frantic now, I turn him back around and pick up my pace to a jog in the direction of the border collie and her owner. I'm weaving us through foot traffic like we're the stars of *Fast and Furious 19: Barkio Drift.*

Benji picks up what I'm putting down, and his ears perk forward in excitement.

"Mama's on board, Benj, let's find this broad."

Scouring the feet of the people ahead of us, I look for the prancy paws of the pretty princess with avid attention. There are several dogs—even a few canine ladies—but the scent of the one that got away is fading fast.

Come on, come on.

A man in a windbreaker doing an overpronounced jog.

Two toddlers fighting in the arms of an overwhelmed father.

Two women with their matching Chihuahuas in overcoats.

A messenger on a bike with fingerless gloves riding past a couple canoodling on a bench.

There's a bevy of activity in this part of the park, and yet none of the activity I was hoping desperately to see.

When we reach the beginning of the Mall, she's nowhere in sight, and I'm officially the worst doggo mom ever.

"Oh, gah, Benji, I'm sorry. I'm so sorry." He looks back in distress, then toward the crowd of receding people again, and then back to me, before rubbing up against my legs in forgiveness.

The world doesn't deserve dogs, I'm sure of it. As for me? I deserve this beautiful, good boy even less.

I crouch down and grab his face at the sides. "Somehow, someway, I'm going to make this up to you, buddy. I promise. I don't know how, but I'm going to figure it out, just like you'd figure it out for me."

Benji pushes me until I gently fall to my butt and then climbs into my lap for a round of body-traversing comfort scratches.

I make sure to hit his back and his legs and his belly and his chest with the best part of my nails the way he likes it, nearly devolving into tears as I do.

The mental anguish of my breakdown is so distracting that when my phone rings in my pocket while we're sitting there, I pull it out and put it to my ear without even looking at the screen, caller ID be damned. All I can say is that if this ends up being someone calling about my nonexistent car's extended warranty, they're going to pay witness to the kind of psychotic tailspin that eludes description.

"Hello?"

"Brooke. Wilson here."

Wilson Phillips, my agent. Dear God, this might be even worse timing than the car warranty call.

"Not really a good time, Will. Kind of in the middle of tending to a dog's broken heart. Can I call you back?"

"What?"

"A canine catastrophe, Will!"

"Listen, I don't know what kind of joke you're trying to tell right now, but it's falling flat. If you're testing it for a book, scrap it."

I groan into the receiver. "I'm not making a joke! I'm in the middle of mending Benji's broken heart."

"Still not getting the joke."

"It's not a joke!" I exclaim, both of my hands leaving Benji's fur and pushing out in front of me theatrically. Not even a second later, my doggo nudges my leg with his snout to let me know the belly scratches are not over.

"Oh. Ha." Wilson lets out a little chuckle. "Okay, avid denial of the joke is kind of funny, I guess. I get what you're going for anyway."

I grind my teeth and start scratching Benji's fur again. "I'm not going for anything other than getting off the phone with you."

"Well, then you'd better work on your excuses, Brooke. This one is kind of lame."

I sigh heavily, and when I look down, Benji rolls his eyes and sits between my legs. *Just get this over with*, he says. I have to admit, with the way the conversation has gone so far, he's probably right.

"All right, Will, is there a reason you're calling?"

"You bet your ass, B. Netflix is approaching the premiere date for *The Shadow Brothers*, as you know, and they still think it'd be a good idea if you did a small tour."

"We already talked about this. I can't get on a plane. It'd be a disaster."

"No, I know. I got that from the last conversation. But they've agreed to the motor home tour, so it's all set. You leave from New York on Wednesday."

I blink rapidly. "Wednesday? As in, *this* Wednesday?"

"Yep. This Wednesday, babe. You and a motor home, driving around the country for three weeks to meet-and-greet with your devoted fans."

"Will, that's, like, three days away."

"Yeah, well, if you would've been able to do the plane thing, you would've had more notice," he answers without remorse. "But motor homes take more time than planes, and everything had to be moved up."

Ugh. Is this for real? I'm supposed to go on a tour where people are expected to get excited about me stepping out of a freaking motor home?

Frankly, it's the craziest thing I've heard in a long time, and since I live inside my own head, that's saying a lot.

"Wouldn't the actors be a bigger draw?" I question. "Seriously, Will. Does anyone even know who I am at this point?"

"Brooke," he chastises. "We've been through this. You're a shining star, baby. Plus, the actors will be doing a small tour of their own, and you'll all meet up at the premiere in LA."

My eyes narrow at the thought of me on a freaking RV. "A motor home tour? This is what Netflix really wants?"

"It sure is, and who knows, maybe you'll pick up some groupies like the bands do."

"Me? Groupies?" I snort. "Yeah, right."

"I wouldn't be so quick to dismiss it."

For the sake of my own sanity, I have to ignore the ridiculous possibility entirely.

"I assume I'll have a driver of some sort?" I question, still one hundred percent annoyed with Netflix's ability to problem-solve. "It's not like I have any CDL training, and I don't think a forty-car pileup on the interstate is the kind of headline Netflix has in mind for this publicity business."

"Actually, your editor Chase volunteered for the job. Said it'd be helpful with the edits on the new book, *Accidental Attachment*—one I don't remember hearing about, by the way—and make it easy to liaise with the publisher and Netflix."

Did he just say Chase would be my driver? Surely my ears are playing tricks on me.

"I'm sorry, what?"

"Chase. Dawson. He's going to drive you."

"No." It's all I can say. Just…no. God, no. *Hell no.* That can't happen.

"*Yes.* I've been on the phone all morning and afternoon getting this settled, and it's just been approved all the way up the ladder," Wilson answers with far too much cheer that not at all matches the war that's just broken out inside my chest. Bombs, missiles, hand grenades, it's full-on anarchy.

Just relax; there's no way he's serious about this.

I inhale a deep breath and shake my head at myself and my agent's stupid joke. "My freaking editor driving my motor home tour? Ha-ha, Will, you really got me there. But seriously, you should leave being funny to me. I'm better at it."

"I'm not being funny, Brooke. He's going."

And now… *I'm going.*

Benji jumps up from his spot on the ground, alert to my spiral, and encouraging me to put my head farther between my legs before my blood pressure tanks. My heart rate's speeding down the highway at a hundred and ninety with no regard for reckless driving.

I…I cannot *live* with Chase Dawson on a motor home for *three weeks*. We cannot be all up in each other's personal space like that. I cannot have to face the intoxicating smell of his cologne on a daily basis. Or witness just how blue his eyes look when he first wakes up in the morning.

I wouldn't survive it.

"Maybe I can drive the bus," I quickly chime in through a breathless, weak voice. "I mean, I haven't driven in a few years, but how hard can it be?"

"*Brooke.*" Will's voice is now growing impatient. "It's all set."

When I start to lift my head, Benji gently nudges it back between my legs.

Calm down. Passing out in the middle of Central Park isn't going to get you anywhere besides an ambulance ride. I force myself to inhale a deep breath through my nose and release it slowly out of my mouth.

"Besides being packed and ready to go by Wednesday," Will adds. "There's nothing left to think over or worry about, Brooke."

He couldn't be any more wrong if he tried. There're plenty of things to worry about—such as, is there a shower on that motor home? Because I really don't think it'll be good for my sanity to know Chase is in a shower with water dripping down his sexy body and I'm just a flimsy wall away.

And you thought sending Accidental Attachment *to him was bad. This takes the fucking cake.*

"I can't believe you agreed to this without consulting me first," I mutter, my voice nearly missing in action from all the stress of this brand-new revelation.

"Strange how that feels, huh?" Will replies, and sarcasm rounds out his question.

"So…what?" My chest burns. "This is, like, some kind of pseudo-revenge for turning in a book you hadn't heard about?"

Wilson sighs, and my chest flips over on itself, burning rage officially replaced by nausea. "No, Brooke. It's not. Though, I imagine it is a similar feeling."

Yeah, right. He doesn't know what I'm feeling. He doesn't know what I'm feeling at all. *Turning this book in was the last thing I wanted, compadre,* I want to say. And I want to scream, *If I had any self-preservation at all, I'd have set fire to both my laptop and Longstrand and the internet altogether until no copies remained!*

But instead of going off on him, I find myself muttering, "I'm scared." *Boy oh boy, is that an understatement.*

"Yeah, well, this is the part they don't talk about, babe. Dream-achieving *is* scary. It's grand and unexplored, and it's been a figment of your imagination for just a little too long to seem real. Everything you've ever wanted is coming true. Just enjoy it." His voice lacks sarcasm. If anything, it's soft and genuine, and that only makes me more irritated.

"Right. Simple as that. Just enjoy it. By God, Will, I...I think you've just performed a miracle. A true spiritual moment of epiphany, you know?" I shut my eyes tightly. "Frankly, I think that's somehow done a better job than just telling me to relax. And as we know, that's the reining cure for anxiety recommended by medical professionals!"

"Yeah, yeah, whatever, smartass. Silly me, trying to make you feel better about doing something you obviously don't want to do."

It's on the very tip of my tongue to tell him that he, as my agent charged with representing my best interests, should be trying to get me out of the thing I don't want to do instead of making me feel better about doing it anyway, but a very small, nearly minuscule, rational part of me blunts the edge of my tongue.

If I'd known what I was doing enough to plan this shit *at all,* turning in a book you've never even mentioned to your agent, behind your agent's back, *would* be a pretty shitty thing to do to the guy who's gotten you all the deals you've ever signed. Not to mention, most writers would sacrifice themselves to an evil spirit for the chance to take my place on a three-week tour sponsored by Netflix.

I take a deep breath to bolster the resolve to say the things I *know* I need to say.

"I'm sorry, Will. Really. I know you're trying," I admit and stare down at the pavement beneath my feet. I pick at a rogue piece of grass stuck inside a crack in the concrete. "I'm a pain in the ass with the change and a pain in the ass in the air with the no-flying thing. I get it. You're trying to make it work, and I do appreciate that. I just... I'm not socially gifted, and this is pretty overwhelming for me."

"You're gonna do fine, Brooke. You're a quick-witted, bighearted human. People are drawn to that, believe it or not."

I grimace. "Yeah?"

"Yeah. And if all else fails, at least you've got the dog. People love dogs."

I look down at Benji, and he crooks his head in question. *He is pretty darn cute, and he'd be even sharper in that Captain America costume if I reinstate the order.*

"I'll do the motor home thing." The words just fall out of my mouth.

"With the editor?"

A scoff grows legs and leaps from my throat. "Do I have a choice?"

"Of course you have a choice, Brooke. I'd never dream of putting you in a truly miserable situation."

I close my eyes tight and pinch my brain into a state of frozen blackness. There's not enough fight left in me to stop this—not when a whole huge portion of me, specifically the vaginal region—is in complete opposition to my hesitancy in the first place. The ole hoochie-coochie wants Chase there like she wants her next breath, mental stability be damned.

"I'll do it. Chase can come...drive the bus or whatever. I'll behave. 'You Won't See Me Cry.'"

There's a smile in Wilson's voice, despite my own brand of musical water torture. "Great. I'll tell Netflix."

"Great." *I'll gird my loins.*

"Bye, Brooke."

"Bye, Will."

I hang up the phone and let my head fall back in despair. Benji still watches me closely, thanks to my still-very-present anxiety, but his face has melted right along with mine into acceptance. The fainting, the tour, the unbelievably hell-on-earth-ish three weeks on a bus with the man I'm embarrassingly attracted to—it's all happening.

I give Benji's head a scratch and stand up from my spot on the hard pavement. My ass is numb, I need a moral support glass of wine, and Benji needs some time to himself. We're both going to be busy, busy, busy in just three short days.

Three freaking days, and then I can pretty much officially say that I'm living with the man of my fantasies turned private fan fiction turned soon-to-be published worldwide book.

May my horny, Chase Dawson-infatuated vagina have mercy on me.

Chapter
Eleven

Monday, May 15th

Chase

After I volunteered as tribute to be the driver for Brooke Baker's motor home tour and got it approved by Harold Lewis, Longstrand's corporate travel manager, and the executives at Netflix, news of my insanity evidently spread fast.

Dawn called me first, panicked about how we were going to maintain our day-to-day if I was out driving a bus, and then Frank and Regina started demon dialing me about the notes I left on their desks. Even Mo left me a five-minute voice mail full of metaphors for how surprised she was about the fact that I'd taken her advice.

None were as scary though, as the single text I received from Jonah Perish—
Be in my office tomorrow at 10 a.m.

To say I'm on edge right now, as I stand in front of my boss's desk, wouldn't come close to scratching the surface of my current anxiety. I've been here for two minutes, and my legs are so numb they're liable to give out if I make any sudden movements.

"Well, Dawson, you're nothing if not thorough, huh?" Jonah comments from behind the massive mahogany monstrosity he had shipped in from somewhere expensive.

A desk he rarely sits at, mind you. He's usually too busy in meetings or jet-setting around the globe on the Longstrand company plane.

"I have to say this is the first time that one of my editors has agreed to drive an RV for an author's publicity tour in the name of meeting a deadline," he adds and slides his glasses off his nose and tosses them onto his desk. He leans back in his fancy leather chair and stretches his arms behind his head. "On a book that he put his ass on the line for, at that."

My laugh is two parts nerves and one part *"Am I an idiot?"*

Show no weakness, my mind reminds me.

I run a hand through my hair and clear my throat as I dig deep for the voice that convinced him to give *Accidental Attachment* the green light. "Just like you, sir, I'm a man of follow-through. I stood behind the book because I believe in it, and I know what it's capable of. And I'm taking the highly unorthodox step of driving an author around the country in an RV because I'm going to make sure *Accidental Attachment* lives up to those capabilities. Exceeds them, in fact. This tight deadline and these unusual circumstances are nothing more than opportunity, sir."

A wolflike laugh jumps from Jonah's mouth. "You've got balls of steel, Dawson. I'll give you that."

Balls of steel? Pretty sure balls of steel can't relocate themselves to your stomach.

"You're not going to drop the ball on any of your other projects," he declares, a firm statement of warning.

I nod. "Frank has already been briefed on the Beranski deal, and Regina has agreed to be my temporary point of contact for my other authors. I'll be checking in with them frequently while I'm on the road."

Jonah stares at me, his eyes never wavering from my face, and I just stand there and take it, fighting the urge to look away with every cell in my body.

Show no weakness.

He purses his lips, then leans forward to pick up his glasses again. "Don't make me regret this," he eventually says, and he slides the lenses back over the bridge of his nose. "See you in a few weeks."

Translation: If I fuck this up, I may as well not even come back.

Which, funnily enough, feels a little like double jeopardy. If the book fails, I'm fired. If I fuck up the tour, I'm fired. But I can't imagine I can actually be fired twice. Which means all the Eggos are officially in the same basket. And I'm going to have to hold on to the fucker like Dorothy in *The Wizard of Oz*.

Thankfully, the fact that his eyes are no longer focused on me, but on the screen of his desktop, is his way of saying, *You're dismissed*, and I can get the hell out of here.

"Thank you, sir," I say, even though Jonah is now picking up the phone on his desk. His fingers hit the intercom bottom, and he's already giving his assistant instructions about something related to a business trip overseas to meet with foreign publishing houses in France.

I don't dally any longer, more than happy to take myself off the chopping block, and head out the glass doors of his office without another word.

Discreetly, I wipe away a sheen of sweat that has now taken up residence on my forehead and offer Jonah's assistant a friendly but shaky smile as I move into the main hallway.

It takes the entire walk back to my office for my heart rate to calm back down to a normal range, and by the time I'm behind my desk and back to finishing up all the shit I need to get done before I have to leave on Brooke's tour in two days, I'm silently wondering if I'm an absolute moron.

I mean, what editor agrees to drive their author around in a motor home in the name of meeting a deadline? Me, apparently, otherwise known as the crazy bastard who was on the phone all day yesterday to make that exact situation a reality.

Fuck. Any second, that lady from the street is going to show up and punch me in the dick; I just know it.

My phone vibrates inside my suit jacket pocket, and as I'm pulling it out to check the screen, it vibrates three more times.

All text messages. All from my sister.

Mo: Okay, so we need an organized communication system so you can keep me up to speed on everything that happens on the tour. I want to know what

Brooke says and what she wears and what she eats, etc. I want a fully detailed, nightly report.

Mo: Though, I guess I'd be okay with a morning report.

Mo: Or maybe you should do, like, a morning report and a nightly report. That way, you won't forget anything.

Mo: Oh, and if there's any reader out there who tries to act like they're her biggest fan, I need FBI-style background information on those liars ASAP.

I shut my eyes, lean my head back, and sigh.

Yep. It's safe to say crazy runs in the family.

Chapter
Twelve

Tuesday, May 16th

Brooke

I shove at the stacks of clothes in my suitcase, trying to compress them as much as possible. The FlyerPro Deluxe I picked up from Macy's yesterday is fancy enough to have dual quad wheels and an expander zipper, but there's only so much capacity even the fanciest of suitcases can take.

But three weeks on the road is even worse than two weeks on planes, and the only person I have to blame is myself.

When the clothes stop giving and the sweat starts pouring, I pick up my glass of wine off my nightstand and chug. The pinot burns on its way down my throat, but I know in five to ten minutes it'll balm the wounds in my soul.

I suck air in through my teeth, staring at the suitcase that taunts me from the floor, and try again, shoving and prodding until the combined weight of my ass and Benji's front paws allows the zipper to close.

Still, it's precarious at this point, so much so that if I were going through TSA, it'd be labeled an explosive device, taken out on the back forty, and allowed to detonate.

"I wouldn't stand too close to that thing if I were you," I warn Benji, scooping up my glass and heading for the kitchen to indulge in another heavy pour. Mixed company would definitely consider this wino behavior, but Benji knows me well enough not to judge.

We're in breakdown territory, and anything that makes his job of keeping me alive easier, he's all for.

"I just don't know how I got myself into this pickle, Benj. Turning in the wrong book?" My exasperation comes out as an audible rumble. "And then, somehow, talking my agent and Netflix into trapping me with the very man of my fantasies for three straight weeks, just so I wouldn't have to fly?"

I smack my palm to my forehead with a *whap*.

If I would've known I was this good at making nightmares come to reality, I would've tried my hand at writing horror. At least I'd be in the company of Stephen King, instead of stuck inside an RV for twenty-one days with a man I can't trust my vagina to be around.

I cackle. "God, I'm good at making a mess for myself, huh?"

Benji moans before lying down in front of the couch and resting his doggie chin on the tops of his paws. On the surface, someone might find his behavior a little brusque, but this isn't the first time he's heard this tale of woe in the last six hours. Not even close.

If I'm being completely honest, it's not even the sixteenth.

"I know, I know, Benj. I'm pathetic. But you have to let me get it all out now because it's not like I can spend the next three weeks freaking out in front of Chase Dawson. For as fucked up in the head I am about him, he is my editor. I don't need him thinking I'm some kind of nutcase!"

I roll my eyes at Benji's silent response. "Clearly, I am a nutcase, but I don't want him to *know* that."

I could go on forever, but the deeper I get into this bottle of wine, the closer I get to even my dog abandoning me. I need something to distract myself, and I need it pronto.

I need the kind of love only a relative can give, and I need it from someone who can give it without asking me to expand on my explanation every five seconds, so my mom is out.

Hell, the last time we chatted on the phone, she spent forty minutes telling me a sad story about a woman who was diagnosed with leukemia. She knew the woman's life in such detail, I thought it had to be one of our relatives and I had just missed that part, but as we got further into the nitty-gritty of the woman's weekly chemotherapy routine, I found out it was just some random person my mom found on Facebook and had been stalking her page ever since.

A woman like that, God love her, can't be trusted in this kind of situation.

I need the likes of a supportive sister and someone who shouldn't receive a cyber-restraining order from other people's Facebook profiles. I need *my sister*. I need Sam. Scooping my phone up off the counter, I dial her contact and wait impatiently through the rings.

"Hey, Brookie," she finally answers, and I expect to hear my nephews in the background, but I hear a much larger, far boom-ier voice instead.

"Is that Dad?" I ask, wiggling my tongue against the feeling of tingling on the roof of my mouth. It's fair to say I'm feeling much looser than normal, thanks to the power of the pinot.

"When is it not him at this point?" she retorts, her tone a mix of weary and completely giving up. For some strange reason, it makes me smile.

"You're not going to live there forever, Sammy. It's just temporary."

"It doesn't feel that way."

"What doesn't feel what way?" I hear my dad remark in the background. "Like you're a good Catholic? Because you aren't. Hell, none of us Bakers are. Our family sin card has a perfect score," he mumbles before moving just out of perfect earshot. "Two divorced daughters…"

Something, something, something, I can't hear.

"Dear old dad," I laugh. "The pride is just dripping from his every word."

Sammy laughs. "He really only gets this unbearable late in the day. I think he's crankiest when his sleep stores start to deplete."

He must be in another room because he doesn't say anything back to Sammy's quip, and if I had to guess, that's the reason she felt brave enough to say it.

Our dad is a seriously good guy—he would do anything for us—but no one has mastered the art of complaining while complying like he has.

Life just wouldn't be the same if he weren't telling us all—including himself—how wrong we were getting it.

But when the shit really hits the fan, he is always the first to show up.

He was there when I got drunk at seventeen and called him crying because my friends wanted to drive home.

He was there when I told him I was divorcing Jamie and moving to New York City to become a writer.

In that same year, he was there when Sammy got pregnant with my oldest nephew Seth before her wedding to the douche otherwise known as Todd.

And he was even there two years later when she had to have an emergency C-section to deliver my youngest nephew, Grant.

The man is rock solid when it comes to support. I wouldn't trade him, that's for sure, but if I thought I could get away with it, I'd definitely buy him a muzzle.

"Listen, I'd offer for you to come visit me in the city, but I'm getting ready to go on tour for Netflix. I'm not going to be here for the next three weeks," I say without thinking, my freely imbibed consciousness far less capable of censoring information.

"Holy shit, Brooke!" she exclaims through a snort. "Way to bury the lede! We really do not live the same lives. But man, I'm happy for you. This is so huge!"

I wrinkle my nose and plop down on the sofa, curling my feet up under my butt. "Is it still huge if I don't want to go?"

"What? Why?"

"Ah, I don't know." I groan. "Just…all those people, a motor home for three weeks, having to shower and get ready every day—it sounds like a lot." *Not to mention, my editor—whom I wrote explicit sex scenes about inside a book we're supposed to be editing together—will be driving me.*

"Please don't make me fly to New York just to strangle you. You're doing it. Living it. I mean, *Brooke*, come on," she whispers. "A freaking Netflix tour? You *made* it. You, Brooke Baker, made your dreams come true."

Tears sting my nose unexpectedly, and I rub at it vigorously in an attempt to head off the actual eye liquid. I know she's right—I, better than anyone, know how hard I worked to get here. Still, there's a part of it that doesn't feel real, a part of me that doesn't feel like I belong.

Impostor syndrome, I guess is what a professional would call it.

"I'm scared…going out there with people." I pause and take a deep breath. "They're going to see right through me, Sammy."

"So let them, B. You might not realize it, but all you've done, everything you've accomplished, came from inside you. You, Brooke. Not some hotshot celebrity type—*you*. The people love your books and are going to love the show because it came from your brain. Stands to reason, they'd like all the other stuff that comes from it too, you know? So, let them see you. Let those fuckers use X-ray vision goggles if they want. You've got this."

I'm so touched by my sister's speech, I can't help but give her some hope to hold on to in return through my sniffly tears. "I'm going to send you something in the mail. Cruise tickets for the parental units. Departure: as soon as effing possible."

She hoots. "If you're going to send someone on a cruise, make it me. I'll just tape a note to the kids and run."

"Sounds like a plan." My tears morph into a few soft laughs, but eventually, those laughs turn into a sigh. I rub at the microfiber cream fabric of the couch cushion beside me, but Sam's voice is a soft cut through my contemplation.

"Love you, sis."

"Love you too, SissySam," I reply, using the nickname I gave my sister way back when we were kids.

The nostalgia feels good. Grounding, even. It makes me remember where I came from, which, of course, makes it that much more obvious where I've come.

She's right. I, Brooke Baker, am going on a Netflix tour for the show based on *my* books. By the end of the month, my Shadow Brothers—my sweet, ghostly inventions—will be a household name all over the world. People won't just be dreaming them—they'll be streaming them.

And whether I'm able to admit it to myself or not, that's really something.

I just hope I survive the motor home trip through success.

Three weeks with Chase Dawson while I work on Clive and River. Three weeks of reading hot, skin-flushing sex I never thought I'd confront ever again. Three weeks of looking him in the eyes and keeping my shit together while I pretend this is just like any other book.

Three weeks.

Three. Weeks.

Buck up, Brooke. Things are about to get interesting.

Chapter
Thirteen

Wednesday, May 17th

Chase

An hour ago, I arrived at Liberty Harbor RV Park, where June, the Netflix liaison, made arrangements for the motor home to be dropped off and temporarily parked. The place is located in New Jersey, but it's only a short ferry ride and walk from Lower Manhattan.

Yesterday, the keys and a packet of information were couriered to my office, and this morning, I didn't have too much trouble locating the home on wheels.

And now, I'm sitting at the small kitchenette table of the very place that's going to house both Brooke Baker and me for three weeks as we cruise the country, stopping at public appearances and working on edits for *Accidental Attachment*.

Once I checked it all out, and made sure everything appeared as it should be, I've been waiting for Brooke to arrive.

That wait started about fifty minutes ago.

I'm both nervous and excited, and it's the latter that causes the first. Going on tour with an author is a completely untraditional thing for an editor to do, and as such, I should be feeling awkward about how I'm going to keep myself out of Brooke's space while simultaneously being in it.

Instead, I've found myself daydreaming about endless hours of Brooke's humor and brilliant smile and shared meals over late-night campfires.

It's outrageous thinking at its finest, and that level of unchecked foolishness makes me nervous.

Spinning brown hair is the first thing to catch my attention through the paned glass directly in front of me, followed by very loud cursing.

Brooke's bent in half, her suitcase upright but undeniably precarious on the curb behind her, and Benji is circling her avidly, trying to find a way to help. He's dressed in a Captain America costume and has his own matching backpack strapped over his service dog vest. His backpack, mind you, is more secure, compared to Brooke's leather one that dangles from her shoulders and appears to be mucking up the works even further.

Brooke turns back to her suitcase and flips it up so it only sits on two wheels instead of four, all while trying to wrangle Benji's leash in the other hand, and I can't help but think it looks like an intro to an episode of *The Three Stooges*.

Moving quickly, I head for the door to my right, located directly in between the living room area and the narrow hallway that houses both the bedroom and the singular bathroom at the back. I swing it open and jog down the small metal stairs, walking swiftly in Brooke's direction.

Benji dodges left and then right as Brooke's suitcase gets caught on a pebble first and then the curb and then rocks to a stop in an impressive crack in the pavement. Part of me wants to jump in and help—and the other part wants to see where the bag, the dog, and the woman end up, sans intervention.

But my mom didn't raise an asshole and being gentlemanly takes over.

I rush forward at a jog just as Brooke stubs her toe on the demon curb, bending back the entire front portion of her gold sandal.

"Acckk!" she yells, her voice cracking on the line of consonants.

I grab her arms by the biceps and lift her enough to set her shoe right before giving her back over to the power of gravity.

She's grateful, but embarrassed. I can tell by the pinkish hue of her high cheekbones and the flightiness of her eyes.

"You okay?" I ask simply, wanting to ensure she's good without putting her on the spot with a game of twenty questions.

"Yeah." She nods, tucking a loose fall of hair that's escaped from her ponytail behind the shell of her ear. "Normally, my klutziness results in bloodshed, so the fact that we're not drenched in O neg right now is truly remarkable." She snorts. "Probably your gallantry that saved us that bath, honestly."

I chuckle, only letting her arms go when I notice that our awkward joining is causing her some trouble with the tipped and teetering roller bag.

"Come on, I'll help you get all this stuff on the motor home."

As though she's realizing where she is for the first time, she stops in her tracks and looks up and out in the direction of the huge motor home. "So, this is the thing, huh?"

"Yep." I nod, and my eyes are filled with humor. "That's our girl."

Brooke looks closely over the gold, tan, and black paint job and then cocks her neck to look back up at me. "I don't know what I was expecting, but I thought it'd be more Metallica than Ma and Pa's national vacation, you know?"

I chuckle. "I assure you the inside gives much more of a rock-star vibe."

"Really?"

"No," I answer honestly with a shake of my head. "What you see is pretty much what you get. Don't get me wrong, it's very nicely appointed—with a kitschy, farmhouse feel. Chip and Jo would be in their element."

"You're a fan of *Fixer Upper?*" she asks, an amused smile on her lips.

"I mean, they're highly entertaining," I answer. "Though, it could be said they're slowly turning the entirety of Waco, Texas, into shiplap and barn house doors."

She snickers. "Don't knock the shiplap, Chase. It adds character."

"Glad you feel that way because the motor home is filled with *loads* of character, then. Although, it's more wood paneling than shiplap, but you're a writer. You can probably just imagine it's Chip and Jo's latest renovation on wheels."

"Well…" she hums through a giggle, pausing to scratch Benji on the top of his head. "I did kind of throw them a curve ball. They wanted to send me by plane, but since the thing with the stuff and the people and the trauma, Brooke Baker doesn't take planes anymore."

I raise my eyebrows, and she can feel them without even looking at my face, adding, "Don't ask."

"I'm not saying a word."

"Good. As a reward for your behavior, I will allow you to escort my bag to the bus." I smirk as she continues. "I know, it's very generous, but I've got more where that came from, okay?"

Brooke Baker is one of the funniest people I've ever met, bar none. She's got comedic timing and wittiness, and just enough self-deprecation to give it a genuineness that doesn't include loathing or calls for pity.

I'm constantly amused by her in both live action and print.

Honestly, from the moment I met her, through every meeting and situation, I've never escaped without a laugh. But there's usually a discomfort there too, like she's struggling just under the surface of her skin, and right now, I can't see any signs of that at all. I don't know if she's growing more comfortable because we're starting to be around each other more—*which is about to go into overdrive, considering I've made us roomies for the next three weeks*—but I hope I can keep the ease around.

I take Brooke's bag from her grip and head toward the door of the motor home. She trails behind me with Benji in tow.

Once aboard, I take her suitcase to the bedroom and set it inside the closet. When I turn around, I find she's followed me inside.

"So, this is where the magic happens," she comments, jumping onto the bed and flopping on its big black comforter. Her lavender T-shirt bunches up her stomach and reveals a small sliver of her bare skin. My mind goes to an unexpected place, and I find myself imagining what that skin would feel like beneath my fingertips and what her body would feel like beneath mine if I crawled onto the bed and gently pinned her to the mattress.

What the hell was that? Went there a little too easily, don't we think?

I'm still standing there like a mute when she adds the remark, "Sleep, of course!" with a teasing wink.

I nod—I think, anyway. It's hard to tell with my head this fucked. Quickly, I scurry out of the bedroom and back into the living room, and Brooke once again follows. That's to be expected since she's seeing this thing for the first time, which makes me the unofficial tour guide, but my dick could use a little more time to himself to think about what he's done.

Dick detention, if you will.

I walk all the way to the front of the bus while she explores the living room and kitchen area. It's all open, so it's not like I can get away from her for a few minutes, but I'm far enough away that her perfume isn't going to my head.

Jesus, Chase. What is wrong with you? Stop thinking of your author like this.

"So, there's only one bedroom?" Brooke finally asks, the dull, aroused hum in my brain quieting just enough for me to hear her. There's definitely shock in her voice—and a dash of fear too. The rosiness I've come to know well is back in her cheeks, and Benji is circling her like a turkey vulture.

"One bedroom, yes. But the couch pulls out into a bed, and that's where I'll be." I don't see any benefit to dragging this information out. For all I know, one little tease about sharing a bed and Brooke might pass out, and my dick might consider that some kind of go-ahead to put on his military uniform and stand at full attention.

"Well, okay then." She turns around in the space a couple of times before slumping down on the couch and covering her eyes. "It's going to be a long three weeks, isn't it?" she asks from behind her hands.

I nearly laugh at how defeated she sounds. This woman is about to embark on a three-week Netflix tour—because her books are going to be *on TV*—and she's worried about not enjoying it.

It hits me then that I've inserted myself for my own personal gain, but morally, I have a bigger job to do than just meet a deadline. I feel an innate, nagging need to make this trip enjoyable for Brooke. To give her a taste of just how good it can feel when hard work pays off. To remind her how incredible she is.

Okay, buddy. Pump the brakes again, for fuck's sake.

To remind her how incredible her *writing and talent* are.

"I think it's going to fly by," I reply confidently, walking over to the spot in front of Brooke and holding out my hand. "Now, come on. Let's get on the road, shall we? We've got a tour to dominate and a book to edit, all in three weeks. Dynamic duo for the win?"

Brooke looks at my hand for a long moment before shifting her gaze to my face. I don a smile in an attempt to put her at ease, but she just shakes her head and settles her face into her hands again with a huge, wounded sigh.

"Okay. That's giving more duo-doom than dynamic," I muse softly in the aftermath.

"Oh, Chase. Thank you, truly, for trying so hard," she groans, finally removing her hands and standing in front of me. Without warning, she pulls me into a hug. Her perfume is going to my head again, and I hate how much I like the feel of her warmth pressed against me. "Thank you. Again," she adds. "For fighting so hard for me and my books and all of it."

When she pulls away, I'm once again enraptured by her smell and her smile and her...everything.

"I promise not to be a pain in the ass more than ninety percent of the days, okay?"

I chuckle, despite the fact that I'm still trying to inhale her multinote scent deep into my lungs. It's fresh. And something else I can't put my finger on yet. I need more time to sample.

"Just a quick trip to the ladies' room, and we're on the road."

She disappears inside the tiny space on quick feet, and I'm left standing in reflection.

Do I think it's a bad sign that I just imagined what it would be like to touch Brooke Baker—otherwise known as the most important author of my career? Or do I think she smells like soft citrus on a summer night?

Or do you think that, maybe, you are far more fucked than you even realize?

Chapter
Fourteen

Brooke

I take deep breaths in the bathroom while Benji whimpers at the door. He and I both know I'm on the verge of losing lights and power, but I can't bear to open myself up to the outside world, even if it means Benji can't get in. That would be like fully admitting it, and I'd honestly rather hit my head in here at this point than confront the fact that I just pulled Chase Dawson into a hug without his permission.

Bodies against each other, arms around his shoulders, *hugging*.

Sure, he was stiff and awkward, almost like he was holding his entire lower half away from my lower half, but I can't blame the man. Despite all the literary evidence of my break with reality, we are, in fact, only professionally involved. We share no status that would encourage or explain a hug.

We don't share anything.

He's not my boyfriend—he's not even my best friend. He's my editor.

And even at that, the poor sap is only on this horrid motor home tour because some dummy turned in the wrong facking book that he's got to turn into publishing gold.

How I get myself into these situations, I'll never know.

And now he's waiting on me to—what I can only assume he thinks is—finish taking a massive shit so we can get on the road. For the life of me, I can't think of another reason I'd be in the bathroom this long. Like, even with a shit, we're talking severe gastrointestinal distress at this point.

And yet…I can't stop freaking out!

I don't even know where we're going. Or when we're supposed to be there.

How is it just now occurring to me that I haven't even seen the schedule for this thing? *Three weeks? Sure thing! Don't even need to know where I'm going!* Bloody hell, I'm an idiot. It's times like these I pretend to be British because an angry British person sure sounds better than bitter Brooke.

I inhale three deep breaths, take off my glasses, and lean forward to the small sink to splash cold water on my face. It's one of the only things that'll bring me back from the brink of passing out sometimes. It's like it resets my nervous system or something. Don't quote me on the science, though, because for as long as I've been this way, I'm in no way a medical expert.

Emotionally, though? I am the sensei. Oh yeah, I'm a master in the fallout that usually occurs from these passing-out events in both myself and other people. For me: embarrassment and shame. For others: mostly pity.

Dabbing my face with the hanging towel, I put my glasses back on and finally exit the bathroom to an angry Benji. After assessing me for himself and seeing that I'm beyond his help, he moves over by the couch and lies down, purposely turning his face away from me.

I feel badly, of course, having betrayed him and his loyalty like this, but we'll have to wait for a more private moment to discuss my behavior in detail. "Talks to animals like they're humans" isn't the kind of thing you normally air out so early on in a relationship.

Ha. Ha. You're not in a relationship with Chase Dawson, Brooke. Be one with reality.

Leaving my dog to his pout, I make my way to the front of the motor home to find Chase in the driver's seat, the engine on, and his seat belt fastened.

It would make a funny picture with anyone else—sitting there in the massive recliner-looking driver's seat with the big-ass steering wheel in their hands—but not Chase. His black hair sweeps just right at the top of his forehead, and his strong arms look equipped to steer this wheel and then some. He nods in my direction with his usual, white-toothed smile, puts on his aviator sunglasses, and with little effort, pulls out of the parking lot and onto the road. Off to see the Wizard and all that.

Still, the thought of a book editor turning into my motor home driver is too much of a mindfuck to let pass. I have to comment. I *have* to. How on earth does he know how to drive a giant bus like this, when I barely know how to drive a car?

I don't want him to take my question the wrong way, though, so I try to make myself sound as sophisticated and professional as possible.

"Have you ever operated something this big before? Or are you used to working with small equipment?"

He coughs, and the innuendo of what I've just said hits me square between the eyes. *So much for sophisticated and professional.* I might as well be a producer on a porn set with the way I crafted that question.

How big does your penis measure, sir?

GAH.

Benji jumps up to attention—my now-erratic heart rate his siren call—and runs to place himself next to me as I do my best to worm my way out of my awkward hole without accidentally whipping out a measuring tape. "I mean... what I meant was... See, you're driving a motor home, and that's pretty big compared to a Kia or, like, even a small pickup truck or something, you know? I'm not saying that you can't handle big equipment or that I think you only recognize small equipment or—"

Chase laughs, reaching out to put a hand to my knee. Every ounce of my blood leaves the rest of my body to rush to that one spot I refuse to communicate with at this very moment. *Heart needs blood? Not right now, it doesn't.* My gaze fixates on his long, tanned fingers as they squeeze at my flesh, and all of my basic functions grab their picket signs and go on strike. I have to remind myself to take breaths in and out and swallow every now and then.

"If I'm being honest, I'm probably used to dealing with average equipment in my day-to-day life," he says with a teasing smile that makes me feel nauseated.

Oh my God, this would be the perfect time for the bowels of the earth to open right up and swallow me whole. Sinkholes, quicksand, where are you when I need you?

I cannot find words, not in my mouth or my throat or at the bottom of my stomach. Language, for me, ceases to exist.

Chase doesn't linger in my silence, though, filling it rather with good-natured chatter. "Actually, I've driven a motor home two times in my life—or well, for two, one-week stretches, I guess I should say. When I was a kid, my parents always took my sister and me to Myrtle Beach in South Carolina. Have you ever been there?"

I smile. Holy shit. *Myrtle Beach?* "Seriously? That's where we always went too."

Chase laughs. "I think it was a nineties hot spot."

"I wonder if we were ever there at the same time," I muse, thinking back on all the pictures my mother took of Sammy and me jumping in the waves and boogie-boarding. There were always kids all over the beach, and the thought that one of those children might have been this man is almost unfathomable. I mean, he's so…rugged and manly and masculine. Clearly, men like him had to be kids at one point in their lives, but I'm here to tell you the awkwardness I lived through during my childhood is the kind of thing that lingers. There's no way he wouldn't have at least a touch of it left in him if he hadn't spawned straight into adulthood. Right?

"We probably were."

A shiver runs down my spine as I remember the video I saw on the internet about spirit guides. The lady talking about them was showing a picture of herself on her first day of college, with her now-fiancé completely unaware in the background. She said the spirit guides try our whole lives to bring us together with the people who are important, and little Easter eggs like that picture are their way of making a cute joke.

Could it be possible that Chase Dawson and I are meant to be? And our spirit guides have been teasing us our whole lives with trips to Myrtle Beach and a love for books? Have they even been brushing us up against each other in New York City?

"I don't remember what month we used to go, but I think it might have been

June," Chase remarks, snatching me from my fantasy and seat-belting me right back into the passenger seat of this motor home. The Bakers went in July. Always. "I'd have to ask my sister. All I can remember is that we always went to get ice cream at the shop down the street from our campground. Mo got vanilla bean, and I always went for orange sherbet. I never ate the stuff except when we were there, and I don't think I've eaten it since. But we went twice after I got my license, when my parents weren't really sure what to do with us anymore, and my dad made me drive the motor home. I had to park it in the campsite and everything, and my sister would always be screaming at me not to run into anything."

"Wow. I think that makes you an expert, then."

"I don't know about an expert, but definitely capable of handling large equipment."

A blush steals across my cheeks once more at Chase's playfulness—surely induced by pity—and I turn to look out the window in an effort to conceal it. Benji forgets our beef temporarily and takes a rest right in between Chase's seat and mine. I reach to buckle my seat belt—literally, this time—as we go across a couple of bumpy parts in the road and stare out the windshield at the unbelievable amount of city traffic Chase has to navigate this thing through. I'm stressed just watching it happen, and I don't even have to do anything.

I can only hope my cortisol levels won't be this high throughout the entire trip. Benji won't get to sleep at all, and I'll never hear the end of it.

"So, after we make it out of this urban deathtrap…where are we heading?"

Chase glances at me quickly—you know the look. Flashing, swift blinks before returning his gaze to the road in front of him, his eyebrows slightly drawn. "They didn't give you the schedule?"

I laugh and tilt my head. "Shockingly, no. And I didn't think to ask for it either, so I'm flying blind until you let me in on the details."

He nods then and pauses…almost like he's considering something and the best way to tell me. As a professional awkward exchanger, I don't like the look one bit.

"What?" I ask. "What is it?"

"Well, the first stop is your hometown. *Hometown*, Ohio," he clarifies with a laugh that says he knows I know the name of my own town and its irony, but humor seems like the only way to handle dropping this bomb without getting blown to bits.

"What?" I shriek, detonating the thing anyway. "Why would they do that?"

Chase shrugs. "I thought they'd okayed it with you and it was kind of like a comfort thing. To get your toes wet without too much pressure. June, the liaison I've been working closely with, even said they were going to contact your family about the Hometown tour stop." He meets my eyes, and I can imagine they're currently looking too big for their sockets. "Although, I'm sensing now there are lots of asses by assumption walking around Netflix headquarters at the moment."

He glances at me several more times, frankly taking his focus off the road a little too much, while I try to gather myself.

The first stop on this tour is my old stomping grounds, *and* they're planning on contacting my family to join the party? I'm starting to wonder if the people at Netflix even like me.

"Are you...okay? Is home really bad? Do I need to call someone and make them change it?"

"No, no," I muster with a shake of my head. Obviously, I need to dial back the drama a little bit if Chase is ready to tell Netflix execs how to do their jobs on my behalf. In my experience, the leaders of large companies usually don't like that. "Home is...fine. It's not bad or anything—it's just...small. Intimately knowing, you know? And I haven't been back there in years."

"I get that. I'm officially from Nashville, but I really lived in a town outside of the city, so I understand what small-town life is like. Everyone knowing your business and their business and Tom's, Dick's, and Harry's business. But you're a super-successful author now, and I'm sure they're all proud of what you've accomplished. Towns wouldn't make signs to say what celebrities came from them if they weren't impressed."

I snort. "I doubt Hometown has a sign out for me, but thanks for the pep talk. I'll be okay. I just wasn't expecting it, I guess."

"Well, if it makes you feel any better, we won't be there today. We've got a planned stop at a campground in Pennsylvania for the night before we get back on the road tomorrow. You won't have to face anyone from your childhood for at least twenty-four hours."

"Oh, great," I manage while my mind spins over the fact that Chase and I are going to be alone for the next turn of the planet instead. No Netflix handlers, no readers, no fans—nobody but me and the guy I wrote a book about.

Ha. Ha. Shouldn't be difficult at all.

Chase seems to notice my uneasiness, or I don't know, maybe he just wants me to stop chatting while he's trying to navigate this monstrosity on wheels down busy city highways. No matter the reason, I'm eternally thankful when he suggests, "Why don't you go back in the bedroom and take a nap? I'll get us on our way, and you can just relax."

Still, I don't want to be a Selfish Sandy, so I double-check just to make sure. "You don't mind? I don't want to leave all the hard stuff to you. I can't drive, but I can pull some other kind of weight."

"You and Benji go rest. We'll regroup when we get to the campground in a few hours."

I nod. That sounds like the best plan for everyone. I can stop embarrassing myself, and he can take a break from consoling me.

The Brooke Baker Motor Home Tour is a full-time job.

"Thanks, Chase."

"Rest easy, Brooke."

Oh, if only it were that simple.

Chapter
Fifteen

Brooke

I close the bathroom door behind myself and settle onto the toilet to unleash the kind of pee that shouldn't be possible. You know the one. A wild spring, a pressure-washer, and a raging river combine their forces for world domination of toilet bowls and convene in a half-hour event of relief.

We've been on the road for an undisclosed amount of time—my nap made keeping track of the hours and minutes hazy—but I could tell by the urgency in my bladder as I came out of the bedroom and then overhearing Chase checking in with the front gate of the Pennsylvania campground, that it's been quite a while.

Still, I held it in while I pretended to help Chase pull into the spot and hook us up to all the necessary water and electric or whatever campsites have, and that extra jolt of time not emptying my bladder was enough to make me feel like I might go into the bright light if I didn't take care of it soon.

Thankfully, Chase took off on foot to the camp store to get some supplies and ice or something I almost listened to him explain, and I jetted into this tiny room like a urine-propelled rocket.

I'm telling you, this kind of bladder release is nearly orgasmic, and for the first part of it, my eyes are half shut in what I can only describe as ecstasy.

Eventually, I shift my line of sight from the teeny-tile floor space in front of the sink to the half-closed vent at the top of the shower. Two, beady little eyes stare back at me with unspent aggression.

What the...?

I squint as my brain tries to make sense of what I'm seeing. Call me crazy, but something about being on the toilet doesn't combine well with being *watched*.

The beady little eyes blink and adjust its furry head, and that's when I realize a freaking squirrel is watching me pee.

It still looks angry. Pissed off, in fact, and seeing as we just got to this campground, I don't understand where the beef comes from.

Do squirrels bite humans? Do they have rabies? My mind starts to question all the consequences that could come with being attacked by this animal, and I try to force my bladder to finish up.

"There, there," I coax quietly, hoping to stave off the need for a rabies shot. "Stay calm, little squirrel man. I come in peace." I snort at myself. "Well, *pee-ce* if you really want to get down to it, but *AHHHHH—*"

Glass breaks and babies somewhere in the distance cry as I unleash an unholy scream of epic proportions at the very moment the squirrel lunges right toward me and my marathon pee.

"Ahhhhyyeeeee!" I screech, jumping from the toilet just as my bladder decides it's done and banging my body into the medicine cabinet above the sink like a wrestler bouncing along the ropes.

The squirrel lunges again, this time, I'm convinced, at my throat, and the bathroom door slams open in dramatic fashion. Chase's eyes, wild with fear, fill its abandoned space.

I don't have the time nor concentration to explain, instead hopping garishly to pull up my pants and avoid the squirrel, all while Chase swats an arm toward the offending animal without hesitation. He is in his hero hour, running toward the distressed calls of the damsel in the fire, and I am so close to an out-of-control banshee, I don't even recognize myself.

I'm impressed with how quickly he assessed the situation for what it was and thankful he didn't linger too long on the fact that I was full-on vageen flashing when he first swung open the bathroom door.

Benji is barking like a madman now, but since space is few and far between, he can't get into the bathroom to be Robin to Chase's Batman.

Plus, he's not dressed for the occasion. Captain America and Batman never fight crime together. It's some kind of unwritten DC and Marvel rule.

"Holy hell, he's angry," Chase mutters, still solely focused on pest control, and I am zero help.

"He wants to kill me!"

Benji barks, each woof a verbal, "*Let me at him, bro! I can handle him!*" and I just stand there by the sink, like a woman who forgot how to human.

But the squirrel is still furious and jumping around the bathroom in a way that makes me fear he's going to find a sharp object to stab me with.

"Ahh! OO-ahh! Shhiiiitakeeee mushrooms!" I yell, my coherence lacking and temperament unhinged. It's not that I have something against squirrels. I like them, actually, but from a distance. You know, like, when I'm behind a window and they're hundreds of feet away in a tree.

The squirrel bobs and weaves, and in Chase's single-minded determination to make contact with the ferocious monster, he elbows me in the tit—like, right in the nipple—and I'm shrieking all over again.

"AHHHYEEEEE!"

"Sorry, sorry, I'm sorry!" he yells, climbing onto the toilet and launching himself on top of the shower door when our furry foe makes yet another frantic move.

I rub at my stinging nipple and try to maneuver myself out the tiny door into the hallway. The squirrel dips and dives, and Chase bellows a battle cry that I'm almost positive alerts the FBI.

I finally manage to exit the bathroom, leaving Chase, the adversarial squirrel, and a toilet full of pee on their own in the small space. I also manage to grab Benji's collar so he doesn't slide inside and ramp up this war to a nuclear disaster.

Chase lunges as the squirrel launches, and I shriek unhelpfully as the fluffy-tailed pest comes toward the exit. Benji barks again and pounces toward the furry lunatic, but I'm gripping his collar tightly enough to prevent any progression.

Whipping a one-eighty, the squirrel dives back into the bathroom, rendering all of Chase's hard work up until this point null and void.

"Whoopsie-daisy," I manage before sliding fully out of the way and into the living room. From the sound of things, the valiant fight continues for another minute and a half before the squirrel once again jets out the door. This time, though, without me blocking the path, he makes it all the way to the actual door of the motor home and jumps back into the great outdoors again, bounding toward the nearby trees like he's the one who's been assaulted here.

"Brooke?" Chase calls, his eyes harried as he searches for me upon his own exit from the bathroom. "Are you okay? You're not hurt, are you?"

"Are you kidding?" I breathe. "You freaking samurai-ed that thing! I barely had time to scream before you were going Spider-Man on that squirrel's ass. Although, I think Benji is a little pissed he didn't get in on the action."

We both look to Benji and find that my doggo is currently lying down beneath the small kitchen table with his face between his paws and a pout on his lips.

"Next time, my man," Chase states through a laugh, the slightly winded nature of his breath making it sound raspier than normal.

I walk over to give Benj a scratch between the ears, but he just lets out a groan that lets me know I need to give him some space.

"I closed the vent above the shower so another one can't get in that way," Chase explains. "But we'll have to be careful of the side door. I noticed it was open when I got back and heard your scream, so I'm not sure which way it got in."

"Hot damn," I say through an incredulous laugh. "From New York City to the scene of a squirrel attack. I feel like I slept my way into a new dimension."

"Did I forget to tell you I drove the motor home down Alice's rabbit hole?"

"A little heads-up would've been nice."

"Sorry about that." His tickled smile is nearly too much for my pathetic heart, and my laugh dies to a smile.

Silence stretches between us then, and my smile turns uncomfortable too.

I feel terrible because it's not Chase's fault that I don't know how to just *be* around him. I'm a dancing bundle of nerves where an exciting faint is the finale of my nightly show.

I need to find a way to be normal or neither of us is going to survive.

"Maybe I should—"

"It's going to be dark—"

Chase and I both speak at the same time, and a thrill runs down my spine as my heart flutters into a skip.

"Sorry," we both say simultaneously.

Officially gun-shy, I nod in a gesture of *You go ahead* rather than speaking. He smiles and runs a handsomely veined hand through his thick black hair.

"I was just saying it'll be dark soon, so I'm going to double-check all of our power connections and grab some firewood just in case we want one."

"That sounds like a fantastic plan." And seriously more philanthropic than mine.

"What were you going to say?" he prompts when my embarrassment delays me from filling in the gap.

"Oh, ha-ha," I say nervously. "I thought I might just take a shower."

Not only do I need a reset, but I think some rogue pee might have run down my leg in the mayhem.

"Great. That sounds like a terrific idea. I can shower later," he offers with another smile, turning toward the door with a hook of his thumb and heading out to take care of everything we need to survive without complaint. I notice that he takes time to shut the door securely, even pulling on it slightly to test it before walking away.

My head falls back, and I slap my palms over my face in shame.

God, Brooke, you have really got to get it together here. This is day one. DAY ONE.

Jumping into action, I make a quick trip to my suitcase to get my shower toiletries and then head back to the scene of the squirrel crime. The toilet sits unflushed when I enter, so I take care of that as a first order of business and then crank on the shower knob to full heat.

It's a scientific fact that women's skin is ready and willing to be scalded at all times, so long as it's done in a shower.

And even though my best buddy will be annoyed with me, I give him one final scratch behind the ears, whispering, "You just chill here, Benj, while I shower."

He still looks mad, and his silence and avoidance of my eyes speak volumes, but I'll find a way to make it up to him later.

Once the bathroom door is shut, I strip without finesse and climb in, not even hesitating to shove my face directly into the hot water. It feels so good against my overstimulated skin, and the longer I stand in it, the more I can feel my shoulders sinking down from their place around my ears.

I know this is a stressful situation that no one could have seen coming—not even that fancy, freaky fortune-teller named Cleo I saw when I first moved to the city. But the way I'm handling it so far is manic, even for me, and I *have* to tone it down.

There's one thing that usually brings me back into a steady state without fail, and as twisted as it is that it's directly related to all the things that fire me up and freak me out, I can't think of anything I'd rather do.

Gently, I scoot my fingers down my belly to my pelvis, swirling at the soft, wet skin right above my clit.

You have issues, my mind tries to warn me. But I ignore it, the feel of my fingers against my ramped-up skin far more pleasurable than a mental health check-in.

My head falls back, and my shoulders complete their descent to normalcy, and I know beyond a shadow of a doubt that I'm going to see this thing through to the end.

I need to come, and in all likelihood, I'm going to visualize Chase's face while I do it.

"Bless me, Father," I whisper to myself, "for I have sinned."

I'm officially living with my ultimate inappropriate crush, and the only thing that can calm me down is flicking the bean to his face.

Note to self: Maybe call your therapist after this tour.

But there's no going back now. I'm soaped and lathered and quietly moaning like the closeted whore that I am.

I'm officially "come-itted."

Chapter
Sixteen

Chase

The firewood clunks as I pile it up at the side of the fire ring and then dust off any debris with a few quick swipes of my hands. I've double-checked all the lines and the leveling jacks and the tires, just so we don't wake up with a surprise in the morning, and everything is good to go.

It's been ages since I've been camping in any capacity, but on a weirdly sentimental level, it feels good to be doing it again.

Opening the motor home door with a click of the black handle, I jog up the metal stairs and into the living room, pausing only to close it securely behind me, before settling into the dining booth and pulling out my phone to text my sister.

Me: We made it safely to our first stop.

Mo doesn't normally act like such a mother figure, demanding that I communicate my every move, but then again, I've never driven across the country in an RV with her favorite author either. She's in full fangirl mode, and I am the medium, connecting her to the other side.

Her reply is swift and annoying.

Mo: Good. I'll expect your nightly report before I go to bed. Be sure to include anything interesting Brooke says or does, okay?

I don't hesitate to tuck my phone directly back into my pocket as soon as I read it. She knows everything I'm willing to communicate right now.

Since I can hear the water of the shower running, I take my manuscript and notes out of my tan canvas bag and set them on the table in front of me. I grab a pen from the front pocket and lick my finger to pick through the pages.

Now, I'm aware that most editors in the twenty-first century would be using a computer and Microsoft Word to track their changes and make comments and the like—or hell, maybe something even more advanced than that—but not me. I like to feel the pulped trees and taste the tinge of lingering ink on my thumb when I go to flip the page.

Justin, my ex-best friend, liked to mock me for being old-school, but I never put much stock in that. Good thing too, because as it turns out, he's not a very nice person.

A small bang echoes from the bathroom, and I swear, I hear a whisper of a low, slow moan come from the other side of the wall.

I lean in unintentionally, and then I hear it again, coming from where Brooke is currently in the shower.

Is that… Is she…?

I can't be certain, but I'm pretty sure my heart is now outside my chest.

My ears are on high alert whether I want them to be or not, and a ringing consumes the inside of my skull. But when I hear something else—the sound of escalated breaths puffing through the wall, I swallow hard. *Holy shit. She's doing what I think she's doing.*

Skin tingling, I jerk my back into a straight line, and the ringing in my ears turns to a high-pitched squeal from listening so hard. I know it's wrong on every human level, and yet, I can't turn the stupid things off. They're like heat-seeking missiles, bound for any sound that can turn me on.

Stop listening. Focus on something. Anything else but that shower.

My ears ignore the rational side of my brain and appear to have formed some kind of kinship with my dick.

Brooke moans again, and I am so fixated on what's happening inside that shower that I can practically feel it through the thin material of the wall.

Sweet Jesus.

My instincts warring with my humanity, I find it somewhere in the depths of myself to stand. My legs are shaky to the point of wobbly, and it's everything I can do to stumble my way out of the dining booth, across the short distance of the living room area, and out the side door, into the clammy, cold air of the great outdoors.

Manuscript and work to do—forgotten.

I take three deep breaths to focus all the oxygen in the air toward my brain and will my legs to carry me even farther, away from the motor home to the picnic table on the other side of our campsite.

I don't know what part of my life made me as naïve as I clearly am, but this very simple problem on the first night of our trip has enlightened me to the deep shit I'm practically drowning in.

Three weeks. *Three weeks* of living this closely with her—of fighting my dick's urge to invade Brooke's every personal moment.

I'd like to pretend I had no idea I would even consider a sexual attraction to Brooke, a woman whom I'm responsible for maintaining a professional relationship with. But the truth is, I'm not that good of a liar even to myself. I read every word of *Accidental Attachment* as though she were River and Clive were me.

Every lick, every stroke, every touch and kiss—I imagined them happening between two people who look a hell of a lot like us. I told myself it was a natural thing, with Brooke being as beautiful and likable and relatable as she is and having physical attributes that are similar to the character of River. But after my unconscious behavior tonight, I'm afraid it might be a little more complex than I was keen to admit.

Fuuuuuck.

Scrubbing my hands over my face roughly, I pace the trimmed grass on the far side of the picnic table with mania motivating the quickness of my steps.

I mean, this isn't that big of a deal, *right?*

I'm making it out to be some gargantuan thing, but in reality, I'm a grown man with almost zero control issues. Just because I *think* something, doesn't mean I'm going to *act* on it. I can separate the two easily.

And we're not going to be alone *all* the time. It'll probably be hardly any time at all, really. It's a publicity tour, for God's sake. The whole point is to shove Brooke in front of her rabid fan base and addicted readers at every opportunity. Tonight's an outlier. Everything's just getting started, and the two of us are still figuring out the logistics. I'll just get a routine together where I make a habit of leaving while she's in the shower, is all. Simple.

The trill of my ringtone sounds in my pocket, so I pull it out while still muttering to myself and answer without looking at the screen. Any distraction is surely a good distraction at this point.

"Hello?"

"Chase," the caller breathes seductively, all the air in her body seemingly trapped inside her lungs. I recognize the voice right away, but that shouldn't be a surprise. It's the voice I heard say my name for nearly eight years.

You call this a good distraction?

Apparently, naïveté can strike more than once.

"Caroline," I greet back through terse teeth. *I can't flipping believe I didn't look at the caller ID on this one.* And I thought I was in pain before; compared to this torture, blue balls and a stomach pitted with uncertainty are nirvana.

"Chase, baby, I miss you so fucking mush."

The slur at the end of her statement is jarring and expected all at the same time. The last I'd heard, she was back on the wagon—but I don't normally get phone calls from the sober version of her either.

"Caroline," I say through a rough sigh, a knot lodging itself in my throat. It's not because I'm upset so much as my body has adapted to keep me from saying the stuff that'll end up making me feel like a sack of shit later. But this whole scene…believe me, it's tired. Three fucking years, and it's still not done.

"I can't stop thinkings about you," she whispers, allure in her voice.

Seduction is what Caroline is known for. She's highly skilled at it, and the younger version of me was mesmerized by that power of hers. She just has a way about her. She knows how to use all her sensual tools to spin a web that pulls you straight in.

Men look twice when Caroline is in the room.

And you don't look away when Brooke enters a room.

I don't know why my thoughts go to Brooke in the middle of a call with my ex, but I choose not to linger in the aftershock of it.

"Chase, talks to me," Caroline purrs my name again, and it's a stark reminder of who she is as a person.

This side of her, the sexual goddess she's trying to encompass, is a front for her deep-rooted insecurities and issues. Now that I'm older and wiser and have matured from the superficial tendencies of a twentysomething man, I can see right through it.

Caroline only thinks about Caroline. And she has this nagging need to chase the high she gets when she successfully seduces someone. It goes without saying that is a recipe for disaster when you're supposed to be in a long-term, committed relationship.

The honeymoon phase doesn't last forever. Eventually, couples evolve into something more complex and emotionally rooted that should be treasured and held tight with both hands. Something that means far more than lust and attraction.

But Caroline didn't evolve, and frankly, I don't know if she'll ever be able to. She'll probably always be chasing that high, and every relationship she gets involved in will fail because of it.

"*Caroline*, this is getting old."

"Don't say smy name lick that, Chase," she orders, hardness replacing the seductive purr.

"How do you want me to say it, then? Because I prefer not to say it at all."

"Why do you haves to be so mean?" she questions, her tongue still incapable of keeping up with her words.

"I'm not being mean, I promise you. You'd know it if I were being mean."

"Can't you forgive me?" she whispers then, the tears and dramatics the next stop in her five-step plan.

"Forgive you for sleeping with my best friend for a year and a half right under my nose?" I scoff. "No, I don't think I can."

"You were always sooo perpfect. Mr. Perpfect Chase Dawson. Better than everyone else."

"I wasn't perfect, and I've never thought I was better than anyone. But I do have a moral compass, and having an affair with my significant other's best friend isn't anywhere on it."

Frankly, I wouldn't be surprised if Justin weren't her only affair during our relationship.

"A thousand miles away and you still dunn think you're far enough, do you?"

Damn. A question that makes sense.

"Truthfully?" I retort. "No."

"Thas cuz you still love me, you know."

"No, it's not," I correct her. "It's because you never stop calling."

The thing about my ex is that I am so far past that relationship *and her* that I don't even feel hate for her anymore. I'm mostly just a mix of sad and annoyed.

And this call is about her own self-involvement, not about her really wanting me back. She is a toddler in a room full of toys who is angry that one of those toys was taken away. This is elementary-level selfishness and the furthest thing from love.

"Lossa girls there in New York City, huh? Think you're some hot shit now?"

It's moments like this that make me wonder how I stayed in a relationship with this woman for so long. How I'd planned to marry this woman. But it's also moments like this that have the power to make me lean into my annoyance and lose my cool.

"I'm living out my dreams, working with intelligent, interesting people, and touring the country with one of the most successful authors I've ever met," I grit foolishly, allowing my emotions to get out of check. "So yeah, I think I'm doing pretty fucking well for myself. Better than rotting away with you."

"Chase?" I hear from behind me, the sweetness of that voice altogether different from the one on the phone. I spin fast to see Brooke leaning out the door of the motor home, a towel around her neck as she scrubs at her wet hair. A fluffy robe covers her body, and I find myself silently wondering if she has anything on underneath it. Seemingly noticing the phone at my ear for the first time, she puts a hand to her lips and widens her eyes. "Oh my gosh! I'm sorry! I didn't know you were on a call."

I shake my head, pulling the phone away from my ear even as I can hear Caroline asking things like "*Who the hell is that?*"

"It's okay. No big deal at all."

Brooke's cheeks pink a little bit, but she pushes on. "I just wanted to let you know that the shower's free if you want to use it."

I smile. "Thank you."

"Okay. Well." She glances down at her bare feet and then back at me. "Um, see you in here, I guess," she mutters awkwardly, and it's so fucking cute it nearly makes me laugh.

I wave in response, tucking the phone back to my ear and turning around. Caroline is now losing her mind, and if I didn't know that she'd call back relentlessly as a result, I'd have already hung up the phone.

Still, if I were a smarter man, I probably would have done it anyway.

But when my ex-fiancée calls, unfortunately, I haven't quite figured out how not to answer.

Chapter
Seventeen

Brooke

Refreshed and relaxed from my shower, I step outside of the bathroom, expecting to find Chase waiting for his turn. Surprisingly, he's not.

Habit makes me search my surroundings a few times before believing they're truly empty.

But one peek out the window shows him at the picnic table on the far side of the campsite, so rather than making him wait for me to get lotioned and trussed up and dressed and all the woman things, I go ahead and throw on my robe, and then I jog back out of the bedroom to open the door, pop my head out, and let him know it's his turn.

"Chase?" I call to his back, noticing only when he turns around to face me that he's holding his phone to his ear. "Oh my gosh! I'm sorry! I didn't know you were on a call."

"It's okay. No big deal at all," Chase replies with his phone tucked to his chest as he talks to me.

I glance down at my bare feet and try to smile through the embarrassment—I mean, I did just complete the most relaxing activity known to humanity—and get to the point so he can get back to his conversation. "I just wanted to let you know that the shower's free if you want to use it."

"Thank you." He smiles, and I turn, trying not to stay in his business too long.

Unfortunately, gallant as I may be, I can't turn off my ears fast enough to miss what he says next.

"No, Caroline," I hear Chase say softly.

Caroline? Caroline! *There's a Caroline who Chase talks softly to on the phone, and I am a raging idiot. Holy, holy shit.*

I slink back into the motor home, pulling the door shut behind me. My heart races and my vision tunnels as I think of all the sexy things I've written about this man and me.

Tongues on cocks and cocks on tongues and some of the best penetration the imagination can conjure.

Endless scenes of fellatio and moments of intimacy that make my chest get red.

A whole fucking book of it, along with the completely deluded fantasy that at the end of it all, we move on with our lives together—as husband and wife.

And the whole time, he's not even been available.

Good Christmas, I wrote a whole romance book about another woman's man!

I'm hell-bound in a motherpucking handbasket, that's for sure.

And I…I don't know how to make peace with that. I don't even know how to make chaos with that. I'm so over my head, I don't even know where to start.

Panicking slightly—*boy, that's an understatement*—I rush to the back of the bus, into the bedroom where my phone is sitting on the built-in nightstand. I don't know what I intend to do with it other than summon a witch and a broomstick to fly me away somewhere, but when I unlock the screen with frantic fingers, I find myself going straight to the text thread with my sister.

Benji jumps up on the bed to crowd me into sitting down before I turn this place into a crime scene. I perch on the soft surface of the bed like a cockatoo—as close as I can get to sitting with all this adrenaline running through my body—and type like a maniac.

Me: I need to be talked off the ledge, and I need it now. My toes are among the crumbling rocks at the edge. Quite frankly, I may need to be sedated.

An answering FaceTime call rings on the screen, and I drop the phone like a hot potato. *Is she nuts?! I can't be on video right now! I can hardly even stand to be on Earth!*

I pick up the phone and smash at the screen with my fingers.

Me: DO NOT CALL ME. I CANNOT SPEAK RIGHT NOW.

Sam: What? Why? Are you trying to scare me? Because it's WORKING!

Me: I can't tell you that. I can hardly even tell me THAT. So just do it. Talk me down. Type me down. Whatever. Just pitch me whatever mental health shit you can come up with until something sticks.

Sam: Okay, well…without context, this is going to be a little tough.

Me: SAM!

Sam: Okay, okay. Back away from the edge, Brooke. Back away slowly.

Me: No offense, but you're doing a TERRIBLE job.

Sam: Oh, I'm sorry? Did you expect me to be creative in the environment I'm currently living in? DAD IS SHITTING WITH THE DOOR OPEN RIGHT NOW, BROOKE. WHY, YOU ASK? Because he took all the doors off all the bathrooms! The kids got into the toothpaste ONE TIME, and he's gone fully insane. THERE ARE NO DOORS ON THE BATHROOMS. AT ALL. And you're on a tour for fucking Netflix. So, tell me again, which one of us is it who needs to be talked off the ledge, huh? WHICH ONE??

I survey my emotions again, and in the strangest way possible, her rant worked just as I asked, bringing me back to reality and putting some steady ground under my feet.

This isn't the end of the world—far from it. This is just…life. And it could be a lot worse. Say, having to shit without doors, for example.

In the real world, sometimes we crush on people who aren't available or who we don't actually end up with.

Sure, most people don't go so far as to write an entire book about those things, but I'm an author. Turning my emotions to the page is what I do. It's my outlet, my sanity, my routine. I've just done what I know, and now—now that I know he's with someone else—I can put all of this behind me and focus on making it a good story. Clive and River can just *be*.

Yeah, I'm okay. It's all good. Really. Or at least, I will be in three to five business days after I've left time for "processing." I sink from my roosting place to my butt and try to make my shoulders relax.

I also text my sister back.

Me: Thank you. That was just what I needed. And I'm sorry about the open-air shitting. I really, really hope it gets better soon.

Sam: I'll let you know my check-in date for the psych ward.

Me: And which one, too. Don't forget that. I want to be able to visit.

Sam: Love you, fucker.

Me: Love you too, Sammy.

With that all settled, I set my phone on the nightstand and lean back into the pillows at the top of the bed. I need to get up and do my face moisturizer and change into my pajamas and brush my teeth, but I'll do that in a minute when—

The sound of the door opening in the living room makes me sit up straight, my anxiety spiking all the way into the reddening cartilage of my ears.

Okay, maybe I'm not *that* okay. *I need the processing time!*

"Brooke?" Chase calls from the living room, and it's at the sound of his voice that I understand just how not okay I am. Man, as it turns out, I am *really* good at lying to myself.

Shit. Shit. Shit.

Panic makes me frantic, shifting from one side of the bed to the other to search the little back bedroom for something. I have no flipping clue what I'm looking for, though, because it's not like a weapon will do me any good unless I use it to stab my own self in the heart. *Which…has some merit.*

I can hear Chase's gentle footsteps approaching the door, and Benji sits up to an alert position next to me on the bed. I'm obviously approaching the entrance ramp to passing the hell out, but at this point, I would genuinely welcome it.

The sadistic thought is shockingly helpful, and almost instantaneously, I flop back onto the bed, close my eyes, and do my best impression of a woman fast asleep. As long as he doesn't look too closely at the violent heave of my chest, I think it'll be convincing.

I wait and wait and wait for him to open the door and peek in, but the time never comes. Instead, he knocks lightly—just once in an almost high-five-like gesture—and whispers through the wood. "Goodnight, Brooke."

I wait until I hear the sound of him walking away and then sit up straight again, scratching Benji behind the ears.

"Goodnight, Chase. Goodnight, Dreams. Goodnight, Misguided Crush. Goodnight, Moon," I whisper so only Benji can hear.

His head cranes, and I sigh, speaking so softly, I almost can't even hear myself with my own ears. "I know, Benj. I know. Mama's crazy. You don't have to say anything."

He tucks his head back down in a crease in the comforter and groans. He knows just as well as I do that this is going to be a *long* three weeks. It's going to be hard and awkward and more complicated than I even imagined, and trust me, I imagined it being tangled as fuck.

But it is what it is, and like my sister Sammy said, at least I don't have to shit with no door.

Plus, there's the whole Netflix tour and dreams coming true and even the success of this upcoming book. It's all good, even if it doesn't feel like it right now.

Quietly as I can, I get up off the mattress and pull my pajamas out of my bag, donning them without putting any underwear on and climbing back into bed.

My skin will be dry in the morning, but there's not even a snail's chance in a monsoon that I'm going back out there to the bathroom where my moisturizer is located before the sun rises in the east.

Take me out of the oven and stamp some grill lines on my ass, because if I were a restaurant steak, I'd be D-O-N-E *done* with this day.

Chapter Eighteen

Thursday, May 18th

Chase

Interstates have turned into back roads as I wind the motor home through the Ohio countryside toward Brooke's old stomping grounds—Hometown, Ohio. It's still early enough that the sunlight's angle is soft, and Brooke still sleeps soundly in the bedroom.

My thoughts, on the other hand, woke me early. Brooke was already in bed when I got off the phone with Caroline last night, and as much as I would have liked to have seen her, I think it was for the best. Talks with a drunken Caroline don't usually put me in the greatest of moods, and last night wasn't out of the ordinary. Because for as much as I'm happy with where I am in my career and life in general, I'm not at all where I thought I'd be in love.

I was never the perpetual bachelor type. I didn't long for a flavor of the week, and I didn't need the freedom to explore. Settling down, finding a woman to take care of, and eventually starting a family were all the things on my bucket list.

But spending eight years of your life with someone, only to find out the whole thing's been a waste kind of blows that old bucket to smithereens.

Still, calls like last night's bring the fact that I dodged a bullet into stark relief, so there's at least one sliver of silver lining.

Eager to distract myself this morning, I checked and answered a few work emails from both Frank and Regina before rereading several chapters in *Accidental Attachment* with the intention of making notes. But Clive and River stirred a whole other set of emotions I'm woefully unprepared to talk about.

As a result, I've been keeping to myself. Other than a few more texts from Mo asking about Brooke's breakfast, Brooke's toothpaste, and Brooke's coffee that I haven't dignified with responses, it's been quiet.

The bedroom door creaks, and Brooke curses under her breath as she stumbles out into the living room on untested sea legs. Much like being on a boat, the motor home sways and rocks on the road, leaving anyone trying to walk feeling like they're learning to do it for the first time.

"You okay?" I ask as I hear her bump into something, followed by a sharp bark from Benji. I turn down the Tom Petty song on the radio in an effort to hear her better.

"Shit," she mutters before raising her voice in my direction to answer me directly. "Yeah, yep. I'm good. Feels a little like I went under Derek Shepherd's knife for a traumatic brain injury and am relearning how to bee-boop as a human, but I'm good."

I chuckle as she collapses into the passenger seat like a rag doll. I can only look over for a second, but what I see when I do shorts out the normal circuits of my brain. I grab the wheel with both hands as the bus swerves with the skip of my heartbeat.

Nipples—Brooke's nipples—are right there, for all—me—to see.

Sure, there's a thin layer of white tank top over them, but I swear to New York Fashion Week, it's the frailest fabric ever created. They're pert and, what I can best assess with that quick of a glance at a view under fabric, are a mauvy-rose color. I know that's specific, and no, I don't know how I'm able to come to this conclusion. Regardless, I'm powerless to stop my continued perusal.

The tank top rides up to her navel, and on the bottom, a simple set of men's boxer briefs bunch over her slender, warm-olive-toned thighs. It's a bit of a mindfuck, but I swear they're the exact brand and style I wear.

Rationally, I know she didn't steal my underwear, but…my dick really, *really* thinks she did.

Immediately, I'm thrown into a scene in *Accidental Attachment*, one of the ones I read this morning, where River sleeps over at Clive's apartment for the first time, completely unplanned. River dons an outfit, just like this one, only the underwear and the undershirt tank top are both Clive's. The chapter before is one of the sexiest, most erotic things I've ever read, bar none, and seeing Brooke like this after reading that this morning is messing with my central-penis nervous system.

And if I feel this way for much longer, I'm not going to be able to hide it behind my pants and the seat belt.

"Is that the book?" Brooke asks suddenly, her voice quiet and noticeably devoid of sleepiness as she stares at my bag on the floor between us with the manuscript on top.

The book. That fucking book. It's the last thing I'd like to think about right now.

Funnily enough, it's the whole reason you're here...

Shit. I clear my throat and attempt to morph myself into the professional editor I should be.

"Y-yes." I stumble over my tongue a little. "I was reading a bit this morning before getting on the road. Why?"

She shakes her head back and forth for no less than ten seconds before finally finding some words. "I just..." She shakes her head again, swallows, and then puts together a sentence. "I've just never seen it all printed and in person like that." I don't know if that's the original sentence she intended; somehow it doesn't feel like it. But I can't imagine what else she'd be thinking or feeling, and it's not my job to make assumptions and assertions about other people's feelings.

"You can pick it up and hold it if you want," I tease, nodding toward it while I focus on the road. "I've read it five or six times at this point, though, and made a ton of small notes, so the pages might be a little furled."

"Five or six times?" Brooke asks, shocked.

"I know, it's pretty shameful." I flash a playful wink. "But I have to sleep sometimes. If not, I'd have read it more."

"No, I didn't… I meant…" Brooke staggers to explain until taking a good hard look at my face and recognizing my taunt. "Oh. You're joking."

"Sort of." I laugh. "Frankly, I probably would have read it more if I didn't have to sleep."

Brooke shakes her head. "You're crazy. You're a crazy, editing, squirrel-fighting, motor-home-driving speed-reader, and I don't know what I'm going to do with you." She pauses and gestures out the window in front of us as we approach the main square of Hometown, and she chuckles. "Of course, I'd very clearly be able to do nothing without you, so I'm not going to change anything."

"Wow," I remark at the idyllic street-lining lights with springtime bows and floral greenery wrapped around them with care. A mighty, historic bank sits on the right and a fire station on the left as we approach a large court building at the very center of town. "So, this is where you grew up?"

"Outside of town. But yes. I drove through this square every day on the way to kindergarten through twelfth grade."

"Do you miss it?"

Brooke shrugs, her eyes scanning everything in sight with a great deal of muscle memory. "Parts, yes. I did love the simplicity. But I couldn't have stayed here, not doing what I was doing and seeing who I was seeing every day. I was dead inside. Now, I don't have any friends to speak of—other than Benji—" she corrects as he lets out a little bark, "but I'm beaming bright on the inside. Too bright most days, if I'm honest. The voices are loud."

Shaking my head with a smile, I'm surprised when Brooke yelps and jumps up from her seat in a mad dash and runs toward the back.

"Brooke?" I yell, steering the bus into its designated parking space on the square. "Are you okay?"

"Yep. Just saw my first-grade teacher on the square, and I'd rather he not see me in my pajamas!"

Her response is so endearing and a perfect Hallmark ending to my introduction to her town.

Tonight, though, I'll get to see Brooke in real action with the people who know her best.

And you can't fucking wait.

Netflix is really on top of their event game. The Hometown Recreation Hall is decked out in movie-style posters showcasing *The Shadow Brothers*, along with two tables full of pens and bookmarks and other various forms of swag for Brooke's fans to take as souvenirs.

The instant we walked inside, a handler by the name of Jan greeted us with a big smile. Jan is here to be at Brooke's beck and call. "Anything you need at all," she told her when we first arrived. "Just let me know."

And the Hometown fans have not disappointed. They've shown up in droves, to the point that even two Hometown police officers keep watch on the whole event from their spots at the front doors.

Ninety minutes into this event, and everything is going as perfectly as it can possibly go. And seeing Brooke with her hair and makeup done as she meets and greets fans across a narrow six-foot table, chatting and laughing with them, is a surreal experience.

I find it incredibly hard to describe how someone can be their genuine self without putting on a show, but be doing it *more*…at the same time.

I know I sound confusing, but I'm confused myself. It's the same woman I'm fascinated by—the same woman whose prose captivates and endears me. And yet, she's also playing at celebrity in the most charming way.

I wish I had a better way to explain it, but I'm enjoying watching her so immensely, I have to remind myself that it might look weird if I stare at her without blinking with a garish smile on my face for the whole two hours of this meet-and-greet.

In the interest of human-ing correctly, I find other things to look at every few seconds or so. The people in her line. The old-timey photos of the town on the walls. The wear of the wood floor. They've all got character, that's for sure.

It's not until a man in cowboy boots, jeans, and a flannel shirt approaches the table, a blond woman with snug but conservative clothes on his arm, that Brooke balks at all.

Silent and gulping, she stares at the pair for such a long moment, I start to worry that if she doesn't take a full breath of air soon, her skin is going to turn blue.

I glance down at Benji, who is resting but awake beneath the table. He shows no signs of concern, but without even thinking, I step up beside Brooke, dive right into the middle of the silence, and insert myself. It's a crazy thing to do in every aspect I can consider, and yet...I can't stop it from happening.

"Hi, folks. I'm Chase Dawson," I say with a smile, holding out a hand to the man first and taking his large, callused one in my own. "Brooke's editor."

He glances to Brooke and then back to me. "Jamie Carter. I've known Brooke since grade school."

Brooke snorts then, catching both of our attention, and my eyes flit to hers to find them nearly wild. "Yeah. I guess you could say that, huh?"

My brows draw together, and Jamie shifts on his boots and wraps his arm around the woman next to him.

Brooke looks directly at me, explaining, "Jamie is my ex-husband. Mary Katherine is his new wife. And all three of us went to school together, starting in the fifth grade when Jamie's family moved here from an hour away."

My forehead becomes nothing but eyebrows as the situation's complication spills out all over the space between us. Jamie and Mary Katherine are silent, but Brooke's broken into a rolling laugh that borders on hysteria. I put my hand on her shoulder in an effort to calm her down. I mean, she has every right to freak out, but the sound of Scar's hyenas in the Hometown Recreation Hall is starting to garner a few looks from the crowd.

I gently squeeze at the flesh and bone there, instilling as much comfort as I can into the pads of my fingertips.

And it works, as she pulls herself together remarkably quickly, shaking her head infinitesimally before directing attention to Jamie. "I'm sorry, Jamie. I know this has to be weird for you too, but I really do appreciate you coming. You too, Mary Katherine. Says a lot about your character, truthfully, stepping out to support your husband's ex-wife with a smile. Thank you both."

Jamie's voice is quiet, almost rough, as he answers. "You know I always wanted to support you, even if I didn't understand how best to do the job of it. I figure it's better late than never."

It's the strangest thing, but in that moment—while Brooke's ex-husband, whom I assume she devoted years and years of her life and heart to, is laying an apology at her feet—my brain can only come up with one, brilliant, emotionally shallow piece of insight.

It seems exes run amok these days, but at least this one's not drunk.

Chapter
Nineteen

Brooke

Jamie Carter, my ex-husband, and his new wife are here, being nice and, beyond that, sentimental in the middle of my Hometown public appearance.

I haven't been anywhere close to this memory lane in years—haven't even driven past it. But now, I'm smack-dab in the middle of what feels like an ex-couple counseling session in the psych building at the end of that winding road, while Chase Dawson, the dreamiest man I've ever laid eyes and occasional hands on, looks on from about six inches away.

When I thought I wasn't prepared to be out here doing this, I had *no* idea just how right I was.

Dear God, I was really not prepared for this at all.

"You know I always wanted to support you, even if I didn't understand how best to do the job of it," my ex-husband says quietly, a familiar coarseness in his voice. "I figure it's better late than never."

What does one say to something like that when the person's new wife is standing right beside them when they say it? It doesn't feel romantic or longing, at least, but I don't know what it's supposed to be besides that either.

"I appreciate that, Jamie, but honestly, it's all water under the bridge. It's been a long time, and I didn't even blame you back then. We just weren't aligned, weren't headed on the same path. But it's really nice of you to come here." A soft laugh jumps from my throat. "A little awkward, but really nice."

Jamie starts to smile—a just barely there curve of one corner of his mouth. He was never an expressive person and, other than being a decently good human, is just about the opposite of Chase's outgoing personality in every way. But before either of us can say anything else, the boisterous sound of my family entering the building overtakes everything.

For maybe the first time in my adult life, I'm grateful for their graceless intrusion.

"Jesus, Mary, and Joseph, is there a Fleetwood Mac show after Brookie's thing?" I hear my dad ask from twenty people back in the line. He grunts, under what I can only assume is an assault from my mother's hand to the back of his head, and continues on, volume control a phantom idea meant for other people. "What? I'm just sayin'. There's lots of people here."

I close my eyes for a brief second and then smile. *Ladies and gentlemen, the Bakers have entered the building.*

"What? No way, Sam!" My dad's voice is now the star of the show. "Why would all these people be here to see Brooke? They've seen Brooke every day since she was a month old!"

I nod silently. Just a steady bob of my head and purse of my lips because, yeah, that sounds about right coming from my dad.

It's not that he's not proud of me; he just doesn't understand how being something like a writer can have the magnitude it does. He never has. Even when he was carrying my newly divorced furniture into a walk-up apartment in one of his least favorite cities in the world—not that he has a favorite city, being the rural guy he is—he grumbled and bumbled and questioned every stranger we saw on the street, and he cursed my stairs and my door and my apartment. But he was there. Every step, every minute, every long hour in the ten-hour drive from home—he was there. And at the end of all his complaining, he kissed me on the forehead, told me he loved me, and said to call him when I needed him.

I made it on my own, but if I hadn't, Hank Baker would have been there then too.

It took me a while to recognize all of it for what it was, but my path was one my dad had never taken—a path he would *never* have taken—and it's just not as easy to come to terms with that as you'd think. We're humans. We're not perfect. Even parents.

"Hey, Chase," I turn to ask, touching his forearm to get his full attention. "Can you go back there and bring my family up before my dad makes a full-on scene?"

"Sure thing." Chase's smile is bright, white, and playful.

I can't help but stare at it.

When I turn back to Jamie, he's watching me with interest, and I have a feeling it's because he's familiar with the dreamy, moony-eyed look that's probably on my face as I watch Chase walk away. That look used to be directed at him when we were growing up.

Thankfully, my ex-husband lives ten hours away from me, and aside from right now, I haven't talked to him in roughly six years. After today, I don't intend to talk to him again. Hence, he's not the person I have to provide an explanation to or be concerned that he'll want to discuss why that very look is on my face and directed at my editor.

Jamie, and that part of my life, are truly in the past.

"Thank you again. It was nice to see you both," I tell him and Mary Katherine, effectively dismissing them as my whole band of crazy family approaches the table. My mom, my dad, my sister Sammy, and her two wild offspring are like a band of spider monkeys, swinging through the trees.

They don't even notice that it's Jamie as he and Mary Katherine make their retreat—thank goodness—so we're spared of a dick-whipping sword fight between my dad and reluctant ex.

My dad doesn't hate Jamie—in a twisted way, they're the same type of man—but the old Baker sin card was forever marred by our divorce, which in and of itself, is enough to make Hank throw down.

The Baker gaggle is loud as they approach my table like a swarm of bees at a fruit picnic, but man, my heart feels heavy with warmth.

I never expected it would be this good to see them, but even with my dad's loudmouth grumbling, I jump up and practically over the table to wrap each of them in a tight hug.

My mom smells like she always does—Chanel No. Five and baked goods— and feels like decades of memories. My dad hugs me even tighter than she does, and it's the kind of surprise that reminds me how much he misses me and I miss him. My nephews Seth and Grant hug me at the same time while bouncing on their toes and shouting, "Aunt Brookie!" Although, their attention is quickly diverted when they see Benji beneath the table and start petting him with rough hands.

He's a good sport, his Captain America costume matching his ever-present compassion, and takes it all in doggo stride.

And my sister's hug—well, it nearly makes me cry. It's one of love and joy, but also, flat-out exhaustion. She's been through the wringer recently, and living with my parents while she "heals" isn't exactly speeding the process.

"Oh, Sammy," I whisper in her ear, tucking my face into her hair to keep myself from getting emotional on her behalf. She does the same, and I know it's because she's proud of me.

"You're killing it, Brookie. God, I am in so much awe that this is all for you."

I nod. Me too. Truly, me too. I didn't want to do this at all—I was nervous and unsure—but being here now feels like the culmination of all the fights I've fought to have this career.

The late nights, the deadline crunches, the hours and hours of scheming new ways to market and grow my audience.

It's been a long ride, but I'm here—little Brooke Baker has a Netflix series and a new book deal worth more money than she knew existed when she was growing up.

If that little girl could see me now.

I step back from the hugs and look at all of them—save my nephews, who are now slowly ripping the town recreation center apart—and my eyes get teary.

"I love you guys. Thanks for coming."

My dad is the first to look away, and I know it's because he doesn't want me to see the tears in his big, manly eyes. Manly eyeballs are supposed to be the consistency of sandpaper at all times.

Unfortunately, when he does look away from me, he notes the damage my nephews are doing to old man Galloway's historic paintings, and he turns to my sister with a snip. "Hell's bells, Sammy. Can you wrangle the mulchers before they chew up the wood paneling?"

Sammy takes off at a jog to get the boys, and I'm left with my parents and Chase alone. My mom is staring at Chase like he's on the cover of a magazine, and I can't even be mad at her. *Your homegirl wrote a book about this guy, Mom. I get it.*

"Mom, Dad, this is my editor, Chase Dawson. Chase, these are my parents, Sue and Hank Baker."

Chase sticks out his hand, and both my mom and dad alternate taking it. "It's so nice to meet you. You must be so proud of Brooke. All these people here, just for her. And to think, we've got seven more cities to go, just like this, but even bigger."

I close my eyes briefly and then look down to hide my smile. This bastard evidently heard my dad at the back of the room and very much knows what he's doing.

What a sexy little manipulator my muse is...

Surprisingly, it seems to get through to my dad, who looks at me with a beam of pride. It's almost as if I'm a good Catholic who didn't get divorced for a small moment in time.

"Oh, we are so proud of our girl," my mom answers Chase. "I think Brooke's always known that she wanted to do this, but it took her a little while to get the confidence to know she could. I can personally vouch that she was an avid writer in her youth. She'd spend hours and hours writing in that diary of hers."

I don't know if I want her to keep going or shut up at this point, but all I can feel is the burn from both pride and embarrassment boxing each other inside my rib cage.

"A diary, you say?" Chase questions with a mischievous smirk directed at me. "Sounds like Brooke had the writing bug from early on."

"Oh yeah." My mom's smile is beaming. "The things my girl would put in that little pink diary of hers. I'm telling you, it was—"

"Mom," I find myself saying without knowing what to finish with. *The verdict is in—Sue Baker can shut up now.*

I have only a hazy recollection of the shit I used to put in my diary, but I do recall my entire freshman year of high school was focused on wondering if I was going to grow boobs or not. Teenage Brooke was more of a loon than adult Brooke, and growing boobs and kissing boys was all her literary prose was focused on.

It's safe to say, the internal thoughts of teen me are the last things I need my mother disclosing in the middle of a Netflix-sponsored meet-and-greet.

However, Chase is amused as hell, and I'm half tempted to give him a little nudge in the stomach with my elbow.

I don't, obviously. I can't have my readers thinking I'm a violent person.

Plus, my sister has perfect timing and prevents any violence or diary-revealing by approaching our group again. I glance behind her and see that my nephews are in the back of the room with their iPads. Since the environment of Hometown Recreation Hall is only filled with book people and bookish things, it's low in entertainment value for a four-year-old and a six-year-old, and I think the tablets are a mighty fine solution.

But my dad audibly disagrees with a scoff. "Oooh, screen time. Something new for a change."

I have to bite my tongue as he leans forward and gives me a kiss on the cheek before muttering, "I'll be out at the car. Good job, Brookie."

"Thanks, Dad."

My mom leans in and gives me the same kiss, but then she sweeps her hand over my cheek and begs, "Visit more," before following my dad out the door.

As soon as they're gone, my sister's full personality comes out. Leaning in again and pulling me in for a swinging hug, she howls a little and pats me on the back almost brutally.

It hurts, but in the best way possible.

"I'm so, so happy for you. The only thing that would make me happier is staying with you instead of going back with the SnickleFritzes, but dear God, it's good to see you."

"It's good to see you too, sis." I gesture to Chase, who's still standing dutifully behind me with a smile like he's the most entertained he's been in a long time. "This is my editor, Chase Dawson. Chase, this is my sister, Sam."

They shake hands, but Sam looks at me with wide, *holy moly, he's a looker* eyes the whole time before finally glancing back to him. "Nice to meet you, Chase. I bet you can't wait to pull out of here."

A soft chuckle escapes his sexy throat. "I'm enjoying it so far. But I am a third party, which I've heard greatly improves the enjoyment of family antics."

"Uh, yeah. I'd say so." Sam snorts and rolls her eyes at the same time. "I'm suffering through those exact antics every freaking day now. Every morning I wake up, I wonder how much longer I can survive."

Chase tilts his head to the side.

"Me and the boys are currently shacking up with the parental units," my sister answers his nonverbal question, and he grimaces.

"That's gotta be rough."

"From your lips to God's ears." Sammy nods. "I honestly think the CIA could start using the Baker house as a form of torturing answers out of war criminals."

Out of nowhere—or perhaps, a very crazy place I've never met before—an idea hits me and rolls out of my mouth all at one time. "Why don't I give you the keys to my place in New York?"

Sammy's head jerks back. "What?"

"I'm going to be gone for the next three weeks anyway, and you've never really spent any time in the city but always wanted to. You could stay at my place while I'm gone."

"But…I have the boys."

"I know." I snicker. "They're quiet right now, but I didn't forget they exist. My apartment isn't huge, but there's enough room for them."

"Brooke…I don't… I mean, I want to, but…" She pauses and searches my eyes. "Are you sure?"

I think a little harder about it, and funnily enough, the idea sounds even better. It's not like I've got anything of high value in my place other than my Dolly CDs that a whole generation would make fun of me for using rather than streaming from my phone anyway, and my sister needs this. *Desperately.* Her eyes are sunken, and her skin is pale. Even her usually vibrant red hair has faded to a subtle ginger.

I'd do anything to bring her back to life.

"One hundred percent sure," I respond without a single doubt. "You need some time to rest and rejuvenate away from Mom and Dad." I turn around and grab my brown leather satchel purse from its spot beside Benji under the table, and I dig into the front pocket to get my keys. When I spin around again, Sammy is crying, and Chase has pulled her into an innocently comforting hug.

He passes her off to me, of course, and I pull her tight into my arms. "Oh, Sammy."

"Brooke, you have no idea how much I need this."

"I know. It's okay."

"Thank you," she whispers. "This is…this is something I'll never forget you doing for me."

"Come on," I groan teasingly and try to swallow down the urge to cry. "I actually did my makeup tonight, and you're going to mess it up."

As soon as I pull back and see Sammy's real tears, I devolve into my own. Warm, strong arms wrap around me and pull me close, and I nearly drop right into a faint right then. Chase Dawson, my ultimate crush, is comforting me physically, right now.

Just breathe, Brooke. It's just a hug, not an invitation to touch his penis.

Benji stands up from underneath the table then and perches himself in a seated position right beside my legs.

But all I can focus on is Chase's voice as it vibrates against me as he talks to my sister over my head. "Let me give you my sister Mo's number too. She and my brother-in-law have lived in the city for years and own a restaurant, and I know she'd be really happy to be a friend or a source of information or anything you need as you're getting acquainted there. She probably even knows some people who'd be willing to babysit—or even be willing to babysit herself—if you want to get some alone time."

Goodness, this man. Is he even real?

You have a manuscript filled with a hundred thousand words based on fantasies revolving around him. Safe to say, he is very much real.

I finally find it in me to disengage from Chase's embrace—let me tell you, it's not easy—and address Sammy directly as I hand her the keys to my apartment. "Chase is right. I met his sister once, and she's such a nice person. Really fun too."

Benji adjusts his position. He's still right by my feet, but now he's lying down instead of sitting at high alert.

And my sister stares down at the keys in her hand like she can't decide if they're a mirage or the tool to unlock heaven. "Goodness," she mutters and then looks up at both Chase and me. "Thank you both so much. I seriously cannot believe you're doing this for me, B."

I shrug. "I'm not even doing anything."

"You are, though." She grabs me by the jaw and plants sloppy kisses on both of my cheeks. I laugh and wiggle and wipe at the slobber. When she meets my gaze again, her eyes are seriously somber. "You're doing everything."

"Okay, Sammy, jeez," I complain with a swipe to my eyes and a spin that settles me right back where I started. "Let my eyeballs rest already!"

Sammy snort-laughs, and I pull her in for one final hug. "I'll text you with all the information I can think of that you might need, and I'll send you Chase's sister's number too."

Chase gives a thumbs-up, and Sammy giggles.

I swear, the dark circles under her pretty bluish-green eyes have gotten lighter in an instant.

"I love you," Sammy says as she backs away and points at me. "You're gonna kill this tour!"

I laugh and shake my head as she grabs both of my nephews by the shoulders and leads them out of the entrance door at nearly a run. It's completely different from her entrance, and enough to confirm I've done the right thing. Even if I go home to a Hulk-smashed apartment, it'll be worth it.

"I'm pretty sure you just told your sister she won the lottery."

I nod. "She's been living with my parents for weeks. Trust me, I did."

After Sammy headed out, there were only twenty or so people left to see before the first official meet-and-greet of my Netflix tour in Hometown, Ohio, was over.

And holy shit, am I relieved.

And starving.

There's only one restaurant in town that stays open late enough to accommodate Chase's and my celebratory dinner, but I wouldn't care if I were eating cardboard at this point. The local wing place, Bone and Batter, is even better.

Benji, a true chicken connoisseur, is also thankful for the pieces I keep feeding him under the table.

I take a sip of my beer glass of wine—this isn't exactly a fancy establishment—and Chase somehow manages to make eating wings look dignified. I swear, I've never seen someone twist the bones out of the meat before so that they could eat the wing without getting sauce and scraps all over their face.

Still, after all the personal revelations Chase witnessed tonight, I've been a little quieter than my normal ballbusting self.

I never really thought Chase would meet Jamie—or my family, for that matter—ever. It was a bit of a shock to the system.

"You're not the only one with an ex, you know? You don't have to be weirded out at all," Chase finally says, reading my mind with a freakiness I could easily mistake for some "meant-to-be" shit if I let myself.

"I just… Well, I guess I never expected him to show up there—and I really didn't expect him to bring his new wife." I laugh at myself, and it sounds a little deranged. "He's a good man. He always was. The two of us just wanted completely different things. He wanted what we grew up with. I wanted anything but."

"Well, hey, you're miles ahead of me, then. My ex-fiancée wanted to sleep with my best friend, and in fact, that's exactly what she did."

"What?!" I nearly shriek. "Your ex cheated on you?"

"Yes."

"On *you?* Someone cheated on someone with your face is what you're trying to tell me?" I cluck like a hen. "I can't believe it."

He chuckles a little, but I stare him down, deadpan, and he finally affirms it. "Yes. For about a year and a half. Hell, it might not have been her only affair."

I slap the epoxy-topped wood table so hard it shakes. "Shut the front door right now!"

"I'm serious," he vows, wiping his hands on his napkin and sitting back into his metal-runged chair.

"I'm picking that up from you, I am, but I'm still having a very hard time believing it."

He clears his throat and rubs a hand through his hair for a long moment, seemingly considering me. I don't know what he sees, but he leans forward again, putting his elbows on the table and eyeing me closely. "The phone call from the other night. When you came outside to tell me you were out of the shower."

Realization dawns, and my mouth drops open like a hawk swooping for a mouse. "Nooo."

Chase nods, his pretty features completely belying the facts he's laying out. "*Yes.* Her name is Caroline, and she calls once every month or so."

So, that's who Caroline is…

My heart is a little too thrilled with this revelation, and I clear my throat to strong-arm my concentration on to the conversation itself. You know, like any normal person who doesn't have a long-standing crush that made them write an entire book about a guy would do.

"Why does she still call you?"

"It's all a fucking game." He shrugs. "She pretends she's trying to get me back, but I'm pretty sure it'd be more purely classified as a torture tactic."

"I don't know. I'd buy into the part about getting you back. You seem like a catch to me."

Ha-ha-ha-ha. You're such a liar. He is the ultimate *catch to you.*

"Well, thanks. But she only calls when she's drunk, and nine times out of ten, she's the one to bring up Justin—my ex-best friend."

"Justin?" I ask with a sneer to confirm, and he nods. "I don't understand, I'm sorry. The math ain't mathin'. There's no way someone named Justin had something better going than you. I refuse to believe it. Refuse."

Chase laughs, full-on throat extended, head back, out-of-this-world hotness on display, and all my points are proven. He's the hottest man alive, and I am the Almighty of all powerful things because, I, Brooke Baker, just made him do that.

I pick up a French fry, dip it in mustard, and take a bite to celebrate my victory, but I just about fall out of my chair when Chase leans forward and gently swipes his thumb across the corner of my mouth.

"Just a little residual mustard," he says with a tiny wink, and all I can do is sit there and try to remember how to breathe.

He just touched my mouth. With his fingers. Chase's fingers were on my mouth.

Benji puts his snout on my legs, knowing full well my heart rate is heading toward danger territory, but I fight the power of the syncope and force myself to discreetly inhale a few calming breaths.

"By the way," Chase adds with a grin. "I think the most shocking thing about tonight is the fact that you dip your French fries in mustard."

"Hold up." I quirk one eyebrow toward the ceiling and lift one hand toward his face. "My mustard use is more shocking than my ex-husband showing up at my meet-and-greet today with his new wife? Or the fact that my dad was asking my readers if there was a Fleetwood Mac show afterward?"

"Yep." He nods through a soft chortle. "It's so incredibly strange that I honestly think it's cute."

He thinks my mustard use is cute, and *he touched my mouth.*

Dear God, I'm in so much trouble it's not even funny.

This man is single? And the last woman he was with treated him like absolute garbage? Sounds like a game, set, spike situation for me.

Stop, Brooke. You work with him, the sweet, good-natured angel voice in my head scolds.

But I'm a little afraid that by the time you've written a book about someone, all the bad, troublemaking things are already stuck in motion. Conscience, you sweet angel, you better get used to the dark side, baby. I think we're here to stay.

My mind reels with my next move, searching deep for any certified flirtation or seduction techniques I've utilized in the past that have worked. Sadly, my track record isn't exactly aces. Truthfully, I don't know if I ever attempted to seduce anyone, not in any kind of successful way, that is. My awkwardness always seems to trump my sex appeal.

I start to think about any strong, spicy woman I can come up with in the hope that I can channel her inner temptress.

Angelina Jolie? *She's way out of your league, babe.*

Christina Hendricks? *You need bigger boobs to go this route.*

Jennifer Lawrence? Megan Fox? Kate Upton? *J. Law's goofy, endearing personality has some merit, but still, she's* Jennifer Lawrence. *The OG Katniss Everdeen. You ain't got the clothes.*

"You know what I think we need to talk about right now?" Chase's question pulls me from my brain's "sexy female celebrity" Google search.

"What we need to talk about?" I repeat, my voice trailing off on the last word. *Your smile? How good your eyes look right now, even beneath this shitty lighting? How good your penis would look inside me?*

When I don't say anything, he answers for me. "The book."

Everything inside me deflates like a balloon.

Oh, *that.*

Defeated, my brain closes out of her Google tab and powers down her laptop.

The book. *That damn book.* It's the whole reason he's even sitting in front of me right now, and suddenly, it's the death of any progress my inner sex kitten just made—*sad meow.*

Chapter
Twenty

Brooke

Tucked in the motor home bedroom with a belly full of boneless barbeque wings, I pull my laptop onto my thighs and stare at the blinking cursor at the end of Chapter Twenty. I've got earbuds in with the sultry beat of "Closer" by Nine Inch Nails flowing into my head, and I'm doing my best to heed my dreamboat editor's bookly advice.

"Expand the sex scene in the break room," Chase suggested tonight at dinner. *"I'm afraid if we leave the readers hanging on this one without a climax, we'll have a riot on our hands."*

Hoo boy, do I understand what he's saying on an intrinsic level. The longing, the aching, the *need* for more—my bones are full of all of them and then some.

This much time with Chase has only enhanced my crush because as it turns out, the real-life version of him is even better than the fictional one I made up in my mind. He's considerate and funny and easygoing at all the right times. He's been just pushy enough to keep me focused on work without it feeling condescending or parental in any way, and if he doesn't stop throwing his head back when he laughs and showing me the muscled cords of his long throat, I'm going to spontaneously orgasm in my panties.

I am a frozen Creamsicle, begging to be thawed by Chase's tongue, and if I were still counseling at the high school in Hometown, I'm pretty sure all the students would be bursting into flames around me.

There's absolutely no shame in being a sexy romance author—but at the time I wrote this particular scene, I wasn't that—instead, I would characterize myself as pervy.

The truth of the matter is that when I faded that scene to black, it was because I was so worked up by the fantasies of this poor, unsuspecting man that I needed real-life attention. Sadly, it was from my own hand and a couple of toys, but it was real contact, nonetheless.

Frankly, I'm not surprised this particular scene reads as unfinished because it *was*. And for my own self-preservation, I intended to stay away from it until the end of time.

"Hey, Brooke," the apple of my raunchy eye says, surprising me by peeking his head in the motor home bedroom. I glance down at my lap like I expect to find a mystical, magical vibrator spontaneously inside my vagina simply from the direction of my thoughts, and evidently, the look that puts on my face is enough to make his eyebrows crinkle toward each other. "You okay?"

I pull out one earbud, wave a hand at my very obviously red face, and lie my ass off. "Hot flash or something."

Benji sighs at my fib, just one, single rolling rumble from his comfortable spot on the bed. Luckily, Chase isn't an expert in dog expression yet, and the traitor's snub goes unnoticed.

"You want to come for a walk with me? Maybe get some fresh air. It's at least a little cool outside, so it might help."

He's leaving the motor home?! my inner horndog yells triumphantly. *That means we can flick our bean to the thought of him! YAY!*

It's sad that this is where my mind goes, but it's even sadder that the unsatisfied, throbbing ache between my thighs has made me one hundred percent in approval of this plan. A girl can only be around the hot-as-sin man who revs her engine to the red line for so many consecutive hours before she needs some damn relief.

"I, uh…" My voice starts in a pitch much higher than my baseline, and I have to clear my throat and try again. "Actually, I think I'm going to take a nice cool shower before we get on the road."

"You're…going to take a shower? Like, now?"

"There's still water in the tank, right?"

"Plenty." He nods through a slight cough. "I…uh…just filled it this afternoon."

"Great," I say, trying not to sound *too* excited. Only weirdos do backflips about taking a shower in a motor home. Well, weirdos and pervs like me, I suppose.

We sit there staring at each other like a couple of confused middle schoolers before Chase finally bounces on his heels, breaking the game. "Alrighty, then," he says with an overzealous hook of his thumb over his left shoulder. "I'm going to head out. You…uh…enjoy your shower. Yeah, enjoy your shower." He nods so many times I lose count. "And I'm gonna go on that walk, then. Shouldn't be super long unless I get lost or eaten by a bear or something."

I've never ever seen a bear in downtown Hometown, Ohio, but there's no way in hell I'm going to mention it. Chase Dawson is perfect, remember? If he says there are bears, maybe there are bears.

"Don't run," I say quickly, making his forehead wrinkle and me rush to explain. "If you see a bear, I mean. They say running is the fastest way to get yourself eaten unless you're with someone and they run slower than you do."

His mouth forms this sexy but curious little curve. "Is that really what they say?"

Why do even his facial expressions have to be so hot? I mean, really? This is getting stupid.

"The part about running definitely," I eventually add. "But I don't think everyone throws their companion under the bus like me."

"The bus or the motor home? Just trying to be ready, you know?" he quips, and the smirk on his face puts me closer to the horny edge.

My vagina tingles. My mouth laughs. And a part of me hates how sexy and appealing this man is in all moments of daily life. "Don't worry," I manage to banter back, despite the ever-present ache between my legs. "I can't even start this thing, let alone run you over."

"Good news," he replies, his smile stretching so far into his eyes, it practically takes them over. Just a giant walking mouth, that's Chase Dawson when he smiles like that.

"I guess, I'll…uh…see you after the walk, then," I offer, making him laugh. He knocks on the thin wooden wall beside the door and nods.

"Right. See you after the walk. And uh…enjoy the…uh…shower."

"I will." Dear God, I will. I really, really will.

I listen hard as Chase exits the motor home and the door closes behind him with a soft click, followed by a hard bang. After a thorough post-traumatic-squirrel evaluation, we learned the hard way that if you don't give the thing a hip check after you latch it, it doesn't really latch. Honestly, I'm going to be dreaming about a squirrel mauling my face on the night before every appearance at this point, but hearing the simple sound of Chase booty-bumping the door to ensure the wildlife stays out during my shower makes my face melt into a smile.

Yeah, he really is the perfect object of desire.

Sigh.

Shoving off the bed, I tiptoe into the living room area and take one last peek out the window and watch his strong back as he heads down the sidewalk leading away from our parking spot on the town square. Bill's Flowers and Gifts is quiet to his left, save the twinkle light display in the window, and Pan City, the busiest restaurant in town on most nights until it closes at eight p.m., is dark on the right. There are a million beautiful memories from my childhood here, but none of them are quite as pretty as this—Chase's dark hair, veiny arms, and full butt as he puts one foot in front of the other in the middle of it all.

He moves with such confidence and certainty—qualities I don't think I've ever carried on my tall, lanky frame. I was born awkward, squawking into the delivery room with sounds my mother tells me resembled her childhood pet rooster, Eduardo.

Thanks for that, by the way, Mom.

Un-scissoring my fingers from between the blinds, I let them settle back into place and strip my clothes speedily on the way back to the bedroom. If I'm going to have time to wash and "wax"—if you know what I mean—I need to get moving and pronto.

Goose bumps spread across every exposed surface of my body.

Somehow, the air of the motor home on my naked skin feels completely different from the air in my own home—almost like it knows another person resides in the space. I don't know how to explain it other than it feels like Chase's ghost is lurking somewhere and will somehow see me in all my bareness.

Having forgotten my phone up in the front, I run up there to get it without putting anything on and feel like a criminal as I do. On the way back, I spot the manuscript of my book on the table of the dining booth and pause.

Before the last couple of days, I'd never read anything a second time in that book after I wrote it. I typed it, *pretended* to experience it for myself *by myself*, and moved on. But if I'm remembering correctly, I've got some pretty hot shit in there between the parallel universe that is Chase and Brooke as Clive and River.

And maybe…maybe it wouldn't be a bad idea if I read a little of it right before jumping in the shower. You know, in the name of the work…

Shit. No, Brooke. There's no time. Who the hell knows how fast Chase walks, and after hugging him and smiling at him all day long, I need to come really badly.

I can't chance it. I'll take the book for a spin another day.

I take a quick peek into the bedroom and find Benji still resting on the bed, but he's watching me curiously.

"Just taking a shower, bud," I tell him. "You keep chilling."

I'm pretty sure he narrows his eyes, but I don't hang around to see it. Instead, I sprint straight for the bathroom, lock myself inside, and fire up the water at full heat. I'm learning at this point that it never really gets that hot, so I just blast it right from the get-go.

As soon as it's tolerable, I hop in and wet my hair, quickly running through my wash routine with a single-minded goal of getting to the finale of this show.

It doesn't take much effort to imagine Chase's comforting hug from today, but instead of it simply ending like it did in real life, my mind takes horny liberties and rewrites it.

Wrapped tight in Chase's arms, I lean back ever so slightly to look up at him. My breasts are pressed to his chest, and the warmth of his body makes my skin tingle. He stares down at me, and his gaze flits from my eyes to my lips and back to my eyes.

And then, without warning, he presses his perfect mouth to mine.

It's the kind of kiss that's deep and powerful from the start. He doesn't ease us into it. No, he just kisses me. Hard. And his fingers slide into my hair, even tilting my head back with a little tug to give him better access to my lips.

He growls, as if he can't control himself and the way he needs to consume me, and it encourages a pleasurable wave to slide up my spine. Our kiss devolves into a dance of tongues and leads to him skating his hand up under the hem of my skirt and touching me.

I gasp when I touch myself, the skin already so sensitive it's scary. All this pent-up desire that I've been shoving down every second of every day since we started on this motor home road trip is just spilling out of me in an overwhelming, crazy-with-need, I-have-to-come kind of way.

I slide one finger inside myself and imagine it's Chase's hand doing it, and the power of that visual combined with the sensation of my physical touch forces a moan to bubble up from my throat that I have to swallow hard to keep quiet.

Holy hell, it's not going to take much to fall over this cliff tonight, I can tell.

Swirling gently, Chase slips his fingers out of me and moves them toward my clit to lubricate it before he massages it with precision. He is a greedy, greedy man, and before I know it, he's squatting down in front of me, tossing one of my thighs over his shoulder, sliding my panties to the side, and burying his face between my legs.

I moan. I mewl. My back arches from the red-hot pleasure that his skilled tongue is triggering.

His hands grip my ass, and my hips jolt toward his face, my body restless and needy for the kind of orgasm I know only he can give me.

And fuck, he is unrelenting in the way he eats at me.

Goodness, his mouth and tongue, they suck and swirl and lick against me…

Another moan leaves my throat, and I'm powerless to control it. My head falls back and the water cascades over my skin, and it's like I don't even know where I am anymore.

All I can feel is me and the man of my dreams and a climax that's going to blow anything else I've ever felt right out of the water.

Fade to black? Not anymore.

Chapter
Twenty-One

Chase

The town square is quiet as I make my way back to the motor home. Only a small group of what I think are teenagers remains, and they're too busy doing whatever it is teens do these days to notice my nearby presence.

Part of me wanted to see a little more of the place that raised Brooke, and part of me knew I needed some time alone to get my senses back together. I don't know what's going on with me, but it's like I haven't had a clear picture of what the real relationship between Brooke and me is since we boarded this thing almost forty-eight hours ago.

Add in the dilemma that I can't be in the RV while Brooke is in the shower, and a walk was more than necessary. It was pure survival. Not to mention, if I didn't call Mo back tonight, I was pretty sure she was going to suffer an aneurysm. She sent me no fewer than ten texts during the meet-and-greet alone. All of them revolving around Mo being on some kind of secret-spy-fangirl reconnaissance mission to make sure no other reader loves Brooke's books as much as she does.

I love my sister, but she's obviously off her rocker.

Once I reach the big bus, I climb up the small metal steps to open the door, but just as it swings open, my ears catch the sound of *"Oh God,"* followed by a moan that I know comes straight from Brooke's lips.

To further fuck with my already messed-up head, it's not the soft, barely there moan I heard the last time she was in the shower. It's louder and grabs my attention in ways that are not at all professional.

Panic widens my eyes, and I quickly swing the door back to the closed position before stepping away.

Holy shit, I thought she'd be done by now.

I even walked two miles and stayed on the phone with Mo while she told me about the most painfully boring dinner shift at the restaurant for twenty whole minutes to *ensure* that Brooke would be done by now.

What do I do? I don't know what to do.

I turn to leave, but something at the edge of the sidewalk stops me. A squirrel lurks on a nearby tree, and suddenly I'm faced with the impossible decision to expose my position by slamming the latch on the door so it stays shut or leave Brooke to an uncertain squirrel fate.

I juke back and forth from the toes of my front foot to the heel of my back, and I'm apparently acting so manic, I've caught the attention of the small group hanging out in the square. They stare unabashedly, and I try to calm my movements by running a hand through my hair and considering my options.

Maybe I can just sort of, like, hang out and guard the door without actually shutting the door, so that the squirrel doesn't approach but Brooke doesn't know I'm here either?

I hear another one of Brooke's moans through the small crack in the unlatched door, and every rational thought I've ever had ceases to exist. *Dear God, what have I done to deserve this?*

"*Oh fuck.*" The pitch of her voice is getting higher and the tempo is getting faster as she approaches what I'm absolutely positive is going to be an earth-shattering orgasm. The hair at the back of my neck stands on end, and so does the appendage between my thighs.

Brooke's the kind of woman who's sexy without trying. She is a refreshing— *addictive-as-hell*—contrast to my ex. Hell, to any woman I've ever been with. She doesn't flaunt her body or flash her tits or try to make a seductive act out of anything. She's low-key awkward most of the time, but she's also absolutely adorable in her own skin. Her glasses frame her face and highlight her intelligence, and her wittiness has never missed a meal. I swear she can turn even the simplest thing into a pun or a joke.

She is multifaceted. A mindfuck combination of all the things that turn me on and endear her to my core. *She's the most fun I've ever experienced, and I haven't even touched her.*

"Oh yes," she whimpers. "*Yes.*"

Gahhh, focus, Chase. FOCUS. Now is not the time to get distracted by all the things you like about this woman. Now is the time to get the hell out of dodge before you get in a whole world of trouble.

Because as much as Brooke is a catch and a half, I know that's not the real reason I'm imagining her starring opposite me in the next big porno.

It's the book. It *has* to be the book. Right?

Clive and River's chemistry is off the charts, and the resulting hot scenes are akin to human wildfires. There's intimacy and passion and seriously performative sex, and for a visual reader like me, it can make you believe you're there and that it's happening to you.

Not to mention it's been over six months since I had sex with anyone other than myself, and this kind of drought is not lending a helpful hand in my current situation.

Talking in detail, about a scene where River spreads herself out on Clive's kitchen counter so he can lick her pussy until it makes her eyes roll in the back of her head, at dinner tonight is bound to get a guy feeling like he's on a hair trigger for arousal. Add in cute, sweet, unbelievably kind Brooke Baker moaning like she was born to in the shower just adjacent from my current location, and you've got a recipe for disaster.

As the shower shuts off, my numbered options narrow even further. I no longer have time to decide; I just have to act. Quickly and efficiently, I slam the door closed all the way, ensure it's latched, and power walk in the other direction. I know doing this might make Brooke wonder what I heard or how long I've been there, but I can guarantee if she came out of the bathroom and saw Batman Boner shining his light at the night sky for all to see, she'd know and then some.

Benji barks from the window, but I don't look back. For all current intents and purposes, I am deaf. And for the temporary near future, I am gone until I can get myself—*and my throbbing dick*—in check.

Chapter
Twenty-Two

Brooke

A loud bang sounds from the front of the motor home, and it shakes a little as I step quickly out of the bathroom with only a towel wrapped around my body. On the couch, Benji stands up on his front legs, barking out the window.

"What was that, Benj?"

He doesn't even acknowledge me, and his bark softens to one low, alert growl.

I'm not completely dried off, but not wanting to miss the opportunity to see what's going on, I tiptoe over to the same window as Benji, lean into the counter, and take a look for myself.

There's a small group of people standing at the corner of the town square, but other than that, I don't find anything out of the ordinary. There's no sign of Chase—or anyone else I recognize, for that matter—and as far as I can tell, everything looks normal.

Benji has settled now and bumps me with his butt as he turns around and gets cozy on the couch again.

I take one last glance from side to side before letting the blinds drop back into place as a droplet of water from my hair finds its way down my back. Since the feeling of being anything other than fully wet or fully dry at any given time creeps me out, I hustle back to the bedroom and scrub at my skin and hair with the fluffy towel.

It may seem crazy, but I think in a torture scenario, I'd be very weak if you just threatened to make me wear a damp T-shirt.

Once I'm dried off, I put on my normal toiletries—deodorant, perfume, lotion, face moisturizer—and brush through my thick brown hair with a wet brush. It's tough, even after washing it, thanks to the ten and a half gallons of hair spray I saw fit to put in it before the meet-and-greet today. And for far more than the first time, I wonder how other people learn to do womanly-woman things.

My mom taught me hygiene, how to shave, and that too much blush makes you look like you're on the verge of having a stroke. But the intricacies of hairdos and real makeup with contouring and eye shadow and sultriness completely eluded her.

And by proxy, it's not my forte.

In my lifetime, I can count on one hand the times that I've done my own hair and had it turn out good or had someone compliment me on my makeup. Usually in photos, I look like a shiny aesthetician whose main goal is to show the world her skin in its natural state.

Heck, I watched fifteen hours of YouTube videos on hair and makeup alone in preparation for this tour, and all it got me was a lion's mane of brunette locks that hair spray clings to for an eternity despite a washing.

I sigh to myself and turn in a circle in the small bedroom, waiting for a miracle or some sort of scenario like Jenna Rink landed herself in during *13 Going on 30.*

When neither occurs, I don my pajamas and peek out into the living area of the motor home one more time. Benji is snoring pretty heavily on the couch now, and the rest of the space sits in silence.

Obviously, Chase doesn't owe me any kind of explanations about his whereabouts—we're not a couple. *Ha. Keep reminding yourself of that, chickadee.* But I can't help but worry a little bit over the fact that I don't know where he is or when he's coming back.

Should I lock the door before I go to sleep? Wait up until he gets back?

I'm not sure, and the more I think about it, the more I don't think I'm comfortable leaving the door wide open in the middle of the night when there's a group of strangers not too far from where we're parked. My family probably knows ninety-five percent of them, but somehow, that doesn't make me feel any more comfortable with it. Especially after the loud bang while I was in the shower.

Unless this is a horror flick, the bang had to come from somewhere, and it doesn't include a paranormal entity trying to possess my body.

I close the door to the bedroom, only to have Benji wake up and bark at me for the insult. The two of us are glue, and he's not willing to take the separation very kindly. I don't blame him since the whole basis of his training is keeping me alive, which is a pretty big job for a dog already and doing it at a distance makes it even harder.

I open the door again and apologize as Benji trots through the opening to jump up on the bed. "Sorry, Benj. I wasn't thinking."

He woofs his agreement, and I roll my eyes. *He doesn't have to rub it in.*

All bedroom parties now accounted for, I close the door, jump up on the bed with him, and grab my phone from the nightstand. Part of me feels weird to reach out to Chase in this case, but the other rational part of me knows he's not the kind of guy to get testy about my asking for his whereabouts when I have a good reason.

Me: Hey, Chase. Sorry to bother you, but I was just wondering where you went. Ha. You know, like, I mean…are you coming back soon? I was thinking about going to bed and I didn't want to leave the door open but I didn't want to lock you out if you didn't have the key and

Yikes. Somehow, I've managed to be both awkward and formal and grammatically incorrect all in one text. *Delete.*

Let's try that again.

Me: Hey, buddy, do you have the key to the motor home?

Right. *Vague as hell meets confusing as hell. Delete.*

Me: Heyaaa. Mind telling me where you went and when you'll be back?

Great, now I'm the newest member of OutKast, and they haven't even released an album in I don't know how many years.

Delete.

Come on, Brooke. Just be normal.

Me: Hey, I'm getting ready to turn in for the night and want to lock the door for safety and shit. Do you have the key to get in when you get back?

Not stellar exactly, but the best of the bunch by a mile. I hit send before I can overthink it and flop back onto the pillows at the top of the bed. Benji picks up his head at the jolt of the mattress.

"Sorry, Benj, but you know who you're dealing with. And seeing as we're traveling with the hottest man alive, I don't anticipate that it's going to get better anytime soon."

I've never heard a dog do it before, but I could swear he laughs.

I cover my eyes to escape his doggie scrutiny, but the relief is short-lived. Before I can even take a full deep breath, my phone is trilling on the comforter beside me with the sound of a text.

I pick it up and open the message, clenching my buttocks as I do. I may be a big girl with big achievements, but I'm a scaredy-cat-and-a-half with any kind of regular adulting types of things. Add in my crush, and I'm a flounder.

Chase: Hey, sorry for just taking off. I went for a quick walk and ended up in a decent bar to have a quick drink. I'll be back shortly, but definitely go ahead and lock the door. I have the key.

Is it really possible that this is a real guy in today's world? Not only is he not upset, he's apologetic and forthcoming. Last I checked in the biology books, they'd taken those off the list of possibilities for males.

"Is it any wonder that I wrote a book about this guy, Benj?" I ask my dog, though I imagine we both know he's more of a vessel for self-reflection than an actual conversation partner. I'll admit, though, he's a pretty great one. He never actively disagrees and usually goes along with what I say.

Okay, maybe that's not great for other people all the time, but it is great for me.

Me: Okay, thanks. I'll leave the living room light on for you.

I roll my eyes at myself, but I send it anyway. I am what I am.

Chase: Thanks, Brooke. Goodnight.

Every part of my flesh and bones and organs sighs. Chase Dawson telling me, Brooke Baker, goodnight in what I imagine is a sweet, sultry voice is not how I saw this whole exchange ending, and therefore, I'm not prepared for it.

A very large part of me considers sticking my hand down my pants again, but I fight with all I have to talk myself out of it. I just finger-banged myself to thoughts of this man not even fifteen minutes ago, and already, I'm considering doing it again.

You are a freak.

I'm pretty sure it would be categorized as the kind of behavior that takes you to a thirty-thousand-dollar rehab in the San Fernando Valley with a bunch of sex-addicted celebrities who want to pretend they're doing something about it while drinking fifteen-dollar juice bar drinks and getting massages on the daily.

And I refuse to breach that phase of my life until I have a reality show and five false social media sites dedicated to making up things about me with old pictures. Not a moment before.

What can I say? Everyone's got to have a goal, right?

Chapter
Twenty-Three

Chase

By the time I come back to the motor home after calming myself down with an Old Fashioned at a small bar about a block away, Brooke is asleep, and the bedroom door is shut. Only the living room light above the couch guides my movements.

I close the door as gently as I can manage while still having to semi-slam it and then listen closely to see if I've woken her.

Other than Benji's soft snores, I can't hear anything. I guess it's safe.

With a deep sign, I take a seat on the couch and rest my face in my hands. From the moment I decided to come on this trip in this capacity, in the back of my mind, I knew I was in at least a little bit of trouble.

Let's face it, no matter how important the book is, you don't volunteer to drive an author's RV if you're a senior editor at a publishing house like Longstrand. You just don't.

I knew that, and I did it anyway. More than that, I even went into the lion's den that is my boss's office and stood by the decision under his scrutiny and upped the ante on just how much my job is on the line with this book.

I would laugh at myself if it weren't so sickening.

Regardless, I'm here now, and I'm going on case seven hundred of blue balls—at least, that's how it feels.

And tonight, I have to drive us to our Chicago campsite, so we actually have some time to get work done on the book tomorrow. *You know, the supposed reason I came.*

I roll my eyes at myself so hard I feel them in my hair.

With a sigh and a groan, I get up off the couch and head to the front of the bus to take the sunshades out of the windows and fire it up. Luckily the fuel tank is full since I stopped just before Brooke woke up this morning, so I should be able to cruise the five-hour drive without worrying about stopping.

Without worrying you're going to do something incredibly stupid like climb into Brooke's bed and pull her in for a snuggle.

With the engine warmed up and a fresh cup of coffee poured, I hop into the driver's seat and take off.

Destination: the next random campsite outside of Chicago.

Focus: only the road, and not at all on what Brooke's face looks like when she comes.

Damn, you really suck at lying. Even to yourself.

Chapter Twenty-Four

Friday, May 19ᵗʰ

Chase

I'm still tired this morning from driving last night, but if I don't get up now, I won't get up for a long time. My body craves the kind of sleep that shuts you out from the world for a day and half; I can feel it, but I don't have the time.

Instead, I have my coffee, notebook, and *Accidental Attachment* manuscript set up at the table, and I'm pouring a fresh mug for Brooke when she comes walking out of the bedroom. She's got her hair pulled back and some light makeup on, along with a tight-fitting pair of straight-legged jeans with a white T-shirt and brown boots. She also has a purse slung across her chest, and it's that aspect of the outfit that sends my radar pinging.

I can feel my eyebrows draw together, but I try to keep the wrinkle from getting too extreme.

"Uh, planning on going somewhere, I see, huh?"

Brilliant, Chase. Not a weird way to word that at all. I smile, hoping that'll help.

"Yeah!" Her voice is enthusiastic, and she's nearly bouncing on the heels of her boots as she speaks. "I thought we'd go see the city. Do a river tour! That kind of thing."

"Oh. I…well, I thought maybe we could work on the book…"

She glances to the table then, seeing the coffee and work setup for the first time. Her face melts in disappointment and, if I'm not completely mistaken, terror.

"Oh."

"I don't want to be a stick-in-the-mud," I'm quick to add. "I just know we have a lot of work to do and not a ton of time to do it in."

She nods then, grabbing her purse to pull it off like she's going to give in and sit down, and I…break. I don't know what it is because it's surely not my pragmatism—that part of me knows well enough what's at stake here—but the sight of her looking dejected is too much to bear.

I backtrack faster than a husband who just told his wife her butt does look *kind of big* in her new pair of jeans.

"You know what?" I pointedly shut my notebook. "We can work after we get back or during dinner or something. We're only in Chicago until tomorrow afternoon, so we may as well see the city. Do it up right."

Do it up right? I don't even know who I am anymore. I've never said something like that before in my life.

Brooke's smile is a million watts and a million more times worth it. When she smiles or laughs, it transforms her whole face from something interesting to something that takes the air right out of your fucking lungs. It makes sense why Netflix wanted to do the tour with her—whether she knows it or not, she's enchanting.

"Yes!" She fist-pumps the air and does a little jig of a dance in the aisle of the motor home. "That's the spirit! You know, they say to write what you know, and in order to know, you have to get out there and do! So, let's do, Chase Dawson. Let's do!"

"Do the Dew?" I ask through a teasing grin.

"Do the Dew!" she agrees excitedly, following it up with one more fist pump.

"Do you like Mountain Dew?"

"I do not!" she yells.

A chuckle starts in my chest and makes its way up my throat easily. "You're a lot of fun, Brooke, you know that?"

"I don't get out a lot, but I do keep myself and Benji highly entertained, so hearing the news from you isn't a huge surprise."

Benji lets out a little bark at the sound of his name and comes trotting out from the back bedroom with his service vest intact.

And I rise to my feet, the entire time my eyes taking in the smiling enigma that is Brooke Baker.

Man, I like her confidence. I like her playfulness. Truth be told, I like that my changing my stance on work and agreeing to go exploring in Chicago was all it took to make her feel this way.

But beyond all that, I like Brooke. And if I considered my feelings for anything longer than a second, I think I might realize I like her a little too much.

Chapter
Twenty-Five

Brooke

I come out of the bathroom, final pre-outing pee accomplished and teeth brushed.

Benji is all set to go in his service dog vest, and Chase is packing up the manuscript into a binder and placing it back inside his canvas bag in the kitchenette booth. At a glance, my long-forgotten leather backpack on the other side of the table gives me the middle finger.

Man, I really am a procrastinating fool. The reality is, I'm going to have to make time to work on *Accidental Attachment* eventually. The deadline is coming, and believe it or not, the work will not do itself.

But not today. Today, I've already got a whole other thing in motion. Not even Dolly's "9 to 5" could motivate me to sit down and stare at a computer screen rather than going out and exploring the city of Chicago right now.

"I'll call an Uber," Chase offers, and I wince a little.

"Yeah, see, about that…"

"What?" He laughs with a shake of his head. "You already called one?"

"Well, kind of." I tilt my head from side to side like a Valley girl. "I mean, I might've already called an Uber before I even came out. I didn't want to waste any time, you know, waiting until I could ask you and get an answer and such." He guffaws, and I rush on. "I totally would have canceled it if you'd said no, though!"

"Of course."

"I would have!" I gesture wildly with two hands. "The car was coming from downtown, and it was going to take a while to get here, and I didn't want to waste any of our time, so that we can get back here early enough and still be able to work."

I'm spitballing lies like a stand-up comedian doing crowd work, but if there was ever a time for the "whatever it takes" motto, this is it. I ain't about that "I have a job" life today.

"Oh, I believe you."

I narrow my eyes at him. "Then what's that face about?"

"What face?"

"The one you're making that no human as hot as you has ever made before!" I snap, getting impatient. "Your brow is overly furrowed, Dawson, and it's obvious."

"You think I'm hot?"

My heartbeat hits the shifter and revs my rhythm up to sixth gear. *Do I think he's hot? Pfft. That's like asking if pigs like to roll around in shit.*

"Oh, come on," I grumble. "You know you're hot, and you're stalling. What are you making the face about?"

"I guess I'm just girding my loins for whatever you get me into today."

I chortle. "Trust me, I'm not a wild woman. We're going to get into some deep-dish pizza, at best. No hardened prison stays or the like in our future, pinkie promise." I hold out my most delicate finger, and Chase considers it for a long second while Benji crowds me.

My doggo knows I'm not the cool cucumber façade I'm putting out there. Just like Farmers Insurance, he knows a thing or two, because he's seen a thing or two.

My phone pings with an alert from Uber that our driver is almost here, and Chase shakes his head with a smile again before pushing my pinkie away and pulling me in for a hug.

It's the oddest, most familiar feeling, and there's a part of me that wants to lean in and hold on for the rest of the day. Luckily, Benji barks at the approaching car, and it's enough of a reality check to pull me off the delectable-smelling man before I'm arrested for harassment.

When the car pulls to a stop outside our motor home, I check the license plate for consistency and then wait for the driver to say my name out the window before opening the passenger door.

When you're a single woman, you learn to protect yourself so intrinsically that you do it even when a man is around.

"Brooke?"

"That's me. Leroy, right?"

The driver notices Benji as he's nodding, and I open the door for Benji to jump up first. I do have him on a leash, even though he doesn't really need it, but I don't trust all the strangers in a new city not to say anything. I also put him in his service vest today rather than a costume, and as far as I can tell, it's doing the trick.

Sometimes drivers balk at letting Benji inside their cars when he's not labeled plainly for what he is.

I mean, obviously, he's a superhero to me, but usually no one else gets it.

Chase and I climb in after Benji, and because of the three of us being in the seat together, my leg kind of pushes up against Chase's leg. I'm not at all prepared for how firm and muscular it is, or for the visual of Chase's sweet blush as he touches my thigh by accident when trying to place his hand on his own.

Dear God, how did you make this man? How? I must know the full recipe with instructions for how to complete it. I mean, if I can't have Chase, I may as well attempt to bake a man just like him from scratch, right?

For the sake of my sanity, I busy myself, unlocking my phone and clicking into Facebook to scroll through the NYC Doggie group I joined before this tour started. Benji doesn't know it yet, but I've been on the hunt for his lady friend ever since I let him down that fateful day in the park. The last thing I want to do is break my sweet fella's heart beyond repair, and I swore to him that we'd both have our chance at love.

In my delusions, I'm having my chance now, with Chase, which is clearly not the case, but that doesn't mean Benji doesn't deserve his own happily ever after because I'm completely deluded. I don't want to let him down.

I check my post first, made under my incognito profile, **BrookieCookie**, where I've described the sweet girl with the bow and the man she was with in an effort to jar someone's memory. So far, no one has any leads, but there have been a few friendly commenters championing my efforts.

Carrie Lawson: New York won't sleep until we've found your doggo's soul mate!

Hunter G: I'm so impressed that you're keeping a level head, BrookieCookie. I'd quit my job and go MI Tom Cruise on finding my dog love.

Della Plays: I've been to the park three times this week—no luck so far. Will check back tomorrow.

Chase glances at me several times without prying, but I know for a fact by my angle and proximity that he can see my screen. I know I'd be curious if I were him, so I decide to fill him in a little bit.

"I'm, uh…just doing some secret recon for my BFF, you know? I kind of let him down one day, but I don't want to get his hopes up too soon. I haven't gotten any leads yet, but I'm not giving up."

Chase's smile is both brilliant and bewildered as he looks down at me. "I'm sorry, what? I didn't understand anything you just said. I feel like I'm missing something here."

I glance down at my screen again and back up at him as a blush creeps up my neck. "Oh. You, uh, can't see my screen?"

He smirks and shrugs. "It just looks black to me."

Oh shit, yeah! I smack myself in the forehead, remembering aloud, "I forgot I put one of those privacy screen protectors on it before leaving for this tour."

My laugh is a cackle as I imagine just how crazy I must sound right now after my spiel with absolutely no context.

"Sorry, just ignore me."

Chase considers me a long moment before whispering, "Kind of hard to."

"I know," I reply, sinking my head into my hands and dropping my phone into my lap. "I'm a little nutty these days. Even more so than usual. Thanks for putting up with it."

"It's my pleasure," Chase responds with a smile. "Really."

I shake my head. "You're clearly too nice, and perhaps, worked at Chick-fil-A at some point in your life. I promise I won't hold it against you if you tell me the truth. Or if you want to tell me to stop talking or whatever. Or even if you want to go back to the campsite and just rest instead of getting dragged around Chic—"

"Brooke?"

"Yeah?"

"You can shut up now."

"See!" I shriek through a giggle. "That's totally cool of you to tell me that."

I wrap an arm around Benji and look out the window with a stupid smile on my face as the Chicago skyline approaches. I've always had a thing for skylines, even when I was growing up in rural Ohio on my family's farm. I had several framed watercolors of New York and Chicago and Nashville and London, and if I know my parents at all, I imagine they're still in their places on the paisley pink wall in my childhood room—that is, if my nephews haven't torn them to shreds yet.

And now, I'm a grown woman touring these cities as my books are turned into a series on *Netflix*. If I could tell it all to little-girl me—after I'd have to explain what Netflix is and how Blockbuster went under ages ago—I know she'd be so excited.

I watch the skyscrapers pass by through the window and note how stunning

Chicago looks in the spring. The city puts out an unbelievable effort to landscape the urban streets with beautiful flowers and blooming trees.

I spot a sign for Millennium Park, noting that it's only a few blocks away. During my Uber request, I asked to be dropped off there because it's the only place I've heard of in Chicago.

Ha. Wow. That sounds…crazy.

Holy crapola. I don't actually know anything about this city that I've just convinced Chase to explore…

Benji starts nudging me as I begin to get nervous, and I nudge him back. I know he's doing his job and all, but yeah…not now. I'm going to fight the faint with sheer willpower, even if it kills me.

*I will not pass out and piss myself in the back of an Uber on the way to downtown Chicago. I will not pass out and piss myself in the back of an Uber on the way to downtown Chicago. I will not pass out and piss myself in the back of an Uber on the way to downtown Chicago…*and repeat until infinity.

My best buddy maintains the stare but stops the bumping, and for the consideration, I'll be forever grateful.

After several minutes of silence, the Uber pulls to a stop on Michigan Avenue with a view of the famous Bean, and without much of a choice, I grab Benji's leash and climb out of the passenger door on the driver's side while Chase climbs out of the opposite one.

As the car pulls away, Chase approaches Benji and me with a warm smile and wide arms. "So…what's first on your 'explore Chicago' agenda?"

It's at that exact moment that the wave of everything I'd been fighting in the car crashes over me, and I freak the hell out, dropping to the ground, sitting on my ass, and putting my head in my hands. Benji and Chase both swarm me, although I think Benji is mostly confused because my vitals aren't doing the things they normally do in these situations. I'm light-headed, but it's different. It's, like, *emotional* or something.

"Oh my God, Brooke? Are you okay?"

I shake my head and try to get my voice back, but Chase is too busy running his hands over my limbs looking for injury to realize that every time his flesh touches mine, the silencing lump in my throat grows a little bit larger.

"Brooke, are you okay?" he asks again.

Finally, I find a hole in my shame big enough to explain through. "I-I-I … *shit*… I don't know what to do. It just hit me…just now, that I don't have a plan at all." My face scrunches in absolute horror. Chase stares at me for a long moment, and then he breaks out in the kind of laugh I've never heard from him. Huge, crowing, completely unreserved. It's beyond hot and makes his perfect black hair bounce. Like, *boing-boing*, those strands are jumping.

How can one man have so many good physical attributes *and* a good personality? I don't get it. I thought God tried to spread it all around just a little bit.

Any other man I've ever known would be scowling their ass off right now if they'd just found out I'd dragged them down to one of the busiest cities in the country, when they were supposed to be doing something else, without even having a specific reason or a plan.

Chase makes it to his feet before I do and holds out a hand for me to take and climb up. I take it—honestly, I'm kind of scared not to—and he takes off at a brisk clip down Michigan Avenue.

"Chase?" I question, churning my legs behind him so that Benji and I can keep up. "Are you mad?"

He stops then, turning around to face me, and without hesitation, pulls me into a hug. It's warm and crushing without hurting, and supportive both physically and emotionally. I think this one embrace heals something inside me I didn't know was broken.

"No," he murmurs into the top of my hair. "Of course I'm not mad. I'm taking the lead. If you don't have a plan, am I right to assume you don't mind?"

"You're going to spend the day in the city with me *and* figure out what we do?" I snort. "Are you kidding? That's the best thing I've ever heard."

"Good," he remarks, pulling me away enough to place a kiss on the top of my head where his chin used to be.

Um, excuse me? What is happening?

Did his lips just touch me?

Your forehead, honey. Just your forehead. Relax.

"Then I figured we'd start with coffee," he announces while teenage me scribbles "I heart Chase Dawson" all over her science notebook. "I could really use a cup of coffee."

I tell teenage me to take a hike and nod in agreement with his caffeine plan. "Sounds great."

I also have absolutely no questions about why he might need coffee so desperately. *I* am the reason, and I accept that. Taylor Swift has it so right. *I am the problem. It's me.*

He jerks his head in the direction of the sidewalk ahead. "Then come on. Let's go."

I fall into synchronized step beside him, though my legs are shorter than his, and without a word, he reaches over and laces his fingers in between mine. My hand is so small compared to his larger one, and the feel is so unbelievably intimate, I don't dare say or do anything that might break the spell.

Seas of people on the crowded sidewalks part for him, and I trail in the wake happily as he approaches a place called The Black Crow on the corner of the next block up. It's a modern-looking place on the outside, but upon entering the door, I see it's filled with vintage furniture and crowded shelves with various knickknacks, and maybe best of all…books.

The Black Crow is a combination coffee shop and bookstore, and Chase Dawson found it within five minutes of arriving in Chicago.

That gets me thinking as he very gently drags me to the coffee counter, where a barista stands at the ready. I wait for him to order and murmur my own—*because I'll take caffeine in any form at any time of day, thank you very much*—and then, as the barista goes to make our drinks, I fire off the question that's been sitting on the tip of my tongue. "Have you been to Chicago before?"

"Twice. Both times when I was under the age of eighteen."

"And yet, you found this place in the matter of a heartbeat?"

He winks. "I'm taller than you. I can see farther down the street."

"What?" I ask with a hoot as the barista hands over my coffee first—a white mocha—and then his—an Americano.

"I didn't know this was here until I saw it from a block away."

"Well, sir. You have unbelievable luck then, because this place has coffee *and* books. I don't know of anything better than a combination of the two…unless there's wine. I like when there's wine."

"They probably have wine in the afternoons."

I giggle like a damn schoolgirl and put my cup to my mouth to take a sip, but he pulls on my hand before I have a chance to get any liquid, and once again, we're on the move. This time, into the depths of the store on a mission only Chase knows.

"Where are we going?" I ask on a whisper as we pass a man at a table who appears very focused on whatever is on the screen of his laptop.

"To find a book."

"Oh, cool! Are you looking to read something specific? Maybe we can both pick one out and read it together?"

"I like that idea, but given the timeline with your own manuscript, I have a little bit of a different idea."

"Oh yeah? What?"

He flashes that stupid sexy wink of his at me. "You'll see."

I follow along as he searches the shelves with avid concentration, useless in my ignorance. I don't know what we're looking for, which makes it hard for me to find anything.

"Chase," I call again as he moves into another section and starts scanning the shelves. "What are you looking for? Maybe I can help."

I've barely uttered the words when he grabs a book by the spine and pulls it off the shelf, tucking it to his chest and heading for the front register with long strides of his toned legs.

Unfortunately for the sleuth, I recognize the back cover immediately—as I should, since I spent months figuring out what I wanted it to be.

"Chase Dawson," I snap, following him so quickly that Benji actually has to jog to keep up. "What are you doing with my book? My *first* book, I might add." The pitch of my voice is on the rise without my permission, so I do my best to lower it as I keep whisper-yelling. "Chase! Why do you have the first Shadow Brothers book? What are you doing?"

He doesn't answer me, and I have to admit, for the first time ever, he's kind of pissing me off. Of course, it's still in a playful, fun way, rather than the way most men ruffle my feathers, but I'm absolutely coming out of my skin not knowing what he intends to do with that damn book.

"Chase. Chaseeee!" I hiss as he walks up to the register where a young girl in a black apron is waiting for him with a friendly, customer-service-approved expression on her lips.

"Excuse me," he says to her, his smile fully engaged and his charm oozing all over the goddamn place. "Could you help me?"

She blushes a little, tucking her shoulder-length blond hair behind her ear and allowing the corners of her mouth to curve up just a little. I have no doubt if she weren't painfully shy, her smile would be beaming to the moon right now, but as it is, I can tell she's enthralled.

But who wouldn't be? The bastard is offensively attractive, and he has no freaking clue.

"Um, sure," she replies with a mousy murmur as she takes the book from his outstretched hand.

"Can you tell me what you know about this book?" Chase asks the most ridiculous question I've ever heard. He knows the book. He's *read* the book. "I'm looking to start a new series, and some friends told me this one was good, but I don't know much else about it."

What kind of weird-ass game is he trying to play here?

I almost ask him exactly that, but as I witness recognition of the cover and title hit the young girl's face, my breath catches inside my chest. Her eyes light up, and the book is quickly and gently cradled to her chest.

"Oh my God, yes!" she exclaims in a soft hush. "The Shadow Brothers is one of my all-time favorite series! This is definitely a good choice." She breathes for a second, staring down at my book and turning it in her hands a little bit.

And I take a few steps back, horrified that she might recognize me, and nervously shrink into the background. Benji stays by my side dutifully.

"It's technically paranormal because the brothers are ghosts," she continues on. "But it's not really high fantasy, you know? It's entirely relatable fiction for, I think, both men and women. I'd be willing to bet that'll you be back in here looking for the next two books within the week."

Chase smiles big, and my heart beats like it wants to climb out of my body. *Why is he doing this?*

"Well, thanks," Chase says easily, his whole little dog and pony show creating far less anxiety for him than it has me. "I'm really looking forward to it now. I appreciate you taking the time to explain it to me."

"Of course!" the girl replies, noticeably more comfortable than she was before.

I pace the area behind him with Benji and head for the door once she's done ringing him up.

As soon as he steps out on the sidewalk, I put my hands to his chest and shove, yelling, "I cannot believe you just did that!" loud enough for a half-mile radius to hear.

"Why not?" Chase asks through a laugh, handing me the bag with the book just for me to toss it right back at him. "Wasn't it fun being incognito?"

"Well…yes. Of course it was! I felt like a CIA operative for a minute there, but I also feel like I was lying to that poor girl."

His face is skeptical. "She enjoyed talking about it. You could see it on her face. And you weren't technically lying anyway. I was. Plus, lying is pretty standard practice for all of the alphabet agencies."

I frown and he laughs, grabbing my hand again and dragging me and Benji down the street. "Where are we going now?" I yell, making him chuckle.

"I guess you're just going to have to wait and see!"

I follow him down the street at what feels like a jog, but it's a pretty normal pace if your heart isn't walloping like it's a car on the autobahn and can drive a million miles an hour. And we don't stop until one of the biggest, brightest, deep-dish Chicago pizza places with an all-glass exterior comes into view.

He pulls the book out of the bag and a Sharpie too—that I had no clue he bought, by the way—and hands both to me like he's expecting me to do something with them.

I raise my eyebrows, and he raises his back.

It's mano a mano here, final death match, chicken at its best. I won't break. I refuse.

With the tempting smell of pizza in the air, Benji gets annoyed with our stare down and sits on his hind legs with a groan while we continue the charade.

I raise an eyebrow in challenge as my eyes start to burn, and he narrows his pretty blue ones, which I'm afraid might be a better long-term tactic.

"Chase."

"Brooke."

"Ugh. What are you doing now?" I ask, giving in pathetically quick. It's not so much that I'm a loser as much as it is that I'm starting to feel funny things in funny places from staring at him this long.

"You're going to sign this book," he tells me. "I'm going to put it somewhere while you go in and order pizza, and then, you're going to post about it on social media."

"Okayyy…?"

"And *then*," he adds with a mischievous little grin. "We're going to eat our pizza and watch as people flock to come get it."

"Are you serious? You can't be serious."

"Deadass, my bro. No cap."

I smile despite myself, because hearing him use Gen Z language semi-seriously is too much. And then, I sigh.

"What is your deal today, Dawson? You're normally so easy to be around."

He guffaws. "I'm still easy to be around, *Baker*. I'm just showing you that you're easy to be around too. And that fans love you and your books and that you have nothing to fear on this tour or with this new book or with anything. You're severely talented, Brooke. Seriously, if talent were violent, you'd have leveled everyone around you by now. *Even* Chuck Norris."

"Okay, you're annoying because even when you're annoying, you're nice. And that's more annoying than just being annoying, so you're double annoying with a cherry on top."

He nods, fully accepting it.

I grumble and snatch the book and Sharpie out of his hand, signing the inside title page swiftly and then handing it back to him with a shove to his manly chest.

"I'm going to get pizza. Come find me and Benji when you're done being a weirdo."

He does that hot wink thing again. "Oh, don't worry. I will."

The truth is, I can't wait. This is the most fun I've had in a long time.

Much more of it, and I might really never want it to end.

Chapter
Twenty-Six

Saturday, May 20th

Chase

The sun has barely risen, and I'm already up and a full hour into my day.

Coffee singes at the sensitive skin of my top lip as I take a sip from what I've now claimed as "my mug"—it's got little black dashes on its white surface and a handle that perfectly fits my four fingers.

Yesterday, we spent most of our time exploring the city, and this morning, Brooke will be making a television appearance on *Good Morning, Chicago* to talk about all things Shadow Brothers.

While she's busy getting ready, and since we'll hit the road shortly after she finishes her TV interview, I decide to fit in a little work. Briefly, I check for any Longstrand emails on my phone, and when nothing urgent appears, I slide into the motor home's kitchenette booth to resume my notes on *Accidental Attachment*.

The margins of Brooke's book baby are filled with ideas, suggestions, and scribbles. Someone who isn't familiar with the way I work might think this means there are a million changes to make and burn the manuscript right then.

I'll have to be careful to remind her of this before she gets a wild hair.

But for me, the more notes I make, the better the book is. With books I don't like, I find I have next to nothing to say.

When I love something...I'm the kind of editor who gets so enthralled, so attached, I can't help but comment on both the good and the bad. And not just "more of this" and "less of that" but with the ways each joke made me spit all over my shirt or take off at a dead run with anxiousness. I want the creator of the work to know when I can't breathe because of the tightness in my chest or when a character hits so close to home, I wish I could pick up my phone to call them.

I know the level of work that Brooke and all other authors pour into their manuscripts, and they deserve to have confirmation when their time and effort pay off. Sometimes, they need an editor's reinforcement to be spoken, and I'm more than willing to speak it.

I set my mug down onto the table carefully, pick up my copy of the manuscript, and start to read a chapter about the first time River takes Clive to her apartment. It's in her point of view, and I've read it several times, but it never fails to bring a smile to my face.

I slide my key into the keyhole of my apartment door, but before I engage the lock, I stop and turn to Clive.

"Okay, before I let you in, there're a few things you should know."

"Oh, really?" He tilts his head to the side, but his eyes never leave mine. "Like what? Is your apartment door actually a door to Narnia? Or is your apartment just really, really dirty like that episode of Friends *where Ross is dating that woman who has a rat in her bag of chips? I need some direction on whether I should focus on wonderment or excrement."*

"Neither. But there are several rom-coms on my Netflix account and a Janis Joplin CD in the stereo."

"So, what am I supposed to prepare myself for, then?" he asks, leaning closer to my face and offering up a sexy little smirk. "The sight of a CD?"

"No. You're going to need to prepare yourself for the rules."

"The rules?"

"Yes." I nod. Just one defiant tip of my head. "The rules."

"Okay," Clive responds and steps back in a gesture with both hands held out in front of him. "Lay 'em on me, Riv."

"The only condiment I serve is mustard. Ketchup is for sheep, and mayo is for simps. At least, in my apartment. Feel free to do what you want with your free will otherwise."

He smiles instead of running straight in the other direction, and my heart kicks up in my chest.

"What else?"

"At this late hour, my TV only knows one channel. It will not be swayed, and it will not be changed, no matter how cute you grin."

Speaking of cute grins, his gets even bigger. "And what channel will I be subjected to?"

"TV Land, of course. When someone asks who I love, Lucy will always be the answer."

"Okay, Riv. You've definitely got some 'splainin' to do, but for the sake of getting out of this hallway, I'm going to go with my gut and agree to the rules now."

I pull myself away from the manuscript at the sound of Brooke's bedroom door opening, forcing my mind to reenter the real world. It's not a bad place to be, on a bus with Brooke Baker, but the more I dig into the realm of Clive and River over and over again, the harder it is to remind myself that the flutters in my chest and aches in my cheeks aren't real. As much as they feel like they should be, Clive Watts and River Rollins *aren't* real people.

Convincing myself is especially hard right now, having read this scene with an entirely new context into River's obsession with mustard. Brooke took that one from herself, like all writers do, but as the reader, with little to no contact with the author, you don't normally find out.

I put down my pen and pick up my cup of coffee and wait for Brooke to make her way through the tiny hall by the bathroom and into view. It's not a long walk, but since she's been in there getting ready for a while now, the wait feels painstakingly prolonged.

When she finally emerges, her soft brown hair is swept behind one ear, secured by a pin, and her eyelashes are lengthened with mascara. The sight of her makes my breath catch in my throat.

Clive and River and Lucy Ricardo are officially a memory.

She's wearing a burgundy crushed-velvet blazer over the thinnest, silkiest white lace top I've ever seen. Trim, black pencil-leg pants finalize the outfit and end at the top of a pair of shiny black heels. She looks classy and gorgeous and…a million other descriptors that a book editor with an above-average vocabulary should certainly be able to think of right now.

"Brooke," I start, stopping myself just short of spewing a whole monologue about how beautiful she looks that'll scare her beyond belief.

"What?" she asks, confused by the single use of her name—as she should be. "Do I look weird? I'm trying not to walk like a baby colt on ice, but it's been a while since I've donned a pair of heels."

"You definitely don't look weird." I have to blink to believe she's real. "You look…well, you look beautiful."

Brooke's signature blush climbs into her cheeks at a rapid pace, and she ducks her head to look down at the floor. A smart man who knows his boundaries would have considered the implications of a compliment in a professional setting further, but all *I* can think is that I'm sorry for saying anything now because it's robbed me of her dewy green eyes.

Shit, Chase. Get a grip on this…quick.

I try to find another way around my words, but everything else would be a lie. The fact of the matter is that Brooke *is* beautiful. I can't take my eyes off her.

"Well, thank you," she eventually responds and lifts her gorgeous eyes back to mine. "But I'm too nervous right now to let your words soak into my brain. I'm not exactly an expert at hair and makeup, and this is my first time on broadcast TV," she admits with a little frown. "I mean, I don't even know what they could ask me where the answer isn't supremely frightening."

She changes her voice to imitate that of a TV interviewer, *"What's your daily routine like, Brooke?"* Faux-flustered, she fans at her face and glides seamlessly back into her own voice. "Oh, you know, unwashed clothes and a cycle of self-loathing and talking to myself, mostly, followed by a bottle of wine in the evening. Sometimes two, if I'm on a deadline or feeling extra self-deprecating."

She's always so fucking funny. Still, I can tell behind her humorous façade, she needs something other than laughter to ease her nerves. She needs reassurance. She needs confidence, even if she's not the one to display it.

Thankfully, I've got plenty of reasons to believe that the public is going to love Brooke Baker as much as I...*Benji* does.

"You're going to do great, Brooke, I know it."

"Thank you. I'm glad one of us believes in me."

Benji woofs, and Brooke laughs. "Okay, two." She leans down to scratch at Benji's ears, and he leans in to the attention. "Thanks, Benj. Somehow you've always got my back."

See? Benji's unwavering *love* and support. That's what I was talking about.

Just out of curiosity, how many astronauts on the International Space Station do you think saw everyone roll their eyes at you?

Desperate for a distraction, I glance out the window to see the black town car pulling up, and Brooke follows my gaze.

"There's something strange about a fancy car picking you up from a campground to go be on TV, huh?" she questions on a snort. "I guess that's why they had the planes and five-star hotels thing in mind when they initially planned this."

"I think it gives it character. Just think, you could end up with a pine needle stuck to your shoe instead of toilet paper. Honestly, it seems better to me."

"Better for a sequel to *We're the Millers*, maybe. But better for a Netflix tour? I'm not so sure," Brooke reassesses with a laugh. "It is what it is, though. So, I guess we better get to gettin' on."

I stand from my spot in the booth and take my mug to the sink to pour it out, offering, "Do you want me to make you a to-go cup of coffee?"

She nods yes, but her words don't match. "No. No, I shouldn't. I'll end up spilling some on this blouse right before I go on air."

"What if I make it, hold the cup at all times, and supervise when you take a sip?" I ask, giving her another chance. By the looks of things, she could really use a caffeine ally.

Her giggle is both sweet and satisfying. Some part of me feels summoned to re-create it over and over again. And it's that part of me that's undoubtedly in a lot of fucking trouble.

"I want to, but no." Determined now, she shakes her head. "I don't trust myself. I'm on a clear-fluid diet until I'm done with this thing."

"Vodka?" I suggest, turning her giggle into a full-blown laugh.

"Stop it with the great ideas, Dawson, or I'm going to end up agreeing to one of them."

I shake my head. "Okay. No coffee or vodka…yet. We'll save them both for after the show."

She shoots an adorable finger gun at me. "Now you're talking."

"I think we both know by yesterday that I'm an excellent planner, Baker."

"When you look at your dictionary for the word 'planning,' does it say *be very tricky and slightly manipulative?*"

"Oh, come on," I insist, moving to the door, opening it, and then holding it there so it doesn't slam into Brooke or Benji as they follow me down the stairs to the outside. "You can't tell me you didn't have the time of your life yesterday!"

"Between cardiac events, it was quite splendid. Even when you tricked me into working while I was up to my nostrils in deep-dish pizza."

"All I did was talk about *Accidental Attachment* a little. I mean, that's kind of why I'm on this trip in the first place, you know?"

"That's a funny way to admit to ruining a day, but I guess editors are supposed to be creative with language."

"You really are even prettier when you're pretending to be mad."

"Listen, sir." She points one index finger toward my face. "That line was too smooth yesterday when you were taking pictures of me watching what felt like a hundred rabid readers come search for the signed book you hid on a windowsill in the middle of downtown Chicago, and it still is today. Not to mention, the look on my face in those pictures is probably straight-up fear that I was going to end up in the newspaper for inciting a mob."

I can't deny, once Brooke had taken to Instagram and posted the photo I took of the first Shadow Brothers book I'd hidden on the street, it was a fucking sight to see readers flocking to find it. A sight that I knew she needed to see. A sight she deserved to see.

"Hey now, the smoothness isn't my fault. It's all the Clive and River I've been reading!" I insist. "You're starting to alter my brain chemistry."

She snorts so hard she almost chokes on her own saliva and stumbles her way to the waiting car, Benji's leash still in her hand. He jumps in first, and Brooke follows. And I choose not to think about the fact that that's going to put Brooke *right up against me* in the car just like yesterday.

"What? It's not that farfetched, is it?" I climb inside and shut the door behind me. "To be morphing into the characters I'm spending so much time with? You must do it too."

I meet Brooke's eyes as the driver pulls away toward the front of the campground.

"Oh, Chase," she murmurs, a wry smile on her face I can't quite decode. "You have no idea."

"See. So, stop choking on your saliva and start getting into the River Rollins frame of mind that you, Brooke Baker, can and will be on TV."

"Poetry, that sentence. Absolute poetry."

"Sometimes, in life and in literature, you just have to tell it like it is, Brooke.

It might be boring that she walked to the cabinet, but walk to the cabinet, she did."

Her eyes roll heavenward, but she also lets out a little giggle from her lips, and I probably like that sound way too much.

Pretty sure that's already been established, my man.

The driver glances from the road to the mirror several times, and I avoid eye contact until he starts to stare at only Brooke. His eyes are like glue to her reflection, and I start to wonder if he's even watching the road.

When they finally flick away from her face, I catch them with my own and hold them—my gaze hard and unrelenting—until I don't see his eyes glance in her direction again.

It's not like people aren't allowed to admire someone as pretty as Brooke, but she's nervous enough as it is. The last thing she needs is to look up and find the driver staring at her and eavesdropping on our comfortable conversation. I know Brooke, and that would send her anxiety from a one to a one hundred in a heartbeat.

"You know, Dawson, you're kind of a literature nerd." Brooke's little joke pulls my attention.

"I'm a literature nerd?"

She nods.

"And? So? What's your point?" I retort with a smirk. "I don't see it as a bad thing. I fully own my literature nerdature."

"Very punny." She snorts. "And don't worry, I think it's a good thing." She gently pats my thigh, and I try not to notice how perfect her hand looks right there. "Most of the time anyway. Might want to stay away from the world's roughest ruffians, but around book people, it's endearing."

"I guess it's good news that I don't often find myself in the company of gangsters, then?"

"Likely, yes."

"All right," I comment, pretending to scribble on my hand. "No mob-based activity. Got it."

"Motorcycle clubs too," Brooke suggests. "You should keep them on the list for good measure."

I pretend to lick my finger pen and jot that down before turning to her like an old-timey news reporter. "And what else?"

"Um, basic street criminals?"

"Right, right."

"Prison inmates."

I nod. "Noticing a slight pattern here, but go on."

"Knife makers, gun enthusiasts, psych wards, pyros, general surgeons…"

"Wait. Why general surgeons?"

"I don't know." She shrugs. "But from watching *Grey's Anatomy* for seventeen seasons, I can tell you that most of them seem a little crazy. All that shagging and wanking at work? While people are supposedly dying? Who has the time?"

I can't stop my chuckle, and I don't even try. Brooke deserves to know how funny she is, and smothering my laughter would be an insult to her skill. Still, the amount of enjoyment I get out of her stand-up routine makes the hairs stand up on the back of my neck and my gaze move to the edges of my bent knees.

I lift a hand to rub away the sensation, and by the time I glance back at Brooke, I'm shocked to see that a trail of blood has found a way from her nose to her chin and is, at this very moment, dripping onto the pristine white fabric of her silky shirt.

"Shit, Brooke." I reach over, swiping at the fluid with my thumb without even thinking. "Your nose is bleeding."

"What?" she startles, the information jarring her spine to a much straighter position. "It is?"

I nod and cup my hand at her chin, even as her hands come up to battle mine for placement. "No, no," I order, batting her cute fingers away with my free ones. "It already dripped onto your shirt once. I'm catching it so it doesn't happen anymore. Do you have a tissue or something in your purse?"

"A tissue in my purse? *A tissue?!*" she yells, pausing dramatically to flail her arms. "That's for prepared people! I've got five ones and a Ziploc bag of maple syrup and ChapStick that probably expired a decade ago, for God's sake. I am infantile in maturity. So, no, Chase, I do not have a flipping tissue!"

A fluff of white appears over the break between the front and back seats, courtesy of Nosy Joe Driver, and I grab it with my free hand like the life of Brooke's pretty white shirt depends on it.

"Oh my God, I can't believe I got something on the shirt, and I didn't even have coffee. Or vodka! No coffee vodka!"

"Calm down," I coach in a soothing voice I hope doesn't suggest judgment. I understand why she's freaking out. The whole appearing on a live news show is huge for any normal person without a history of celebrity. Add in a bodily fluid, and the ante really ups. "I'm going to fix this. When we get to the studio, I'll get the stain out."

"What? How? It's blood, Chase! Blood! Not even that OxiClean guy is confident he can remove this stuff!"

"I'll get it out, I promise. Just concentrate on stopping the bleed." I rip off a piece of tissue and ball it up before lifting her lip and shoving it underneath. She's shocked by the intrusion. "Here. Keep this under your lip, right there on your gums, so it puts pressure. I got elbowed in the face playing high school basketball, and the athletic trainer taught me this trick for stopping a nosebleed."

"You were a basketball star in high school?" she asks, amazed. I can't help but laugh at the insinuation, as well as how easily her mind is distracted.

"Star? Uh, not so much. I played, but that's about it. I'm only six one, and I didn't get to be that until my senior year. In the basketball world, I was practically a runt."

Brooke looks me up and down, her lip sticking out like an adorable chip-munk, thanks to the tissue in there. "You don't look like the runt of anything."

My chest puffs up and my eyebrows waggle, but the truth is, I'm just lucky Brooke doesn't have access to my high school yearbook. My growth curve was slow at best, and I didn't get to the point of musculature I am at now without the help of a personal trainer teaching me how to use the gym when I lived in Nashville.

Both in literature and the real world, perspective can be faked. With a little effort, making people see what you want them to see is easy.

I don't feel the need to mask my past with Brooke, though. She's nervous of-ten, but she doesn't let the nerves stop her from being authentic. I don't know that she realizes just how lovable that is, but I think the fact that I'm willing to put myself through several rounds of Stain Removal Medical School via Google and YouTube just to ensure her shirt goes unmarred on television speaks for itself.

"Gah," she breathes, looking down at her shirt before covering her eyes with her hands. "I can't believe *this* is what I look like before my very first TV ap-pearance. I look like I got bad lip filler, punched in the nose, and stabbed in the chest with the world's tiniest knife all at the same time."

The drama queen in her is on full display. Any other woman and I'd prob-ably be annoyed, but not Brooke. If anything, I'm fucking amused. "It's not as bad as you're imagining it, and it's all temporary. When we get there, we'll head straight for the bathroom, and you can give me your shirt. I'll work some magic and bring it back to you within a couple of minutes, I promise."

"Great," she murmurs softly. "Undressing in the ladies' restroom while you do triage on my blouse is exactly what I envisioned when I woke up this morning."

"If that's true, you might want to look into some facts on being gifted with a sixth sense. Because that's pretty impressive," I tease.

"I'm pretty sure that's reserved for ghost kids and the Bruce Willises of the world." She shakes her head. "But if I had it, I'm certain I would have used it to avoid a few things on this tour already. Benji would have a lover, and I'd have moved to New York before the whole hassle of divorce."

"Well…it's a new gift, maybe?"

"We're here," the driver calls, thankfully releasing us from this weird state of holding. As tempted as I was to rip her shirt off right there in the car and start working, somehow, I think that might have made things worse.

Just a theory, but I'd put money on it.

Brooke frowns as I hustle her out of the car and into the back doors of *Good Morning, Chicago*'s studio with a hand at her back and Benji at our side. I shield her as though there's a gaggle of paparazzi flashing away with their cameras, even though there most definitely is not, and rush her toward the bathroom after hurriedly asking someone for directions.

Once inside the restroom, I take Benji's leash from her hand and push her into the stall gently.

"Eep," she yelps, frowning as she closes the swinging door. I smile and look down at her best friend with a wink.

I know he's a dog, but I swear the ends of his mouth curve up into a grin.

"Just pass it over the top of the stall," I tell her confidently, still not completely sure how I'm going to fix it but determined enough to know that I will.

I catch the blouse as it comes flinging over the door, and I let go of Benji's leash with a small nod. He woofs lightly, confirming he gets the message loud and clear—he'll take care of our girl, who's clearly spiraling, and I'll take care of the shirt.

"Sit tight. I'll be back with it in ten minutes tops."

"Ten minutes!" she shrieks. "And what am I supposed to do for ten minutes?"

"Listen to one of your favorite Dolly songs on your phone?"

"Listen here, mister. Do not bring Dolly into this."

"But I thought you said she was the answer to everything?"

"*Chase!*" she exclaims, full-on exasperated now.

"I'm sorry," I say through a chuckle. "I don't know what you should do. Hang out naked? I can only solve one problem at a time."

"Ugh. Fine."

I laugh at Brooke's grumble and take off out the door at a near run. I told her I could only solve one thing at a time, but the fact is, I'd be willing to do more.

A lot more. And I'll be damned if that's not alarming.

Man oh man, you just might be in trouble.

Chapter
Twenty-Seven

Monday, May 22nd

Brooke

The Brooke Baker Motor Home Tour doesn't quit.

The last few days have been an absolute blur. We've been from Chicago to St. Louis, from St. Louis to Memphis, and now, we're on our way from Memphis to New Orleans.

I'm exhausted, and I've barely even done anything other than talk to people, sleep, and put effort into hair and makeup, so I can't even imagine what Chase is feeling.

I swear, I've never seen the man sit still. If his ass is on a seat, it's because he's driving or working or ordering me food in a restaurant in which I've demanded we eat. If he's not working on the book, he's cleaning a bloodstain from my silk blouse.

Truly, he's multifaceted.

And I don't know whether to award him or sedate him, but tonight, since he's once again driving, I have to settle for doing my best to keep him awake and entertained long enough to make it to New Orleans.

But the farther we drive, the harder I have to try because, as it turns out, I started running out of funny things to say somewhere around Arkadelphia, Arkansas.

Searching my suitcase for props, I flip through everything I own three times before deciding that I'm no old-school Carrot Top—you know, before he got all weird and muscular—and I should never try to entertain someone with props.

But when I glance to my right, Benji's bag peeks out from the closet, and I have the brilliant idea to end all brilliant ideas.

Sure, Benji and I are a slightly different size and, you know, shape, but there's got to be something from one or two of his costumes that will fit me if I really try for it. And Chase *has to* think a woman in a dog's superhero costumes is funny. Right?

I dig and pick and flip through everything, tossing the things I think could work onto the bed and trying them on one by one.

Captain America's cape fits just right with Batman's ears, and I'm even able to slide Hulk's arms over my own. Benji stairs at me from the floor, slightly horrified. "I don't look nearly as good as you do, bud, but hopefully we'll give Chase a laugh."

Even if his laughs stem from secondhand embarrassment for my ridiculousness, it at least has to be enough to give him a zap of endorphins to keep driving. I have no qualms with playing the clown in this "keep the driver of our motor home awake" game.

Benji hops on his front feet until I lean down to give him a scratch, and then he rubs up around my Hulk arms with what seems like a doggie laugh.

My doggo gets my humor maybe better than anyone else—as he should with how many jokes of mine he hears on a daily basis. But honestly, if it weren't for him, I'd have never narrowed down the one-liners to use in *The Shadow Brothers*, and we might not even be here at all. Plus, I'd probably have split my head open beyond repair at this point, so he's really been helping me from both angles.

Basically, I don't trust anyone like I trust him, and if he isn't shaking his head at me with shame right now, I can't be on too wrong of a path.

With some quick application of makeup, I hastily turn my face into a mix of the heroes I'm wearing and head for the front of the bus where Chase is doing the responsible task of driving us.

He's facing forward and looking at the road—which is obviously a good thing—but that also means I have time to stumble up through the rocking aisle and sit in the passenger's seat before he notices my getup at all.

Once my butt hits the captain's seat beside his, Chase looks once and then triple takes so fast his head looks like a cracking whip swinging between me and the road.

His chuckle is instantaneous and throaty, and I immediately think of five more dog costumes to order off the internet pronto. I won't since the moment is completely topical, but *man*, to make him laugh like that again, I would do nearly anything, including spending a large portion of my life savings on apparel meant for a canine.

"Only you could look as good as Benji in that stuff, Brooke."

I pick up my ass slightly and Hulk smash on the dashboard, and Chase's laughter renews all over again. "Sit down, sit down. I'm laughing too hard to have you that close to the windshield."

I pretend to fly back into my seat, and Benji barks his approval from his current spot on the couch behind us.

"What are you doing, crazy lady? Playing dress-up?"

"Well, *Robin*, Batman's job is to lead and save those who need saving, and I could see that you were on the brink of exhaustion." I shrug. "But of course, our dynamic duo has cities to save, and we can't stop, so I thought I'd entertain you for a bit. It's the least I could do after you ShamWowed my blouse into working condition again, hooked us and unhooked us from every campsite we've entered, and fought off a squirrel villain to boot."

"Oh man. All that, and I don't even get to play Batman for just a little bit?"

I scoff. "You're good, but I'm very obviously the star of this show, Chase. I mean, look at me."

"You got me there." His throaty chuckle is back. "Everything is as it should be. You're the star of the bus, and River is the star of the book."

My breath catches in my throat. The blockage is a combination of nervousness—something any mention of this freaking book always brings to the surface—surprise, and maybe just maybe, a little bit of awe.

"You think River is the star of the book?"

"You don't?" he asks in reply, glancing from the road to me and back again while his big, strong arms hold on to the wheel and make adjustments as needed.

I don't know what to say to that. I mean, I sure as hell didn't write it that way. Clive and his every Chase-ism is the character I adored. The one I gave most of my attention and love to. I didn't know how to write River any other way than to base her entirely on myself, and that was mostly for pervy and selfish reasons.

"Oh, Brooke, come on. The scene in the break room where she uses all of the people's lunches to put on an impromptu play?"

I still don't say anything. I can't. Sure, that was funny, but it was mostly the crazy ramblings of a woman who lives alone and is by herself ninety-five percent of the time. When you're talking to yourself, even the food starts to have a personality. I took that scene directly from the near-hallucinatory masterpiece I'd enacted for Benji in my apartment that night.

"And the review River does live on air for food she's allergic to and hasn't even tasted?" he adds, and his eyes light up with humor. "I lost my shit over that. It was funny and heartfelt, and somehow didn't even insult the chef."

Again, I took that from a food review I did on Benji's new dog food—*for Benji, mind you*—when I was a bottle of wine deep and procrastinating like a mothertrucker on *Garden of Forever*.

"River takes nothing and turns it into something, Brooke. And *that*, that's what star power is."

For a second, I don't know how to exist anymore. Because those words are some of the most book-worthy I've ever heard, and Chase Dawson was the one to come up with them.

At a loss for any other option, I do what I do best—deflect. "Okay,

Shakespeare, whoa. Do I have your permission to use that line in the book without fear of vindication, cries of plagiarism, or a lawsuit for a byline?"

"Oh, come on." He rolls his eyes all the way through a chuckle. It's a big eye roll since I can see it, even though he doesn't reroute his gaze from the direction of the highway.

"What? That was a great line! For real. I'm using it. I suggest you just go along with it if you don't want to face the consequences."

He side-eyes me from his periphery. "And those would be?"

"I'm not entirely sure, but I heard it's probably something violent. And messy. And filled with loads of paperwork. Incidentally, what are you afraid of most in this world? Because that's involved as well."

"You have access to rattlesnakes?" Chase asks with a chuckle.

"Yes," I reply with impressive seriousness. "It may not be common for most New Yorkers, but I've got a whole den of eastern diamondbacks shake, rattle, and rolling on my outside terrace."

He glances away from the road long enough to look me up and down, goes back to the road, and then does it again before saying anything. I let him have his moment of observation, but the wait is absolutely terrifying. I'm sitting here in Benji's dog costumes, for goodness' sake. It's not exactly the ideal getup for a situation like this.

"Brooke...you are..." He shakes his head and bites into the plump-y flesh of his lower lip. *His lucky, lucky lip.*

"Insane?"

"One of the funniest humans I've ever met in my life. I don't know how you do it, but I'm pretty sure this smile is branded into my features at this point."

I sit back into my seat and stare out the windshield with an audible howl of disbelief. "I think what's happening here is that you're slowly becoming delirious and your standards of humor are too low."

"If that's the case, I've known a lot of really unfunny people in my life. Like, startlingly unfunny. Because you're miles above them."

"Okay, okay, cool it, Mr. Complimenter. All of this is going to go to my head, and my joke-writing skills are going to be locked up tighter than a sex-toy drawer in a nun's room."

"No way. I have a hard time believing Brooke Baker lives in any state other than perpetual hilarity. In fact, I refuse to believe it."

I snort. "I spend a fair amount of time in the states of 'pathetic' and 'wallowing' too. Just ask Benji. He'll confirm."

Benji lifts his head from the couch and opens his eyes into the tiniest slits before falling back into the lulling coma only a house on wheels can provide.

"Okay," I mutter to myself. "Maybe now isn't the best time to ask him. But I'm telling you, it's true."

Chase opens his mouth to respond, but when his phone starts to ring, vibrating and shaking in the cupholder between our seats, his attention is redirected. He reaches for it, glances at the screen to identify the caller, and then groans aloud.

My eyebrows draw together at his sudden and obvious disdain while he tosses the phone back into the cupholder unanswered and replaces both hands on the wheel.

"Spam? The other, *other* meat? Calling about your car's extended warranty, perhaps?" I ask playfully, and it's the perfect shield for my unbridled and unhealthy curiosity.

He laments. "If only."

"Wow," I remark. "Worse than the car warranty people? Must be really bad."

He runs a hand over his face and ruffles the top of his hair before letting out a big exhale. "Caroline. My ex-fiancée."

My heart does a flip in my chest. Even just hearing him use the word fiancée is enough to send my completely unfounded and unearned jealousy nerve into a tailspin. "Oh, schnikes. That is bad."

He chuckles dryly. "Yeah. It's best if I just don't answer."

I nod. I can see the merit of that completely. Out of sight, out of mind.

But *on the other hand*, this is the second time he's dealing with her on this little adventure alone, and we've barely even started, in the grand scheme of things. Maybe Caroline doesn't need to be ignored. Maybe she needs the opposite.

And maybe it's wrong and completely overzealous, but I pick up his phone from the cupholder and scroll into his recent calls with ease. The screen hasn't even slept since he put it down, so I'm beyond needing a password.

I hover over her name and look to him for permission. "Do you mind?"

"Mind? I don't… What are you going to do?"

I shrug. To be honest, I'm not entirely sure. My heart is beating wildly, and my tongue has taken up residence in my throat. This behavior is completely outside of the bounds of what I'd consider normal for myself, and yet, I can't stop.

I don't know what I'm doing. I just know that Chase doesn't need to be dealing with a woman who slept with his best friend repeatedly if he doesn't want to be. Period.

"Call her back. That's…kind of as far as I've thought it out."

"Holy shit."

"I know." I cringe. "You can totally tell me no, and I'll respect that. I have no idea how it's going to go, and you didn't exactly order a rogue agent to act on your behalf. Smacking me in the face is totally allowed, too—for this time, and this time only."

He thinks it over for a long moment—like, a long, long moment—and I start to wonder if his contemplative stare at the road will ever end. It's hard for me to keep my mouth shut that long, but I do it, for him.

"Yeah. Okay. Do it," he concludes finally, his shoulders rising and then sagging even lower than before. "Honestly, it's not like it's going to make it worse than it already is. So…what the hell. Call Caroline back."

He doesn't have to tell me twice.

I drop my thumb to the she-devil's name on his call list and then put the phone up to my ear as it starts to ring. I'm sure Chase would rather me do this on speaker, but I'm not entirely sure I'll be able to maintain as much of a badass façade if he's listening to every word of the exchange. And if I don't make the call right away, I don't know that I'll have the confidence to do it at all.

On a general basis, I'm about as nonconfrontational as you get. I'm the girl who won't go back to a fast-food restaurant when they completely screw up her order. I'll just take the bag full of wrong food home and pray I like it.

But this…for Chase? Feels different.

"Hello? Chase?" Caroline answers, her voice a ball of breathy excitement. I feel like she's trying to seduce me before I can even buy her dinner.

"No, sorry. Chase can't come to the phone right now."

"And who are you?" The purring of a kitty cat in need of my milk is gone, and her voice turns cold as ice. And I'm talking the bad kind of ice. Not the good kind that's perfectly crushed in easily chewable nuggets. This is jagged, sharp, and blizzard-worthy.

I almost give her my real name, but a light goes off just in time to save me— and my career—from the complications that could cause. "River Rollins. I'm Chase's girlfriend."

My eyes bug out of my skull, and so do Chase's as he glances over at me and then back to the road again frantically.

"His *girlfriend?*" she screeches. "Excuse me? I'm his *fiancée.*"

This poor, deluded woman. I know it's got to be hard, losing a catch like Chase and accepting that it's a forever kind of thing, but she did it to herself. And I've got absolutely no mercy for a woman who can fuck another man behind her fiancé's back willfully and repeatedly.

"No, Caroline, you're not his fiancée," I correct her. "You pissed all over that and then some when you slept with Justin over and over again, don't you think? You're not anything to Chase Dawson anymore, so I think it's a good idea if you stop calling him."

"You don't know what you're talking about. Chase and I are—"

"Absolutely nothing," I cut her off before she can spout more bullshit. "You threw him away when you had an affair with his best friend, and I know—I *know*—that has to be hard to hear. But, sweetheart, the facts aren't changing because of your feelings. Stop calling him. Stop taking advantage of him being a nice guy. Stop trying to insert yourself into his life, and stop thinking you have a shot of getting back together. That shot is less than a shot in hell. It's literally roaming around at the core of the earth. It's. Not. Happening. He's very happy."

"Oh yeah. He's happy with you?" she retorts. "You think you're immune from where I am? You think you're the woman who's going to tie him down? Yeah, right. You have no idea what kind of pressure there is living up to a man like Chase Dawson. After a while, I promise you, he won't be as interested in you as he is right now."

"No, Caroline. You're not getting it. I'm not saying he's happy *with me*. I'm saying he's happy. Period. And no amount of groveling on your part is going to change that. Maybe he and I will be together forever and maybe we won't, but the point is, he's never going to go back to you."

Wow, Chase mouths, a small smile curving up the corners of his perfectly full lips.

I smile back, desperate to crack Caroline with an even bigger hammer if it'll make him smile like that again.

"I don't believe you." She continues to delude herself. "Chase needs to be man enough to tell me himself—"

I open my mouth to return fire when the phone is very suddenly but gently ripped from my ear. Chase puts it to his own, his jawline carved out of the very finest of stone. Marble, perhaps.

"Cut the shit, Caroline. I'm tired of hearing it."

I would wonder how he heard what was going on enough to take over the call, but the glaringly obvious answer from the receiver held slightly away from his ear when Caroline speaks tells me all I need to know. Hell, I might as well have put the dang thing on speakerphone for as loud as the conversation is anyway.

"Whatever, Chase. Is that why you're having your new girlfriend fight your battles now?"

"Caroline," he says, and her name is mingled with a sigh that even makes my stomach drop. "For the longest time, I've let my pity for you trump my sanity."

Pity? *Hol-ee shit.* That's a stinger.

"Pity?" she nearly shouts. "Why would you pity me?"

"Because everything about you makes me sad," he answers, and my eyes are back to bugging out of my head again. "I know that's hard to hear, Caroline, but it's the truth. Because of your insecurities, you're too fixated on being the center of attention or numbing yourself with alcohol that you keep ruining all the good things that you have in front of you."

Oh, momma. Someone call 9-1-1 and send them straight to this chick's house because this shit just turned into a five-alarm fire.

Caroline is silent, probably because she's currently trying to fan out the flames consuming her, but Chase keeps going.

"I'm sorry for you, Caroline. I actually am, but I should have put your ass in line ages ago. And truthfully, I'm sorry for myself I didn't. But I'm glad River gave me the nerve today. It's been three long years of your bullshit, and I'm done," he declares. "Don't call me again because I'm not interested in hearing from you. I'll be blocking your number and hanging up if you try to call from any others. I'm done living in the past. I'm done catering to your supposed guilt. I don't owe you anything. And most importantly, I'm done talking to you now. Goodbye, Caroline. Forever."

He pulls the phone away from his ear, ends the call, and his eyes are only slightly less wide than my own. I don't know how I expected that to go, but I swear, I never could have imagined it would be quite that badass.

"Okay, Dawson," I tell him, my smile growing by the second. "You are *officially* Batman for the day. I hope New Orleans is ready with the signal."

Chapter
Twenty-Eight

Chase

I turn off the water and step out of the shower, grabbing the fresh towel I placed on the one and only hook inside the sardine-can-sized bathroom of the motor home.

We've been driving for what feels like all day, only arriving in New Orleans about an hour ago when the sky was already dark and the clock was nearing 10:00 p.m.

Since Brooke deferred on taking her shower until in the morning, I figured I could use a good clean and scrub. It's odd how driving for hours can make you feel like you just spent a week in a hostel with no AC and only one pair of underwear, but there's just something about when you finally reach your destination that makes a shower feel like nirvana.

Six straight hours on the road, with hardly any stops, is typically enough to make anyone go insane, but against all odds, Brooke managed to keep Benji and me entertained. At one point, she came out of the bedroom in a mashup of his superhero costumes, and I laughed so hard I nearly swerved off the damn road.

I'm convinced she could take on Ebenezer Scrooge and the Grinch and walk away with the two bastards cackling.

Nonetheless, she looked hilarious in Benji's superhero costumes, and it was just the energy boost I needed to see the rest of the drive through. Not to

244 | m a x   m o n r o e

mention, an additional adrenaline rush came in the form of a purposefully ignored call from Caroline turning into Brooke *calling* Caroline back.

That conversation ended in me finally telling my ex what she should've heard a long-ass time ago—*she needs to move the fuck on.* The instant I hung up, I didn't feel upset or mad or angry. I felt relief. It was as if I'd been carrying dead weight around for the past three years and I finally unloaded it at the proverbial garbage dump.

All thanks to Brooke.

I dry myself off with the towel, scrubbing at my hair for a few seconds before making quick work of the rest of my body. But when I go to grab a clean pair of boxers to slide on, I realize I have zero clothes inside this bathroom.

Well, *shit*. I know I got my clothes out of my bag, but apparently I didn't bring them in with me.

Not very helpful for a guy who's not auditioning for a role in the Broadway production of *The Emperor's New Clothes.*

Quickly, I wrap the towel around my waist and open the bathroom door, laser-focused on the pile of clothes on the pullout sofa. But I only make it two steps toward the living area before I run right into something. Run right into *someone*, actually.

"Ahhh!" Brooke screeches and drops an arm full of different foods to the floor. She teeters on one leg from the impact, and I reach out with two strong arms to pull her steady, but the momentum of my determination mixed with the opposing direction of hers combined with the fall makes our equilibrium all wonky. Her chest bumps into my chest, and her hands reach up to grip my shoulders to help her body overcome gravity's pull.

We finally rock to a stop in a full-body lock, her one ankle even trapped between the two of mine.

"You okay?"

"I think you saved the day, Batman," she responds, but her words soften to a whisper at the end of her sentence as those big green eyes of hers look up and into mine.

All the air gets pushed out of my lungs.

She's beautiful. *Scary beautiful, I mean.*

I should have a response here, but since the earth has stopped spinning and time has frozen, I don't say anything at all. I just stand there, with my hands still clutching Brooke's waist and her arms holding tight to my bare shoulders.

Her chest rises and falls in dramatic waves, and my lungs find it difficult to play their role in the carbon oxygen cycle.

She searches my face, and I don't miss the way her gaze moves from my eyes to my lips and back to my eyes before repeating that circuit three more times.

Her body is *so* close to mine that not only am I consumed by her citrusy scent, but I can also tell she isn't wearing a bra. Her breasts are pressed tight against my bare chest, and I can feel the hardening of her nipples through her flimsy T-shirt.

God help me.

It only takes a nanosecond before all the forbidden, completely unprofessional, dirty things I want to do to this woman start rolling around inside my brain. My head might as well be scrambled eggs, and my dick thinks it's high time he joins the party.

This is too much.

I need to back away, I know I do, but my pesky limbs won't seem to move.

I pull my gaze from her eyes instead, as sort of a first step, if you will, but without explicit direction to get the fuck off Brooke completely, it goes to her mouth, and I witness her white teeth dig into her bottom lip. It's coy and sexy as hell, and I want to slide my tongue across the indents her teeth make in the rosy-pink flesh.

You want to know what that mouth of hers tastes like.

Fuck. Fuck. *Fuck.* She is too warm, too soft, too beautiful, too tempting…just *too much* for me in this moment. If I were a better man, maybe I'd be able to resist her pull, but I can feel my body moving toward hers.

She is a magnet and I'm metal, and *poof!* goes all my control.

I think I want to kiss her. *No, you want to kiss her, no "think" to it.*

My lips. *Her* lips. It might as well be the apocalypse right now and we're the last two people standing.

I grip her waist and pull her closer to me, my mouth gravitating toward hers.

Inch by inch, I close the distance until I'm hardly a breath away from knowing what Brooke's mouth feels like. What she *tastes* like.

Bang!

A loud sound cracks into the air, and we jump away from each other like two teenagers at a school dance. It takes my brain a good ten seconds before I can put the puzzle pieces together and understand that it was just a car door slamming near the motor home, but the moment has left the building.

Thankfully, I think. *I mean, I am her editor, for shit's sake.*

Benji's bark is deep and ferocious as he rushes out of the bedroom and starts surveying every window he can access.

Brooke jumps into action to calm him, pulling him back from the window soothingly and rubbing his head between the ears.

All I can do is just stand there, like a dick flagpole, covered only by a towel.

Benji barks a few more times before he's completely assured that there's no murderer in our midst, but he finally gives the all clear by heading back into the bedroom on an annoyed huff.

Brooke shoves to standing in his absence, her index finger rubbing a barely there, mindless line across the plump center of her bottom lip.

The silence between the two of us is deafening until we both try to cut through it at the same time.

"I left my clothes—"

"I needed snacks—"

"So…that was…" A nervous giggle jumps from her throat. "Sorry about that."

"I think we both surprised each other."

"Yep. Yep. Yep. I was definitely surprised. *Super* surprised." She nods so many times I fear she's going to pull a muscle in her neck.

"Well, I guess I better—" I start to say, but she cuts me off with an *"Oh, man!"*

I follow the path of her gaze to the floor, where various bags of chips and cookies and candy are scattered on the carpet between our feet.

"I think I went a little wild with the snacks!" she exclaims at a volume that is way higher than needed for our close proximity. "Pretzels! Doritos! Oreos! Chips Ahoy! A bag of gummy bears!" She rattles off each item as she reaches down and grabs them from the floor. "It's like I had too many options or something!" Her laugh is borderline maniacal, and she rises to her feet again, clutching all the snack baggies to her chest like they're a life vest. "Can I interest you in a snack, sir?" she asks and hesitantly meets my eyes. "It's quite possible I've grabbed way too many from the kitchen cabinet."

"I'm good, but thanks." I offer what I hope is a reassuring smile. "And I should probably get dressed." *You know, because my dick is still hard and all I have on is a goddamn towel.*

"Cool. Cool. Sounds like a plan." Her eyes flit to my waist, but then she quickly averts them to the floor. "And I'm going to go eat these snacks, but not, like, all of these snacks. Just some of these snacks. I mean, this is way too many snacks, you know? But way to go, Netflix, on making sure we were set with snacks!"

I have no idea how many times she's said the word snacks, but yeah, it's a lot.

"Actually," she keeps rambling, "I should probably go call my agent now and let him know about the snacks and how great the snacks are and how great the snacks and Netflix are. Yep! That's what I'm going to do! I'm going to go call Wilson Phillips—my agent, not the band—and you can get naked…" She pauses, eyes wide, and quickly clears her throat and shakes her head at the same time. "I mean, *dressed*. You are naked. Well, not completely naked because you have a towel, but you know what I mean. Ha! Yeah. Better go make that call now!"

She spins on her heel, heads straight for the bedroom, and promptly shuts the door behind her. She even drops a bag of Lay's potato chips on the way but doesn't backtrack.

And I'm left standing in the middle of the hallway, wondering what in the hell just happened.

You were about to kiss Brooke.

I let my head fall back for a brief moment before snapping myself out of it and snagging my clothes off the sofa and walking back into the bathroom.

But I don't get dressed right away.

Instead, I stand there, with my towel pitched like a fucking tent, forearms bracing the small sink, and stare at my reflection in the mirror.

Can't be sure, but it seems like you are fucked beyond belief…

I shake my head at myself and redirect my thoughts like they're the only thing capable of saving me from whatever just happened outside this bathroom.

It's no big deal, *right?*

Brooke and I are basically living together on this motor home. She's a beautiful woman, and any man would find it hard to resist the situation we just found ourselves in.

Yes, I almost kissed her. *Almost,* though. No line was crossed.

The only thing I need to do now is focus on the book and driving this motor home to ensure that Brooke gets to all her publicity stops. That's my job. It's why I'm here, and it's exactly what I'm going to do.

Pretty sure these could be categorized as "famous last words," my man.

Chapter
Twenty-Nine

Tuesday, May 23rd

Brooke

The sun gawks at me through the small, accordion blinds of the bedroom, but I'm already awake.

Truthfully, I've been awake for hours. Sleep did not come easily last night, but that's probably because I'm suffering from a case of Post-Almost-Kissed-Chase-Dawson Stress Disorder.

PAKCDSD, if you will.

I don't know what happened or how it happened, but I was simply heading back from the kitchen after raiding the snack cabinet and ran smack-dab into Chase while his perfect, muscular, bare chest was on full display and only a white towel was secured at his waist.

He was fresh out of the shower—basically, naked—and my snack-focused mind rapidly switched course, taking a hard left and heading straight for Hornyville, USA.

Chase Dawson. *In only a freaking towel.* To say that messed with my head and only widened the circumference of my crush would be an underexaggeration.

I *felt* his bare, warm chest pressed against mine, while his eyes were so close I could make out every tiny facet and little detail that makes them so blue. The

base of his irises is blue, but tiny flecks of aqua glitter are scattered throughout, and *that* is what gives the color such pop and dimension.

Aside from my up close and personal with the eyes, I also saw the outline of
his *ahem* through his towel. And let me tell you, that outline wasn't "average"
equipment. It was far bigger and thicker than to be described as a run-of-
the-mill penis. No way. That penis is running the fucking mills. President,
King, and CEO.

And his lips. *Have mercy, his lips.* I wanted to kiss him. Thought about doing it a thousand times in the span of a minute. And for the briefest of moments, it even felt like he might've wanted to kiss me too.

But the almost-kiss bubble was popped by a loud noise from outside the
motor home.

I pretty much turned into a crazy person after that, rambling about God
only knows what before making a mad dash for the bedroom and locking
myself inside.

Which is where I've been since last night, stuck in this small room and feeling too awkward and unsure and afraid to leave it.

But now, I'm reaching the point where I have to attend to basic needs like
emptying my bladder and feeding my growling stomach, and doing the first
in here sounds like a whole other problem I don't want to have to fix.

Just go out there and act normal.

My mind is kind of cute when it's being stupid. When have I ever been able
to achieve normal? Add in my ginormous, huge crush on Chase, and it's a
damn joke to think I can pull off two notches below semi-sane.

Benji looks at me from his spot near the pillows on the bed. Lord knows he's
tired of watching me try to amp myself up to walk outside of this bedroom.
He would also probably like to empty his own bladder and get fed breakfast.

"I'm trying, okay?" I whisper toward him, and he just lets out a little huff
from his snout.

Eventually, though, when my bladder's urge becomes too strong and Benji
gives another huff that I think says, *we're getting close to dog abuse, crazy lady,* I

know I have to woman up. It's that, or else I'm going to have pee in an empty Gatorade bottle on the nightstand by the bed and Benji might take to shitting in my favorite pair of boots.

I can't be sure, but bottles full of piss might raise some red flags, and shit-boots certainly won't make me more comfortable.

On a deep, deep, *deep* inhale, I force oxygen into my lungs as I stand up from the bed. My knees wobble a little, but I exhale through the nerves and step to the door.

Hand wrapped around the knob, I pull it open slowly and peek my head out toward the hallway, trying to see if I can gauge the situation from right here.

I spot the back of Chase's head as he turns from the coffee machine with two mugs in his hands. Instantly, we make eye contact, and it takes everything inside me not to slam the door and go hide under the comforter.

"Morning," he says, and his voice is friendly and natural and not at all weird.

He is fully dressed, and a smile sits on his lips.

I don't know what I was expecting to see. I mean, it's not like he was still going to be out here in his damn towel. That'd be nearly as weird as me starting a collection of urine bottles in the bedroom and walking around in shit-boots. But for some reason, him acting entirely normal after a moment I've made this big in my head almost feels the strangest of all.

"Go—" I start, but I stop to clear the frog out of my throat. "Good morning."

"How about a caffeine boost?" he asks and lifts one of the mugs toward me.

Okay, this is good, Brooke. Really. Him acting normal gives you a sane lead to follow. Just do the same.

"Yes, please." I nod and open the door the rest of the way, walking into the hallway and toward the kitchen. Benji is quick to follow my lead.

"Sleep well?"

"Mm-hmm." *You are such a big, fat phony.*

"Glad to hear it," he says and places the mug into my hands.

"Thank you." I take a sip before setting it down on the small kitchen table. "Now, if you don't mind, I'm going to head off to the bathroom for a brief moment. Fingers crossed, I don't have to fight off any squirrels while I pee. And then, I'm going to take Benji out before he starts bitching at me."

A soft chuckle escapes Chase's lips as he sits down in the little booth, his notebook and manuscript for *Accidental Attachment* already out on the table.

I head into the bathroom and make quick work of emptying my bladder. And when I get back from letting Benji out, everything still feels pretty normal. Chase starts pushing me about the book. I start procrastinating from doing work on the book.

We fall back into what has become our typical routine on this motor home. The almost-kiss might as well have never happened.

Which is good…*right?* Everyone loves normalcy.

Yeah, but everyone isn't wondering if they missed their chance to kiss the man of their dreams.

Chapter
Thirty

Brooke

It's official. I'm buried in a live grave, and the dirt is piling up.

For the entirety of the morning and most of the afternoon, I've used all my best avoidance techniques to keep Chase off the book path.

But I can no longer avoid working on it without checking him in to a psychiatric facility.

Hell, I've managed nearly a week of including him in my procrastination, but I can see the tiny indentations of crow's-feet starting to radiate from his eyes as a result of the stress, and to be the one to mar his perfect face would be an unrecoverable tragedy.

So, here I am, in the kitchenette booth, my previously abandoned backpack open and my laptop front and center on the table in front of me. I've got a cup of coffee poured in one of the mugs from the cabinet and a blinking cursor on the screen, begging me to make magic.

Sure, I wasted forty-five minutes in the NYC Doggie Facebook group, trying to find more leads on the border collie of Benji's dreams—without luck, unfortunately—but now I'm ready to get down to serious business. My actual job—*finishing a damn book.*

I scrub a hand down my face, silently hoping I can survive the pressure of this thing—otherwise known as the huge, gargantuan mistake that's led to me going through edits on a book that I didn't intend to let see the light of day, all while being stuck on a motor home with the apple of this book's eye.

If working on a contemporary romance book while simultaneously living through a real-life forced-proximity trope isn't irony, then I don't know what is.

Although, if this were a romance book, you should've already experienced the big, explosive moment that ends with Chase's super-sized McPenis inside you.

I roll my eyes at myself, and from his spot on the floor near my feet, I'm certain Benji rolls his eyes too.

Shaking my head to clear the monsters out of it, I start to read the chapter I'm in, doing my best to detach any understanding of the words from my physical body enough to keep my syncope from taking me to the floor.

It's a scene close to the beginning of the book, when River has her first on-air experience at KKBY. She's an experienced anchor, but she has no practice with the object of her fantasies looking on while she does it. It's nearly shocking how well I wrote this part before living it.

"Good afternoon. I'm River Rollins, and this is KKBY with your local news," I greet viewers, my voice carrying the deepness of speaking from my diaphragm—better known as my "work" voice. "Today, we'll be visiting local small businesses that are sharing their struggles to find a new normal in a social-media-driven world. Pat and Belinda Bryce, for example, have been baking pies for nearly fifty years for the community of Oxboro, but recently, their sales have dried up. They say they've tried to find a presence on Instagram, but the technological world is changing too quickly. I spoke with them directly, and this is their touching story."

Clive signals to me with a point and a smile, sending the live shot to the camera roll of the interview with Pat and Belinda I conducted just a day ago.

I take a deep breath and fix my hair that's sticking behind my shoulder, and Clive looks back at me with a thumbs-up and a wink. I'm so rattled, my foot slips off the bottom rung of my stool, and a clanging ring explodes in the middle of the otherwise silent and waiting studio.

My eyebrows grow to ten times their normal height as everyone redirects their gazes directly to me.

Great, River, I think to myself. First day on the air and you're already causing a scene worthy of—

A gentle tap on the shoulder is all it takes to send my stomach straight to the inner lip of my asshole, locked and loaded and ready to be shat in a fiery spray of nerve-induced diarrhea.

Instantly, *Schitt's Creek* comes to mind, but instead of *Ew, David*, it's *Ew, Brooke.*

"Whoops, sorry." Chase laughs shamelessly at the startled expression on my face, but he doesn't look contrite at all. Rather, he looks amused.

"You're taking your life into your own hands, sneaking up on me like that! Jeez." Exasperation puffs from my lungs. "Did you get some new, soundproof orthotics I'm unaware of?"

An additional chuckle jumps from his perfect mouth, but I choose to ignore his plump-y, most likely incredibly soft lips that I still wonder if I almost had the chance to kiss last night.

"I wasn't even being that quiet, Brooke. You were just entrapped in the book so fully you didn't hear me." He waggles his eyebrows, the bastard. "It's good, isn't it?"

I realize in some shallow part of me that his remark is a compliment to both me and my work, and yet, still, it feels like a jab. He may as well be saying, *Ha-ha, I told you working on this would be fun!*

But two can play at the game of redirection, and I remembered to pack my cleats. Not, like, literal ones, of course. I'm no Sporty Spice.

"Not as good as a day spent on Bourbon Street, I'm sure, but I guess if this is how you like to get your kicks, I'll fall in line."

He nods to my coffee mug as he takes another one out of the cabinet. "Good. I'll let you keep using my mug, then."

"Your mug?" I scoff. "Aren't these all the community mugs of the motor home, sir?"

"They were until I claimed that one. I've used it every morning and night since we got on this bus. But, just this once, I'll let you use it," he offers faux magnanimously.

I look down at the white mug, covered in dashed marks and imagine all the times Chase's lips have encompassed the rim. Suddenly, his silly mug seems like the kind of thing I'm going to have to talk myself out of taking to bed tonight.

You are a sick, sick woman.

Desperate to separate myself from *the thoughts*, I offer up the mug with a lift of my arm. "Here. You can have it back, then."

He considers me for a minute before accepting it, but accept it, he does. *How cute*, I think. *The little weirdo has formed an obsession with the mug.*

That's totally something I would do and, at the same time, completely unexpected from him. He seems so dignified, so mature, so well-adjusted. Turns out he's just faking it way better than I am.

Satisfied, I've nearly turned my attention back to the scene and River's faux pas when, out of the corner of my eye, I catch sight of Chase putting the mug to his lips and taking a sip before pouring it out in the sink.

My coffee. *My* backwash. *My* lingering lips on the rim.

Holy shit. My abdomen spasms, full-blown arousal threatening to make me come right then. And I don't even think he knows he did it!

Just a mindless sip from a mug he's established as his own.

If only my body would recognize it as that innocent, but my mind is too busy playing memory lane with last night and imagining what it would've felt like to kiss him.

Don't go there. Disengage.

I busy myself with absolute bullshit for the five minutes it takes Chase to wash out the mug and refill it with his own coffee and return to the table. I'm still trying to make my eyes focus on my computer screen enough to read the words when he taps me on the hand, a frown pointed in my direction.

"Are you upset we're not out exploring right now?" he asks, clearly misreading my fucking off for something deeper than a spontaneous-combustion orgasm.

"Huh?" is my eloquent response.

"You seem sad. And I don't like the idea that I've made you sad like some kind of work-pusher. You're a grown woman, and you're allowed to make your own schedule."

I wave him off with a dramatic arm. "Oh, it's fine. You're right to make me work. I may be grown on the outside, but my maturity and responsibility are slightly lacking around shiny things."

He smiles as I continue.

"It's no big deal, really. I've been to NOLA before, so it's not imperative that I get boots on the ground. Work does need to get done."

He nods, considering me closely before pushing a little harder. "How about the flaws for Clive? Have you gotten a chance to work on those yet?"

"I, uh…well, I attempted it."

"And?"

I cringe. "I failed."

"Brooke," he chides gently, and I sink my head into my hands.

"I know, I know! But it's the next item on my agenda. Just getting myself re-established with the story."

Liar, liar, pants on fire! You know these characters better than you know the folds of your labia, and thanks to writing this story about Chase Dawson, you know your meat flaps quite well.

My God, I've turned shameless. I didn't even think about how duplicitous this whole thing is before spewing something to get him off my back. I don't want to have this attitude—I don't want to keep hiding something this important from him—but my God, how do you even begin to explain this to someone without both scarring them for life and ruining their opinion of you?

"That's fair," Chase answers, completely unaware of the half-cooked monologue in my head. "Do you want to brainstorm through some of the notes I've made at this point? See if you're open to accepting any of them?"

I'm just about to say yes when Chase's phone rings from its spot on the table, drawing his eyebrows together until he gets a look at the caller. I catch a glimpse before he picks it up, and I recognize the name straightaway.

President of Longstrand himself, **Jonah Perish.**

Yikes. It never feels good when the boss is calling, and it feels even worse knowing I've been fighting Chase's ability to do his job at every turn. I really, really hope he's good enough at bullshitting to keep himself out of trouble.

But his face is incredibly stalwart, given the circumstances, and I'm impressed as he manages to offer me a smile and a wink before stepping out of the motor home's front door to take the call.

When it closes behind him with a click, I let my head fall back in dismay.

The time has come when avoidance is no longer possible without seriously fucking with the man I have an enormous crush on and, quite possibly, ruining his life. I can hem and haw and pretend to try to work on this stupid scene some more, or I can get down to the meat and potatoes of what I know I have to do.

And I do *have to.* No book is complete without depth, and by its nature, that means the characters have to be layered.

All of the characters. Including the ones modeled after Chase Dawson.

Ugh.

I have to make a flaws list for the most perfect man on the planet's fictional character.

But before I can do that, before I can let it go, I'm going to have to face the reality that Chase is a rounded person, and even if I find him the most charming in every way, there are things about him that could be considered flaws—or at very least, supply him with a quirk.

Knowing I'll never be able to stand immortalizing the heinous act of speaking ill of the man of my dreams by typing it into the digital world and saving it as a file, I dig around in my backpack until I find a notebook with some loose-leaf pages to tear out and a nearly inkless pen to scribble on them with.

I write a title at the top of the page to get myself in the spirit.

Chase's List of Flaws:

I nearly roll my eyes at the obviousness of it all, but ridiculous is as ridiculous does, and forcing myself to break down a man who is probably the best man I've ever met for the sake of publishing a book I never wanted published is about as farfetched as it fucking gets.

I groan. *Good grief, I don't want to do this.*

And it's not because it'll make me think less of him or recognize the parts of him I wouldn't be in love with if I just considered them harder. I know Chase has flaws; the problem is, I'm pretty sure I find every single one of them endearing.

I don't want to do it because it makes me think less *of me* for dragging his innocent soul into this whole mess in the first place.

It'd be one thing if Clive were just a character, but the Lord and I know he's so much more than that and then some. He is the reincarnation of Chase Dawson, and since I never thought this manuscript would see anyone's eyes but my own, I didn't even bother to hide it.

One might wonder how Chase doesn't see that when reading through his copy, but I get why. It's the limited sight of our own reflections that's keeping him from figuring it out himself.

Just like with a mirror, there are parts of ourselves we can't see. Some are good and some are bad, but when it comes to Chase, I know for a fact that he's completely missing the parts that show just how great he is.

Maybe they're taped to his back or strapped to his feet, and he's only got a half-length mirror, but as far as I'm concerned, he's one of the finest humans I've ever met.

And I'm about to search the depths of my soul to make a list of things that are wrong with him, even though I like everything about him—the good, the bad, and the literature nerd in between.

Ugh.

I take another deep breath in through my nose and let it out through my mouth while I gather myself with a quick crack of my knuckles.

Slowly, ever so gently, I pick up the pen on the table beside my no-frills sheet of loose-leaf paper and count off from number one.

1. Doesn't understand how handsome he is.

I laugh at myself at first, but I keep trying before getting discouraged, adding, **This makes him oblivious to his "pretty privilege" and deaf to the struggles of those without it.**

Ughhhh. I really, *really* hate this.

Still, I push onward.

2. He uses a fake broadcaster-type voice when he's on the phone with important people to make himself sound more authoritative.

3. He's pretty fucking pushy about a book that's ruining my life.

And even though he does it with some of the nicest compliments I've ever heard—periodt—it's still kind of annoying to have someone drag you to the depths of your own personal hell.

4. He forced his way on to this tour with me without asking if I'd be okay with it.

5 He's so work-minded that sometimes he forgets to have fun.

6. He flirts without thinking of the fallout.

Gah. *This is seriously so hard. Just make it to ten, and then we can quit. Just get it over with before he comes back in from the call. Just doooo it,* I practically yell at myself. *And make them good ones, Brooke. Don't hold back!*

7. He practically martyred himself for this stupid book I didn't even mean to write.

8. He let his ex walk all over him for a long, long time.

9. He's arrogant in his ability to make this book what it needs to be.

10. With an ex and a best friend who went behind his back for a year and a half, his judge of character is questionable.

It feels like razors are dancing under my skin as the vitriol I can barely even stomach pours out of me. I let out an involuntary scream as my pen finishes the last stroke, and I shove the sheets of paper into my bag in a rush.

I need it gone, covered… I'd even burn it if that wouldn't completely defeat the purpose.

I take a huge breath and let it out, forcing my shoulders back down from around my ears as I close over the top flap of my leather bag.

It wasn't easy, but at least it's done.

As far as I'm concerned, that sheet of paper will die in that backpack, returning to the earth in a million years or so as both of them decay into nothingness.

But when Chase asks, I can say I've done it with truth in my heart, and now, all that's left is trying to find a way to implement them into the story. No pressure, huh?

Triple *sigh.*

Now, I've only got about three weeks left to turn this book into something worthy of reading.

I guess I better get to work.

Chapter
Thirty-One

Wednesday, May 24th

Chase

Brooke shifts nervously and pulls at the collar of her bright-pink shirt as the producer for *Wake Up, New Orleans* counts her and the hosts down to the live shot right in the middle of the French Quarter.

Behind them, a live audience watches on with avid eyes, sidewalk cafés bustle with breakfast traffic, and a line of fancy, colorful buildings are highlighted with scrolling cast-iron balcony rails.

Ron Weakly, the lead TV personality here in NOLA, introduces Brooke to the viewers both in person and watching from their living rooms, and I look on as Brooke's face lights up with one of her most captivating smiles. It's subtle and a little nervous, but it illuminates the dewy grass color of her eyes in the prettiest of ways.

This week kicks off the annual Crawfish Festival, and the show notoriously spends the whole week right in the mix of the downtown action doing their broadcast. And with Brooke as the main guest this morning, they've invited her to sit in on pretty much everything. She'll do an interview, cohost a few fun events, and even sample from the cook-off between half a dozen restaurants at the end.

I can still picture her improv routine in the car on the way here this morning.

She impersonated Guy Fieri, Anthony Bourdain, and Gordon Ramsay one after another, the nerves about being a foodie on TV starting to get to her.

"Welcome to Flavortown, fish man!"

"I'm not afraid to look like an idiot, but this crawfish makes me smart."

"You think this is a crawfish! My gran could do better! And she's dead!"

Of course, that led to an explanation about the Food Network phase of her life, and how she unintentionally gained twenty pounds pretending to be a food critic. She said it without fear of judgment or self-critique, even joking about how Benji got jacked during that time to ensure he'd be able to spot her on a fall.

I smiled more in that twenty-minute car ride than in the entirety of my relationship with Caroline, and Brooke wasn't even trying.

She doesn't realize it, but she really is something special.

"She's great, isn't she?" the producer whispers to me as Brooke says the forty-fifth witty thing of the hour. I have to work to drag my eyes away from her huge smile and bright-green eyes, but I finally do to meet the producer's gaze directly.

"Oh yeah. Brooke Baker is definitely the real deal."

"So, if you don't mind my asking, how long have the two of you been dating?"

"Dating?" I ask dumbly, not understanding the question. Though, if I'm completely honest, I'm a little distracted watching Brooke too. Just because this woman has decided to have a conversation with me doesn't mean I'm ready and willing to miss anything Brooke might say in the interview.

"Oh, I'm sorry," she apologizes with a frown. "Are you married? None of her info said she was married, but that could be my mistake."

I have to clear my throat as I laugh, glancing between Brooke and the female producer until my brain can process exactly what she's saying. And after it manages that, it screams under the pressure of figuring out the right way to phrase my denial so it doesn't sound offensive or defensive or any of the -fensives, really.

"Oh, okay. No. Sorry. I was a little slow to understand." I chuckle with what I think sounds like ease. "I'm Brooke's editor. I know it's a little unorthodox for me to be tagging along, but we're working on a pretty tight deadline with her next book to be published."

Her eyes widen, and her glance mirrors the one I just performed moments ago. Back and forth, back and forth, from Brooke to me and back again until she looks like a bobblehead in an earthquake. "You…the two of you aren't an item?" she asks again, her voice damn near disbelieving.

I shake my head while maintaining a smile. *What isn't she understanding here?* I really don't want to have to go *Fight Club* to convince a stranger that we're not together, but if we keep talking about it much longer and my chest gets any tighter, I just might have to.

"No, we're not dating. Just professionally linked." I shrug. "And friendly, I suppose. She's a lot of fun."

The woman nods a few more times and then walks away, but not without me hearing her talking under her breath as she does. "Man, I want friends who look at me like that."

Friends who look at her like what? How am I looking at Brooke?

I turn back to the stage in the middle of the festival, where Brooke is sitting with the two hosts and gabbing back and forth about the Shadow Brothers and what inspired her to write them. I first heard this story in Chicago when they asked her about it, but I have to admit, it's just as enthralling the second time.

"This is a little scary to admit so publicly, but the Shadow Brothers were my young imagination spicing up death. I've dealt with vasovagal syncope for my whole life, and while it's not actually considered a life-threatening condition, for a young girl, it felt like one. When I wondered what an afterlife might look like—or what I wanted it to look like, rather—I always imagined a group of dreamy ghost men to protect and entertain me."

It takes almost fifteen full seconds of listening to Brooke talk and getting lost in her words to realize what the producer was talking about. How am I looking at Brooke? I have no way to describe it other than *loudly*.

My face is like a fucking spotlight. I can feel it from the pressure in my cheeks to the strain at the corners of my eyes—I'm smiling like the Joker on uppers, and I'm doing it all while staring directly at a woman I'm in no way involved with.

Lord help me.

I spin away quickly like that'll somehow change anything and scrub a hand over my face. Am I...am I developing a literal *crush* on Brooke Baker?

I know I've always thought she was cute and funny, and she's obviously a brilliant writer, and my dick is kind of becoming obsessed with her lately, but that's all just...just...

Goddamn. *I'm totally fucking crushing on Brooke Baker!*

And not the crush of an adult man with mature feelings and a plan of attack, but that of a high schooler—with hormones and impulsiveness and dick-ruled decisions taking an unjustified lead.

Holy shit, I'm so stupid!

This is the woman whose novel I've put my ass and career on the line for. This is the woman with whom maintaining a professional relationship is of paramount importance. This is the woman it would be monumentally stupid to get emotionally involved with because if something happened and we became *unemotionally* involved, it would ruin everything that I've ever worked toward in my whole thirty-three years.

But what if it worked out?

No. No. God, Chase, that is such stupid thinking that you cannot do. Lying to ourself about the gravity of the complications is only going to get our ass roasted like a rotisserie chicken at KFC. Do we understand us? DO WE?

Fuck. It's never a good sign when you start arguing with yourself.

I turn back at the sound of Brooke's full-blown cackle laugh, and I catch the line of her throat extending as she throws her head back. I swallow hard to distract myself from the fact that I can't look away—that I am *not* looking away, despite a colossal amount of mental effort.

The male host reaches out to pat Brooke's arm through his chuckle, and my vision tunnels on the contact. My veins heat and my skin tingles, and holy fucking hot wheels on a plastic track, I'm *jealous*. Just like I was in the car on the way to Chicago, just like I am whenever another man looks in Brooke's general vicinity, I'm realizing.

Oh man, Chase. You've really done it now.

Benji shifts back and forth in front of the interview table, his keen canine eyes pointed directly at me. It seems unlikely that he'd be able to sense my heart rate from way the hell over there, but he's sure acting like he can.

I turn and walk away, pulling my phone out of my pocket and putting it to my ear.

"Hello?" I say to the nonexistent caller. "Of course," I say with a fake chuckle that embarrasses me to my very core. "I always have a minute for you."

Oh my God. This really is a new low point. And frankly, a little unbecoming of how emotionally mature I consider myself to be.

I churn and burn with my legs, searching for a closet or a room or, I don't know, a hole to crawl into so I can quit pretending to be on this fake phone call and do some deep-breathing exercises while I come to terms with my newfound discovery.

When I finally find a quiet alley to duck into, I drop my phone back into my pocket, lean against the brick wall, and let my head fall back with a smack. It hurts a little, but the reality check of some physical pain seems entirely necessary right now.

How on earth did I let myself get here? Openly crushing on Brooke to the point that random strangers are making note of it? Getting jealous of an innocent touch from some schloppy news anchor? Actually walking away on a fake phone call so I don't have to explain the beet-red color of my cheeks to anyone in passing?

Almost kissing her the other night after you got out of the shower...

Truth is, if it hadn't been for the loud distraction outside the motor home,

I know I would've kissed Brooke. I would've kissed her, and I have no idea how far I would've let that kiss go.

Oh, you know how far you would've let it go, but you don't want to accept it.

I'm really on the cusp here of fucking things up for myself. *A lot, a lot of things.* I left Nashville behind with a clear mind and no women to speak of. I had goals—big ones—and my priorities were clear. I was ready and willing to put in the hours and the sweat equity and the creativity, but all of a sudden, I find myself on a three-week tour with one of my authors, driving the fucking motor home from city to city?

It sounds nuts. And at this particular moment, I can't seem to convince myself that it really was the book that drove me—and not some insane need to be dangerously close to Brooke Baker for an extended period of time.

Like, did I know I was crushing and wasn't willing to admit it? Or is this something new? Forced by the proximity and intimacy of living with someone for three weeks?

I really, really wish I knew.

But even more than that, I wish I could come up with a plan for how to stop it.

My phone buzzes in my hand—for real, this time—and I pick it up to look at the screen. An ill-timed message from Mo sits front and center.

Mo: BRO. WTF. I'm DYING here. It's been a week since you've texted me back or answered my calls! You've got to tell me something, Chase! Are you avoiding me on purpose, or are you just too busy falling in love with Brooke Baker?

The real answer? Both. And oh baby, does the truth hurt.

Because if I don't want to ruin literally everything, this cannot and will not happen. I can't let it.

Brooke Baker is my author and nothing more. And that is fucking that.

Chapter
Thirty-Two

Brooke

Lights dance through the windshield as Chase navigates the motor home through the outskirts of New Orleans on our way to San Antonio. It's about an eight-and-a-half-hour drive, and thanks to some networking—aka an invitation to a late lunch and wine bar—with the people from *Wake Up, New Orleans,* we didn't get packed up and on the road until about forty-five minutes ago.

And every minute has been filled with the soft sounds of the radio and zero conversation.

Six in the evening is not an ideal start to a long drive, so I can understand why Chase has seemed a little quiet. But still, I hate to be the kind of pain in the ass that turns a wholly good-natured man into a grump.

I thought about suggesting that we just wait until the morning to get on the road, but I didn't want it to seem like I was questioning his system. He's managed to get us everywhere we've needed to be on his own just fine, and he hardly needs me trying to tell him how to do it now.

I make my way to the front and slide into the passenger seat beside him with a groan. Benji lies down right behind my captain's chair and tucks his head into the crook of his crossed paws.

Chase doesn't look away from the road, and I feel the crease of a frown settle into the thin skin between my eyebrows. Not getting a smile stings, and even I know that's a bit ridiculous.

Damn, you're not even halfway into this tour with the guy and you've already become a glutton for his attention.

Instead of getting discouraged, I throw myself on my sword of apology. "I'm really sorry we got held up today. I can only imagine the last thing you feel like doing right now is driving across a state and a half, or however far it is to San Antonio."

"That's all right," he says, still staring at the road intently. "I arranged to stop at a campground about halfway, so we can take a break in a few hours."

"Ah, that's the overachiever I'm beginning to know and love," I say playfully, reaching out to give him a small shove in the shoulder.

The corner of his mouth curves up, but just barely, and he regrips his hands on the steering wheel without looking at me again.

I look down at Benji, who's picked up his head and is staring at Chase too.

Evidently, I'm not just imagining it. The vibe has considerably chilled from this morning, and I'm not sure why.

Shrugging at my canine pal, I stand up from the seat and offer to take my leave.

"I think I'll go back in the bedroom and do some work, maybe call my sister, if that's okay with you. I don't want to leave you hanging up here by yourself."

Unfortunately, it helps, which is just about the last thing I want.

"That's okay. It's probably a good idea if you get a little work done on the book, and I'll be able to concentrate on the road since it's dark."

I nod. Okay, then. To the bedroom, it is, I suppose.

After one more longing look at the uncharacteristically stern side of Chase's face, Benji and I retreat to the rear of the bus, step into the bedroom, and close the door. Benji hops up onto the black comforter and lies down while I lean my back into the door and let my head hit the surface with a thud.

I don't know what's going on, but whatever it is, I really don't like it. I'm a people pleaser base case, and when it comes to Chase Dawson, I'm apparently a whore for affirmation.

I need something to cheer me up, and I need it stat. And given the limitations of my motor home bedroom confines, calling a free-from-parental-prison-and-staying-at-my-place-in-NYC Sammy is the best medicine I can think of.

The last I spoke with her was via text message a few days ago, when she was letting me know she and the boys had made it to my apartment without any issues.

Climbing onto the bed next to Benji, I grab my phone off the nightstand and dial the only contact I ever use with any regularity.

It rings three times before my sister answers with a breathy, happy voice I haven't heard in ages.

"Hi!" she practically shouts, and the sound of her giddy claps in the background makes me grin. "I'm so excited to hear from you, B! I wasn't sure if you'd have the freedom or time to call a lot while you're on the tour."

"Oh yeah," I reply. "People are whistling and catcalling for my attention from sunup to sundown."

Sammy laughs, and I cling to keeping the conversation about her as a means for my escape from the crappy way I'm feeling about how things with Chase have been for the last few hours.

"How's New York going? Are you settling in okay?"

"Are you kidding? I haven't had to listen to Dad talk about shitting in days, Brooke. I'm doing fucking fabulous."

I can't help but laugh. "And the boys are doing well?"

"We haven't had to call the fire department and your valuables are all intact, if that's what you're asking."

"It's not." A small grin appears on my lips. Because this, right here, is exactly what I needed. "I was really just curious about how the boys were doing in a big city. But, I will admit, I'm glad they haven't torched anything yet."

"I think they really like it. I don't know how long it'll last, but there's always something going on, so even just people-watching out the window has been more entertaining for them than Ohio," she updates, and I can hear the huge smile in her voice. "I'm feeling really good, Brookie. The best in I don't know how long."

"Oh, Sam. I'm so glad."

"Me too, sis. Me too. This might sound crazy, but I'm thinking…about moving out here when you get back. You know, finding my own place."

"Really?" I yell excitedly. Sammy is the only family I would want that close—that I would work to make it happen.

"Yeah. I mean, I know it's really expensive here, and I know it's not always going to be easy raising kids in the city like this. But I was talking to Chase's sister, Mo—who's awesome, by the way—and she said that she and Vinny could set me up with a job at their restaurant until I got on my feet. They also know some people who would be willing to sublet great places while they're away summering."

I snort. "*Summering?*"

"I know!" she hoots. "I told Mo I didn't think I'd be able to afford a place owned by people who 'summer,' but she assured me they'd give me a deal as long as she talked to them for me."

"That all sounds amazing, Sam. I'd be over-the-freaking-moon if you moved to New York."

"Honestly, I feel…invigorated. I haven't felt this good in a long time. I was actually starting to question if the divorce was a good idea while I was living at home with Mom and Dad, but I think I was just missing my independence, you know? Because I definitely wasn't missing Todd. The asshole."

"Well—" I start to respond, but my sister yelling at the top of her lungs stops my progress.

"Grant and Seth Brown!" Sammy shouts. "Get away from that stove right now. I told you it's hot!" I suck my lips into my mouth and wait as she gives my nephews hell. "I don't care! If you burn your fingerprints off on an open flame, Spider-Man's web building isn't going to matter all that much, I promise!"

I chuckle to myself, but Sammy doesn't even pause before switching gears right back to me. *Ah, the life of a mother.*

"How about you? How's the tour going?"

Well, *hell.* I am the last thing we should talk about right now. "Uh…it's fine."

"Fine?" she questions. "Just *fine?* Brookie, what's going on? You're on a tour for a Netflix show about *your* books, and you don't even sound thrilled. And trust me, I know it's not because you're getting negative attention. I was at your first stop and witnessed *all* those people waiting to see you. And I've been tracing your moves. Every article and social media post I've read and every interview I've managed to find on YouTube has been nothing but insanely positive."

"I am thrilled," I tell her, but I don't sound convincing. "It's just some things are…complicated. And hard to explain."

"Well, good news, sis, because those are my favorite things. Lay it on me."

I groan. "I don't know if I can, Sam."

"Sure, you can. Remember who my sons are. Nothing scares me."

"Okay. Well…" I scratch at the comforter anxiously and then move my hand to the top of Benji's soft head to give it a rub. "I've been having a really good time. Like, maybe the best time ever. Until today."

"What changed?"

"I… Oh God, this is embarrassing." I pause, grinding my teeth in consideration. *Am I really going to open this can of worms? Spill this pan of beans? Brew this kind of tea?*

"Come on, Brookie. I highly doubt anything can be as embarrassing as the time I shit my pants during the homecoming dance and had to leave my soiled underwear in the high school bathroom trash can. If I can live through that, you can live through telling me this."

Ughhh. I hate that she's right. Sharting your panties at a high school dance pretty much trumps anything else you can have happen to you.

"Fine." I sigh and drop my voice lower just to be sure the man driving this motor home can't hear me. "I…well… I have a huge crush on my editor Chase."

"Valid," she says without pause. "I've seen him. He is quite dreamy."

"Thank you for that." I blush, dropping my head into my hands. No one knows how to cut through the bullshit and make me smile like my sister.

Well, no one but her and, usually, *Chase.*

"Okay, so you've got a crush on your editor. People get crushes all the time, babe," she remarks. "So, what's the problem?"

The problem? Oh man. The weight of this feels like *a million and one* problems.

"Well…" I pause, take a deep breath, and try to find a way to explain this insane situation of mine. "We've been having a great time. Actually, once I got past the urge to faint every time I spoke to him, and we got used to being in each other's space, we've been having a *really* great time. I…think we even came close to kissing at one point the other night? We bumped into each other as I was going back to the bedroom and he was coming out of the bathroom, and we just kind of…froze. Like, right there in each other's arms, heavy breathing and all that. My boobs almost swelled their way into his throat. We only separated when we heard a loud noise outside the motor home, and even then, it felt like pulling magnets apart."

"Oooh, this is getting juicy-juice! I like it!"

"Don't get too excited," I huff. "Something has shifted, and today, he's barely said a word to me. I did my appearance in NOLA, and now we're driving to San Antonio. Well, *he's* driving, and I'm locked inside the bedroom trying not to turn into a lunatic, because I swear, he can't even look at me now. I don't know what I did or what happened or… I don't know. But I'm freaking out all over again, and to be honest, I'm sad. Like we had a fight or broke up or something. Which is completely batshit crazy pants because we were never anything, Sam!" I slap a palm to my face. "I don't have rhyme or reason to be any of these things."

274 | max monroe

"Oh horseshit, Brookie," she retorts. "Sure you do. Maybe you weren't an official couple, but you're allowed to mourn what you thought you had going on. Still, if he can't see how great you are, then fuck him. There will be plenty of fish knocking on your very successful door from now until the cows come home."

"Yeah, well, that's great and all, and I truly appreciate the solidarity and use of so many animals to express it, but it's a little more complicated than that."

"Why? Because you work on your books together?" she snaps directly into the phone. "No big deal. You focus on the work, plain and simple."

"Ha. Ha. Ha." I can barely keep myself from sounding hysterical as I laugh into the phone.

As expected, Sammy's completely lost. "What am I missing here?"

"Okay, well, see…" I pull the phone away from my ear, lift a pillow to my mouth, and let out an unholy smothered scream into the foamy material. When I put the phone back to my ear, my voice is hoarse from it. "I can't believe I'm going to admit this, but…I kind of wrote a book about him."

She's silent.

"And me."

Nothing.

"And what we'd be like together, as a couple, sexually and such."

I close my eyes and take a deep breath before dropping the biggest bomb of all.

"And well, when I was supposed to be turning in *Garden of Forever*, I kind of, accidentally, attached the wrong file to the email and sent him the book about us, which, incidentally, he loved and fought for with the publishing house, and now that book is the next big thing in my contract. And we're working on it. Together. Now. On this trip."

"Wow."

"I know!" I whisper-scream, banging my head back into the pillow.

"Okay, here's what we're going to do," Sammy says authoritatively, making me sit up straight and listen. "First, you're going to take ten deep breaths until you don't feel like screaming anymore."

I nod. "Okay."

"Then, you're going to make sure the door to your bedroom is locked and take out your computer."

I do both quickly, clinging to her confident instructions like a lifeline. "Okay, what's next?"

"Now, you're going to email me the manuscript so I can read it."

"Sammy!" I shout, annoyed. "Be serious! I'm in the middle of a crisis."

"I am serious, Brooke! I need to know what we're dealing with here. What kind of damage are we talking? I can't make an assessment without the facts. Now, send me the file. And hey, make sure it's the right one."

I roll my eyes as that sound from TikTok plays in my head. *It's a good joke, a great joke even.*

"Sammy."

"Send it, B," she demands. "I've got my email pulled up on my phone, and I'm waiting."

Reluctantly, I scan through my files until I find the right one and attach it to an email addressed to her. Before I can overthink it, I hit send. She shrieks in delight when she receives it.

"I'll be expedient with my research, I promise."

I shake my head. "I don't know if I should be thanking you or mad at you right now."

"You should be loving the hell out of me because I certainly love the hell out of you, and it's the whole reason I want and need to read this manuscript."

"Yeah. Yeah."

"Now, I want you to go splash your face with cold water, brush your teeth, and go to bed, okay? Get some rest and wake up in the morning on a new day."

"That easy, huh?"

"For now? It's the best we can do, kid."

I nod. For now, hoping that Chase is just having a bad day and will be back to his normal teasing self in the morning is the best I can do.

And it really, really sucks. Because whether we were anything romantic or not, we were definitely having fun—fun I haven't had with a real, live human in a long time.

I miss my friend.

Chapter
Thirty-Three

Thursday, May 25th

Chase

Avoiding Brooke for the last eighteen hours has been the longest seventy-two hours of my life. I know that doesn't make logical sense, but if you felt what I feel, you'd get it. Uneasiness has been heavy in my chest the whole time, and now, I'm even starting to feel nauseated by it.

A terrifying prospect, but true.

My head is foggy and my stomach is churning, and if this is how I have to spend the rest of the trip by avoiding her and preserving the security of my job, I think I'd rather have to start my entire career over.

Tossing the manuscript onto the table of the dining booth, I scoot out and shove to standing, momentarily swaying on my feet with a little bit of dizziness. I *have* been working for a while now, trying to move my notes from paper to digital so they'll be easier for Brooke to follow when she's making any technical changes. I also haven't eaten, but I'm not usually impacted by high stress and low calorie intake this much.

As much as I shouldn't, I follow this routine a lot, fueling myself with empty caffeine rather than any nutritious or useful calories in the mornings so I can get started on my work first thing.

This morning, though, with all the raging thoughts in my head about Brooke and the crack-of-dawn drive I had to finish to get us to San Antonio, is proving to be too much. I have to do something about it before I'm the one passed out on the floor—without the excuse of vasovagal syncope.

I have to fix things, and I have to do it now. Detrimental or not, I have to find a way back to the ease and humor I've established with Brooke and let this whole headcase freak-out about *falling in love* or something equally ridiculous go. Between the producer's assumptions and Mo's teasing text message, I got thinking too hard about a simple crush on a truly great woman.

So what if I like her? That doesn't mean I have to act on it. I'm a grown man, for shit's sake. I can lean into the fun of her company without letting it go too far. I've got willpower, right? These are the situations that we have it for.

Determined to meet my discomfort head on by booting it in the face, I take out my phone and send a quick message to answer Mo's text from yesterday.

Me: Sorry, we've been pretty busy! The tour is going great, and Brooke's impressing people all over the place. So far, I've yet to find a reader more obsessed with her books than you.

I don't bother to clarify that the people she's impressing include me.

Me: And I bet you can find the Wake Up, New Orleans show from yesterday online if you look hard enough.

She responds in thirty seconds flat.

Mo: OMGGGGGGGod, I can't believe you're finally texting me back! I saw the show! I even saw you in one of the shots when the camera panned!

Danger! Danger! Warnings flash in my mind about the perilous road the rest of these messages could travel, and I shove my phone back into my pocket without remorse, even as it buzzes over and over again.

The last thing I need is to read something from Mo that sends me back into a Brooke-ignoring tailspin. I haven't even fixed the damage from the first time yet.

I swipe a hand at my sweat-beaded forehead and set out to find Brooke. The only good part about a motor home is that there aren't many places to look when the object you're trying to detect is a full-sized human.

The bathroom door is open but the bedroom door closed, so I start there at the back of the bus with a soft knock on the wood. "Brooke?" I call through the somewhat-thin barrier, feeling like the knock isn't efficient enough.

There's a light bark from Benji, followed by the rustling sound of bedding, and then a door-muted murmur from Brooke. "One second!"

I back away from the door, fully out of the tiny hallway and into the living room space beside the dining booth to give her some room. The space between the end of the bed and the door is already tight when you swing it open, and my looming presence in the hall would only make it worse.

It might also cause a redo of the other night... My mind tries to remind me about the last time Brooke and I were confined too closely—when I had just gotten out of the shower—but I squash that fucker like a bug.

When she finally emerges, she's wearing an oversized sweatshirt, leggings, and the puffy skin of someone in distress. I hate it so much—especially the thought that I might have caused it—that I start rapidly spewing words.

"Hey, Brooke. Good morning. Do you think we could talk for just a minute?"

Her eyebrows lift, but after a moment of consideration, she nods. I extend an arm in offering toward the booth, and she walks forward with her eyes tucked closely to the floor.

I miss them instantly.

She takes a seat, and I go straight to the coffeepot, grab a mug out of the cabinet above it, and pour her a heavy cup.

I add her preferred amounts of cream and sugar, and then set it on the table in front of her before sliding into the side across from her.

She lifts the mug to take a sip, and I dive right into clearing my conscience.

"I want to start by apologizing for...well, the last day or so. I know I've been acting a little weird, and I don't want you to think it has anything to do with you."

Like it would have anything to do with anyone else, considering you've been fused together as a twosome on a three-week tour...

"I think the combination of stress and sleep loss and all the driving was getting to me."

Her face is one of relief, and oddly enough, that makes me feel worse. Because that means I was taking it out on her unjustly, and she's been feeling noticeably ostracized this whole time—which is not the ideal feeling I want for someone I care about.

"Are you feeling okay now?" she asks then, her brow crinkling sweetly with concern. Her green eyes flit over my face several times before adding, "No offense, but you don't really look like you're feeling well."

"I've definitely felt better." I shrug. "I think I just need to go get some breakfast if you're up for it. Maybe on the River Walk?"

Her ears perk up, and as a result, so do Benji's. They really are a cute duo, and Benji really is one of the best good boys. He takes care of Brooke so wholesomely, and he always knows when to keep to himself if he's not needed in that capacity.

"I'll take the foaming at the mouth as a sign that your answer is yes," I tease and she giggles. *Fuck, I've missed that sound.*

"Am I that obvious?"

"It's safe to say we've been hanging out enough now that I'm starting to understand your facial cues."

"And this one was…what?" she asks with an amused lift of her brow. "Drooling onto my chin?"

I laugh, and the tightness in my chest unclenches its fist. My head is still dizzy as fuck, but man, I'm already feeling so much better.

"I think I might have also seen your tail wag."

Benji barks at that, thinking I've confused the two of them, and Brooke's smile grows to three times its original size.

"I got your email with some of the changes you made last night, by the way," I update her. "I'll take a look at them later today."

Brooke nods but also looks away to focus on Benji as she scratches his head from his position beside the booth.

"I've also spent this morning moving my notes to the doc digitally for you. I know that's a lot easier to follow, but I can't seem to get away from the old habit of working with pen to paper first."

"I get it," Brooke replies, looking up from Benji to me again. Her mouth is curved in an adorable smirk.

"You do?"

"Oh yeah. I get it good. First the mug, and now this? Even Chase Dawson is a weirdo like the rest of us."

I snort. "Gee, thanks."

"Don't worry about it. It means you're human. Before this, I wasn't so sure." She winks, smiles, and stands up from the booth. "Now, how about we go get our River Walk on and get you some breakfast?"

My answer is easy. "Count me in."

Brooke gets ready faster than any woman I've ever met—especially when something she wants to do is involved.

I swear, hardly five minutes passed between her downing the mug of coffee I gave her, jumping out of the booth, and flitting between the bedroom and bathroom as she got ready. She even had an Uber called and a map of the River Walk pulled up on her phone in the two minutes after that.

And only now, after five hours of walking the cobblestone paths, periodically stopping at artisan booths and restaurants for a quick treat, and purchasing and donning a new custom-made pair of sandals, is she starting to slow down.

I, on the other hand, am a little worse for the wear. Don't get me wrong. Mentally, I'm soaring. Freeing myself from whatever stupid distance I thought I needed from Brooke was one hundred percent the right move for my mental health.

But my physical health, by comparison, doesn't feel like it's doing so hot.

I haven't felt this bad in years, since I had the stomach flu during my first year at my Nashville publishing house, Brentwood Books. I'm clammy and weakening by the minute.

Brooke's asked about me several times, so I know I must look rough, but I haven't had the heart to cut her day short while she's having such a good time. I figure I'm either going to feel bad here or in the motor home, and I don't see all that much of a difference.

At least, I didn't until now.

My head is spinning and my heart is racing, and I feel like I can't keep standing much longer without falling to the ground. I can see the hazy outline of a bench up ahead, and I stumble my way over to it and settle my ass into the seat and put my head between my legs. I sway from one side to the other, trying to keep myself from falling forward onto the cobblestone.

Brooke's face is in mine quickly, her body crooked and kneeling to get low enough.

"Oh my God, Chase. Are you okay?"

I shake my head to clear it, but the fogginess won't dissipate. I do my best to reassure Brooke through the confusion. I don't want to scare her. "I…yeah. I think I'm all right. I just…need to sit here for a minute."

I feel a paw hit my back and Benji's nose as he licks at my cheek. I try to push him away without offending him too much, but Brooke grabs my elbow to stop me.

"Benji is alerting on you. Your blood pressure must be really low. Keep your head between your knees while I go get you a soda."

I try to laugh. "That's one I've never heard before."

"Just stay there!" she yells as she jogs away to somewhere unknown, leaving Benji to sit and monitor me.

I don't know how much time passes between that moment and the next because I'm busy trying to keep myself from collapsing onto the unwelcoming stone ground, but when she comes back, I can feel the cold, condensated surface of the soda as she presses it into the skin of my palm.

"I know you're struggling right now, but drink this if you can. The hit of sugar will really help."

"I'm not sure what happened. I'm just really not feeling good."

She pushes a hand to my forehead that feels like ice, and I lean into the feeling subconsciously. "That feels really good."

"I think you have a fever. You feel pretty hot to the touch."

"Aw, thanks," I say pathetically, the lameness of my joke practically written in the stars.

"Just lie down for a little bit." Brooke's hands move to my biceps, and then the soda leaves my hand as she eases me down until I'm lying on the bench. It feels a little better, but I'm definitely not firing on all cylinders yet.

Brooke almost looks excited when I glance up at her through the fogginess. "What?"

"I'm sorry, really. I *know* this isn't an exciting event. It's just…I've never been the one not passing out before. It's a *whole* different experience."

"Pffft," is all I manage when she leans forward and lays her head on my chest with a cackle.

"I know, I'm sorry, it's terrible. My therapist calls them intrusive thoughts for a reason, I guess, huh?"

"You're so comfortingly real, Brooke. And if I weren't still fading in and out of consciousness, I'd probably kiss you right now."

I'm just unaware enough not to freak out at saying that, and Brooke's just busy enough taking care of me not to react.

Carefully, she puts the soda to my lips and gives me a few sips while I try to make heads or tails of anything around me. I'm woozy and uneasy, and I really think I need to lie down somewhere that isn't a bench in the middle of San Antonio.

"Do…do you think you can help me get back to the motor home?" I ask weakly as I push myself back to sitting. "I can't be sure, but I have a sneaking suspicion I might be sick."

Brooke laughs so hard that if I had any control over myself at all, I swear I'd snap out of it. It's that good of a sound.

But I don't, and the best I can do is cooperate as Brooke arranges my arm over her shoulder and shoves to standing for the both of us. I'm not great on my feet, but with a grit of my teeth, I make a promise to myself not to take Brooke down with me.

Just get to the motor home. Just get to the motor home. It's the only thing my mind can focus on.

I have no idea how long we walk or where we're going. I can barely keep my head up, and my eyes can't focus on anything but my feet.

Plus, I'm certain the heat in Texas is only adding to my delirious state.

Some kind of black SUV is waiting by the time we get to the entrance or exit or whatever it is, and just about the last thing I remember is falling into the back seat after Brooke tells me it's our Uber.

Only one thought haunts me.

Man, I hope I don't puke all over her new shoes.

Chapter
Thirty-Four

Friday, May 26th

Brooke

Yesterday, Chase told me he wanted to kiss me.

Well, *sort of.*

He was halfway unconscious and coming down with some kind of virus, but he *did* say it, and my ears—they can't unhear it.

But for the last sixteen hours, he's been mostly sleeping, and I've been like a mom with a newborn for fifteen hours and fifty-nine minutes of them.

Checking his chest for breathing movements, touching his clammy forehead nine hundred times to see if he's broken his fever, and putting a cool washcloth on his neck after he got back from a puking session in the bathroom are just a few of the things I've been busy with since we got back from the River Walk last night.

I am Mary Poppins, and he is my charge.

I don't think Ms. Poppins had these scandalous thoughts, though, so that's definitely a different dimension. And I'm not even addressing the fact that I didn't give a shit about germs and might have...sort of...pressed my lips to his—*just barely I swear!*—after I got him settled in bed last night *or* that I spent twenty minutes talking myself out of masturbating when I got situated on the pullout couch.

Nope. It's a new day, and I'm focusing on the now.

The very real now where Chase is still asleep in what I would consider *my* bed. I don't technically own it, but I *have* slept in it for the last week and a half, so if it fits, it sits and all that.

He had a rough night, but it's been several hours since he had to sprint to the bathroom, and I'm certain he broke his fever at around one this morning.

How would I know that? Because I was checking his forehead every five minutes like a psychopath.

I give Chase a gentle shake, my body leaned over his and casting him in shadow as I try to let him know that I'm about to head out for my TV appearance here in San Antonio. I know he needs the rest, but I don't want him to wake up and panic that I'm gone either.

Not that he would…but hell, I don't know. I don't even know what direction *up* is at this point, so I only have my own feelings to guide me. And if I were in his shoes and woke up to an empty motor home, I'd be calling the National Guard, the FBI, and at least seven local police agencies.

He doesn't stir after my first two attempts, and his face looks so at rest, so peaceful, that I decide waking him isn't worth it. He's likely more rational than I am and won't try to contact the president if he wakes up to a vacant motor home. And on the off chance that he's not, I'll write him a note.

But there's an unhinged part of me that can't stop staring at his thick, perfect black hair and fantasizing about running my fingers through it.

Don't do it, Brooke. Don't do it.

My fingers wiggle against the tingling urge, and I have to push myself back by a foot to get my head to clear.

Still, from this angle, the hair looks even better, and before I know what I'm doing, I'm launching forward and softly running just one solitary hand through his midnight locks.

"Ahhh," I moan involuntarily, scaring myself when my special place sends a zing all the way up my spine and down again—*just from running a hand in his hair.*

"Lord forgive me," I whisper, jumping away from the sleeping, sexy man I should *not* be touching, and spinning my body in a frantic circle. I even have to bite my lip to stop myself from screaming over my own temporary insanity.

Faster than I've probably ever moved in my life, I bolt out of the bedroom, grab my purse from the counter, and dash out the door and down the metal stairs.

Benji can barely keep up with me. Thankfully, I was smart enough to put his safety vest and leash on before I decided to get handsy with my patient in the bedroom and make myself freak the hell out.

And while I did ensure the door was latched with a quick hip check, I forgot to write a note. But that's why God—or whoever—invented the iPhone, so I can text him instead.

The black town car is already there, and the driver standing at the door is wearing one of those fancy driver hats and a suit and everything.

Suddenly, it's as if I'm in the movie *Pretty Woman*, and I'm the gussied-up prostitute.

I know my life probably seems fancy to some people, but on a day-to-day basis, it is the exact opposite. I am usually in stained pajamas and barely shower and do thankfully remember to brush my teeth, but contact with real people doing swanky things like driving me to a morning show to talk about my upcoming TV series is not the regular.

I am so out of place, it's not even funny.

I don't know how to behave, other than to be so painfully nice it's concerning. Like, if my driver runs over a pedestrian on the way to this thing, I will assume all responsibility and turn myself in to the police for premeditated manslaughter, regardless of my innocence.

I do not know to handle myself as a mature adult, and I cannot fathom how anyone else knows either. Is there a secret school I don't know about? Private lessons like I would do with a personal trainer for fitness?

I mean, I don't do sessions with a personal trainer either—the most exercise

I get is during a deadline crunch when I can barely see my hands as they furiously type—but I can at least visualize it in that context, you know?

"Good morning," I say in greeting as the driver opens the door for me and steps to the side. I smile and he smiles back, and I mentally attach a gold star sticker to my Normal-Interactions-with-People chart for the day.

Once I've safely tucked my legs inside and Benji is settled beside me, the driver shuts the door, rounds the car, climbs into the driver's seat, and fires up the engine.

I give Benji a few pets to the head that we both know are more for my benefit than his own and settle into the cushy leather to scroll my phone.

I won't do anything productive—even though I know I should—but distracting myself with social media seems like a good idea on a morning when my two main mental streams are being impulsively pervy toward my editor and turning myself in to prison for a motor vehicle accident that hasn't happened yet.

I know. I'm not mentally well. But my whole career enables and encourages the rampant presence of voices in my head, so I'm not sure that expecting anything different is reasonable.

I move from TikTok to Facebook and scroll into the NYC Doggie group, looking once again for a lead on the border collie.

I don't have much faith at this point, so my scroll is halfhearted at best, but when a new comment from someone makes it from my eyes to my brain, I gasp aloud.

Holy, holy shit!

I read the comment again, slowly this time, so I can confirm if I'm losing my mind or not.

Ella Rose: I found her! Her dad lives on the Upper East Side and takes her on walks in the park every Sunday because it's the only day he has off from work. But today, he took a personal day, and he was there! I think I scared him when I went up to him, but once I explained the situation, he agreed to give me his number so you guys can get in contact! DM me, BrookieCookie, and I'll send you the digits! Just remember that you HAVE to update us on what happens when your doggo sees her again!

It takes everything in me to keep my vitals in check so that Benji doesn't know something is up, but I do it because I have to. I can't get his hopes up before I know he's going to see her again for sure, and I can't do that until I've made actual contact with the owner.

I force air in through my nose and out through my mouth and faux casually click the commenter's username to DM her.

From as far as I can see out of my periphery, Benji's eyes are facing forward, and he's none the wiser.

My fingers shake slightly as I type out a message in ninety percent capital letters and hit send. Since I don't expect a response right away and I'm certainly not capable of handling any more emotional roller coasters before I go on TV this morning, I lock the screen of my phone and tuck it in my purse before sitting back into the seat.

Man, what a wild twenty-four hours this has been, I think with a shake of my head.

And while I'd love to just sit here and daydream about Benji seeing his border collie crush again—or your *crush confessing his undying love for you and kissing you like his life depends on it*—I know I have to focus.

Next stop, *Good Day, San Antonio!* with Debbie Digger.

Chapter
Thirty-Five

Chase

My head pounds and my throat is scratchy as I sit up and automatically grab at my chest. It feels like I had reflux all night, and my eyes are sore from what must have been a gargantuan headache.

I don't know much of what happened past the bench on the River Walk, but I imagine I had to at least walk under my own power because two miles is a long way for someone Brooke's size to drag me.

Still, I don't really remember anything.

Thankfully, for as much as my body is dragging, I *do* feel considerably better. Whatever knocked me on my ass appears to have made its exit, and I'm willing to wager that a shower would go a long way in these circumstances.

But first, I need to find a bottle of water because my mouth is drier than the pussy of a woman who's been married to a narcissist for twenty-five years.

I shove to standing, and it's only then that I realize I'm not on the couch— I'm in the bed. *Brooke's bed.* In the back of the camper. God, now that I'm paying attention…it smells like her.

Fuck. Did she sleep on the couch last night? Or did she sleep with me?

I search my memories for clues and can vaguely recall her telling me good-night and leaving the bedroom. Which is good. No matter how grand the idea might sound to the irrational side of me that *really* likes Brooke, there's no way she should've been sleeping in the same bed with me in the condition I was in.

If anything, she should've donned a hazmat suit and turned this bedroom into an isolated infirmary.

I stumble out into the hallway and over to the refrigerator first, grabbing a bottle of water and swigging the whole thing down in six or seven gulps. My throat feels better instantly, and my eyes start to clear too.

I'm always amazed the destruction that dehydration can cause to the human body and how the simple act of hydration can spur what feels like a miraculous change. *Like, maybe if I read that book by Ann Rule about Ted Bundy, I'd find out he wasn't really meant to be a serial killer at all. Maybe he was just really dehydrated and not good at keeping up with his water intake.*

The camper is quiet save the sounds of my gulping, and I start to worry for Brooke's whereabouts.

"Brooke, are you here?" I call stupidly, smacking myself in the forehead just after I do. If she's not been promptly found already, she's probably not going to pop out at the sound of my voice. This place is two hundred square feet, tops.

Instead of devolving into mania at the absence of her, I try really hard to make my brain do the thing it was designed to do again—think.

It takes some concentration, but the clock on the microwave tells me the time and a little hard analysis confirms that her schedule would put her at her appearance in downtown San Antonio. Honestly, she's probably wrapping it up by now, if she's not done already.

I start searching for my phone and eventually find it on the nightstand in the bedroom—along with all the other normal contents of my pockets—and I pick it up to find two texts from Brooke that came in about four hours ago.

Brooke: You looked like you were finally resting this morning, so I left you to it. I'm doing the whole famous girl thing, you know, but I'll see you—a commoner—when I get back.

Brooke: But text or call if you need anything. I mean it! If I find out you needed something but didn't call me, I'll force you to listen to forty-eight hours of

Dolly Parton during our next long drive. No breaks. Just you, me, and Dolly 9 to 5'in the whole way.

She never ceases to make me laugh. Even last night, when I felt like I was dying, I have the vaguest memory of her hitting joke after joke and making me smile through the pain and nausea.

You also remember her giving you a soft kiss on the lips as she was tucking you in to her bed…

That insane thought pulls me up short. I wasn't exactly lucid last night, so I have a feeling the whole kiss thing was a fever dream.

I mean, there's no way that could've happened, right?

Fuck, I don't know. I scrub at my face and refocus on getting myself back to one hundred percent. I don't need to think about any kind of kisses with Brooke before I've had a nice shower and a brush of my teeth, at the very least. I'm nasty from the fever sweat, and I can taste just the tinge of vomit in my mouth, which kind of makes me want to yack all over again.

I can't remember if I actually got sick last night, but I hope to God I didn't put my star author in the position to clean it up for me.

That's not exactly the kind of talent coddling Jonah is about at Longstrand Publishing. Now, me cleaning up an author's vomit? He'd be all for.

In fact, I'm pretty sure Frank Bowman tells a story about having done it before.

Quickly, I gather some clean clothes from my bag in one of the kitchen cabinets and head for the shower. As soon as Brooke gets back, it'll be time to drive.

Destination this time: Viva Las Vegas.

Something tells me I'd better hold on to my hat for what's to come in Sin City.

Chapter
Thirty-Six

Brooke

My interview with *Good Day, San Antonio!* went swimmingly.

I faked my way through being a professional, capable woman who can speak in full sentences and didn't make a single thing awkward for Debbie Digger, the host.

Which, I can't deny, with a name like Debbie Digger, it's like she was born to be a news anchor. Or a porn star, if I'm being honest, but clearly, she's made her choice.

Still, though, once my spot on the show was done, I declined an invitation to join a few of the staff for an early lunch of wine and apps and headed straight for the motor home. The mere idea of drinking booze and eating potato skins while Chase is under the weather felt wrong on all accounts.

Truth be told, I'm still feeling like a mother hen when it comes to him.

I've checked my phone no fewer than six hundred times to see if he's texted me with an update on his status, but since I've received nothing in response, I'm on edge.

Even Benji can tell. His head has been in my lap, my own personal weighted anxiety blanket, for the whole drive back to the campground.

There's a large part of me that wonders if leaving Chase to go do that interview was the right thing. Sure, I'm technically contractually obligated to

Netflix to attend each of the appearances they have scheduled for me on this tour, but that all seems inconsequential when the thought of something bad happening to Chase is at the forefront of my mind.

The friendly man who drove me to the studio this morning pulls the car to a stop right outside the motor home. I barely give myself the time to thank him before hopping out of the back seat and jogging up the metal stairs with Benji in tow.

I push through the door like a member of a SWAT team heading in to case the place for hookers and blow, but I'm shocked to find Chase smiling at me from his spot in the dining booth.

His appearance is a freshly showered man, wearing clean clothes, and not at all the sickly person I was taking care of last night. There's color in his skin again, and his blue eyes are back to that brightness I've adored since the first moment I met him.

"Wow… You look great, Brooke." He greets me with words that threaten to make my knees buckle. But he doesn't give my body any time to melt into a puddle on the floor because he follows that up with, "How'd it go?"

"Uh, thanks, and…it went well," I respond, and refusing to let myself over-think his "you look great" comment, I swiftly divert to the priority at hand. "You're feeling better?"

"I definitely am," he answers, and I note zero misery in his voice. "Though, I'm wondering how bad I made the night for you and if I owe you an apology…?"

"No apology necessary." I shake my head. "You were a perfect patient. Listened to all of my instructions. Even made it to the bathroom successfully every time you had to throw up."

"So, I did puke." He groans. "Damn, I'm so sorry, Brooke."

"I refuse to accept that apology," I tell him with a point of my index finger. "For one, Benji here has an issue with trying to eat his own puke, so you're miles ahead of the worst I've seen. And two, you'd do the same for me."

"I definitely would. No cap." He winks, and I try not to think about how quickly he agreed to that statement. Or what it would be like to have him take care of me when I'm sick, you know, like a boyfriend would do…

Goodness knows, he's handled all of your passing-out episodes like Dr. McDreamy, so it's—

Focus, Brooke. I clear my throat and redirect myself to the most important thing—making sure Chase is doing okay.

"Have you eaten anything?" I ask, and his smile hits me square in the chest.

It's full and vibrant and not at all the weak, barely there grin he was able to give me when he was delirious with fever and nausea last night.

"Managed to get a bagel down and an insane amount of water, too. Even showered about an hour ago."

"So, you're, like, fully mended, then?"

"Yep. Completely recovered and ready to get us on the road," he says, and all of a sudden, it feels like relief and disappointment are battling each other for the top spot in my stomach.

Why on earth would I be disappointed that he's feeling better?

Because you're a sad panda that you don't get to keep taking care of him like some kind of crazy mother with Munchausen by proxy.

Holy hell. It's looney toons thoughts like that that make me wonder if I need to get my head checked pronto.

Uh…ya think?

"You feelin' okay?" Chase asks, his eyes observing my face a little too closely. "God, I really hope I didn't get you sick."

He's evidently mistaken my internal mental breakdown for something else.

"I'm good," I respond and push a smile to my lips. "And super-duper happy that you're feeling better." Sure, there's a part of me that wanted to keep playing nurse for the man of my dreams, but all in all, I'm relieved that Chase came out victorious on the other side of whatever was kicking his ass last night.

"Me too," he says with a self-deprecating chuckle. "You have no idea."

"So, it's settled, then? You're feeling good enough to drive us to Vegas as planned?"

He nods. "Yep."

"Are you sure? Because it's really no big deal if—"

"Brooke, I'm positive."

"So positive that you'd pinkie promise on it?"

He laughs, stands up from the booth, and does exactly what he did the last time I asked him to pinkie promise. He gently pushes my hand away and pulls me in for a hug. "I'm good to go, Brooke. And most of that is because of you. Thanks for taking care of me."

"You're welcome," I whisper, and I discreetly inhale the perfect scent that is a mixture of Chase's body wash and cologne and *him*.

God, he smells good.

When I start to fear that my deep inhales are a little too loud to be secret and my body is liking his warmth and embrace way too much, I gently disengage from the hug and put a few steps of distance between us.

"Alrighty roo, I guess it's time to get this show on the road." I fist-pump the air like a buffoon. "Viva Las Vegas, here we come!" I even step toward him to give him an abrupt high five that makes him chortle.

"Love the enthusiasm," he adds with a smile that makes my chest want to light itself on fire. "I'm just going to finish up with a few work emails, and then we'll head out."

"And I'm, uh…going to change into something less TV and more motor home."

That smile is still present on his face, and I decide it's best to give myself a breather from it. I head into the bedroom to change out of my fancy clothes and into something I can stand to survive in for the long, long drive from Texas to Nevada.

But once Benji and I are closed off in the bedroom and I've managed to toss on a pair of leggings and a comfy T-shirt, my phone pings with what feels like a billion text message notifications.

Brow furrowed, I pull it out of my purse and find that my sister is in the middle of bombarding my text inbox.

Sam: I just finished the book...BROOKE BAKER!!!

My asshole puckers. *Oh boy.*

Sam: HOW COULD YOU NOT HAVE WARNED ME? I pretty much forgot about my kids for the past forty-eight hours because I couldn't put it down! I kind of hate you.

Sam: But if River is you, I also think I might be weirdly attracted to you, which is a serious mindfuck because you're my goddamn sister!

Sam: I also think I understand the Immaculate Conception now because I think your book got me pregnant. Me and Mary, we're on a whole new wavelength!

Sam: Dad would be so proud. Of the Biblical understanding. Not the pregnancy.

Sam: But seriously, what the flocking flock, Brookie???? The book is so good. SO GOOD. I can't even begin to fully express my love for it.

Sam: Just...HOLY SHIT, B!!!!

Sam: If Chase is Clive and you're River, then slap me sideways and call me Sally because I am cheering this on. Like pom-poms and megaphones and shit.

Sam: I'm OVER THE TOP in love with Clive and River, so I guess that means I'm in love with you and Chase then, too.

This is so unlike my sister it's not even funny. Don't get me wrong, she's funny, but she's also the rational one out of the two of us.

But her feedback? It's bullshit—not sensible in the least. I mean, I'm thrilled to hear she loves the book, but I didn't send her the manuscript for a pleasure read!

This crap isn't helping me figure out how to solve my problems in the least, and her next texts proves she knows it.

Sam: GAH. This probably isn't what you were hoping to get from me reading the book, huh? You're probably looking at these messages right now and contemplating strangling me for making things more complicated for you. I'm really, truly sorry about that, Brookie. I am. But hell's bells, if you guys are the real-life Clive and River, then my jaded heart NEEDS you to be together.

Shit, Sam. What are you trying to do to me here?

Sam: And I think, maybe, you should tell Chase the truth about the book? Like, I don't know why, but I just have a gut feeling that's the way to go. I'm also hoping by you telling him that and confessing your true feelings, he's going to do exactly what Clive does when River lays it all out there. GAH. That scene. It was EVERYTHING.

Sam: Or maybe you shouldn't tell him? Fuck. I don't know. I just know I think you should go for it. If that man is anything like Clive, he's worth putting it all on the line for. And that's coming from me, Ms. Divorced with Two Kids.

It's one thing to tell me she enjoyed reading it, but it's another to encourage my delusions.

Sweet Lucifer, I think the book broke my sister.

And now, I'm starting to wonder if there's something inside that book that makes people lose their damn minds. Like, maybe *Accidental Attachment* is an actual health risk for readers.

Sam: Now, I'm pretty sure you're going to need some space from me, and I get that. I really do. Plus, I have this fun, new life in New York now because of you, so I'm getting ready to head out with the boys to go to Central Park. So…just…you know…call me when you're ready to talk about how I really, really want you and Chase to be together now.

Sam: But like, for real, if you and Chase get together, your ass BETTER call me.

Sam: Love you. Don't hate me for too long.

Well, *shit.* If I thought my crush couldn't get any more out of control before, my dear, insane sister just shot that assumption right to hell.

Chapter
Thirty-Seven

Sunday, May 28th

Brooke

Driving for the past two days straight could have—and by all accounts, should have—been miserable. I'm not that much of a traveler on a regular basis, and nineteen hours riding in anything isn't for the weak.

Not to mention, the two days before that were some of the weirdest I'd ever experienced. With all that combined, I never would have expected to have the kind of fun Chase and I had on the way here.

We talked and joked and took turns singing radio karaoke, along with making several stops at some of the United States' greatest landmarks.

The World's Largest Ball of Yarn.

A plastic longhorn cow the size of my apartment.

The Thing in Dragoon, Arizona.

And perhaps the least impressive of them all, Sedona.

Ha, kidding. Sedona was clearly amazing, and both of us remarked on the fact that it'd be worth a whole trip of its own one day in the future.

We didn't make any actual plans, but it'd be safe to say I've been hanging on to it ever since.

We also worked on the book, which is a huge accomplishment, given my track record so far, and I'm starting to feel like it may come together into a real story. Sure, I'm still convinced it will leave me with some form of chronic PTSD and inflict emotional scars until I'm rotting in a grave six feet under, but other than that, I can breathe a little easier.

Finally, though—*finally*—we made it to Vegas this morning, and instead of staying locked up in the motor home, we promptly made our way out to explore the city.

I didn't even have to convince Chase to play tourist with me. He was just as ready as I was when we arrived. Though, it could be said the long drive gave him the nagging itch of seeing something other than the inside of our bus for a little while.

And it only took two casino tours, three bodegas, Planet Hollywood, the Bellagio fountain, and some really sore feet later, for the frozen milky goodness of my favorite dessert to call my name loud enough to bring us here— to Serendipity3.

Chase sits in a chair beside mine, and the famous frozen hot chocolate sits right in front of my greedy face. I take a sip through the straw and practically moan. "It should probably be illegal for anything to be this good."

"I gotta say, I've never seen a dessert that big in my life," Chase remarks, swiping at some of the melting ice cream from my drink with his long index finger and slipping it into his mouth in an erotic move we're not going to talk about right now.

"You've never eaten at the Serendipity in New York? I thought when you said you hadn't eaten here, you just meant *here*, the Serendipity3 in Las Vegas."

He shrugs one casual shoulder. "Sorry to say I meant all of the Serendipitys collectively. Frankly, I didn't know there was more than one."

"Well…I guess you've just proven yourself to be something other than a woman who was growing up during the most crucial time in her life when the movie *Serendipity* came out."

"Which movie was that again?"

"Oh my God, you're killing me, Smalls." My jaw drops in shock and then snaps shut on a scoff. "Kate Beckinsale? John Cusack? Relying on destiny to bring them back together? Ring any bells?"

He shakes his head.

I let my hands fall to the table with a *whap!* and lean toward him with narrowed eyes. "Molly Shannon and Jeremy Piven as the tortured best friends? The gloves? The five-dollar bill? The pivotal ice-skating rink scene with the snow?" My voice rises with each mention. "The search for the copy of *Love in the Time of Cholera* that she put her name and number in?"

"Nope." Another shake of his head, but this time, a laugh follows. "I'm sorry. Really, I am, because I can tell my not knowing this is traumatic for you, but no, it's not sounding familiar."

"Traumatic is an understatement," I retort on a sigh and slouch back into my seat. "Chase, this movie was a formidable part of my life as a preteen."

Another laugh follows. "I really am sorry."

"Yeah, well, you can apologize by rectifying this mistake and watching the movie." I tsk my tongue at him. "Until then, we'll just have to be on civil terms, I guess."

He smiles all the way into his eyes, and truthfully, so do I. Even with his limited knowledge of one of the great rom-coms of our time, he's still so handsome it hurts.

"I'll watch it tonight," he promises sweetly, before digging in his pocket for something. I observe him struggling to get his hand all the way in, and his upper body contorts as a result.

"What are you doing exactly? An interpretive dance in the meantime?"

He chuckles as he finally frees the object he's been after and tosses it to the table between us.

Instantly, I recognize that it's a hotel room key, and both my heart rate and my eyebrows climb to the ceiling when I see it's for the Venetian.

"Uhh," I slur, trying to find the part of my brain that's responsible for language while all the blood takes a road trip to my vagina.

Chase laughs, choking as he rushes to explain. "Oh. No. I mean, yeah, I see how I've confused you, but yeah, I just…" He takes a deep breath and closes his eyes before opening them again and finishing with a smile. "I did get us a room—and it is one room—but only because that's all they had. It's two beds, though, but you mentioned more than once on the drive over that you'd never stayed in a fancy Las Vegas casino, so I thought…"

"Oh my God!" I yell, jumping up and bumping the table as I dive to give him a hug. "That's seriously so thoughtful. Thank you. Thank you. Thank you! I can't believe you were even paying attention when I was babbling on and on during hour umpteen of the road trip that almost never ended."

He tucks me close, his arms squeezing in a way that both comforts and terrifies me, and I can feel his breath in my hair as he answers, "You're welcome. It's no big deal. I just thought you deserved something fun."

This guy. Could he be any sweeter? Any more thoughtful? Any more perfect?

According to the book you wrote about him, the answer to that question would be no. He's the ultimate. Your *ultimate.*

"Wow. Just…thank you," I whisper again, but I make a point to disengage from his embrace before I start getting all dizzy and light-headed. "And crazily enough, I think I already know what I want to do with our wild hotel night."

He quirks a brow, and I try to ignore the sexual innuendo that could be mined from my words.

"Can we sit at the slot machines and order sodas all night?"

I would order wine, but the last time wine-sloppy Brooke and Chase were paired together, I sent him the wrong file for a book that's been trying to ruin my life ever since. So, I think I'll stick to soda.

"If you want. I mean, some sleep might be nice too, but—"

"Oh. When I say *all* night, I mean an hour, tops." I wave a hand in the air. "I live with a ten-p.m. bedtime cap, and I'm not about to change that now. It would throw Benji off completely."

His chest vibrates with humor. "I guess we'd better get back to the hotel and get started, then. Time is ticking with that kind of curfew."

I clap with glee in front of my now scarily happy face, and Chase bites his lip in response. That, of course, makes me think of his mouth and reminds me of the tiny, unconsented taste I took that night he was sick. My cheeks heat to the fiery temperature of blown glass.

Thankfully, he doesn't notice and stands first, taking out some of the cash Netflix gave me for expenses—we both learned early on it'd be a much better idea for him to carry it—and paying the bill while Benji and I stand from our seats and try to gather ourselves.

My canine buddy is definitely tired of walking. I can tell by the heavy way he drags along on his leash as we head out of the restaurant.

"Sorry, dude. Not too much longer," I reassure him as we weave our way onto the sidewalk. "All we need to do is go back to the camper and get our stuff, and then we'll be able to chill at the hotel."

Chase clears his throat behind me, and both Benji and I turn to look at him as a result. The sun is directly above his head, though, so I have to put a hand in front of my forehead to shield it as he explains, "I already had our stuff brought over by a car service. I hope that's okay. I just thought it'd be better than having to go all the way back to the campground."

I shake my head with a smile. "Look at you…taking scenes right out of *Accidental Attachment.*"

It's safe to say that my mind-mouth connection wasn't all that strong on that one, and before I know it, I'm blushing and looking down at the sidewalk again. *What a stupid thing to say.*

Chase, oblivious to my mental meltdown, of course, doesn't take any offense. But, I mean, why would he? I'm still lying about every aspect of the fact that I fictionally cloned the man and made him the main character in the book he's working his ass off to get published.

Even my normally sane sister wavered on what I should do. And when I called her yesterday, while we were stopped at a gas station, she still didn't know. Sammy was still too high off Clive and River; she could only focus on finding out if anything had happened with Chase and me.

Ugh. Sometimes it feels like I'll be trapped in this web I created forever. *Probably because unless you do something about it, you will be.*

I need Dolly, and I need her now.

Mustering up the courage to look at Chase again, I meet his sweet blue eyes before asking cautiously, "Would you mind if I put in one of my earbuds and listened to music on the walk back? I don't want to be rude."

"Not at all. What are you planning to listen to?" he asks.

"Dolly Parton, of course," I reply with a breathiness even I can hear.

"You sure love Dolly, huh?"

"More than is healthy sometimes."

His smile is dreamy. "I'll have to remember that."

I hope you do, Chase Dawson. I hope you do. Goodness knows, I remember everything about you.

Of course, the song that starts playing inside my ears, from my Dolly Greatest Hits playlist, is "Marry Me."

She sings about a boy with sky-blue eyes and a big heart and how he's going to marry her, and if I were the kind of woman who obsessed over signs, I'd probably feel like this is a sign that Chase and I are some kind of star-crossed lovers destiny is intent on putting together.

But I'm not that woman. I'm just a girl who is walking down the streets of Vegas with the most handsome man she's ever laid eyes on while Dolly sings about getting married to the man of her dreams, and it doesn't mean a thing.

Nope. Not a thing at all…

Chapter
Thirty-Eight

Monday, May 29th

Brooke

I've survived twenty-four hours of Vegas with Chase, in the *same* hotel room, and I didn't spontaneously combust.

Truthfully, sleeping in a hotel room with my editor should have been considerably more awkward than it was, but I guess two weeks of being on the road together prepared us for this moment.

Last night, after a few hours of drinking sodas at the slots, Chase and I made our way back to our room, tucked ourselves into our individual beds, and went to sleep like a couple of babies.

I think all the hustle of the tour and constant driving across the country had us both exhausted, if I'm honest, and made what could have been a tenuous situation less so.

I know I should have been freaking out, that's for sure, but against all odds, I finally managed to get a good night of sleep and then some. And I think Chase did too.

When I woke up this morning, he was at the gym, and in an effort to thank his thoughtfulness, I tried to be considerate in my own way, working on the edits he'd emailed me.

And I even managed to get through a whole ten chapters!

I know, I couldn't believe it either. For once in my life, I've had a productive Monday.

Now, Chase is in the shower, and for the first time since we entered this swell little hotel room in the Venetian, my good and normal and non-awkward feelings are starting to wear off.

I can hear the water splashing and splatting as he washes his naked body, and I can smell the aroma of his shampoo steaming through the bathroom door.

Add that to the fact that he's currently getting ready to take me to a fancy dinner and club—an outing he planned as a surprise for me—and I'm feeling an unjustly bit romantic.

Like, this feels like a date. It not only feels like it, it *reads* like it.

If I were writing this scene between Clive and River, they'd definitely be having sex when they came back to the hotel room. *Definitely.*

Stooping above my suitcase to pick out my panties and bra, I hesitate. I've got a nice selection ranging from period wear to sexy, and yet, somehow it feels like I have no options at all. If I choose the granny panty variety as a safeguard, but then by some miracle or the universe's design, this little scene between Chase and me does end in a book-worthy fashion, I'd be embarrassed until the end of time and beyond.

But if I go with the sexy stuff, the sheer lace, high-cut, low-coverage black set I bought on a whim from the internet, and come back here, only to put on my pj's and climb into our individual beds like last night, I'll feel like a fool.

Gah. Why does it have to be so complicated?

I'm enjoying my friendship with Chase. Sure, I spend pretty much every moment fantasizing about that friendship turning into a marriage and eventual babies and a whole happily-ever-after scenario for Benji and me, but that's okay. Life doesn't have to be all or nothing—and neither does underwear, I suppose.

I grab my middle-of-the-road, nude, no-slip, no-line thong that'll be a good fit under the dress I have planned and a matching bra and call it a day.

This is my official commitment to an "I'll take what I can get" attitude. Enjoy the night, see where it goes, *without* expectations. *That's* my plan.

Resolute, I don my garments quickly as the shower shuts off behind the classy, beige wallpaper-covered wall to my left.

Benji lifts his head from his nap, noticing both the change in noise and my vitals. Seeing as I'm only in my bra and thong, I'm hurrying now, and I'm also back to getting nervous.

Good nervous, I think.

Anticipatory, you know? Still, I don't know that my body fully knows the difference between that and one of my episodes because words like *woozy* and *light-headed* are some of my most relevant descriptors.

I manage to pull my dress up to my waist before the feeling becomes too much for Benji, and he approaches me in a hurry, crowding me and pawing at my leg until I slouch down onto the bench at the end of one of the beds and lean forward.

I put my head in my hands in an effort to get it below my heart and breathe deeply for a few long seconds. The first thing to interrupt my view of the hotel carpet? Chase's bare feet.

I'll be the first to admit that a man's feet can go either way. They're either craggily goblins from the center of the earth or the finest crafted veins and flesh—like the feet of gods in ancient times. Some small part of me was holding out hope that Chase would have the first—an unignorable turn-off that might at least temper my attraction—but no…they're perfect. Just like the rest of him.

Dammit.

"Brooke, are you all right?" he asks, crowding me so much that I can feel the terry of his white towel rubbing up against my bare knees.

I try to respond positively, but the only thing I get out sounds a little like a growl.

The next thing I know, he is sitting on the floor below me, nary a thing on his body but the flimsy wrap of bath fabric.

It's like the almost-kiss run-in from the motor home, but only, I'm also half naked. If syncope weren't trying to hold my hand, my horny level would be a twenty-five on the Richter scale.

Yeah, I know, that's for earthquakes, but once you see Chase Dawson's hard, muscular body in only a towel, you'd understand.

"What happened?" he asks, his voice grave with concern. "What can I get you?"

"I'm okay," I finally manage to say, lifting my head just slightly. Benji woofs for me to put it back, so I do. Of course, I let out a beleaguered sigh first, as is my right, but I do what he says.

"Okay. Just stay right here until you feel better. I'll go get you a Coke," Chase offers, scooting across the floor to leave. I don't know what comes over me, but before I know it, I'm reaching out to take hold of his bare arm and stop him.

"No!" I snap, with way more fervor than intended. "Just stay here with me. Please."

Chase agrees without hesitation. "Of course."

I leave my hand on his arm as I work to regulate my breathing, squeezing at his flesh with the normal heart rhythm I'm targeting.

It takes the three of us sitting quietly there in a jumbled group for what I'd estimate to be five minutes or so, but I eventually feel better. Normal, as it were.

I let go of Chase's arm that I've been holding on to like a Vulcan, and Benji trots back to the other side of the room to lie down. I didn't get to give him any good-boy pets, but I'm pretty sure he knows me well enough to understand that I'll catch him later—when I'm not in direct contact with the man of my fantasies in nothing but a towel.

"I'm good now," I promise, lifting my head and scooting back on the bench as I pull my dress up over my bra. "And I don't think I even made us late for dinner."

Chase smiles at my teasing remark, but that's about as much as I'm going to get, I think. For some reason, he doesn't seem to find it very funny when I almost pass out.

Strange.

"Just take your time getting up. You don't need to rush, okay? I'll call the restaurant if I need to and explain the situation, but I won't let you miss dinner."

I force a laugh. It's not that I don't think he's funny, but I think I need a little more than a silent smile to convince him I'm okay. And right now, anything other than breathing through my throat takes effort. "Well, thank you. I think you know that food is what's truly important here, and without it, the night will be ruined."

Chase chuckles in return and climbs to standing, which positions his mostly naked body directly in front of me. This isn't the first time I've seen him without a shirt, but with his close proximity, I'm starting to realize I short-changed ole Clive on the physical descriptors.

My God, his abs are defined. Long, sweeping ridges compartmentalize the sections of his abdomen, and bulging, sculpted delineation feeds my gaze right to Crotch Arena. I can see the swell of his not-average-equipment penis below the knotted waistline of his towel, but I do my best to look away.

The movement is dragged from the depths of my soul, but somehow, I manage to look back up to his eyes. Embarrassingly, they're dancing.

Shit. I guess he noticed me looking, huh?

Chase reaches out and lifts my chin with the gentle touch of a single finger, and my breath catches jaggedly in my throat. The feeling of him touching me like this, the two of us barely clothed, is beyond overwhelming, especially since I don't know why he's doing it.

His voice is a whisper as his gaze meets mine, a mix of seriousness and fondness swirling in his bright-blue irises. "Do me a favor?" he asks.

I nod.

"Take care of yourself, okay? I don't know what I'd do if something happened to you."

One second, he's there, and the next, he's gone, back to the bathroom, my dumb bobbing head and gaping fish lips all that are left in his wake.

Was that an intimate moment between people who care about each other? Or the plea of an editor who put it all on the line for an author who keeps trying to bust her head open on him?

I'd like it to be the first, obviously, but the rational part of me knows better than to rule out the second.

I stand slowly, reaching down to my side to pull up the zipper on my forest-green dress and contorting myself to hook the doohickey to the eye below my armpit. I have to hop around in a circle doing a funny dance, but finally, I get it. I step over to the full-length mirror and admire my attempt at "put together."

It's not bad, actually. Though, I could still stand to spend a couple hours on YouTube learning how to contour.

I move back over to the bench and put on my nude heels, clasping the buckle on each of my ankles before standing up again and heading back for the mirror. Benji climbs to standing from his prone position across the room, showing off his Captain America costume.

My buddy. He always but always makes me smile.

I'm taking one final look at the length of the back of my dress—assuring it covers the bum and hoo-ha, when the bathroom door opens, and Chase steps out, his reflection robbing my attention from my own in the mirror.

My turn to face him feels like it happens in slow motion.

His normally loose hair is styled in a perfect swoop, and a crisp black suit, white shirt, and black tie cover his spectacular body.

Normally, I might be disappointed to go from seeing so much skin to none at all, but with the way he looks right now, it's hard to be disappointed about anything.

"Wow," we both say simultaneously, looking at each other.

"You look…" he starts then, pausing to press a light hand into the fabric at his chest.

"Really good," I finish for him with a smile. "You look really good."

He nods. "Yep. That's what I was going to say."

My smile is big and toothy, and I don't even bother to try to temper it. It's probably best to get it out now before it shows itself in some other insane way later tonight.

"Are you ready?" he asks, holding out an arm in gesture for me to precede him to the door.

"Let me just grab my purse." His long-fingered hand flashes out to grab me by the wrist gently, stopping my forward motion with a shake of my head. "Tonight's on me. Not Brooke Baker. And not Netflix."

"Longstrand?" I ask for clarification boldly.

He shakes his head. "Me."

Does that mean Chase Dawson and Brooke Baker are on a date? Like, an actual date?

He gestures me forward again, putting a hand to the small of my back and guiding me out the door while Benji trots dutifully beside me. As the door shuts behind us and we head down the hallway toward the elevator—and dinner and dancing—one slightly mocking thought stands out.

Is this a date? I guess we'll know soon enough.

Chapter
Thirty-Nine

Monday, May 29th

Brooke

Neon lights flash. Drinks flow. People gyrate on the dance floor in the center of the massive space. And music pounds from the hanging speakers inside the club that Chase chose for the night.

I honestly can't even remember the name of it, but that's probably because I've been too busy gawking at my…date?

Yeah. I still don't know what to define this as, but I do know that dinner was at a swanky steakhouse with candlelit tables and soft piano music and the kind of romantic vibes that made it feel very…date-ish.

And Chase, well, he's the best date-ish dinner and nightclub partner a girl could ask for. Handsome, funny, intelligent, and charming to boot, he could've fed me my steak from the palm of his hand, and I would've gladly eaten it that way.

Besides the booming volume of the music in this club, I wouldn't change a thing about my current situation.

Maybe it's because I'm the oldest thirty-one-year-old woman who's ever lived, or because I almost never come to places like this, but I can't deny the music inside this joint is…a bit over the top in its magnitude. Nearly overwhelming if you're trying to have a conversation.

"It's really loud!" I yell over the music, pretty much directly into Chase's eardrum. That's the only way to hear in a place like this when you're over thirty, I'm convinced.

Don't get me wrong, the club itself is beautiful and, on top of that, filled with hordes of gorgeous people. I can tell it's popular for a reason and would even say that Chase did an excellent and thoughtful job of picking it out with the number of times the DJ's mixed in snippets of Dolly songs with the pounding house music.

But that doesn't make either of us any younger.

"You should be proud!" he yells back into my ear canal, in the world's saddest game of elderly telephone I've ever participated in.

The lights swirl, and a very heavy beat that makes my chest pulse has Benji moving even closer to my feet. We got a table and bottle service, of all things, and I feel like the biggest impostor that's ever postored before. But we needed a spot out of the way so that Benji would be able to chill out from under the trampling feet of real clubbers, and I don't think I'd make it more than ten minutes standing on these heels, so sitting was a must.

It just feels like an out-of-body experience to be having this much "fun" after what I was doing in my own apartment before I left for this tour—power cleaning, chugging wine, and tripping over a chunky knit blanket that's several days past its need for a washing.

"This is a huge accomplishment, Brooke. *Huge.* There are so few writers who make it to the slop."

"The slop?" I ask, confused.

He nods, confusing me more. "The very slop. Statistically, you're probably in the highest half-percent of writers."

"Ohh. The *top!*"

"I won't stop! You deserve to hear this stuff aloud!"

I can't help it. A laugh starts in my stomach and bubbles all the way up my throat until I'm cackling, hunching over, and slapping at my chest to keep myself from choking on my saliva.

We're like a couple of geriatrics who got lost on their way to bingo in here. But God, even old man Chase is sweet.

And he just sits there, looking at me with a quizzical smile. He's handsome as hell, but then again, that's always to be expected with him.

"Thanks for doing this," I lean in and try to say clearly and directly into his ear. "Tonight, I mean. Dinner and this. It's been a long time since I've treated myself to anything quite so special."

He nods. "That's to be expected, I think. Anyone who makes it to this level is bound to get at least a little existential."

I have no clue what he thinks I said, and quite frankly, I don't even care anymore. My smile is so big it hurts, and he smells so good. We need to try something other than talking.

Dancing.

I shove to standing and hold out my hand, rather than trying to communicate verbally, and he takes the hint pretty well.

He accepts my proffered hand humbly, but by the time we make it out of the booth and down the steps toward the dance floor, he's rearranged us so that he is in the lead, pulling me with gentle confidence right to the center.

I look back at Benji, who's jumped up on the booth seat to have a better view of me, and I give him a nod of confidence that it's okay. He sits but doesn't relax any further.

His message is clear: he'll be watching me.

I'm not entirely sure if it's the message of my service canine or my overprotective best friend. My superhero Benji knows my heart better than anyone—and not just the way it's supposed to beat.

Chase's hand is firm as he spins me around to face him, his hands coming to my hips to position my body against his. From the speakers, a bass-thumping mix of a Depeche Mode song that I've loved for as long as I can remember vibrates the air. It's called "Enjoy the Silence," and it's like the DJ chose this song just for me.

The lyrics are powerful and poignant in a way that makes goose bumps roll up my spine.

The music is heavy with need—and so is my vagina.

And all I can think of is the dancing scene I wrote between River and Clive, and how amazingly close I was to getting it right.

The feelings River had, the sensation of Clive's hands on her, the staccato pant of her breath—it's all real and then some as Chase moves us to the music, swaying our hips as one.

We are as close as two people can get without having sex. And his confidence is enough to keep even the rhythmless on beat, and as a member of that particular club, I'm super thankful not to be looking like a wounded turtle.

But mostly, I'm just *consumed*. By the feel of his hands on my hips and the warmth of his skin beneath his white collared shirt.

I run my hands up his chest, and his eyes stare down at me. That blue gaze of his is locked with mine, and for the first time, I don't feel nervous or awkward or like I need to look away. I want to wrap myself in the ocean that is his eyes and stay there forever.

And even though the song lyrics say that *words are unnecessary*, I feel the opposite.

I *want* to say something—I want to say something badly. About how I'm feeling or, I don't know, how much I want him, but with the volume of everything around us, I'm pretty sure it would fall on deaf ears.

But maybe…maybe that's a good thing. Maybe I can say all the things I'm feeling—all the thoughts that are screaming inside my head—and not even have to face the consequences.

If he's not going to be able to hear me anyway…what's the harm?

Wanton and wild, I throw caution to the wind and tell him all the things I haven't been able to get out of my mind since the first day I met him.

"I'm so, so into you, Chase. Your body, your personality, your wittiness— God, I think it's all so sexy."

Time slows between one moment and the next, and before another cognizant thought can enter my mind, Chase's lips are on mine, and his fingertips press deeper into the flesh of my hips as he pulls me even tighter against him.

Panic at the thought that he obviously heard me is quickly squashed by the feel of his tongue on mine. *Sweet Jesus, this is…everything.*

Supple and demanding, his tongue leads the kiss on a journey of exploration and taste that even I, a creative, couldn't have imagined. It's skilled, but not stuffy or formal or formulaic in any way. It feels like he's got the blueprints to my mouth and has been planning a heist of it with the crew from *Ocean's Eleven* for at least a month.

I…I can't believe I'm not dreaming.

Chase Dawson is kissing me. Chase Dawson is kissing Brooke freaking Baker, and I didn't even have to kidnap him and hold him at gunpoint to make him do it.

He moves his hands from my hips to my face, directing my attention back to the kiss in the hottest, most commanding way. I swear it's as if he knew my mind was wandering and, even better, knew how to get it right back on track.

I moan into his mouth, vibrating the air around us and making the skin of my neck pebble with goose bumps. My nipples are hard beneath my dress, and a throbbing, undeniable ache has set up residence between my thighs.

His hips are still pressed against mine, making the bulge of his arousal unmistakable.

God, I want him so badly; I don't know if I can stand here much longer without my legs giving out.

I don't know if Chase can read my mind or if he's just feeling the urgency himself, but he grabs my hand and drags me toward the front door of the club in a hurry. I glance over at Benji in the booth, and he's already jumping down to follow us.

We weave through the crowd of people with ease—Chase must have a map for that too—and are out the door and on a dash to the elevator and our room in no time.

I don't say anything; I can't. He doesn't either. At least, not with words.

But the hold of his hand is tight and strong, and the hard line of his jaw is practically carved from the letters s, e, and x.

My stomach turns slightly as we step into the elevator, and I have to shake my head to stop it.

Surely it's just nerves, wrapping themselves around the opportunity of a lifetime that sits before me. The opportunity to make a man I've been fantasizing about mine for the night.

The cart zooms up to our floor, and when my stomach does some kind of backflip combo, I swallow hard against it.

A ding rings out into the quiet but otherwise intense silence when the elevator arrives at our floor, and Chase pulls us out of the cart in a hurry. His long strides guide us down the hall toward our room, and Benji, my goodest boy, trots quickly and dutifully behind us.

It might be a little weird to have him here, but if ever there was someone I'd expect to be cheerleading from the sidelines, it'd be this little fella. He's had to listen to every insane thought I've had about Chase Dawson for months. As far as he's concerned, I bet it's about damn time.

The door opens easily enough, and Chase pulls me inside to shut it behind us. His body covers mine against the door, his fingers gently tucking a strand of hair behind my ear as he looks me in the eyes and studies me in a way that makes the butterflies in my stomach go crazy.

My God, I'm in love with him. I'm in stupid, ridiculous, overachieving love with every single part of this—

My stomach gurgles and, without warning, triggers a reaction in my esophagus.

Oh no, my mind silently shrieks.

But my stupid stomach is determined with its response. *Oh yes.*

Time stills. Horror-movie actors scream in the nonexistent background. And vomit climbs the path of my throat in painstakingly slow motion.

"Oh no," I say out loud this time, shoving Chase away nearly violently, and sprint toward the bathroom. Luckily, I'm hugging the bowl just in time to lose my hundred-dollar steak, baked potato, and every bit of the five mai tais I drank at dinner.

Clearly, the liquid confidence I thought I needed then has turned out to be a really, *really* bad idea.

How. Embarrassing.

Gah.

From hurried hands to hurling, I've really made this night a memorable one.

Great job, Brooke. You've really outdone yourself, babe.

Chapter
Forty

Tuesday, May 30th

Brooke

My head hurts, but my pride…well, that little girl stings like a son of a bitch.

Waking up this morning to find myself in the same bed as Chase Dawson, an ache behind my eyes and our bodies fully clothed, after coming so freaking close to finally feeling what it'd be like to have him inside me was a real kick to the groin I could have done without.

Last night, he was so sweet and understanding, of course, switching gears from hot sex to cool washcloth in a heartbeat. But the feeling of *what could have been* lingered in the air long past the time that I stopped ralphing into the toilet and he got me settled into bed.

To be completely honest, I can still smell it now.

Ughhhh.

Timidly, I roll out of bed so as not to disturb him—his dress shirt unbuttoned and untucked in the cutest, disheveled way—and tiptoe to the bathroom to wash my face free of both sweat and bitterness.

I have a television appearance this morning on *Las Vegas Morning Blend* that I have to find a way to pull myself together for, and a whole tour to finish out with a man I don't know how I'm going to look in the eye again.

I mean, we were moments from having sex, and I...*puked*. Several times.

Fucking hell.

But things are happening, the Earth is spinning, and life is moving on—even without the penetration we both so expected last night.

After one more long look in the bathroom mirror, I sigh and get down to the business of getting myself ready. Face, hair, teeth, shower—it all has to get done, and from the time on my Apple Watch, it has to get done quick.

I crank up my pace and get moving on each individual task, one at a time, until I'm finally through them all and somewhat put together.

My arm opens the bathroom door on a slow pull to exit, and the squeak of the bed springs as I do tells me all I need to know—Chase is awake.

"How are you feeling?" is the first thing the considerate bastard asks as I come into view, and it takes everything inside me not to crumble.

He really is too good to be true, and at this point, I see very little hope of ever talking myself out of love with him.

I'll just have to be one of those spinsters, talking to her dog and dreaming of the man who got away.

"I'm better, thanks," I say, carefully carrying my dirty dress and toiletries over to my suitcase.

I'm squatted down and concentrating so hard, the feel of Chase's hand on my shoulder is a startling surprise.

When I look up to meet his eyes, they're soft with compassion. "Hey. Let's not let this be weird, okay?"

I laugh. It's very dry, and he can tell.

"No, really," he challenges, pulling me up to standing and guiding me to the foot of the bed to sit next to him on the bench. "I'm serious. I don't regret anything. Everything that happened was...well, I've been thinking about it for a while."

I snort. "Even the vomiting?"

He shakes his head with a smile and reaches up to push my hair out of my face, even bumping my glasses back up to their place on my nose since they've started to slip. "Maybe not the puking," he affirms with a wink. "But everything right up until that moment and beyond…" He shrugs. "I feel privileged just to be around you, Brooke. No one makes me smile like you do."

My skin tingles, and the inside of my nose starts to sting with a warning of incoming tears.

"Chase…"

"Just relax, okay? Get ready for the show this morning. Be your awesome self. I'll go get the motor home ready to head for Los Angeles after."

"And everything else?"

"I've got a strong feeling everything else is going to work itself out too." He smiles, and I'm pretty sure this one, right here, is my most favorite of all his smiles. "Now, go show Las Vegas why Brooke Baker is so lovable."

A buzzing warmth fills my chest.

Is it really possible…that writing a book about this man and accidentally sending it to him…is actually going to work out in my favor?

Chase leans in and kisses my cheek before getting up and heading for the bathroom.

"Good luck on the show, Brooke. I'll see you after," he says with a wink before stepping inside.

I smile as the door shuts behind him.

He sure as hell will.

Fate is going to give me another opportunity.

And this time, I'm going to try really hard not to vomit.

Forty-One

Wednesday, May 31st

Chase

I tuck Brooke's phone into my back pocket as she sits down in yet another interview chair, and she nods her thanks, her smile growing wildly as I wink.

Damn, I love that smile of hers.

We're currently in Los Angeles, inside the Beverly Hills Hotel, where several stations are set up with journalists for Brooke to sit down with and discuss the big premiere of the Shadow Brothers series on Netflix.

Dressed in a blue dress and with her stylish glasses and her gorgeous hair hanging past her shoulders, she looks beautiful, *as always,* and she's handling each and every interviewer like a pro.

And since Monday night's *almost,* I've made it my mission to turn off all the alarms in my brain and just be. If I want to tell her that she's beautiful, I do. If I want to flirt with her, I *definitely* do, and if Brooke says something that makes me laugh, I don't hold back my amusement. I haven't pressured her at all, and with how busy we've been for the past forty-eight hours getting to Los Angeles and doing all of her publicity things, we haven't even kissed again.

But I can feel the inevitable in the air, and I think she can too.

Trust me, I want to be with her. Fuck, do I ever.

And somehow, someway, when the time is right, Brooke Baker and I are going to be together in the most biblical sense of the words. And the anticipation of not knowing when it's going to happen is the most excitement I've felt in years.

Well, that, and planning a surprise for her that will occur at the end of the tour, on our way back to New York.

My phone dings in my hand, and I look down to find a text from my sister. She's been working on getting some of the details of that very surprise set up for me since I came up with the idea yesterday morning.

Mo: Okay, White Limozeen is officially booked for Sunday night like you asked. I had to talk fancy to get them to agree to such short notice without even an estimated head count, but they finally sent over the contract five minutes ago, and I signed it.

White Limozeen is a rooftop bar in Nashville, and one that I know, without a doubt, Brooke will lose her mind over. A Dolly Parton theme just might be involved.

Me: Thank you, Mo. It's appreciated. I know I've put a lot of this on your shoulders, but I can't exactly do the heavy lifting myself and keep it a surprise.

Mo: It's okay. If I'd do this for anyone on the planet, it'd be Brooke Baker. And since you're going to get me an early copy of the manuscript as soon as edits are done, PLUS give me the inside scoop on how in love with her you are when you see me in person again, I figure it's a pretty good deal.

Good grief, my sister is truly skilled at talking out of her ass.

Me: I didn't say anything about giving you the manuscript or being in love.

Mo: Trust me, you did. Everything you've said since the moment you called me yesterday has screamed those two things.

Me: Mo!

Mo: Yes, baby brother?

I sigh heavily before typing, figuring the best way to shut her up is to give in to one of her requests.

Me: Fine. I'll see if I can get you the manuscript.

Mo: And tell me all about being in love with Brooke Baker!

Apparently, I was wrong. If I give my sister an inch, she'll attempt to take a goddamn mile. After thirty-three years of dealing with her, you'd think I would've known that.

Me: Mo.

Mo: Fine, fine. I'll let you deny it a little longer if you want. Men are always slow anyway. Oh! And I also forgot to tell you that I got a call from Glenn. Something about you leaving my number as an emergency contact.

My response is swift and instant.

Me: What the fuck? I didn't leave Glenn any emergency contact numbers. And my address book was in my room.

Mo: Well, I'm assuming the rest of your stuff was still in your room too, but that didn't stop him from moving it to a storage unit in Brooklyn and sending me the address.

If I had the power to strangle that freaky bastard telepathically, I'd be tempted to do it right now.

Me: HE DID WHAT?

Mo: I guess he didn't tell you, huh?

Me: No, he didn't tell me! Do these messages seem like the messages of someone who knows?

Mo: Come to think of it, no, they don't.

I swipe an irritated hand through my hair and text her back with an equally irritated but short and succinct one-word response.

Me: Mo!

Mo: Relax. I called Brooke's sister when I got the info from Glenn, and she was able to go to Brooklyn and check it out. Your stuff is really there. Even packed in boxes. So, at least there's that.

At least there's that? Pfft. The fucker was in my room, going through my shit and moving me out of my own place—albeit temporarily—without my permission. I see no silver lining in this scenario.

Me: My ghost roommate moved me out of my apartment, and I'm supposed to relax??

Mo: Well, yeah. You're not supposed to live there long-term anyway. And your apartment has to be close to done. Have you spoken to Angelo?

I inhale a sharp breath through my nose, trying like hell to contain my emotions enough not to call attention to myself while Brooke is in the middle of these interviews.

She looks up to my face and frowns, so I paste on a smile, waving it off and hooking a thumb toward the door to the lobby in the universal gesture of "I'm going to take this outside."

Something tells me I ought to find a little more privacy before making my next call to my contractor.

Me: I'm calling him now.

Mo: Okey dokey. Let me know if I can do anything else or if I should arrange to have Brooke's belongings delivered to the new place too.

I roll my eyes. I also don't humor her with a response.

Instead, I start scrolling through my contacts until I find my contractor Angelo's number, and I do my best not to lose my shit in the lobby.

When Angelo answers on the third ring, I have to steel my voice against being angry.

"Hello, Mr. Chase," he greets in his thick Italian accent. "How you doing?"

"I'm okay, Angelo, but I've been better. I just wanted to call and find out what our status is on the apartment. I just got some news that means I really need to be in there sooner rather than later. How's it looking?"

"We're getting really close here, Mr. Chase. It's looking very good."

I furrow my brow. "What do you mean by getting close exactly? Like, what is done and what's left to do and how many days or weeks does that mean it'll be until I can get in there?"

"These things, Mr. Chase, they are hard to say very specifically for many reasons."

Is it just me or do contractors never seem to be able to give an exact timeline?

"Give me an estimate, then," I say through a stiff jaw. "Are we talking days or weeks? Because you promised me I'd be in two months ago, Angelo."

"Yes, yes, I understand this. But it will only be days, I am pretty sure."

"Pretty sure?"

"Pretty, pretty sure."

For fuck's sake.

"Okay," I say through a deep sigh. "Well, I'm going to be back in town in under a week, Angelo, and I expect to move in when I get back."

"One moment, Mr. Chase," he states, and the sounds of drilling and hammering reverberate from his end of the line.

While I'm waiting for him to respond, Brooke's phone pings in my pocket, and I pull it out to check if it's something important. There's a Facebook message on the screen from someone, so I make my way back over to the door that leads to the conference room Netflix reserved for Brooke's interviews and quietly step back inside so I can give it to her as soon as I'm off the phone.

"Sorry, Mr. Chase. I'm back." Angelo's voice is in my ear again. "One week. I think this will be no problem. We finish all the finishing things."

Brooke laughs out loud—it's her cackle that makes her mouth go wide and her hand cover her lips—and even with my being on the phone, it catches my attention from across the room. The interviewer is also in stitches, and I can only imagine the kind of thing my girl might have said to set this off. I wish kind of desperately that I'd heard it.

These days, I've grown greedy to hear just about everything she has to say, both aloud and on paper.

"Mr. Chase? Are you there, Mr. Chase?"

I pull my attention away from the stunning woman in blue momentarily and focus back on the phone call. "Just get me in by the time I get back, Angelo. Please," I tell him as quietly as I can. "I cannot express over a phone call how dire my roommate situation is while I wait for this place to be done."

"Oh, oh, Mr. Chase, I understand. I remember you say something about him. Remind me of one of those ghosts like Shadow Brother. Very freaky."

I can't help but laugh at Angelo's unknowingly relevant reference. "Yep. It's just like that."

"Of course, of course. I get this done for you, Mr. Chase. I promise. Be spick-and-span and beautiful when you get here. I make sure, okay? Not to worry, okay?"

By the time I hang up the phone, Brooke has moved on to the next interviewer, and she's making this one laugh all over again. Her blue velveteen dress looks like an icy snow in low daylight, and I have a hard time remembering that she doesn't do these public appearances every day. I know one of her main worries was about being natural in this kind of environment, but I think someone needs to break the news to her that she was born for this.

She can't see it, but I could imagine her being on her own show one day—she's that magnetic.

I glance at my watch to see what time it is in New York, which is three hours ahead of us, and then jump to text my sister again before she gets busy in the restaurant. It's three o'clock there, and things start picking up around four.

Me: Angelo has assured me I'm going to be able to get in when I get back. Please, pretty please, if you can, arrange to have my stuff delivered to the apartment from the storage unit the day before I get back?

Mo: Brooke's too?

I roll my eyes.

Me: Mo.

Mo: Love you, brother. I find I especially like you when you owe me so much.

Me: Oh yeah. It's one of my favorite things too.

Glancing up from my phone just in time to see Brooke's current interviewer get up to leave, I tuck my cell into my pocket and wave down her attention.

She holds up a finger and smiles at the next journalist before stepping around all the wires and lights and walking over to me quickly.

I hold out her phone to explain. "Sorry to interrupt, but you got a Facebook message, and I thought you might want to see it."

She snatches it eagerly and scans the screen, her smile growing with every devoured word. "Oh my God," she whisper-yells, reaching out to grab my hand and squeezing it before letting it go. I miss the contact instantly.

"Remember the thing I was looking for in the Facebook group that you couldn't see on my screen in the car that day?"

I nod. Amazingly, I do, in fact, remember. But I tend to remember just about everything about Brooke.

"Well, I got a lead from someone and sent a message, and I just got a message back!" she explains excitedly. "It's really happening! I found the *thing* I was looking for," she adds cryptically, widening her eyes and tilting her head toward Benji. "You know, the *thing*."

I'm still not entirely sure I understand what's going on, but I'm happy for her, nonetheless.

And my current full-toothed smile at her joy undoubtedly shows that.

She searches my face, and her eyes shift from excited to something else that reminds me of the way she looked when we were dancing in that Vegas nightclub…right before I kissed her.

Without thought or planning, our bodies gravitate toward each other. She digs her teeth into her bottom lip, and it's this sexy little move that does nothing for the tight control I'm trying to maintain.

Fuck, I'm looking forward to being alone with her again tonight.

"I really can't wait for these interviews to be done," she whispers to me, and I lift my hand to discreetly place it at her waist to give it a squeeze.

"Me too."

Her cheeks turn rosy, and she starts to open her mouth to say something I'm unquestionably riveted to hear, but a disruption in the form of someone else stops her.

"Sorry to interrupt," a voice says from right beside us, startling both Brooke and me out of an intense stare. I clear my throat, and Brooke tucks a piece of loose hair behind her ear while she turns her head to a woman by the name of Rhonda—who just happens to be the Netflix executive in charge of this whole deal.

"I just wanted to update you really quick before I have to take a conference call in the other room."

"Oh, okay," Brooke says, nodding.

"We've got quite a few more interviews to get through here in the next couple of hours, and then, Brooke, I've taken the liberty of setting up a meeting for you and me with our CEO," the female executive updates. "He's eager to meet you for dinner tonight and even had his assistant book you a hotel room right by the restaurant so you don't have to worry about traveling back and forth to the, um…motor home. Your glam squad will meet you in your hotel first thing tomorrow morning to start getting you ready for the premiere. And I'll have my assistant send you all the details via email, okay?" She squeezes Brooke's shoulder gently. "Can't wait to see you at dinner tonight."

Brooke doesn't even get a chance to respond before the woman swiftly walks away.

So much for being alone tonight.

Brooke turns to me, her face sunken like I imagine is the unmasked version of my own. Still, I recover quickly before she can catch it.

Having dinner with the CEO of Netflix and going to the premiere for a series based on her books are once-in-a-lifetime opportunities. It's why she's here. If I have anything to say about it, I'm going to be around for a while, so no matter how badly I want and need a night where I have her all to my-self, our plans can wait.

Brooke needs to go, and she needs to do it without worrying about me. She needs to do it and be there to experience it all in a way that lets her witness and enjoy the fruits of her labor and talent.

"It sounds terrific, Brooke." I smile and then inconspicuously lean forward to whisper into her ear, "And don't worry, I promise our plans will wait."

Brooke leans back to meet my eyes, and her smile is grateful and sad at the same time. Seeing her sad isn't something I ever thought I'd be happy about, but right now, it's the balm to every drop of uncertainty I need.

Brooke Baker and I want each other enough to wait. *A couple days, tops.*

Chapter
Forty-Two

Thursday, June 1st

Brooke

I am in a fancy LA hotel room surrounded by ten other women, here to help me get ready for the big red-carpet premiere of *The Shadow Brothers*. *Holy, holy hell.*

Needless to say, I'm anxious, and my current indecision is showcasing that fact.

I pick up both bottles of nail polish again, considering them carefully with a purse of my lips consistent with Miranda Priestly.

It's a big decision, although I'm fairly certain it shouldn't be this earth-shattering, and the manicurist just barely stops herself from rolling her eyes at me. I can feel it.

"I swear I'm not normally this annoying. Truly. I just can't decide what's going to look best on the red carpet because I've never been on a red carpet or even on any red-hued floor at all, you know?"

Becky's stern frown melts, and she takes one of the bottles from my hand with ease, holding it up in front of me. "This one."

I sigh, relieved. "Bless you, Becky. Bless you."

She goes to work polishing the light pink color on, while another woman starts working on my hair. In the corner of the room, a pretty blonde steams my dress, holding it up to the light of the hotel window to ensure she's getting all the wrinkles out of the delicate silk fabric.

I'm both grateful and horribly out of place, and I wish so badly that someone were here to do it with me.

It isn't a minute after I have the thought that a soft knock echoes off the hotel room door, and another woman opens it to Chase. He steps inside with a big smile and a bouquet of light pink roses in his hand.

Every part of me melts.

I haven't seen him since before I had to go to dinner last night with the Netflix CEO and a few important executives, and I'd be a liar if I said I wasn't missing him like crazy.

This guy is every bit as special as I wrote him to be and then some. Truthfully, I'm not entirely sure I deserve to be experiencing all he has to offer.

I mean, at the bottom of it all, I'm still lying to him.

Not maliciously, and not on purpose. But as he walks toward me with a grin that includes his eyes and puts the roses down on the empty chair beside me, I can't help but think he doesn't deserve to be lied to at all.

If there weren't all these people in here with us, I'd consider telling him right now. As it is, I'm afraid the kind of scene that would result from telling him everything this publicly would be even worse than continuing to keep it to myself for just a little longer.

"Good morning, Brooke," he greets and reaches out to gently squeeze my shoulder. "It's the big day, and you're already looking beautiful. Are you excited?"

I smile with a shrug as Benji huffs out his own sentiments. He's borne witness to it all. All I can do is admit, "It's possible I've been a bit of a basket case."

Chase's responding smile is so, so comforting. "I wouldn't dream of it going any other way."

"Par for the course, huh?"

"It's you," he whispers then, a reverence in his voice so obvious that even the manicurist raises her eyebrows. I do my very best to ignore the vulnerable feeling.

He stares at me for a long moment before nodding once, a mere resolute jerk of his chin. "Okay, then. I'm going to leave you to it for now. But I'll see you tonight. I'll be in the car with you on the way to the red carpet, okay?"

Gah. I really want him to stay.

"Where are you going now?" I ask, a desperation in my voice no one could miss.

Chase smiles, and Benji moves from his spot by the sofa to crowd my legs, just in case. "To work on Clive and River."

My breath catches again on the feeling of my lies lodged in my throat.

"And then to get ready for your big night," he adds with a little wink.

All I can do is nod.

Chase bites his lip with a shake of his head and then reaches out to squeeze my shoulder again. "Can't wait to see you tonight."

Oh, Chase Dawson. Can't wait to see you is an understatement.

Photographers gesture toward us, pulsing their arms together to suggest we should slide into an embrace, and both Chase and I pause to check with each other before doing so.

It's both awkward and cute, and I appreciate that someone is feeling as out of place as I am right now. Once in proximity, though, Chase wraps a warm arm around me and tucks me into the side of his body. His tux is crisp, fancy fabric, and I can feel it through the cutout in my lavender silk gown. Both that, and the warm smoothness of his long-fingered hand.

As the night goes on, the distance between us is closing.

When we started the red-carpet walk upon our arrival, Chase hung back for most of the time, smiling when I would look back at him in sheer disbelief at the whole dog and pony show.

I was on a red carpet tonight.

Me, Brooke Baker, on a freaking red carpet in the middle of an LA premiere for *The Shadow Brothers.*

Famous actors walked next to me, even pausing and asking to take pictures with me every now and then.

Photographers yelled toward me, and several red-carpet interviewers stopped me to ask questions. It was all so surreal.

Perhaps most dreamlike, however, was seeing my very own Shadow Brothers come to life on the big screen. It was all I could do to sit through the screening without crying loudly enough to disturb everyone.

Thankfully, I had the two best men any girl could ask for by my side the entire time.

Benji stayed put by my feet, and Chase held my hand while two very palpable tears carved rivers down my fully made-up cheeks and I didn't care.

This is big, dammit, and for the first time since I landed the deal, I let myself *feel* it. I forgot about my makeup and the lavender dress I picked out because a certain someone told me he liked that color on me.

I didn't worry about what anyone thought of my tears.

I just let myself savor the moment.

I mean, I wrote a book that they turned into a show. Just a small-town girl from Nowhere, Ohio, living the biggest of fucking dreams. And tonight at midnight Pacific Time, it's going to be live everywhere in the world, for all the people to watch.

Every time I've let myself think about it since those tears inside the theater, I've started to shake.

I did it. Just like Sammy said, I really did it.

Chase and I smile for the cameras a few more times before stepping away from the crowd and walking off the red carpet and climbing into the waiting car that's ready to take us away from the Hollywood glitz and glamour and back to the motor home, just outside of the city.

The moon is full and the stars are big, and I've got full-blown hearts in my eyes as Chase scoots closer to me and we drive away.

He is quiet as he takes my hand in his own and holds it tightly, rubbing his thumb against the line of mine. I breathe deeply into the silence while Benji watches me from the far side of the limo.

"Do you ever…" Chase starts to ask into the otherwise silent car before stopping himself. He shakes his head, but evidently, the motion isn't enough to clear it. "Do you ever imagine what it would be like to be Clive and River?"

His eyes search mine as though the answer to his question can be found inside, but I know by the ever-present longing on his face, it can't.

Oh boy, if it could…

Every day I spend with this man, working on characters I based on us, I get a little heavier with guilt. My conscience, reminding me it's there and not, you know, on a six-month hiatus to Siberia like I'd like it to be.

And while I can appreciate the motherboard of my soul not being fried to smithereens in a way that makes my reflection seem cloaked in sixes, I wouldn't know where to start when breaking the news of this whole debacle—and I don't think Chase would be ready to hear it even if I did.

It's big—gargantuan, really—to find out you've had an entire novel written about you without your knowledge. That someone studied you closely enough to create an entire world revolving around you—without your consent.

Ugh. It's not good. *I know it's not good.* But I feel absolutely nauseated at the thought of experiencing the effects of truth serum in living color. *What would Chase say? What would he think? Would he drive the motor home straight to the nearest psych ward?*

Instead of divulging the secrets of my heart, I stick to the surface of the truth. It's real. It's raw. But it doesn't score me wide open without the safe haven of a surgeon to put me back together.

"Yes. I do."

Sweet merciful Jesus, do I ever, Chase Dawson.

He swallows and nods, and within the flash of a second, his concentration has moved from my eyes to my lips.

Heart beating wildly, I shiver under the intensity of his gaze and beg of myself to stay alert. Benji picks up his head from his spot in the front of the limo, but I will him with every shred of my nonexistent superpowers to stay put just a little while longer. The womanliest part of me *needs* this moment—to feel *sexy* and *alive* and *grown*. The truth of the matter is, I haven't craved a man's touch the way I do Chase Dawson's at any other singular time in my life.

Not on the night I lost my virginity. Not on the night I married Jamie.

Not ever.

Fuzziness enters my vision, and Benji stops hanging back. I can feel his body as it pushes against my legs with urgency, but Chase doesn't move out of the way. He doesn't back up; he doesn't balk. One moment, I'm on the brink of unconsciousness, and the next, his lips are on mine.

Chase. Dawson's. Lips.

An organ I've written a literal sonnet about before. *Yes, really. Yes, I know I'm pathetic. Yes, I burned it.*

The shock of his swift action is enough to defibrillate my heart back into a normal rhythm, and all the fog in my head clears by magic. My feelings are crisp and clear, and my stomach feels like it could fly to the moon.

I am found in this moment.

My confidence, my self-love—they're both renewed with fervor. I deserve this culmination of my fantasies. I deserve to feel the warmth of his lips on mine. I *deserve*—

Shock tingles through my limbs as Chase pulls back so abruptly it feels violent, and he sets me away by the flesh of my arms. My throat no longer feels warm and right; instead, it feels dry and empty.

I can't speak, can't move—not even to run and hide. All I can do is stare.

He rocks from one side to the other and then does an entire one-eighty spin before running angry hands through his beautiful, dark hair. Even agitated and fresh off rejecting me, he is the embodiment of my perfect male specimen.

It's confirmed: I'm so, so pathetic.

And then suddenly, I'm not.

Chase closes the distance quickly, pushing our bodies together until they feel almost entirely like one. I take a deep breath that tastes like him, and his eyes flare infinitesimally.

"I'm sorry," he whispers.

"For what?" I ask raggedly.

"For pulling away. It's not because I don't want you."

"Then what is it?"

"It's because I want you so badly I'm afraid I won't be able to control myself. I don't want to hurt you."

A thrill runs down my spine at the growled words I never wrote in the book.

Right now, Chase Dawson is no Clive Watts.

No.

Right now, Chase Dawson is even better.

Chapter
Forty-Three

Very Early Friday, June 2nd

Chase

Her teeth tug at my lip, and I shove a hand into the back of her long hair as the limo pulls away. Locked together, the two of us stumble to the stairs of the motor home, and I pull her toward me with one hand while the other works at the door handle. I can't get close enough fast enough, and from the way her legs are trying to climb my own, I'm thinking she's feeling the same way.

The door finally opens with a rattle and a pop, the plastic screen separating from the solid frame just enough that I have to fight the complication of the two behind Brooke's back until they finally stick together again.

I pick her up and wrap her legs around my waist to climb inside, Benji fighting for his life in a tangle of our feet, and I pull the door slammed behind us and walk her straight to the bedroom.

Swept up in the chaos, Benji stays close as I drop Brooke to her back on the bed and climb on top of her, hiking the sweet slit of her silk dress even higher on her thigh and skating my hand against the newly revealed warm skin.

Benji groans a little, retreating out the door to a place, I can only assume, that won't scar him quite so much. Still, I don't want him to leave if Brooke should have him here for her safety.

I pull back slightly, as much as I don't want to, and ask her about it. "Benji... do you need him to..."

She snorts. "There's no way my blood pressure is dropping right now. I'll be fine."

With the way my own blood is pumping at this point, I understand her confidence.

"Okay, if you're sure. If you need him to—"

"Chase," she cuts me off, gripping my jaw tightly and pulling my face to hers again, the weight of my hard chest pushing into her soft one. "I appreciate the concern, truly. But please, please, *please*, shut up and kiss me."

A clear request, not to be denied.

My smile is obvious against her lips as I take them in the kind of kiss that would melt the paint off the walls if this weren't a cheaply wallpapered motor home. It's intense and deep, and I can feel the want in every shift of her hips as my tongue dances along the edges of hers.

Her body feels so fucking perfect, I can hardly stand it. We've been waiting so long, fighting this so hard, that to finally be at the inevitable stage of completion almost feels like a fever dream. If I'm not careful, I'm going to miss it.

I mean, I'm here, and I'm feeling, but if I let it, the adrenaline of my excitement could very well make the details hazy. And I want to remember every single second.

I want this to be a core memory that I remember for the rest of life and afterlife and a million afterlives after that.

Slowing down, I pull back and sit up, sliding a tortured hand from Brooke's neck to her collarbone and then down through the drapey fabric at her chest. Up and down with the motion of her ribs, her breathing comes in heaves.

"Shh," I soothe, running my hand down her belly and around her hip and over the split fabric at her thigh.

Brooke's eyes are wild, wide and restless, and rapidly becoming sick of my shit. I shake my head with a smile. "Relax. I want to take my time."

"Oh really? Because time sounds like a terrible idea. Alexander Graham Bell should be fired."

"What's he got to do with this?" I ask on a near snort, my dick jumping in my pants at the sound it fell in love with—Brooke Baker being funny.

"I'll tell you! Alexander invented the phone, and the phone is full of numbers, and time *is* numbers. And since his name is the only one I can remember right now while all the blood in my body is partying down south, the very loose connection between the two makes him at fault. Period."

"I see," I say with a nod, gently moving the fabric of Brooke's dress into a bunch in order to slide it up her legs.

She looks down at me with a scowl, and I can't help it, my grin grows.

She's just so fucking cute without even knowing it.

As I scoot her back with a thrust, she squeals and throws up a hand behind her head as I push her into the pillows. Quickly and with ease, I slide my hands under the fabric at her hips and lift, forcing her dress up around her waist and exposing her pretty lace panties completely.

"I thought you wanted to go slow."

"Sometimes slow is fast, and sometimes fast is slow," I tell her through a smirk, dropping onto my stomach until I'm at the perfect angle to put my lips on her.

"Okay, Lightning McQueen," she teases on a scoff. "Whatever you say."

Without hesitation, I rip the delicate fabric in two and pull it apart until I'm left only with bare skin. She's completely waxed—something I didn't imagine I would find on Brooke. I don't care either way, but from everything I've learned about her, she never struck me as the type.

She laughs then, explaining the answers to my thoughts without even knowing it. "I'm going to have to give Helga at Body Sensations a big kiss for talking me into adding the Brazilian on to my eyebrow and partial wax."

"Brooke," I say with a shaking laugh.

"Sorry, sorry. Just thinking aloud. Please proceed."

I know the rambling is a direct result of nerves and an inability to concentrate on anything else. I work hastily to give her something else to think of, spreading her thighs with the palms of my hands and licking a long, slow line right up the center of her.

She's warm and wet and so fucking tasty. I groan.

Excited, my dick swings like he's next at bat, fighting to escape the confines of my pants and the pressure of the bed. I deny him entirely. For now, this is all about Brooke.

I make soft, smooth movements with my tongue, savoring the taste of Brooke's skin and excitement. She dances in her spot, grasping at the comforter and my hair and my shoulders and pretty much everything she can get ahold of.

I love it so much that I almost don't realize at first…I've taken some of my moves directly from Clive without even meaning to.

The way he holds his hands on River's pelvic bone to answer her hip thrusts. The way he positions River's legs over his shoulders. The way he escalates the motion of his tongue to match the pace of her breathing.

I've done all of that tonight—and the results are outstanding.

Brooke's back hasn't un-arched since the curve started, and the sound of her moans is getting louder and louder with every lick.

It reminds me of when I heard her touching herself in the shower, and I feel like the luckiest son of a bitch that I'm about to be the one to make her come.

And I know from the feel of her on my tongue that she has to be getting close. Slow and easy, I add two fingers to the mix, working them inside her until they're seated to the hilt.

She freezes for a long moment at the intrusion, and so do I, other than working my tongue at the sensitive clit above them.

"Chase," Brooke whispers, her voice thick with need and rushed by want.

"I know," I say softly against her, letting the warm air and vibrations from my mouth add to her sensations. "I know, baby. Just let it go."

Back and forth, her head shakes against the comforter, and her hand latches into my hair, pulling several of the strands at the root. The demanding sensation is all I need to get me to push.

I lick and swirl and suck and pulse with my fingers until she's mewling so loudly, the thin walls feel like they'll shake down.

Her pussy is tight around my fingers, grasping and gulping until it finally releases into an earth-shattering quiver that fills my mouth with her release.

She tastes almost exactly like she smells, like a citrusy, warm summer night, and it's all I can do to keep myself from coming right inside my still-fastened pants.

I'd be a harsher critic of that high school level of hormonal control, but Brooke is the kind of woman who tests a man's willpower, no matter how tough he is.

Long, lithe limbs, sultry eyes, plump, pouty lips, and a body that could be on the cover of magazines are just the tip of the iceberg. Physically, she's perfect. But she also makes it impossible to forget the rest of her—the humor, the heart, the passion.

She's got so much packed into one relatively small human body, and to be the one experiencing a connection with her feels like the highest of privileges.

I push up on the bed and stand, shucking my clothes in what feels like slow motion. Brooke's gaze is set, fixed on my every movement while she's splayed on the bed recovering.

Pants, underwear, shirt, and bow tie removed, I climb back onto the mattress and sit, scooping up Brooke's body and setting her astride me. Her eyes widen, but I don't pause before scrunching the silk of her dress until most of it is contained in my hands and pulling it up and over her head.

"You're even more beautiful than I imagined," I say quietly, running the tip of my finger along the delicate lace covering her breasts.

She reaches behind herself to unclasp her bra, which pushes her chest toward me. I don't miss the opportunity to catch one of her perfect nipples in my mouth.

She gasps, and I move from her breast to her mouth to catch it in a kiss. The feeling of her surprise against my lips might just be the second-best thing I've ever tasted. And it's only topped by the other thing I've had tonight.

I kiss at her cheeks and her collarbone and her shoulder and along the length of her arm and then move back to her neck while pulling her close to me.

Her head falls back on a whimper, and I whisper against the most delicate of skin. "You're so fucking perfect, Brooke."

She shivers slightly, her spine curving her body toward me to protect against the feeling.

And I feel almost drugged; the sensation of so much of her skin on mine is potent.

Reaching gently to the pocket of my suit pants, I grab the condom I bought presumptively for this opportunity and set her back just enough to slide it on myself. She watches avidly as I roll it down, her white teeth biting into the fleshy pink of her bottom lip.

The look is erotic and all-encompassing, and I want to be inside her so badly, I feel like I might explode.

Sitting up, I pull Brooke back onto my lap and offer her the opportunity to climb on me. I don't know what it is about her personality, but I'm absolutely desperate to see what she does when she's given control.

Brooke, smart as always, doesn't need an instruction manual to understand what I'm thinking, and excitingly, doesn't need any encouragement to follow through either.

With one gentle hand on my shoulder and the other at the base of my dick, she climbs into a straddle atop me, sinking down until I'm fully seated inside her.

I can say without a shadow of a doubt, this is the singular best feeling I've ever had in my entire life. It feels complete. It feels right. It feels…like magic.

Her head falls back, exposing the pronounced line of her collarbone, and I rain kisses across the entire thing before she makes even one move. Her heart is beating fast, I can feel it at the pulse of her neck, but she's utterly calm.

In fact, I don't think I've seen her this unflustered in the entirety of the time that I've known her.

What a fucking turn-on.

Brooke moves slowly, lifting herself with the power of her thighs and sliding back down ever so slowly. I wrap my arms around her body, and she answers by putting both her arms over my shoulders and closing them.

Our mouths are together and mingling, and goose bumps pebble the flesh of my neck. The air around us feels stagnant, as if the entire world other than the two of us in that moment is immobile.

Unhurried and precise, Brooke strokes herself on me until her limbs begin to shake, and a single drop of sweat catches on my hand as it runs down her spine.

I swear I could stay locked in this moment forever. Just here, on this side of what I can tell is going to be the biggest climax of my life.

Focused, I pull one of my hands up to dig it into her hair, and I hold her stare with mine while our lips bump together.

Down, down, down, her strokes end on a deeper grind every time, and the tightness around me amplifies.

She trembles softly and then violently, all at once, and her head shoots back in a blast of pressure to my hand as her pussy squeezes all around me. Her mouth is a silent *oh*, her breath gone entirely in the warm air between us.

My climax follows hers, and I unleash a profane groan while I bite into the flesh of her shoulder just enough to leave a tiny indentation.

I've never been more sure of one irrefutable fact.

On paper and in person, Brooke Baker is matchless.

And it doesn't matter anymore whether I should be doing this or the implications. Because now, I can't go back.

I'm forever changed in ways that are irreversible.

Chapter
Forty-Four

Brooke

A scratching sound grates at my ears as I try to pull myself from the hold of sleep's clutches. My eyes are hazy, and my head feels heavy. Even my body feels nearly impossible to separate from the mattress, and I don't know why.

I open my eyes slowly and repeatedly until my vision clears enough to get a view of the ceiling, and once again, I try to sit up.

But my ab curl is futile even with the benefit of sight, and my brain starts to get discouraged at its inability to perform its tasks.

I grunt and try again, and it's only then that the pressure at my stomach releases, freeing me to sit up…and I watch as Chase rolls to the other side of the bed, still asleep.

Ohhh. Okay. So it was the weight of another human that was stopping me. Got it.

Thankfully, the scratching persists, completely distracting me from dealing with the momentous, giant elephant-schlonged man in the bed. Instead, I jump up and run to the door, afraid I know exactly where the noise is coming from.

Benji's judgmental frown is a little hard to accept when I swing open the door, but in the interest of not waking Chase just yet, I shush Benji out into the living room to apologize.

Oh, and by the way, I'm still completely and utterly buck naked.

"Heya, Benj," I whisper, trying to sound casual even in the face of the very obvious absurdity of the situation. "How'd you sleep?"

He tilts his head with a pop, the attitude equivalent to that of a teenage girl with a hand on her hip. I cave immediately.

"Okay, okay, I knowwww. I'm really sorry. I locked you out for your own good, okay? Sometimes what's good for mommies is traumatizing for their babies."

He groans and jerks his chin toward the door. It's, I think, both an act of dismissal and a plea to go potty all in one, but I'm currently, as a reminder, *butt-ass nekkid*. I don't think I can take Benji out for a walk like this.

"Okay, buddy, just one second. Let me cover my vageen, okay? I don't think the good campers of Los Angeles Wilderness LLC paid enough in admission for the full monty."

Quietly, I move back to the bedroom in a hurry and start searching the still slightly dark room for any form of clothing. The first thing I come to is Chase's shirt from last night, so I pull it on over my head and wriggle around looking for my underwear.

I bend down and up and basically wallow on the floor, but it's only when I pop back up empty-handed to Chase's open eyes watching me avidly, that I remember my underwear from last night no longer exists.

No, the happy-go-lucky, easygoing, considerate, kind, thoughtful man of my dreams…vaporized them with a single rip and pull.

He tore my panties. To shreds. And fuck, if that wasn't beyond sexy.

Goodness, just the thought of how hot he was last night gives me a tingle all over.

He was controlling but gentle. He was generous but demanding. He was eighteen inches long.

Okay, not really, but I had a serious existential crisis in the moments before slipping him inside me about whether he'd fit without an episiotomy. In some weird way, the first time seeing his dick is the only time I've actually considered his inability to decode his role as Clive's muse as credible. Because I *way* undersold fictional him.

Regardless, he did fit—thankfully—and I can officially say that all my fuck-ups have culminated in a successful ending.

Or at least, a successful climax. In a traditional story arc, there's usually a bumpy road ahead before we can call it good and done.

"Brooke," Chase finally says with a laugh. A laugh that tells me perfectly that as much as I like to think my inner monologues run on some other space-time continuum that's faster, they don't.

And he's been sitting here staring at my nearly naked, crouching ass the whole time.

I drop my head into my hands on the edge of the bed, right next to his chest, and groan. "Oh God, I'm being really weird, aren't I?"

"Strangely, it doesn't really feel that way. I think I'm getting used to you," he teases. I smack at his chest in response, and he grabs my wrist. All the air leaves my lungs as he laces his other hand into the back of my hair and pulls my lips to his for a kiss.

It's moment-halting and earth-shattering all at once, and I can feel all the tension in my shoulders I didn't know I was holding leave them.

"Good morning," he whispers when he's done, right there against the ridge of my lips.

I nod, making our foreheads bump just a little. "Good morning."

Benji woofs at the door, practically making a show of crossing his legs, and I jump into action once more. "Sorry," I say to my dog before turning back to Chase and repeating the sentiment. "Sorry!"

He laughs and pushes me back out of the way as he climbs to standing. He's still naked, and my eyes nearly bug out of my head at the sight. He notices and turns me toward Benji with a shove. "Go. Take Benji out, and I'll start getting everything ready to get us on the road."

I nod three times without moving, and it's only then that Chase lifts me over the bed and sets me by the door with another laugh and a pat on the butt. "Go."

I finally follow orders, grabbing Benji's leash from the counter just in case, and then leading him out the door with a scowl on his handsome face.

When he gets down the stairs, he takes off for the grass on the other side of the site, over by a desolate tree, and lifts his leg immediately. He pees like I peed the day the squirrel attacked, and at the sight of it, my guilt is renewed.

I have to make it up to him, the poor guy. He's such a sport for putting up with me all the time.

When he comes back to me by the door, I stop him from climbing the steps and jerk my head toward the picnic table. He looks at the table and then back at me, and then he just stands there.

I sigh before leading the way and sitting down on the bench, pulling Chase's shirt under my bare ass enough that I'm not going to get any splinters in a delicate place.

Benji reluctantly follows, jumping up on the bench beside me and settling to sitting.

I pet at his head as I figure out how to work my way toward the good news. "Listen, I know you're mad at me. I get that. You should be mad at me. But you're my best buddy, and I can't allow this fight to go on. I need you in my corner. I don't know what I'd do without you other than go crazy. Because I know I can be self-centered and in my head sometimes, and I know that's not fair to you."

I sigh, and Benji looks confused. I don't blame him, with as much sense as I'm making. But I can't help it. My thoughts are all jumbled.

Maybe it's best if I just get to the point.

"So yeah. You remember that day we were in the park and I was kind of in my head and we lost the girl of your dreams?" I ask him.

He doesn't nod, but I'm pretty sure he gets me.

"Well, I've been trying to make that up to you while we've been touring, and I've been searching for her and her owner. And well…I found them. Or someone on Facebook found them. Whatever. The point is, when we get back to New York, I've arranged for us to get together with them, and you can have a date!"

Benji's tail wags as he jumps up and paws at my shoulder before licking me on the face. I don't know for sure, but I think he's excited.

Chase comes out the door and down the steps, but when he spies the scene between us, offers nothing more than a smile and a wink before going about the business of packing in the camper to get it ready for the road.

I still can't believe the man is this observant—so much that he'd recognize a special moment between me and my dog enough not to interrupt it—but I'm grateful, nonetheless.

Right then, I start thinking of ways to pay him back for the next few days while we're driving. It's going to be a long time on the road, and he's going to spend a lot of time at the wheel. The least I can do is make sure he's as entertained as humanly possible.

Chapter
Forty-Five

Brooke

As Chase pulls the bus into the first stop of the night—Albuquerque, New Mexico—I climb onto the bed in the bedroom and twist my legs into the criss-cross-applesauce position. Benji takes a spot beside me, lying down and closing his eyes with a groan.

I can't blame him. It's been a long day.

Eleven hours of driving and countless entertainment bits, and Benji and I are just about spent. After making up this morning, Benj and I teamed up to do a variety show of sorts while Chase drove.

We donned costumes and I painted my face with seven different kinds of makeup, and I sang an entire Shania Twain album at the top of my lungs.

The finale, though, well, that was where I really took it to the edge, turning myself into my girl Dolly with the shiniest outfit, biggest hair, and most pushed-up boobs I could manage by using three of my bras on top of one another.

I know Chase is exhausted too, but as a certified recluse, I'm not used to using this much of my social tank in one go.

If I'm going to have any hope of impressing him in the bedroom tonight— which is, of course, my highest of priorities—I'm going to need to get refreshed, and to get refreshed right quick.

When I spy the goodie bag from the premiere party last night on the nightstand, I drag it onto the bed and start pulling stuff out.

There's some candy and merch for the show and a designer change purse, but the stack of beauty products at the bottom puts a twinkle in my eye.

I never spend the money on this stuff myself because I'm usually home alone, but just the look of the products in the packaging is giving me a tingle of excitement that only free beauty products can.

Scouring through each thing carefully, I pull out the coolest-looking item in the bag. "Vandalay Fusion Face Cleaner," I read aloud, flipping over the packaging to the side to see what it does.

"T-sonic pulsations that lift away dirt, oil, and dead skin cells," I read, summarizing as I go. "Firming massage with silicone touch points for a hygienic experience and a shrewd design that you don't have to replace. Made in Finland."

"Perfect!" I squeal in delight. "Those Finnish are all so beautiful. Surely they've got to know what they're doing in the beauty industry." Given the fact that I've been very stupidly sleeping in my makeup most nights on this trip, I'm willing to bet my skin needs a good scrubbing. And just like her influence, Dolly's makeup is tricky to get rid of.

I dig down in the bag and fish around until I find a big bottle of micro-foam cleanser to use with the cleaner thingie and get to work firing this bad boy up.

It vibrates in my hand, and immediately, my eyebrows shoot up. *Is this thing really a face cleaner? Or did I read the wrong package…?*

I test out the feeling of it on the palm of my hand.

Holy shit, this thing really moves…and vibrates. *Like, the kind of good, good, good good vibrations The Beach Boys would be proud of.*

I try to turn it off, but it starts pulsing harder instead, the sound ringing out into the otherwise quiet space like a siren.

When smothering it with my hand is unsuccessful, I start stabbing at the power button again, trying to make it tired or something.

It just winds up more, though, going on a setting so intense, I swear it's going to start to shake the motor home if I can't turn it off.

The door opens with a bang, and Chase comes flying through in Cosmo Kramer fashion. I know my face looks guilty—I can feel it—even though there's absolutely nothing going on in here other than a facial scrub.

"I'm not doing anything, I swear," I blurt unexpectedly, sending my face into a crimson bloom so intense I can feel it in my ears.

"What exactly are you doing nothing with?" he asks then, spying the face scrubber tucked under my leg—and still running at full speed. His smirk is mischievous, and his eyes dance as he crawls onto the bed beside me and pulls out the scrubber to hold himself.

"It's a face cleaner!" I declare, rushing to explain. "I was going to use it to scrub all this Dolly off, but I can't get it to do what I want! It's got a mind of its own!"

Chase smiles and leans back onto the pillows with the scrubber in hand. He pushes the power button several times, cycling it through all manner of pulsations until it finally shuts off. He looks satisfied, like he's mastered the operation of it completely within a few short seconds.

He smirks again, putting it in his lap and reaching out to grab my hips. He pushes me into the pillows beside where he just was and climbs to his knees. I watch with painstaking attention as he pulls at the waistband of my pants, sliding them and my underwear down and off my legs in one smooth motion.

"Chase. What are you doing?" I ask, just as Benji takes his own leave of the room. Down and off the bed, he's gone in a flash.

"Maybe Dolly can stick around just a little longer."

My eyes narrow as he climbs down between my legs and grabs the face-cleaning machine from the bed.

He spreads my thighs with his hot palms, and then, with the push of a button, turns on the pulsating thing once again.

Obviously, not only am I naked from the waist down, but I'm utterly riveted now.

"Okayyyy, so this is getting interesting…"

He winks at me and drags the vibrating device gently up the innermost part of my thigh and then stops, right on the bikini line, holding it there for a long second and then lifting it away right when I start to squirm.

Sure fingers stroke at the bikini line on the other side, and my blood starts to pound in my ears.

He makes that same pattern again. And again. And again. Until I'm practically panting and barely there fingertips ghost over the sensitive bud at my center.

My eyes roll back, and my breath catches so hard in my throat, I have to gasp to breathe.

My hair whips into my face and tickles at the overly sensitive skin as Chase climbs my body, finds the line of my collarbone, and kisses a path that eclipses the length of it.

Even that is enough to send me careening toward an orgasm at high and reckless speeds.

From this moment on, I will never, ever be convinced that the whole body isn't an erogenous zone if the right person is using it. Fingers, toes, no matter where he goes—I'm the proud owner of a new fetish every time.

Chase moves back again to the space between my legs, taking off his pants and rolling on a condom in several short movements. I watch avidly, blinking only when he settles into the space there and pushes himself inside.

He's so big—it's an intrusion every time—but I suppose he's used to wielding it. He pauses, giving me time to adjust.

Honestly, on a spiritual level, I'm perhaps more convinced of a divine power than ever. Because God's plan makes total sense here, Chase having a monster dick and all. Only a considerate man can understand how delicate he has to be with its powers and not use them against the constraints of a woman. And Chase is the ultimate solicitous man.

He hands me the face scrubber while I'm relearning to breathe, and my eyes widen even more than they already were.

"Use it," he instructs simply. "Make yourself feel good."

I have to say it; I can't help it. "Well, the cock's a good start."

Chase laughs, and the motion of it sends a thrill through one hundred percent of my body, the feeling amplified ten times at the root of our connection. My head falls back and my hand to the bed, and Chase reaches over to redirect the device to my clit.

Taking it momentarily to get it good and vibrating, he puts it back in my palm and then reiterates, "Make yourself feel good, Brooke. Chase your orgasm."

I might need to be told twice, but I certainly don't need to be told a third time. Doing as he suggests, I place the vibrating wonder at my clit and nearly scream at the instant and intense sensation.

"That's it," he coaches easily. "That's my girl."

Okay, then. Safe to say I'm into the whole praising thing.

Slowly, ever so slowly, he starts to move, in and out and in again until he's seated to the hilt. I'd never have guessed I could fit the trunk of an elephant inside me, but I guess with the proper lubrication, many things are possible.

I push at the pulsing device in my hand, adding pressure to my clit and grinding my hips up and into both the device and Chase.

His breath is hot on my neck, and I want nothing more than to feel the sensation going down my throat. I reach up to push his chin back, and he relents immediately. I put my lips on his, sucking in everything I can get of him. I'm hoping to make it all the way to his soul, but we shall see.

Over and over and over again, we rock together in perfect rhythm, the squeaking of the bed singing a song for all around to hear.

I grab at his hair as the peak of my climax overwhelms me, and he sends a growl so savage down my throat I almost forget how to function.

Chase Dawson and Brooke Baker together.

Let me tell you something…it's worthy of a book and then some.

Chapter
Forty-Six

Saturday, June 3rd

Chase

The Albuquerque RV camp is still quiet, and Brooke is still sleeping, but my scheming and I are both alive and well this early morning.

Not only do I have to use this time to get through the reworked *Accidental Attachment* chapters Brooke has sent me because of our looming deadline, but thanks to my brilliant idea to surprise her with a party in Nashville at the ultimate Dolly-inspired rooftop bar, White Limozeen, Mo's and my text messages are burning the candle at both ends.

I don't think my sister has been awake this early in ages. As a restaurant owner, being a night owl is more her style.

Me: Did her family give a final head count?

Mo: Reluctantly, her sister Sam says both her mom and dad are coming along with her. I'm going to watch the boys so she can have the flight and party to herself.

Me: Wow. That's really nice of you, Mo. I'm impressed.

Mo: Sam's had it rough. And Vinny and I love the chance to be goofy with people who appreciate it.

Me: Children?

Mo: Exactly.

Me: So, what else needs to be done? I can try to make some calls myself, but I don't know that I'm going to get much accomplished since we're both going to be trapped in the bus all day long driving.

Mo: Don't start worrying about taking some of the burden now. We're in the home stretch, bro. I've got this. Assuming, that is, that the manuscript is going to be in my inbox soon.

I roll my eyes, but to be honest, she's earned it. Because of my close quarters with Brooke, Mo has made all the arrangements with the hotel and bar, picked the catering and drink menu, arranged for decorations and invites, helped get people who needed travel arrangements set, and on top of all that, is watching Brooke's nephews for the night so her sister can come without having to worry about being a mom. I feel a little badly that Mo's not getting to come to the party herself, but I'll make it up to her.

If things keep going between Brooke and me like they are now, I might even be able to give her the ultimate sister-in-law.

Okay, Chase, now you're getting ahead of yourself.

I know, I know. We've only slept together twice, and this is all so new and there are so many unknowns…but I really, really like her. Heading home like this is a stark realization that pretty soon, I'm not going to be with her all day, every day. Pretty soon, she's going to go back to her apartment and routine, and I'm going to go back to mine.

Almost as if by design, Brooke bounds out of the bedroom right then, and I click the screen on my phone to lock it. Her hair is down and sleep-messy, but her eyes—her eyes are alight and dancing.

She shimmies and shakes and does a little hop, skip, and a jump until she lands on my lap. The table of the booth jabs into her side, and she howls aloud like a beagle.

"Holy hell, Brooke! Are you okay?" I ask, trying my best to soothe the injured part of her side with my fingertips.

"Yes, yes," she lies with a groan and a laugh, both of which make me smile.

"I'm fine. Just clumsy." She leans forward and puts her lips to mine then for the softest, most intimately gentle kiss. When she pulls away, her voice is a sweet whisper. "There. All better."

My God. I really might be in love with her.

Satisfied with our hello, she climbs from my lap once again, grabs Benji's leash off the counter, and then opens the door for him to fly outside and pee. She winks before shutting the door behind her, and everything inside me misses her the moment she's out of sight.

I have to wonder. *If I miss her this much when she's just outside, how much am I going to miss her when we get home?*

Chapter
Forty-Seven

Sunday, June 4th

Brooke

At Chase's direction, I'm sitting on the passenger side of the motor home, wearing heels and a dress, my makeup done and proper, as he pulls up to the curb of a side street in downtown Nashville and shuts off the engine with a twist of his wrist.

He looks yummy too, having made a stop just outside of Memphis to shower and change himself before instructing me to do the same while he drove. I didn't know how far we were going or where we were stopping, but I never expected the glitz and glam of a downtown Nashville hotel.

Dinner, maybe? I thought when he was making suggestions about what I might want to wear.

But now that I'm looking closer at where we're stopped…I realize where we are, and a loud squeal jumps from my lungs without my approval.

Holy flocking sheep! He brought me to White Limozeen—*otherwise known as the Dolly Parton-themed bar of my adolescent dreams.*

Maybe someone else wouldn't realize where they were with the immediacy I have, but as someone who's dedicated a frightening amount of her time and life to the music of Dolly Parton, I knew when they decided to open this place and name it after her 1989 album very shortly after it was announced in the paper.

"Chase freaking Dawson, where are we?" is all I can manage, and beyond that, I can only do it in a whisper. I also keep looking at the sign of the Graduate Hotel, the home to the Dolly-inspired rooftop bar, blinking several times to make sure what I'm seeing is real.

Chase, though, he's all relaxed and calm, just sitting there in the driver's seat with a big-ass smile on his face.

"Tell me this isn't what I think it is. Tell me we're not where I think we are," I beg dumbly, unable to handle the raw emotion of twentysomething years of obsession culminating in this moment.

A chill runs the entire length of my spine as he reaches over to grab just the top of my knee. And his voice is unbelievably gentle and understanding as he replies. "We are where you think we are. And we're here to celebrate you."

"What do you mean?" I demand, bouncing up and out of my seat. "What do you mean we're here to celebrate me?"

Chase stands with me, pulling me into his body just enough to stop my shaking. "The premiere in LA was about Netflix. Sure, they were very welcoming to you, and you were a part of it, but overall, it was a celebration of their success…of their milestone."

My nose stings as tears enter my eyes uninvited.

"This…tonight…is a celebration of you—Brooke Baker—and your success. Your milestone. You have a show on Netflix!" he nearly shouts, hugging and shaking me at the same time. "This is big, Brooke. Huge. And there was no way in hell I was going to allow you to let it pass you by. And I couldn't think of any better place to celebrate you than here."

I launch into his arms, wrapping my legs around his hips and raining kisses all over his face. It's enthusiastic and overzealous, and I don't care. I'm so fucking thankful that this man exists.

"You!" I yell, directly into his face while clamping his jaw with my hands. "You are something else! I would totally take you back to the bedroom to ravish your whole body right now if I weren't so damn excited about the bar! I'm sorry for that! And I'm sorry for yelling this loud and for possibly injuring your eardrums also!"

"You're welcome, Brooke." His response is a soft chuckle and one of my fa-vorite Chase smiles. "Now, how about we get inside and see it?"

Putting Dolly Parton before sex without argument?

It's official. He really is the *perfect* man.

Everything feels like magic tonight. The air is somehow thick but translu-cent, and it makes me feel like I'm riding a cloud with a view of the city. My family is here, along with a few publishing friends I've made over the years, and Dolly's huge bust sits in the corner of the rooftop and pink umbrellas festoon every third foot. White tassels hang from the edges, and women in cowboy boots deliver frilly drinks to people in their finest rhinestones.

I look down at my own outfit of fringe and festivus—the very cowgirl-es-que outfit Chase encouraged me to wear—and I can hardly believe where life has brought me. A rooftop Dolly-themed bar like this was something I dreamed about back in the sterile classrooms of my high school in Podunk, Ohio. A launch party for a creation of mine with people swirling their well-wishes and good times around me while the show based on *my books* plays on TVs in the background is beyond anything I could fathom.

If I could talk to the young girl inside me and make her see what was truly possible, maybe I wouldn't have struggled so much with my anxiety. Maybe I would have seen the value in myself enough to know that I deserved this moment and, more than that, that I would think myself worthy of the dream-boat of a man at my side.

Maybe Chase wouldn't feel unattainable at all. Maybe he'd just feel like my destiny.

Sammy bumps me from behind, getting my attention before pulling me into the hug of a lifetime. I can feel both her own joy and her happiness for me radiating through her, and it brings comfort on a level I can't describe.

"Hey, SissySam," I say with a rock and a tease, pulling her hair from her shoulder and draping it down the center of her back. "Thanks so much for making the trip all the way here for this. I can't believe he put all this together!"

Sam's smile is bright and easy and just a touch knowing. "Are you kidding? I wouldn't have missed it! My sister is a rock star with her very own groupie," she says with a waggle of her eyebrows and a jerk of her chin toward Chase.

"Oh, come on."

"You come on, Brookie. You can't be that slow on the uptake on this one. I wasn't entirely sure what I was going to find here after the last time we spoke, but that's a man in loveeee. Okay?"

"Shhh," I hush her, embarrassed. "Don't talk so loud, someone might—"

"Hear me?" she interrupts on a laugh. "Brooke, look around you, would you? I don't think anyone needs to hear me say it to understand that this whole party is written like one giant love letter. He had to use Mo to get a lot of this shit done because he was with you the entire time, but trust me, this whole thing is designed and approved by Chase Dawson himself."

"Okay, Sammy, stop. Really. Before I freak out."

She eyes me closely before narrowing her gaze and hitting me with some honesty. I don't know that I'm ready for it, but I'm pretty sure I need it. "Maybe you need to take a closer look at *why* you're freaking out. Like, what's holding you back at this point, Brooke? You've got the success, you've got the talent, you've got the personality, and the looks… Why wouldn't a man, any man, but especially that man over there looking fine as hell, want you? Reality check, baby, you guys are a match made in heaven, okay? Why do you think the book you wrote about the two of you reads so good? It's because you really are the real-life Clive and River."

She nods as everything she's saying plays out across my face.

"Mm-hmm. Maybe, just maybe, you need to set aside the freaking out for a night and take a little trip to reality. He'd be a fool not to love you, babe. And you'd be a fool not to tell him you feel the same."

Tears hit my eyes, and she hushes them away. "Now, come on. Don't start crying. Get yourself together, and then get over there and tell that man that you've very clearly been having a taste of that you're in love with him, would you?"

Sammy leaves me with a bump and a nod, and I watch the biggest TV in the back of the bar for a long moment as my Shadow Brothers pester and tease each other with ease. The life that I breathed into that series? It's there and then some. I know sometimes seeing your work transition to another medium can be scary and worrisome, but the job they've done with this show—the success I'm certain it'll have—brings me the most all-encompassing good feeling.

She's right. I did this. I got myself a show on Netflix, taught myself to do some makeup, and survived nearly a month on the road talking to and interviewing with all manner of people.

I've made Chase laugh over and over again with my jokes, and with the way he's looked at me the last couple of nights, I must have something that's working for me.

I deserve this. I deserve him. We're almost at the end of our adventure, and I want the happy ending so badly I can taste it.

Steeling my spine, I set my course. Chase is in the corner chatting with someone from the staff of the bar, but I'm on a mission now, and I won't be stopped.

Benji follows me closely, but I don't glance down at him even once. I know he won't take offense, though. He gets it. He has to get it.

If I don't seize this moment—if I don't give in to the burn in my chest and the temptation in my heart in a moment like this—I never will.

And I don't want to look back in twenty years and wonder if my own story could have had a happily ever after if I'd taken my nose out of my books long enough.

With determination and pure adrenaline driving me, I weave my way through the crowd—past my drunk and happy parents, past my previous editor, past my sister watching from the corner—and walk right up to Chase, who's just ending his conversation with the manager of the bar.

His attention comes to me right away, and without hesitation, his eyes light up.

That's the final boost of confidence I need.

"Chase, can I talk to you for a bit in private?"

He nods, and the manager steps away with a smile. "We're all set anyway, Mr. Dawson." She looks to me. "Enjoy your night, Ms. Baker."

Fingers crossed, I will.

Chase takes my hand and pulls me inside the doors that lead to the indoor section of White Limozeen, and then he walks me around the bar to the other side of the room. It's much quieter in here, and that's both good and bad for a woman who's trying to fill that gap in noise with the single most important three words of her life.

I take a deep breath as Chase pulls me to a stop and turns me to face him. For a minute, all I can do is study the man on my mind.

Swooped, perfect black hair, brilliant white teeth, hard but forgiving jaw, and the sweetest smile that seeps all the way into the pretty blue of his eyes. He's wearing a navy velvet suit coat, a black shirt, and black dress slacks, and he's still only as handsome as he normally is.

Funny thing about perfection—it's hard to beat.

Add the fact that he hasn't even once tried to rush me during this whole perusal, and I'm officially convinced that I'm doing the right thing.

Complication or not, I'm in love with Chase Dawson. And I think it's about time that I told him.

"Chase…"

"Brooke."

I nod. *Okay, okay, get on with it.*

But maybe…maybe just a kiss first.

Rolling up to the tips of my toes, I take his face in my hands and his lips under mine. He reacts swiftly, putting his hands to my hips and fusing my body to his while I run the tip of my tongue along the length of his. He groans at the sensation, and my head spins with arousal.

I can hardly make myself stop, but when I do, I'm winded and out of breath. He holds me close, putting his forehead to mine, and remarks teasingly, "Is that what you wanted to talk to me about? Because I could say a thing or two myself."

Laughter rolls between us as I rock my forehead back and forth on his. "No, actually. That was a split-second decision."

"Okay, then. Those are good, too. Let's make more of those."

"Chase!"

"What?" His smirk is addictive. "You need me to take the lead? Because I can definitely take the lead. Pretty sure I proved that in Chicago."

I set him away with a snort and a shake of my head and then point with a finger in his face. "You. Stay right there while I tell you this. No sudden moves."

He chuckles incredulously. "*You* kissed me!"

"I know. But now I'm trying to tell you something, and if I don't get it out now, I don't know if I'll get it out ever, and I have to get it out. I have to before it eats me alive."

"Okay. What is it?"

"First, I just want to thank you for…well, everything. But especially tonight. I'll never get over this as long as I live, and I don't know that I'll ever feel this special again. You just… You're the best."

He smiles so big, his cheeks threaten to leave his face. It's beautiful. He also tries to open his mouth to speak, but I put a hand over it just in time.

"Ah," I buzz with a shake of my head. "Just…not yet. Let me finish."

He nods. His smile is still present against my hand.

"The second and most important thing I wanted to tell you…the reason I brought you over here…basically my reason for everything at this point…"

He raises his eyebrows.

"I know. I'm rambling. But the reason I'm rambling is because I want to tell you that I love you."

His eyes widen—just slightly—and my heart and blood pressure take a dive that even the dutiful Benji at the couch behind me isn't prepared for.

Chase catches me just as I'm falling, and then he lifts me into his body and squeezes so tightly I can hardly breathe.

It's enough to keep me just on this side of consciousness, though, and Chase makes sure to use the time efficiently.

"Brooke, I need you to look at me right now, and I need you to listen. Do not pass out, do you hear me?"

I try to nod, but God, the pull is strong.

"Do not pass out before I can tell you I love you too."

Everything freezes, and a jolt of electricity rights the rhythm of my heart. I am suddenly, wholly, impossibly aware.

"You...you love me too?"

"More than I'm comfortable admitting."

"Chase..."

"Brooke, when it comes to me and what I'm looking for in this life? You're it."

"Chase," I whisper his name again, nearly undone.

"You're. It." He brushes his lips softly against mine, and even though I'm definitely conscious and I'll remember those words for as long as I live, I might as well be a puddle of love-struck, moony-eyed goo on the floor.

He loves me.

Holy hell. Somehow, someway, I turned my life into a self-fulfilling prophecy.

And bagged the absolute finest man on the planet.

Tonight, my life is an actual dream.

There's only one little problem.

At what anniversary is it safe to tell your husband that the book you published together was actually about him? Fiftieth?

Asking for a friend.

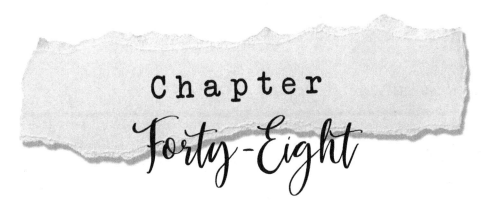

Chapter
Forty-Eight

Monday, June 5th

Chase

Freshly showered after our third round of lovemaking inside our hotel room at the Graduate Hotel in Nashville, I wrap my towel tighter around my waist and wink at Brooke through the glass wall of the shower.

She's a fucking little goddess in there, her naked body on full display and my eyes refusing to miss a second of it. I've been inside her for what feels like hours tonight, but when it comes to Brooke, I don't think I'll ever be satisfied.

I don't think I'll ever have enough of her.

"I'm not one to rush people, but I'm telling you, if you take too long in there, I'll just end up joining you instead."

"We need to eat!" she exclaims on a laugh.

"Then I guess you need to find your way to some clothes."

"You're incorrigible." She splashes water at me over the top, and I laugh as I dart out of the way to avoid her fire. But I don't leave the bathroom just yet.

"And you're beautiful."

"Chase Dawson." She points one defiant index finger in my direction. "I swear, if you keep smooth-talking me like that, I'm going to end up inviting you back in here. And then Benji is going to have to be on guard for both of us."

"Fine." I hold up two hands in the air on a smile. "I'm going."

"Aw, man," she whines, her lips turning down at the corners into the most adorable little pout, and I can't not smile.

"Woman, you drive me wild." I take in her gorgeous body and her pretty eyes one last time. "But I'm really going."

She giggles and draws a heart in the steam on the glass, and I step out of the bathroom and into the bedroom to get dressed with a permanent smile on my lips.

We've already planned to find sustenance after we're both done getting ready, but my stomach growls as though I'm starving, thanks to the whirlwind of the last, I don't know, hundred hours or so.

Brooke told me she loved me last night, and I can still hardly believe it—can still hardly believe how lucky I am.

Now, I know that sounds sappy, but after the absolute shitshow of my relationship with Caroline, I didn't know that I'd ever find someone I wanted to try with again.

I didn't know that the reward could ever be worth the risk.

But all this time spent with Brooke has flipped everything I've ever known on its head. It's taken my preconceived notions about hard rules of professionalism and keeping your personal life separate to a different stratosphere—to a planet where that's not only impractical, it's impossible.

Because sometimes life brings people together for a reason. Sometimes life knows better than you and teaches you to throw caution to the wind. Sometimes life reminds you that there's more to it than a job.

This was a major issue for Clive and River in Brooke's manuscript, but the more I've lived it myself, the more I've come to realize that all that bullshit is just that—bullshit. If it's in the way of happiness, get rid of it. If it's worth it, it'll find a way to work.

After I toss on my clothes, I grab a granola bar from my backpack on the chaise and unwrap it to take a bite.

I smile as the shower shuts off, and I snap my backpack clasps back into place.

I spin away from the chaise lounger in our hotel room, wanting to be ready to catch sight of Brooke before she covers herself in clothes, and in the process of my haste, I accidentally knock her brown leather backpack to the floor. It upends, and the contents scatter across the carpet with impressive distance.

"Shit," I mumble, stooping down to pick it all up and put it back together as neatly as I can.

There are several pens and a bevy of notebooks, but there are also a handful of loose-leaf pages of paper with colorful notes scratched on every line of them.

I don't mean to look at them, but when I see my name at the top of one, I can't help but read through that line and then…keep reading for the entirety of the page.

Chase's List of Flaws:

1. Doesn't understand how handsome he is.

2. He uses a fake broadcaster-type voice when he's on the phone with important people to make himself sound more authoritative.

3. He's pretty fucking pushy about a book that's ruining my life.

4. He forced his way on to this tour with me without asking if I'd be okay with it.

5. He's so work-minded that sometimes he forgets to have fun.

6. He flirts without thinking of the fallout.

7. He practically martyred himself for this stupid book I didn't even mean to write.

8. He let his ex walk all over him for a long, long time.

9. He's arrogant in his ability to make this book what it needs to be.

10. With an ex and a best friend who went behind his back for a year and a half, his judge of character is a bit questionable.

A burn simmers in my chest, and my cheeks heat with unchecked embarrassment, all the things Brooke thinks are wrong with me laid out for me to see.

I don't know how to breathe, can barely force my throat to swallow as Brooke comes stumbling out of the bathroom, a towel wrapped around her body and a huge smile on her face.

A mere two minutes ago, that smile would have led to feelings of lust and charm and endearment, but now…now, it feels like a smirk that hides all the things I don't know.

Why would she make a list like this? Why would she write it down? And why on earth does it hurt so much to read it?

It doesn't take her all that long to notice the sheet of paper in my hand or the hard line of my jaw, and from the looks of her frown, I'd say she knows *exactly* what I'm holding. The guilt is written all over her—in her hesitant gaze, in her timid feet, and in the way her hands grip her towel.

"What is this, Brooke?"

She swallows hard and pulls the towel even tighter around herself, smoothing some of the wet strands of her long hair behind one ear. "I…"

"Speak up," I hear myself chastise, and a pink hue rushes to her cheeks.

I feel badly, but I won't let myself be swayed by the way I feel—the fact that I love her—right now. I have to know what in the hell is going on. I have to know what in the fuck this means.

I have to know *why*.

"Um…" She clears her throat. "W-when you told me the characters had no flaws, I did an exercise to get myself in the habit of picking out flaws. I was…having a hard time with Clive, and I needed somewhere to start."

"Why on earth would you start with me?"

She steels her spine then, and it doesn't take a body language expert to understand that what she's about to say next isn't going to be something I want to hear.

"Because…Clive is you."

I blink, and then I shake my head, trying to understand. "What do you mean?"

"Clive Watts is Chase Dawson. And River Rollins is Brooke Baker." She closes her eyes. "With a few improvements. But…I wrote the book about us."

"I don't understand." When she turned in this book, we hardly knew each other.

Her laugh is a mix of a scoff and a sneer, and I don't know what to make of it. "Of course you don't understand. Because why would you? It's an insane thing to do, writing a whole book about someone without their knowledge or permission. But you know what's even crazier, Chase?" She doesn't pause for me to respond. She doesn't even pause to take a gulp of air. "Turning that book in to your editor by accident because you were too drunk to distinguish the files the night your manuscript was due. That's crazy. And then, you don't tell your editor what you've done. Instead, you go along with it, and you let him take that book to his boss and pitch it like it's the most normal thing in the world to turn in a book the publisher isn't expecting. And then the crazy finale! They decide to publish it!"

"Brooke—"

"Yep. That's the truth, Chase. The unvarnished shitshow! I've fucked you in my head since the moment I met you, and now I've fucked you in way more ways than the one I always fantasized about. How's that for flawed?"

My jaw is firm, and my heart is sore as I consider the implications of all the things she's saying to me right now—of all the lies she's told me for weeks and weeks.

"I'd say it's pretty fucked up," I admit, my voice hard even to my own ears. Talking to Brooke like this…it's unnatural. My stomach is literally turning in on itself.

But even that—feeling the drive to protect her—is a behavior built on falsehoods. Who is the woman I thought I knew?

Who is Brooke Baker at all?

"For someone who claims to have written a book about a crush on me, you sure seem to have found some things to hate," I say, shaking the paper in my hand.

"No, Chase. No. I don't think those things at all—"

"Oh, come on, Brooke. You wrote them, didn't you?"

"Yes. I did, but—"

"But nothing, Brooke," I cut her words off before they can put on gym shoes and run all over me. "They're your words, your truths, and I think they tell me more than the rest of the time we've spent together. Time, I see now, was all some part of a sick game or something."

This is too much for my brain and heart to comprehend. The hotel room feels like it's growing smaller by the second and my only option for survival is to escape.

I toss the papers down and grab my backpack, headed for the door.

She's blocking the path since the bathroom is at the front of the room, but I don't stop even when she grabs my arm.

"Chase, please. You're getting this all wrong. Let me explain."

"Explain? Now? After you've tricked me and lied to me all this time?" I shake my head. "I don't think so, Brooke. The time to explain was a while ago. Maybe the night I asked you if you ever felt like Clive and River. Before you spewed some bullshit about loving me."

"But it's not bullshit," she cries, grabbing at my arm again as I open the door. She says more, but my ears can't hear it. My mind can't process it.

I can't do anything but leave this hotel room before it suffocates the life out of me.

Thinking I had the world in my hands, only to find out I don't know anything at all, hurts way too much. Looking at the woman I thought I knew enough to love—to risk my entire career for in half a dozen ways—feels like twisting a hot knife in my chest.

I can't stay here another minute. I can't and I won't.

I shove through the door and walk as fast as I can.

Away from Brooke Baker and everything I thought she was and back toward reality.

Love hurts. But losing it before you've even really had it? That burns like a bitch.

Chapter
Forty-Nine

Brooke

Chase's back has never looked bad in all the time I've known him, but it looks pretty fucking shitty right now. His lines are hard and his gait steady as he walks away from me toward the elevator of the hotel at a near run.

And I'm just standing in the hallway, with wet hair and only a towel covering my body, and it feels like I'm watching my heart walk away from me.

His long legs have no trouble extending the distance between us, and with each long step, my breathing gets a little bit shorter.

I want to call out—to say something worthy of him turning around and bringing those long strides back toward me. But what do you say to a man you've been lying to for basically the whole time you've known him?

A man you involuntarily dragged into your twisted fantasies so far that he put his career on the line to support them. A man who's been your everything for the last month, taking care of you in ways you never dreamed a man could or would—without even being your boyfriend.

I don't know that there's a bouquet of flowers in the universe big enough to right the wrongs I've perpetrated against him.

I'd love to claim it wasn't intentional—but I knew from the moment he said the names Clive and River in his office that I had absolutely no intention of letting him in on the joke.

I just…I can't even begin to figure out how to apologize. How to make it right. This isn't exactly the kind of thing normal people do. Suzanne Somers did not give life advice for this one in her guide to life book, that's for sure.

As Chase disappears on the elevator and the desolation of the situation comes into focus, I close the door and sink to the floor with my back against it, unable to stop the huge, bucking sobs of fat tears.

What…what have I done? How did I ruin the best thing to ever happen to me so quickly?

And maybe most important…am I ever going to be able to fix it?

Chapter
Fifty

Tuesday, June 6ʰ

Brooke

The whole motor home shakes with a repeated bang on the door, startling me awake. I've been here since yesterday around checkout time from the hotel room, just waiting and hoping for Chase to come back and talk to me.

It's the worst kind of feeling, being helpless to do anything proactive.

Aside from texting and calling his phone a couple of times, which either went straight to voice mail or was left unanswered, I haven't even been able to form any other thoughts aside from a wallow.

I know how pathetic that is—and trust me, my dog has given me more than enough looks to confirm it—but my sister is already on her way back to New York, my parents are probably already in Ohio, Chase is gone and I don't know if he's coming back, and *I don't know how to fix this.*

If there was any part of me that could come up with some kind of a solution, I'm sure I'd be doing better, but as it is, I'm just surviving. Benji is dog-tired, no pun intended, and I've been on the brink of unconscious more times in one night than I've been in years.

As it turns out, handling this level of hysteria with my condition isn't something I have exactly worked out.

I jump up off the couch, catching my leg in a tangle in the blanket I fell asleep sobbing into last night. I have to twist like a toy top to free myself, before I can lunge for the door.

I don't even bother to check myself or wipe the slobber from my chin before jerking it open with a painfully hopeful, "Chase?"

The unknown man's eyebrows climb almost to his receding hairline, and he takes a step back in the shock of my aggression. "Uh, no, ma'am. I'm Mark. Your driver for the trip back to New York?"

His inflection is in a question, almost certainly because this is information he expected me to know, but I'm too much of a mess to know anything.

If the call wasn't coming from Chase, I didn't answer it. If the message wasn't him answering my apologies, I wasn't reading it.

And since he didn't call or message me back, I haven't talked to anyone besides Benji.

In the interest of safety, I know I should check that Mark is who he says he is before letting him aboard. But I'll be honest; I'd rather take my chances on being brutally murdered than speak to Wilson Phillips at this juncture. I can't imagine he'd be impressed with the mess I've created out here, even without the use of planes.

I step aside and hold the door open, but Mark hesitates before filling the opening. I don't blame him. I'm a ball of unblown snot and tear-streaked skin, and the statistical chance that I'll latch on to any living point of comfort in the next thirty seconds is incredibly high.

As he steps inside and begins the routine of readying the camper for the road, memories of Chase doing the same the first morning after we made love flood me. The smiles, the winks. The teasing looks and touches as I dared him to flex his muscles.

Oh God. It hurts.

I drop into a ball on the sofa again, and poor Mark works around me with wide eyes. I can't even pretend not to cry, though. The pressure in my ducts is just too damn strong.

A sob escapes my throat, and Benji curls up next to me. As ridiculous as I am, my best friend can feel the very real and raw pain in the place my hysteria is coming from.

Chase isn't coming back. Not now, and maybe not ever.

And I've got the next fourteen and a half hours to myself to think about it. Just hysterical Brooke Baker and her new driver Mark.

A sob breaks free again, and I bury my puffy face into the blanket in my lap as a very scary realization dawns on me.

This story…my story…may not have a happy ending.

Chapter
Fifty-One

Wednesday, June 7th

Brooke

My bag bumps along the sidewalk behind me as I walk the final block to my apartment building from the train. After fifteen hours on the bus with a man I didn't know—and still don't know, thanks to the off-putting nature of my complete mental breakdown, or as I like to call it, *Menty B*—he parked in the lot downtown and sent me on my way to take the subway home.

Several people stared at me on the ride, which is really saying something in a city like New York, so I know I must look pretty fucking terrible, but I wouldn't dare tempt confirming it with a mirror right now.

Instead, I've resigned myself to what I am, a sobbing disaster that hiccups with a new cry every fifty feet or so.

Believe it or not, it's a vast improvement over yesterday. Just ask Benji.

I shove open the front door to my building and hold Benji's leash to shuffle him inside first before following, my bag clattering over the change in elevation presented by the threshold enough to get my doorman's attention.

He lifts his head from whatever he's working on at the front desk, a smile at the ready, but when he catches sight of me, any and all familiarity vanishes. I'm pretty sure if it weren't for the Batman costume-wearing dog beside me, he'd be detaining me while the police found their way to our building.

"Ms. Baker…are you all right?"

I open my mouth to speak, but nothing more than a shrill cry escapes, so I shut it and hustle to the elevator as fast as my heartbroken body can take me.

I'm not suitable for conversation right now, dammit!

My backpack slides off my shoulder with the speed of my spin and knocks me off-balance, but Benji crowds my legs enough to catch me before I can bang my head into the elevator wall. With manic fingers, I push the button to my floor and the door close button simultaneously and over and over again.

When the door finally closes in front of me, I sink into the back rail and then past it, until I'm flat on my ass.

I know it's dramatic, but I swear, I don't feel even an ounce of strength in my body.

When the elevator does make it to my floor, I have to crawl to my door, dragging the suitcase behind me like a corpse—a painfully accurate representation of the way I feel.

I reach up with one hand to put my key in the lock, and I have to make several attempts before getting it. When I push the door open with the knob, I slink my way forward like the snake that I am.

Snot coats just about every inch of my upper body at this point, and my eyes are so puffy I can barely hold them open. I'm not delusional enough to think I look normal, but I still try for a smile when my sister catches sight of me slithering in the door like I've lost the use of my legs.

"Jesus Christmas!" she yells, likely horrified by the terrifying sight of me as we make eye contact. "Grant, Seth, go in the bedroom now!" she orders unequivocally, and the two of them take off running. She recovers from her horror quickly, though, jumping up from the couch and running toward me as I collapse into a heap on the floor. I roll over to my back, staring up at the tiles on my drop ceiling while I cry.

"Brooke, what happened? Oh my God, what's wrong? Did someone die?" Her voice is both loud and discreet in the way only a mom with small children can be, and Benji crowds the two of us as Sam pulls me into her arms.

"Brooke, tell me what's going on so I can help you. Do I need to make funeral arrangements or plan a hit? Give me a clear path to work."

"I…I…I'm smo dove."

"Smo dove? Smo so? So dove so done? So dun dun dum dumb, so *dumb*. You're so dumb!" Sammy yells out her successful translation excitedly, making me scowl. I mean, I understand that I'm not the most coherent I've ever been right now, but I'm in the middle of a crisis, for shit's sake. Sammy notices my discontent and corrects her face immediately. "Sorry. Really sorry," she apologizes, running a tender hand over my hair and twisting at the ends like our mom used to do when we were kids. "Take a deep breath, Brookie. Get it together, so you can tell me what's wrong, okay?"

Get it together? Ha. I'm so far from being able to get it together it's not even funny. It's tragic.

She strokes my hair gently, alternating running a finger over my cheek every time another tear escapes. "It's going to be okay, I promise. Nothing you and I can't fix, okay?"

My breathing is short and choppy for a lot longer than I'd like to admit, but under her quiet direction and undeniable patience, I eventually overcome the frog in my throat and put together a coherent sentence.

"I…I really messed things up with Chase. I had a chance, an actual chance at being with the guy of my dreams, and I blew it."

The words are no more than just clear of my mouth when I devolve into my four-hundredth round of tears. Saying it aloud—admitting how big my fuckup really is—has me spiraling into a full-on breakdown all over again.

And I thought poor Mark saw me at my worst. I'm reaching new levels of breaking down as we speak.

"Oh, Brooke." She hugs me. "You know as well as I do that no low is unrecoverable. No wrong is unrightable. I know you as a person, and, I'm guessing, so does Chase. There's nothing you could have done that you can't fix, sweet girl. Because you're not vindictive, you're not willfully hurtful, you're not mocking or petty or cold. Anything you've done is nothing more than a mistake, and I'm going to help you figure out how to fix it. I promise."

"I wouldn't have thought those things about me either. But, Sam," I cry, "he...he...found the list of shitty stuff I wrote about himmmm."

"Shitty stuff? I'm confused. I read the book, and you didn't say one shitty thing."

"I know!" I sob. "That was the problem, he said. Clive was too perfect." I sob harder. "So I wrote a list of awful things to try to get myself in the frame of mind to rough him up around the edges, and now..." I hiccup. "And now this!"

"Did you explain to him why you did it?"

"I tried! But between telling him the book was about us and the list and having just told him I loved him, he—"

"Wait...you told him you loved him?" Sam interrupts eagerly.

I appreciate the sentiment, really, but now is so not the time. "Sammy!"

"Right, right, I'm sorry. Maybe later."

"With everything he was finding out, I just think it was too much, you know?" I cover my wet, snotty face with my hands. "He couldn't take any more, and he didn't want to hear anything!"

"Maybe he just needs time, then, babe. I mean, it had to be a shock, you know? It's not like the book is abstract to him. The man's been actively into it, reading it, working on it for weeks."

"I know," I cry again. "I know."

"So, just give him some time. Get together a plan for when he is willing to talk and go from there."

"You really..." I pause through a stuttering breath. "Think he'll forgive me?"

"I don't think it, B. I know it. Look at everything you've done for me." She gestures around the apartment and smiles softly. "You're going to get this karma back, and I'm going to make sure it's in the form of mending your broken heart, okay?"

I nod through my tears. I want to say so much more, but I just can't.

"Now, let's start by getting you in the shower because you are absolutely disgusting. And then, we'll get us a plan together, okay?"

"I love the sound of a shower and a plan." I hiccup through a breath. "I just don't know if I can come up with a plan good enough to fix this, Sam. It feels…impossible."

"Brookie," she whispers and hugs me tightly again. "Do you love him?"

"More than I've ever loved anyone or anything." I nod so many times my neck starts to feel like it might snap in half.

"If you love him like that, babe, then nothing is impossible. That kind of love doesn't fade away, and I know for a fact he feels the same way about you. I saw it with my own eyes in Nashville. He loves you and you love him and while things aren't great right now, I know they will be. Love like that is rare, B. It's rare and it's beautiful. Use it to give you the strength you need to overcome this."

I know what's happened between Chase and me has been a whirlwind. It's been this all-consuming thing I've felt since the moment I laid eyes on him.

I know it's not the normal pace of a relationship.

But I also know that it's the realest, most precious thing I've ever felt.

I can't walk away from this. I can't walk away from him.

I *have* to find a way to fix this.

"Now, how about that shower, yeah?" Sam reminds me of the basic necessities that are required to human properly. Lord knows, I've been slacking in that department ever since Chase walked out of our hotel room.

Frankly, I don't even remember the last time I ate or drank anything.

All I can do is nod, and she helps me to my feet.

And Sam stays there, by my side, her calm, rational, and gentle approach providing a tiny balm to my aching chest.

I strip out of my clothes and step under the hot spray of the shower head, and before I can even start to think about shampooing my hair, a lightbulb just clicks on.

I think I know what to do. I just hope it'll work.

First: finishing this shower.

Second: a date with my first love…my computer.

God, I hope it works.

Chapter
Fifty-Two

Thursday, June 15th

Chase

The long walk back from Jonah Perish's office is bittersweet.

Yesterday, I turned in the final edits on *Accidental Attachment,* and today, Jonah called me into his office to celebrate with a bottle of champagne and more than a little back-patting.

"I knew you had it in you, kid. I'm glad I gave you the reins."

My God, talk about a kick in the balls. It's the confirmation I was craving, the ending I knew was possible with a book as good as this one—and yet, I can barely even swallow my saliva when I think about it.

A book about us—Brooke and me—just doesn't sound as sweet when the ending in real life is in the shitter.

Truthfully, it took everything inside me to be able to send it to him. I didn't want to. It felt wrong in all the ways it possibly could. But when I think about what it would've done to Brooke's career had I not turned it in, I didn't have any other option but to send it off.

At this point, I don't know if I even give a shit about my own career. The simple act of forcing myself out of bed each morning is enough of a task for my mind to focus on.

I brush past Dawn and into my office, and when I spot the well-used, gently worn paper manuscript for *Accidental Attachment* that I've been carrying around with me for weeks on end, I shove it off my desk and toward the garbage can in an uncontrolled moment.

Tears prick at my eyes, and I sink down into my chair and drop my head into my hands.

Fuck. The pain I feel is a deep, gnawing, ache that spreads from the center of my chest to the pit of my stomach. It is ever-present and there is absolutely nothing that provides relief.

I think about Brooke, but I'm always thinking about Brooke. The terrible thing about love is that once you fall in love with someone, you can't force yourself to fall out of love with them.

Once your heart is in it, it's ride or die, no matter the consequences.

Hell, even though I left her in that hotel room in Nashville with no intention of looking back, I still made sure to call Wilson Phillips with enough of an explanation to get him to hire a nice man by the name of Mark to drive her and the motor home back to New York, just to make sure she was safe.

Every instinct inside me still wants to protect her. Still wants to be the man standing by her side.

A timid knock sounds from the glass wall next to my door, and I look up to see Dawn stepping inside my office.

"Sir? Are you...are you..." She clears her throat, reconsidering calling me out on the tears directly. "I, um...is there anything I can maybe help you with?"

I smear the moisture from my eyes down across my nose and then swipe at my mouth when a smidge of the salt hits my tongue.

God, I'm a mess. One little book and the woman who wrote it have turned my life *upside down.*

I've been from one extreme to the other and back again in the last month, and I hardly even know who I am anymore.

I just want to feel normal. I want to feel happy. I want to go back to before I knew all the shit I know now.

With a heavy sigh, I swing my chair around to my computer and click haphazardly until my email is open.

Without looking at her directly, I dismiss Dawn as politely as I can manage. "No...thanks. I'm all right."

I can practically feel her pause before she turns to leave, and on a last-minute shout, I order, "Shut the door on your way out."

I wait until it closes all the way to take another full breath. I knew, without question, that when I let it out, it would be shaky.

I scroll through my email, dragging the ones I know are junk to the trash and starring the ones I know I'm in no way ready to face right now—other authors, potential manuscripts, correspondence about the editors' meeting. I can't concentrate on any of it at the moment.

Once all the emails are cleared, I lean back in my chair and unfurl the knot in my tie, hoping it'll make it easier to breathe. It doesn't alleviate the choke hold on my throat completely, of course, but it's better than nothing at all.

Shoving my chair back on a roll, I start to stand up to go for a walk or leave for the day or anything other than sitting here, but the population of an email at the top of my inbox stops me.

The sender? *Brooke Baker.*

My heart stops. My lungs tighten. And I rub my fingers on my palm for five seconds, considering what to do before I find myself clicking it open with a quick tap of my mouse.

The contents, I find pretty quickly, are our breakup scene. *Ours.* Not Clive and River's. Chase and Brooke's...from her point of view.

There's no intro or apology or explanation before it starts. Instead, the email dives right into the scene...and so do I.

Monday, June 5th

Brooke

I stumble out of the bathroom, the man of my dreams on my mind.

Last night, Chase and I exchanged I love yous.

Three months ago, I would have never thought an outcome like today would be possible. I was happy, but lonely, and after many discussions with my canine sidekick, had pretty much decided it would stay that way.

None of the men in New York came even close to what I wanted in a life partner, and to be honest, none of the men in Ohio did either. I had started to wonder if I might be the problem or if my standards might be too high or if maybe I'm just supposed to be a one-woman-plus-canine show for the rest of my life.

But enter my new editor Chase Dawson, and my whole world flipped on its head. I know it's crazy, I know, but I don't even completely know how it happened other than to say…the day I met Chase Dawson was the day the earth stood still.

There were bright lights and powerful auras, and I'm pretty sure the whole "circle around the sun" thing paused for ten to fifteen solid seconds.

He was everything those men weren't and then some. He was polite and gracious and charming and sweet, and he had the eyes and body of my fantasies! And I, lucky girl, was going to be working with him on my next book for several weeks at a time.

Add that to the fact that my current work in progress, Garden of Forever, was lacking in just about every lust I'd ever had for writing, and my mind was crying to cling to the creativity of an innocent crush.

Maybe that's why it was so easy to build a fantasy around Chase after the first time I met him. I don't know. But writing that book was one of the greatest escapes of my life, and to find out now that everything I wrote, everything I wanted so desperately, could be true?

Well, I think it's safe to say I'm beside myself.

Playful and prancing, I round the corner from the bathroom into the main room, ready to pick up where we left off only minutes ago and convince Chase that food isn't that important right now. I can't get enough of him, and I know it's more than just the physical. Emotionally, I'm obsessed, and for women, that's the ultimate turn-on.

But I'm met with a frown, the normally perfect lines of Chase's friendly face turned down with the kind of hurt I wouldn't wish on my worst enemy. He's holding a sheet of paper, and unfortunately, I know immediately what the lines of it hold.

It's the only loose-leaf I've used the entire trip.

Chase's List of Flaws. The single-handedly hardest and most awful creative experience of my life.

"What is this, Brooke?" Chase asks, the pain of betrayal raw in his deep voice.

Every part of me aches with the absence of an answer. The truth is, what I've done is inexcusable. Because I could argue that the exercise itself wasn't my choice, or that I was doing it for the good of the book, or that I didn't mean one bit of it—which I didn't.

But I'm the one who dragged Chase into an imaginary world he didn't have any say in. I'm the one who used his likeness to heal something inside myself. I'm the one who couldn't separate the man from the character at first.

I swallow, cinching the towel at my chest and tucking some hair behind my ear. "I..."

"Speak up," Chase snaps, and embarrassment permeates my every pore.

I'm so, so embarrassed that I've done this to us. That I've put us in the position to fail.

"Um..." I clear my throat. "W-when you told me the characters had no flaws, I did an exercise to get myself in the habit of picking out flaws. I was...having a hard time with Clive, and I needed somewhere to start."

"Why on earth would you start with me?"

It takes everything in me, but Chase deserves to know the truth. The whole, undistorted, ugly truth.

"Because...Clive is you."

He blinks rapidly, his pretty blue eyes a blur. "What do you mean?"

"Clive Watts is Chase Dawson. And River Rollins is Brooke Baker." I close my eyes. "With a few improvements. But...I wrote the book about us."

"I don't understand." I know he doesn't. It hardly even makes sense to me. But God, I would give anything to show him that the way I feel about him and my motives for writing this book are two different topics entirely.

I laugh, but there isn't any humor. I'm sad. I'm so, so sad that I'm hurting the person I've fallen so hard for. "Of course you don't. Because why would you? It's an insane thing to do, writing a whole book about someone without their knowledge or permission. But you know what's even crazier, Chase? Turning that book in to your editor by accident because you were too drunk to distinguish the files the night your manuscript was due. That's crazy. And then, you don't tell your editor what you've done. Instead, you go along with it, and you let him take that book to his boss and pitch it like it's the most normal thing in the world to turn in a book the publisher isn't expecting. And then the crazy finale! They actually decide to publish it!"

"Brooke—"

"Yep. That's the truth, Chase. The unvarnished shitshow! I've fucked you in my head since the moment I met you, and now I've fucked you in way more ways than the one I always fantasized about. How's that for flawed?"

Lying to Chase about anything will forever be the biggest mistake of my life. Because he's better than the book.

Chase Dawson, plain and simple, is the shit.

"I'd say it's pretty fucked up," he growls, making my chest squeeze. "For someone who claims to have written a book about a crush on me, you sure seem to have found some things to hate," he spews, shaking the paper in his hand.

The craziest thing is that those "flaws" I wrote—well, I don't even think they can be considered flaws because I find every single one of them endearing.

But that's how it is when you love someone. You love all of them. Every single part.

Me, on the other hand... Well, my flaws are fucking disgusting. And right now, I have the pleasure of facing them head on through the pain in Chase's eyes.

"No, Chase," I try to explain. "No. I don't think those things at all—"

"Oh, come on, Brooke. You wrote them, didn't you?"

"Yes. I did, but—"

"But nothing, Brooke. They're your words, your truths, and I think they tell me more than the rest of the time we've spent together. Time, I see now, was all some part of a sick game or something."

Before the paper even hits the chair, I can feel his intention to leave. His intention to leave me standing here with nothing but my mistakes to keep me company.

"Chase, please. You're getting this all wrong. Let me explain."

"Explain? Now? After you've tricked me and lied to me all this time?" He shakes his head. "I don't think so, Brooke. The time to explain was a while ago. Maybe the night I asked you if you ever felt like Clive and River. Before you spewed some bullshit about loving me."

"But it's not bullshit!" I yell, grabbing at his arm one last, futile time. "Chase, it's not bullshit! I was scared! Scared of what you'd think, of what you'd say. I'm sorry! Please, let me apologize!"

He doesn't stay, though, and he doesn't listen. I watch as the door closes behind him, and Chase walks out of my life forever.

And I don't even blame him. He may not think he knows me, but I sure as hell know him.

And he doesn't deserve this.

He deserves someone with their life together, their head on straight, their heart on their sleeve.

One thing is for sure, though. No matter what, no matter how much time passes, I'll miss the tiny taste I had of his perfection until the depths of forever.

Because God, I love him. Frankly, falling in love with him is the easiest thing I've ever done.

Chase will never be someone I can get over. He'll always been the most important someone I lost. And he might've walked away from me, but my heart is still with him. And truthfully, I don't think I can ever get it back.

When I reach the end of the email, my heart is in my throat, silently screaming over this terrible ending.

Because it is fucking terrible. There is no closure. There is only deep-rooted pain and sadness that I can certainly relate to.

Walking away from Brooke felt like the hardest thing I've ever done in my life because I love her. And just like she said, falling in love with her was the easiest thing I've ever done. She's endeared herself to my soul. She's imprinted herself on my heart. She encompasses all the things I want in my future.

The love I feel for her isn't a flash in the pan. It's fucking forever, and it is very much inside me, always there, always present.

Fuck.

I lean back in my chair, hardly able to breathe as I put my hands to the back of my head and let out a yell that startles Dawn to her feet.

Truth be told, the hardest part about reading this email is the fact that I can't pull Brooke into my arms and make it all okay. I can't wipe the tears from her eyes. I can't tell her I love her. I can't do anything but sit here like a fucking schmuck.

All the steady-headed, career-minded, logical things I'd have considered in the past to be deal-breakers just…don't matter anymore.

I'm in love with Brooke Baker. Her laugh, her smile, her words, both in person and on the page—she's everything and then some.

Clive and River are the shit. I knew a good book when I read it. But they're the shit because we are. Our chemistry, our humor, our personalities meshed together—it's all a recipe for sensation.

And it's time I get that back. Right fucking now.

Chapter
Fifty-Three

Saturday, June 17th

Brooke

It's been two days since I sent the scariest email of my life, and I've yet to get a response.

Sammy has been careful to talk me off the ledge every time I get hysterical. She's tried to tell me he's a really busy guy, and that I'm probably not the only email he got that day, and that when she talked to his sister, Mo said he was so busy that he'd hardly even slept.

All of that is barely comforting. I feel like if he read the email and he wanted to talk to me, wanted to see me, he would've already done it.

But that doesn't negate the fact that I miss my friend. I want to see him again. And the not knowing if that'll ever happen again is driving me crazy.

Truthfully, I'm starting to lose hope. I'm starting to reach the point where I'm just bracing myself for the inevitable—that Chase is really done with me, and soon, Longstrand will be letting me know I have a new editor. Or worse, they'll be letting me know they can no longer publish my books.

I have no idea what happened with *Accidental Attachment* after I sent the final manuscript to Chase a little less than a week ago. I don't know if Chase turned it in or if he told Jonah Perish that I'm a terrible human being that Longstrand should no longer represent.

I don't know and, sadly for my career, I don't even care at this point.

The only thing that made me finish the work on the book at all was him. Knowing how much he'd fought for the book to happen—how much he'd put on the line at his job.

No matter how distraught I was, I knew I couldn't leave him hanging.

But the only thing I can seem to care about now is Chase and what he's doing and what he's thinking and if he read my email and if he still loves me or if he's really, truly done with me.

I click off the stereo that's been playing Dolly and make my way back over to my computer to check my email again.

Sure, I get email notifications on both my phone and my watch, but sometimes they're delayed or something and I don't see them right away. I'd hate to think there's an email from him just sitting on my computer without my knowledge.

With several clicks and a beleaguered sigh, I return to the couch unsatisfied. There's no email. There's no call. There's no answer from Chase.

Maybe this is the time I need to accept it for what it is—done.

I cover my head with the blanket from the couch and pull Benji's warm body a little closer. He obliges, like any good friend would, but I can tell his body's a little too stiff to be enjoying it.

It takes effort to let him go, but eventually, I do.

He barks immediately, and I'm surprised when the door opens and Sammy steps inside. I sit up straight as a rod, concerned. "Aren't you supposed to be at work? Isn't that why you took the boys to Mo's place?"

"Yes. But I actually have to run an errand for her, and I want you to go with me."

"Ugh, Sammy," I groan. "I'm not really in the errand-running mood."

"No kidding." She snorts. "You're not really in the apartment-leaving mood these days. But I'm not giving you the option. Get up, go brush your hair, and put on something decent."

"Are you for real right now?"

She nods. "The realest. Now move it, or we're going to be late."

With a roll of my eyes that makes her scowl, I climb from the couch and head down the hall to my bedroom. Sammy's air mattress is between me and the closet, and normally I'd walk around it, but with the way she's annoying me, I trudge right over it.

Without even really looking, I grab a pair of jeans and a T-shirt and run a brush through my hair before putting it in a ponytail.

Since my glasses are also caked with smears from my frequent crying jags, I run them under the faucet and clean them with soap too before putting them back on my face and heading back to the living room.

Sammy peruses me seriously as I enter the space. I answer her suspicions with a sarcastic remark. "Is this good enough for you, Your Highness?"

"I'm going to ignore that since this is a traumatic time for you."

I stop myself just shy of sticking out my tongue.

Gah, I'm a real peach when I'm depressed.

"All right," I agree with a groan. "Let's go."

Benji jumps up off the couch and follows me to the door, where Sammy festoons him with a plaid bowtie she bought him a day or two ago. I chortle. "What? Even the dog has to dress up?"

She doesn't answer, rather shoving me out the door and forcing me into the elevator and through and out of the lobby.

The streets are bustling and the sun is shining, and the whole thing feels like a giant lie. Earth and planets and the sun—they're a bunch of fucking liars.

Sammy, Benji, and I walk the two blocks to the subway in silence, and then we climb down the stairs to wait for the train. I don't bother to pay attention to anything other than my own two feet and my canine friend.

Not even the line we get on. Nothing. I don't care about any of it.

Hell, I don't even know what errand we're running. Sammy could be leading me to an empty field to bury a body and I'd be none the wiser.

I sit grumpily while the train bumps along for nearly twenty minutes, and I only look up when Sammy grabs me by the elbow to lift me out of my seat. "I guess we're getting off here," I say smartly to a complete stranger on the other side of the car. In true New York fashion, they ignore me entirely.

When Sammy pinches me, I decide not to piss her off any further—since she's basically all I have left at this point—and follow her up the stairs, down the block, and into an apartment building I've never seen before.

She's annoyingly cryptic, even as we step on to the elevator and head for the sixth floor—something I know only from the illuminated button she pushed. "So, where are we going for Mo exactly? Drug deal? Illegal adoption? Picking up some sort of extinct animal to put in the soup special tonight?"

The elevator dings, and the doors open directly in front of the open door of an apartment. As a result, I can see clear inside.

Roses are strewn across the entirety of the light wood floors all the way to the floor-to-ceiling windows, and in the middle of it all, stands the man of my dreams.

Sammy leans into my ear mockingly. "What do you think? Is it time to shut up now?"

I nod. I can't do anything else.

Every single part of me is focused on Chase in the middle of the room.

He's perfectly coiffed and shined, and his heart is in his eyes from the first moment I catch them.

What I see inside them is a man who doesn't want to fight with me any more than I want to fight with him. We're lovers, in every sense of the word. *And, oh my God, I'm going to cry.*

I step forward eagerly, stopping myself after only a couple of steps and pulling my arms into my chest. I don't want to push too fast. I'd give anything not to ruin this.

"God, Chase," I start, tears forming in my eyes without pause. "I'm really sorry—"

"Don't be. I told you to do it."

"To write the book?"

He laughs. "No. To write the flaws." He shakes his head. "The book was all you, but baby, you did a fucking bang-up job."

"*Chase*."

"They're perfect in all their flaws, Brooke. Because they're us. Just like you wrote them to be. I thought I loved this book before, but I had no idea how much more it could be." He smiles, really, truly smiles at me. "Now, get over here and kiss me."

Between one moment and the next, I'm in his arms, my legs around his hips and my face in his neck. Sobs rack my body, and he squeezes me tightly against the onslaught of them. His warm hand is a comfort as it rubs at my back, and his very being is a comfort to my soul.

I've missed him so much.

He kisses my tears away as I pull my face out of his neck, and I chase after his mouth with my own until I land it. The taste of him mixed with the salt of my tears is the only solution I need to mend my open wounds.

"I love you so much," I whisper against his lips.

"I love you too, Brooke."

It's a long, emotional moment before I can look at anything but the man in my arms, but when I finally do, I realize I don't even know where we are.

"What is this place?" I ask, just as Sammy steps out the front door and closes it behind herself.

"It's my new apartment," Chase says with a smile. "The one I've been renovating, and it's finally ready."

398 | max monroe

"Wow," I whisper, looking around at the sleek hardwood floors and gorgeous warmth the sunlight provides through the windows. "It's beautiful, Chase."

"I know," he whispers back, but when I look over to meet his eyes, he's not looking around at his apartment. He's looking at me.

"I know this is going to sound crazy, baby, but I'm starting to realize nothing we do is conventional, you know?"

I tilt my head to the side, and he continues.

"When I see this apartment, this fresh beginning, it doesn't feel right unless you're here too."

"What are you saying?"

"I'm saying I want you here, Brooke. With me. Us, together, in this apartment, waking up to each other every morning and falling asleep beside each other every night."

I'm pretty sure my heart just escaped my throat and ran across the floor and entered Chase's body. "You want me to move in with you?"

"Yes. I miss living with you."

I nod. I miss living with him too.

"So you will?" he asks to clarify, and I break down into tears yet again. This time, though, they're very, very happy.

Sure, it might seem insane for me to move in with him, but when you know you want to spend the rest of your life with someone, you don't wait.

You *shouldn't* wait.

The rest of your life starts right now.

Which is why my answer comes easily and excitedly. "Yes!"

He covers my mouth with his own once more, taking me in a kiss that I could write another entire novel about. And with the way this one turned out, I might not even stop myself from doing it.

"That's good," he murmurs against my lips when we finally pull apart.

"It is?"

"Yep. Because Sammy, Mo, and Vinny already went to get your stuff."

God, I love him.

I smile and stare deep into his eyes. "And they lived happily ever after?"

"*Definitely,*" he answers before giving me the kind of kiss that tastes like forever.

Okay, God. I'm good right here.

Hurry. Someone say "The End."

Epilogue

Saturday, October 21st

Four months later…

Brooke

Oh, what a magical night. Twinkle lights dance in the windows of The St. Regis Roof Ballroom, and a view of Fifth Avenue and Central Park lies beyond them.

Accidental Attachment is officially one with the world, and to my greatest shock and early horror, the world is one with it as well. It's been out for almost two weeks and, in that time, has sold an incredible five hundred thousand copies.

Pink paperbacks with scrolling yellow letters saturate the hands of subway riders and sidewalk walkers alike, and women rave about Clive Watts on every inch of the internet.

It's officially a hit, and tonight, Longstrand is hosting this swanky party to celebrate.

And with Chase at my side, I'm excited about all of it.

Yep. My cup runneth over and then some. Because as of now, Brooke Baker has it going on.

I mean, it's not every day you write a book about your crush, work on that book with your crush while you spend nearly a month on a motor home together, find yourself falling in love with your crush, and then, not only do you publish that book, but you do it with that very man standing beside you the entire time, as a couple.

In the world of romance novels, this is what you'd call the ultimate meet-cute turned HEA.

And to be the girl who gets to experience the kind of love I feel when I'm with Chase, well, it goes without saying that I'm blessed.

We are that Lana Del Rey song "Lucky Ones" come to life.

Sigh. Yeah. We really are the lucky ones.

Through the crowd of drink-holding partygoers, I spot a flurry of white-and-black fur prancing through the main doors of the ballroom, and with the way my Spider-Man-costume-wearing buddy at my side starts to fidget, I can tell I'm not the only one.

Benji barks at Dolly to say hello, and without warning, she rushes the leash and yanks it out of her owner Noah's hand. He laughs, thankfully having had the good sense to let go before it could pull through his palm and singe off his million-dollar, anesthesiologist hands.

Dolly is beautifully trussed-up with a big pink bow, and Benji's immediate crowding is a sign that he appreciates his pretty girl's effort.

I have to say, I appreciate it too. It's pretty thoughtful of a sweet dog like Dolly—and her overtly masculine owner, who's wearing a pink tie himself— to have taken the time to match the theme of the release party for the newest #1 *New York Times* best seller, *Accidental Attachment*.

Yes, that is the sound of me screaming loud enough to be heard in all five boroughs, thank you very much.

And evidently, the spirit guides, the rulers of destiny, never miss. Not only did they lead me to Chase, but they've brought a woman into my best buddy's life who's full of class and confidence, just like her namesake—yep, Dolly Parton.

It's freaky how the world works sometimes and, to be completely honest, how good of a friend Noah has become. Since our initial meeting with him in Central Park, just three short days after Chase's and my emotional reunion, we've gotten together at least two times a week, every week, no matter our other obligations.

All in the name of Benji and Dolly's budding doggie romance.

Having had my heart broken by forced distance from the man of my dreams, I know the very last thing I'm going to do is keep my buddy Benji from the woman of his. Anytime I can find a way to unite the two love doggos, I do it.

And thankfully, Dolly's owner has been on board with this plan since that fateful day we brought the two of them together.

"Hey, Noah," I greet cheerfully, reaching down at my feet to give Dolly a rub-down worthy of her cuteness. "Thanks for coming tonight!"

His answering smile is just about all I need to know about my secret plans for meddling for next week. *Eek!* I'm not normally the type to force people into things, but in this case, I can't even bring myself to feel bad.

I know to my core that my sister and Noah are perfect for each other, no matter how good they seem to be at avoiding actually meeting. And this eager beaver isn't waiting any longer.

It's time my big sis finds her happily ever after. It's time she finds a man who's worthy of how awesome and special she is.

And now that she's settled in New York a little more, I think she's ready. I *hope* she's ready.

Goodness knows, Dr. Noah Philip has a Grey's Anatomy hot factor that can't be denied. Add in the fact that he's rich, successful, charming, and raised a good little girl like Dolly, and I feel like he's the perfect man for Sam.

All that's left is me shoving them together and—

Chase puts a squeezing hand to my hip, sensing the excited wandering of my mind like only he can, and pulls me back from the rabbit hole.

"Congrats, you guys. Dolly and I wouldn't have missed it," Noah answers, reaching out a hand to shake Chase's in that man-bro-ish, *I'm saying hello with my body language* way that only a couple of stone-cold foxes like the two of them can pull off. "I'm sorry I have to take off in a few minutes, but I'm glad Benj and Dolly will at least get to enjoy each other's company for the night."

I smile and lean down to ruffle Dolly's cheeks again. "Are you kidding? I'm so excited I'm going to have a girlie sleeping over!"

Benji gives me the side-eye, displeased with my misguided belief that Dolly will in any way, shape, or form be *my* guest. I squint and stick out my tongue at him, but his doggie disdain doesn't change.

"Yeah, well, I'm sure she's excited too." Noah smiles. "I've been talking about how much I don't want to go to this fundraiser for the last week and a half, and she's been the unfortunate sounding board for the brunt of it."

"If she's anything like Benji," Chase intervenes, "I'm sure she's used to the mental load."

"Excuse me?" I scoff playfully with a bat of my eyelashes and a hand to my chest. "Just what exactly are you trying to say, Mr. Dawson?"

"You're a writer, baby." Chase chuckles and wraps his arm around my shoulders, tucking me close to his manly, strong chest. "You're supposed to be adorably verbose."

Noah smirks. "And what's that say about me?"

Chase doesn't even blink. "All of Brooke's characters are in her head. All of your patients are asleep. Makes perfect sense to me that both of you would spend ninety percent of your time talking to your dogs."

Noah smirks. "Well, thanks again for inviting me. And a huge congratulations! I swear, all the nurses I work with own a copy of *Accidental Attachment*. It's all they rave about." He glances down at the fancy Rolex on his wrist. "*Shit.* Well, I wish I could hang around, but…"

"Duty calls," Chase finishes for him before giving another bro-worthy slap to Noah's upper arm.

Noah steps away with a flick of his fingers and a last rub to Dolly's head before disappearing right back out the door through which he came.

And I'm left standing there, annoyed that my sister has, yet again, not shown up in time.

My pout must be obvious because it isn't but a few seconds before Chase is pulling me into a hug and whispering in my ear. "Don't look so sad. You already have a plan, remember? He and Sammy are going to meet next week."

"I knooow," I cry, with only my charm to save me from my petulance. "But I wanted to lay the groundwork tonight, you know? Get a head start."

Chase pulls me back and places a gentle kiss on my lips. "I have an idea."

"You do?" I ask excitedly.

Chase nods, his forehead brushing against mine. "How about for tonight, just tonight, you focus on yourself and this book and the absolutely enormous accomplishment of hitting *number one* on the *New York Times* list?"

Properly redirected, I laugh, shrugging as nonchalantly as I can manage for this performance. "Yeah, okay. I guess that's, like, a decent idea."

"I love you, Brooke."

Chase's smile is so bright, I'm afraid if I don't do something to smother it, all the planes going to JFK are going to start to divert toward us by mistake just from catching a glimpse of it through the window.

"Yeah," I reply with a wink. "I'm pretty into you too."

We're still giggling and kissing when his assistant clears her throat from behind me to get our attention.

"Dawn!" I say with a yell, spin-diving into her arms and almost taking her off her feet. Chase pulls the two of us to a steady position again, and Dawn wraps me in the kind of genuine hug I'm convinced only someone like her can give. For most people who work at my publisher, this kind of behavior would be a little too much, but not for Dawn.

My first impression of her was right. She's the bee's fucking knees. I'm pretty sure I have a girl-crush on her.

We hug and sway for a long minute before separating, at which point Chase leans in to give her a light, professional hug, with back-patting and everything.

It makes me laugh so hard I snort, and that, of course, is the moment my agent, Wilson Phillips, approaches. "Well, I guess that rules out my theory that making the *New York Times* list multiple times would somewhat calm your personality."

"Oh, Wilson, come on, now! 'The Dream Is Still Alive'!" I hoot with a fist pump. "We've got many years to come together and, hopefully, many best sellers. There's still 'A Reason to Believe'!"

Chase smiles, pulls me into his side, and adds, "I know she's 'Impulsive,' but 'In My Room'..." He turns to look at me, "'Ooh, You're Gold.'"

"It never ends." Wilson groans, turning to Dawn with the hope of camaraderie. "Can you believe these two?"

Dawn just smiles. "I'd 'Give It Up' if I were you. At this point, it's in their 'Flesh and Blood.'"

"I should've known," Wilson huffs and eyes me pointedly. "I should've fucking known you'd manage to turn them against me, too."

"It's only because I love you, Wilson," I reply. "I don't tell you this enough, but you're 'Everything I Need' in an agent."

Chase attempts to cough through his laughter. Dawn pretends to choke through hers. And I'm holding my giggles in so tight it's making my cheeks puff out like a blowfish.

"Yep. That's my cue to mingle. Far, far away from you three." Wilson takes off before we can toss another song reference at him, heading in the direction of the open bar, and the three of us are left laughing so hard, I have to bend over and hold my stomach. "I don't know why that's so funny, but it really, really is."

"It was fun," Dawn agrees, almost sheepishly. "I wish I'd have thought to do this to him a long time ago."

"Listen, feel free to do it every time you talk to him from now on, okay?" I nod with wide, you-should-totally-do-that eyes. "I think it's good for everyone involved if we spread this as far as possible."

"You got it," Dawn agrees, leaning in to give me one more hug. "Congratulations," she whispers sweetly in my ear. "On the book...and the man. I am so happy he found someone as great as you."

A little bit of a sting hits my nose unexpectedly, and Dawn winks as she shoves Chase in the shoulder gently and then steps away.

"Proud of you, baby." Chase presses a soft kiss to my forehead.

"Like, how proud?" I question, batting my eyelashes at him and dropping my voice so only his ears can hear me. "Like, 'I could hug you all night' proud? Or 'I want to do dirty, wild, sexy things with you when we get back home tonight' proud?"

He smirks down at me, his eyes heating in a way that makes a thrill of excitement run up my spine. Lips to my ear, he whispers, "All of the above, baby."

Yes, please.

I'm just about to open my mouth to keep this conversation going, but our alone time is cut short by more people stopping by our little circle to offer their congratulations.

Frank and Regina, two of Longstrand's other senior editors.

A few of Longstrand's other authors I've become friends with over the years.

Several employees in the marketing department I've worked closely with on the *Shadow Brothers* and now, *Accidental Attachment*.

And then, the big man, Jonah Perish himself. He almost feels like a movie character, he's so perfect for his role.

"Well, Dawson, you were right about this one. I really like when someone I believe in lives up to my expectations."

Chase's smile is huge, and it should be. Frankly, he deserves all the credit for getting this book to the number one spot on the list. I may have written it, but Chase Dawson is the one who believed in it.

"Thank you, sir. As someone who's grown in the industry admiring the way you work, it's truly an honor to have your recognition."

Jonah's smile is playful, and I swear it takes a whole ten years off his handsome but hardened face. "You don't need my recognition, Dawson. You've got the recognition of readers worldwide. Congratulations," he finishes, turning to me and flashing a smile. "To both of you."

I thought at first that Chase's and my relationship might be a problem at

Longstrand, and to be honest, Chase and I went back and forth for an entire contentious week about whether we should keep it a secret. He was ad-
amant that Jonah Perish was a man of sound mind and rationale, and that a
relationship between the two of us wouldn't be a problem as long as it didn't
affect the work.

I, however, as a watcher of many an episode of *All My Children*, feared there
would be a clandestine scheme to break us up, involving one or many of the
following: poison, a train accident, hit men, several days caught out in the
cold of a snowstorm without shelter, and an evil twin of his or mine.

Chase, obviously, won. And surprise of all surprises, the world didn't end.
Jonah didn't fire Chase or cancel my book, and well, here we are…at the top
of the heap emotionally and professionally.

Still, the air lightens immediately when Jonah finally steps away to go rub
elbows with some of the other important people, and Chase takes a deep
breath only someone standing as close as I am would know he was holding.
I smile and draw him into a hug, wrapping my arms around his shoulders
to pull him close.

"Now that, my love, *that* was an attaboy!"

Chase laughs and picks me up off my feet, only to have me wrestled out of
his arms by a woman three-quarters his size.

Sammy screech-yells and pulls me into a hug so hard that we tumble to the
carpeted floor of the ballroom without a touch of grace. Thankfully unin-
jured, we both laugh ourselves stupid as I untangle my dress from hers and
climb to my feet with the help of my man.

Once I'm settled, he reaches down to help my sister up too, and the two of
us fall into a hug all over again, this time much more controlled.

"Oh, Brookie! I'm sorry I'm late. The restaurant was absolutely crazy tonight!"
She looks over my head as though she's talking to Chase. "Mo and Vinny
will be here soon, I swear, but it was really hard to leave."

I pull away and wave her off with a smile. "It's fine! We've got all night, right?"

Sammy's success here in New York has been a sight to behold. She officially took over my old apartment when I moved in with Chase, and she and the boys have been flourishing ever since. In fact, she proved so valuable at La Croissette that Mo and Vinny promoted her to the general manager position. I swear, sometimes when I look into the pretty aqua-green of her eyes, I don't see any evidence of her ex Todd Brown's assholery at all.

I just see my happy, confident, thriving sister living the life that she deserves.

Well, besides the whole "I really think she and Noah would be a good match" thing. Everything else is set. Just that one tiny thing we still need to achieve.

I look from Sammy to Chase when both of them are suspiciously quiet, but just as I'm about to ask them about it, Chase lunges in to kiss me.

"Whoa—" I start to say in surprise, but his lips cut me off.

And it's a good kiss—a great kiss, even—so every thought in my head escapes in a blink, confusion forgotten and replaced by the sweet feel of Chase's tongue against mine.

When he finally pulls away, I feel like the human version of the heart-eyes emoji. Just a giant head with two big red hearts for my eyes.

"Wowee, Mr. Dawson, sir. Now *that* was a kiss. I have no idea what it was for, but I don't care. Kiss me like that for the rest of my life, and I'll be a happy girl." I spin in a circle of pure happiness; I can't help it, and Sammy and Chase both laugh at my performative gestures.

But it's moments like this, standing here with two of my favorite people in the whole wide world, that make me feel so damn thankful for how everything has turned out.

Chase and I are both on top of the world at work, we're happy in our relationship together, and Sammy is so settled in her new life in New York that I don't think she'll ever get knocked off her feet again—except when we hug, maybe.

I'm one happy girl. The happiest, really. Ninety percent of the time, I can't believe this is my life.

Sammy's expression changes, her excitement growing, and she points to the front door of the ballroom dramatically. "Oh look, Chase! There are Mo and Vinny now!"

I turn to rush toward them, Mo having become a fast best friend since Chase and I got together, but I'm surprised when I'm jerked backward, the resistance of Chase's hand too powerful to overcome.

"Hey, what are you—" I start to ask, my eyebrows pinching in a frown as I whirl to face him, only to be cut off by the literal evacuation of *all the air* from my lungs.

There, on bended knee, Chase sits poised with a tiny, velvet box that a girl who grew up on rom-coms and spends her time creating literary "happily ever afters" knows the sight of all too well.

I'm already crying. Just big, fat, happy tears sliding down my face.

"Oh my God. You're gonna—"

"Yep." Chase nods, the natural ease of his handsome smile during such a huge moment a memory I'll remember forever. "I'm sealing the deal, locking it up, making the coolest woman on the entire planet mine forever." He pauses for a brief moment—just enough time for me to wipe the bubble of snot forming at my nose away—and then continues. "That is…if you'll have me."

My throat is clogged, and my heart is full. I have never, and I mean never, felt so sure of something in my entire life. I want to scream it from the rooftops, but I force myself to stay quiet long enough for him to finish saying what he has planned.

"Brooke Baker…lover of Dolly, master of words, queen of humor and my heart…will you, please, be my wife?"

"Yes!" I exclaim. "Yes, a thousand times. Yes, before you even asked me. Yes to forever."

Benji barks and his girl Dolly joins him in the celebration as the whole room erupts into a roar of applause and cheers, but with my pounding, pulsing ears, I barely hear them.

All I can see, all I can sense, all I can feel is the man in front of me.

I lunge forward, just as he pushes to standing, brushing the ring out of the way to put my arms around him tightly. My nose finds a place in his neck and stays there, intent to breathe everything he is in this moment deep into my soul.

"I promised my sister I'd wait until she was here," Chase whispers softly, a roll of laughter from his chest making him sound out of breath. He untucks our heads to look me in the eye. "So, I did. But I couldn't wait even a second longer."

I take Chase's face in my hands and press my lips to his, completing our fairy-tale moment entirely.

I've only pulled away an inch when I hear someone not too far away muse, "You know, they kind of remind me of River and Clive."

My smile grows a mile, and Chase's eyes light with wonder.

"Sending the book was an accident," he says softly. "But you and I? We were meant to be."

I kiss him again, letting him know with everything inside me that I agree. We *are* meant to be. It is as simple and as complicated as that.

I've made a lot of mistakes in my life, but my most favorite mistake will always be accidentally attaching the wrong file in an email to Chase Dawson at Longstrand Publishing.

Otherwise known as the man of my dreams turned man of my life.

Man of my future. Man of my forever.

My guy.

I couldn't have written this better if I'd tried.

THE END

Need more of Brooke and Chase and Benji and Dolly?

Of course you do! That's why we have EVEN MORE fun for you in an *exclusive Accidental Attachment Extended Epilogue.*

And, we can't deny, you're going to love every second of it.

Download **Accidental Attachment's EXTENDED EPILOGUE at dl.bookfunnel.com/fk665py5ex**

It's completely **FREE** and not-to-be missed!

Need EVEN MORE Max Monroe?

Grab *The Bet* to read all about how an anti-commitment bachelor meets a happily ever after-focused woman who has the power to bring him to his knees. It's the first book in our best-selling romantic comedy standalone series—*The Winslow Brothers Collection*—about four brothers who go to a fortune teller and she predicts how they'll all fall in love.

Trust us, you won't regret it. ;) ;)

BEEN THERE, DONE THAT TO ALL OF THE ABOVE?

Never fear, we have a list of nearly FORTY other titles to keep you busy for as long as your little reading heart desires! **Check them out at our website:** *www.authormaxmonroe.com*

COMPLETELY NEW TO MAX MONROE AND DON'T KNOW WHERE TO START?

Check out our Suggested Reading Order on our website!
www.authormaxmonroe.com/max-monroe-suggested-reading-order

WHAT'S NEXT FROM MAX MONROE?

Stay up-to-date with our characters and our upcoming releases by signing up for our newsletter on our website: *www.authormaxmonroe.com/ newsletter*!

You may live to regret much, but we promise it won't be subscribing to our newsletter.

Seriously, we make it fun! Character conversations about royal babies, parenting woes, embarrassing moments, and shitty horoscopes are just the beginning! If you're already signed up, consider sending us a message to tell us how much you love us. We really like that. ;)

Follow us online here:

Facebook: www.facebook.com/authormaxmonroe

Reader Group: www.facebook.com/groups/1561640154166388

Twitter: www.twitter.com/authormaxmonroe

Instagram: www.instagram.com/authormaxmonroe

TikTok: www.tiktok.com/@authormaxmonroe

Goodreads: https://goo.gl/8VUIz2

Acknowledgments

First of all, THANK YOU for reading. That goes for anyone who has bought a copy, read an ARC, helped us beta, edited, or found time in their busy schedule just to make sure we stayed on track. Thank you for supporting us, for talking about our books, and for just being so unbelievably loving and supportive of our characters. You've made this our MOST favorite adventure thus far.

THANK YOU to each other. Monroe is thanking Max. Max is thanking Monroe. Yes. We know. We're like a broken record at this point, but we can't help ourselves. We simply *love* writing books together.

THANK YOU, Lisa, for being an editing Queen (please, don't edit the Q to lowercase because you very much deserve the capital) whom we can't live without. We love you to infinity and beyond.

THANK YOU, Stacey, for always accommodating us with kindness and grace. You are a goddess, and we appreciate everything you do! Especially, for being such a good friend and for making the inside of this book so pretty! We adore you!

THANK YOU, Peter (aka Banana), for working your ass off on this cover and making it everything we wanted and need it to be!

THANK YOU to every blogger and influencer who has read, reviewed, posted, shared, and supported us. Your enthusiasm, support, and hard work do not go unnoticed. We love youuuuuuuuuuuuu!

THANK YOU to the people who love us—our family. You are our biggest supporters and motivators. We couldn't do this without you.

THANK YOU to our Awesome ARC-ers. We love and appreciate you guys so much.

THANK YOU to our Camp Love Yourself friends! We love you. You always find a way to make us smile and laugh every single freaking day. You're the best.

As always, all our love.

XOXO,
Max & Monroe

Printed in Great Britain
by Amazon

22033797R00235